CHRISTMAS MIRACLES AT HEDGEHOG HOLLOW

HEDGEHOG HOLLOW BOOK 6

JESSICA REDLAND

Boldwood

First published in Great Britain in 2022 by Boldwood Books Ltd. This paperback edition first published in 2023.

1

Every effort has been made to obtain the necessary permissions with reference to copyright material, both illustrative and quoted. We apologise for any omissions in this respect and will be pleased to make the appropriate acknowledgements in any future edition.

A CIP catalogue record for this book is available from the British Library.

Paperback ISBN: 978-1-78513-794-5

Hardback ISBN: 978-1-80162-443-5

Ebook ISBN: 978-1-80162-447-3

Kindle ISBN: 978-1-80162-446-6

Audio CD ISBN: 978-1-80162-438-1

MP3 CD ISBN: 978-1-80162-439-8

Digital audio download ISBN: 978-1-80162-440-4

Digital audio MP3 ISBN: 978-1-80162-441-1

Large Print ISBN: 978-1-80162-444-2

Boldwood Books Ltd.

23 Bowerdean Street, London, SW6 3TN

www.boldwoodbooks.com

This book is dedicated to my very own Christmas miracle – my beautiful daughter Ashleigh. With love and hugs xx

This whole series is dedicated to all the amazing people who help hedgehogs – owners, employees and volunteers at rescue centres, fosterers, fundraisers, campaigners, anyone who has found a hedgehog and called for help, and those who put food and water out and provide a safe haven in their gardens. What a difference you all make xx

Recurring Characters from the Hedgehog Hollow Series

Samantha Alderson, aka Sam or Sammie
Owner and full-time manager of Hedgehog Hollow. Married to Josh

Josh Alderson
Veterinary surgeon and partner at Alderson & Wishaw Veterinary Practice. Married to Samantha

Fizz Kinsella
Full-time veterinary nurse at Hedgehog Hollow

Yasmin Simms
Fizz's girlfriend. Artist/sculptor

Natasha Kinsella
Fizz's mum. Runs events and catering business and works in partnership with Samantha

Hadrian Kinsella
Fizz's dad. Police sergeant

Barney Kinsella
Fizz's older brother. Farmer at Bumblebee Barn

Phoebe Corbyn
Trainee accountant. Volunteer bookkeeper at the rescue centre. Lives at Hedgehog Hollow

Darcie Flynn
Eight-year-old neglected by the Grimes family and adopted by
Phoebe. Lives at Hedgehog Hollow

Jonathan Wishaw
Samantha's dad. Veterinary surgeon and partner at Alderson &
Wishaw Veterinary Practice

Debs Wishaw
Samantha's mum. Aspiring gardener. Identical twin to Chloe's
mum, Louise

Chloe Turner
Samantha's cousin. Married to James. Runs Crafty Hollow with
Lauren at Hedgehog Hollow

James Turner
Samantha's ex-boyfriend. Married to Chloe

Samuel Turner
Chloe and James's son (two years old)

Louise Olsen
Samantha's auntie. Chloe's mum. Identical twin to Samantha's
mum, Debs

Simon Olsen
Samantha's uncle. Chloe's dad

Lauren Harbuckle
Josh's auntie. Non-identical twin to Connie. Runs Crafty Hollow
with Chloe at Hedgehog Hollow

Riley Berry
Lauren's boyfriend. Manages Bloomsberry's (family-run garden centre)

Kai Berry
Riley's son (twelve years old)

Connie Williams
Josh's mum. Counsellor. Cub leader. Non-identical twin to Lauren. Married to Alex

Alex Williams
Married to Connie. Cub leader. Dave's uncle

Paul Alderson
Josh's dad and former business partner. Veterinary nurse at Alderson & Wishaw Veterinary Practice. Lives at Alder Lea – the veterinary practice house – with his family

Beth Giddings
Paul's girlfriend. Josh's ex-girlfriend. Part-time receptionist at Alderson & Wishaw Veterinary Practice

Archie Alderson
Paul and Beth's son (three years old)

Lottie Alderson
Paul and Beth's daughter (two years old)

Thomas Mickleby
Elderly widower befriended by Samantha. Left Hedgehog Hollow to Samantha in his will on the proviso she ran it as a hedgehog

rescue centre

Gwendoline Mickleby
Thomas's wife, whose dream it was to run a hedgehog rescue centre

Rich Cooper
Good friend of Samantha. Partner of Dave. Ambulance paramedic

Dave Williams
Good friend of Samantha. Partner of Rich. Builder

Hannah Spiers
Samantha's best friend. District nurse

Toby Spiers
Hannah's husband. James's best friend

Amelia Spiers
Hannah and Toby's daughter. Samantha's goddaughter (three years old)

Tariq
Josh's best friend from university. Veterinary surgeon at Alderson & Wishaw Veterinary Practice

Rosemary Norris
Good friend and former neighbour of Phoebe's. Has a guide dog called Trixie

Celia
Rosemary's long-standing best friend. Lives with Rosemary

Terry Shepherd
Good friend of Samantha and Josh. Has brought in several rescue hedgehogs/hoglets. Has a springer spaniel called Wilbur

Zayn Hockley
RSPCA inspector. Volunteer at Hedgehog Hollow

Javine Dafoe
Former Head of Art & Design at Reddfield TEC. Art tutor at Crafty Hollow

Jeanette Kingston
Community leader in local villages and friend of Samantha

Robbie
Friend of Fizz's. Architect and illustrator

Hayley Grimes
Darcie's biological mother

The Grimes family (Tina, Jenny, Cody, Brynn and Connor)
Relatives of Gwendoline's with a vendetta against Samantha. All currently in prison

THE STORY SO FAR...

After discovering that Hedgehog Hollow's bank account had been emptied, Samantha and Josh's wedding plans looked shaky, but the generosity of the local community and their good friend Terry helped save the rescue centre and Samantha and Josh said 'I do'.

Josh's Auntie Lauren was delighted for the happy couple, but the wedding made her reflect on her own two divorces and her decision to remain single.

While Samantha and Josh were on honeymoon, Lauren received the shock news that the job she loved would soon disappear in a work restructure. Her future career wasn't the only source of confusion, with Lauren finding herself drawn to Riley Berry, the man who'd given her the redundancy news.

Lauren's past returned to haunt her when her first husband, Shaun, made contact twenty-six years after walking out on her. She agreed to meet him and discovered the reason he'd left, which gave her closure and helped her move forward. Riley was exceptionally supportive during this time and Lauren finally felt ready to love again.

Samantha had told Josh on their wedding day that she was

ready to start a family but had a panic attack on honeymoon when she thought she might be pregnant. Back home, she was on edge until Lauren convinced her to tell Josh so they could face it together. Josh was as supportive as ever but, when Samantha found out that she wasn't pregnant, she felt disappointed and began to wonder if she might be ready for a baby after all.

Terry brought an injured fox cub to the rescue centre, prompting Fizz to share that her dream job was to work full-time in a rescue centre. Samantha wasn't opposed to extending their work beyond hedgehogs but said there wasn't the staff or funds to do so. Keen to show her gratitude to Samantha for welcoming Darcie and her to Hedgehog Hollow, accountancy whizz Phoebe showed Samantha and Josh the financial viability of running a larger operation with paid staff.

A few months later, Hedgehog Hollow played host to another wedding when Josh's mum Connie married Alex. So many of Samantha's friends and family had now found happiness, but there were a couple more people Samantha felt deserved to find their happy ever after.

It's now October, one year later, and a lot has happened at Hedgehog Hollow...

1

SAMANTHA

I opened my eyes with the first gentle beeps of the alarm clock, pressed the snooze button and settled back under the duvet.

Josh snuggled up against me and lightly kissed the top of my shoulder, stirring the butterflies in my stomach.

'Happy birthday, Sammie,' he said, trailing his kisses up my neck.

'This is how all birthdays should start.' I adjusted position so his lips could touch mine. 'Actually, it's how every day should start.'

'That can be arranged.'

'Ooh!' My hands flew to my stomach. 'That was a big one. Someone's awake.'

I guided Josh's hands so he could feel it too.

'We might have a footballer in there,' he said, laughing as the baby kicked once more.

'Or a martial arts expert.'

'Just think, next time either of us celebrate a birthday, we'll be parents.'

I entwined my fingers round Josh's. 'Only twelve weeks to go. It's getting very real now.'

'How are you feeling?'

I squeezed his hand. 'Still in a good place.'

I'd initially struggled with the idea of becoming a parent, fearful of having the same difficult relationship with my child that I'd had with my own mum. A combination of discovering that Mum's behaviour arose from a shocking incident in her past rather than being my fault, counselling support, and building a fresh relationship with Mum had helped allay my fears.

When Josh and I were both ready to try for a family, it didn't happen immediately. Each month that passed brought fresh disappointment but, looking back, that extra time worked out for the best because there'd been so much work to do in progressing our plans to expand Hedgehog Hollow into a wider wildlife rescue centre. At the start of this year, Hedgehog Hollow Wildlife Rescue Centre was established as the charitable division of Alderson & Wishaw Veterinary Practice in which Josh and Dad were partners.

Fizz was now qualified as a veterinary nurse and we were both salaried. Having Fizz working full-time and the additional flexibility to draft in staff from the practice had eased the pressure on me.

In early December, I'd be stepping back and going on maternity leave. In theory. We all knew that I wouldn't be able to resist spending time in the barn helping out until Bublet arrived, Bublet being Darcie's name for the baby – a combination of hoglet and baby. Organising the nursery was the project for the half-term holiday the week after next and, once that was done, what else would there be for me to do but sit and wait for the little one to make an appearance? Might as well make myself useful in the barn.

Darcie and Phoebe were both so excited about having a baby in the house once more. It was mid-October now, sixteen months since Josh's dad Paul and his family had moved into Alder Lea –

the house at the veterinary practice – and we all still missed having Lottie and her older brother Archie around for regular cuddles.

'Do you still think you know Bublet's gender?' Josh asked as the baby kicked again.

'Yes, but you're not getting it out of me. Wait until fourth of January or whenever they appear and, at that point, I'll tell you if I was right.'

'You're such a spoilsport!'

I laughed at his childish whine, knowing he was joking really. We'd made a joint decision not to find out the gender, eager to enjoy that special moment of surprise when Bublet arrived.

'I'd best get over to the barn to give Dad a hand,' I said, reluctantly pushing back the duvet.

Dad had been on overnight hoglets duty. Hedgehogs typically produce a first litter of hoglets in the spring following post-hibernation mating, but there's a second round of births – autumn juveniles – in September and October. As with the spring births, this resulted in a phase of hand-rearing the tiny hoglets who'd been abandoned, so Josh, Dad, Fizz and I took it in turns to stay in the barn and feed them overnight.

'I'll do that,' Josh said. 'Why don't you have a lie-in and a long shower?'

'A lie-in would be amazing but there's no chance of me getting back to sleep with Bublet doing their morning workout. The long shower sounds good, though.'

'Phoebe and Darcie should be up by the time we're done in the barn so we can give you your presents.'

Josh kissed me again then slipped into the en suite to brush his teeth and freshen up while I rolled myself off the bed and padded over to my cheval mirror.

Each time I caught sight of my reflection, the baby bump still took me by surprise. I lowered the waistband on my pyjama shorts and lifted up my T-shirt so I could see it more clearly.

'How are you doing in there, Bublet?' I asked.

The reply came in the form of another kick.

I still had moments when the responsibility of raising a little human felt overwhelming, but I knew that was completely normal from conversations with Chloe, Hannah and Beth. Josh had moments too which gave me reassurance that we were in every part of this together.

* * *

I'd only just pulled on my maternity leggings and a tunic top when I heard giggling outside the bedroom door.

'Happy birthday!' Phoebe and Darcie cried when I opened it.

Phoebe was holding a tray containing tea in my favourite hedgehog mug, a couple of warm pain au chocolats, which smelled delectable, a bowl of chopped fruit and a pot of yoghurt.

'Thank you. That looks delicious.'

I settled onto the bed and Darcie snuggled up beside me. Phoebe was about to pass me the tray but we both started laughing, realising that eating off a tray while pregnant wasn't going to work.

'I'll just pop it on here,' she said, clearing some space on my bedside drawers for the tray then perching on the edge of the bed.

Misty-Blue, my grey and white tabby cat, jumped up, closely followed by her best friend Luna – a black stray who'd become our pet last year after being found on Fizz's brother's farm, Bumblebee Barn, feeding some abandoned hoglets. We hadn't been sure if Luna would adjust to life inside, but she spent more time indoors than Misty-Blue did, usually curled up on Darcie's bed on the top floor of our three-storey farmhouse.

'How are you feeling about the shorter hair?' I asked Phoebe.

She ran her fingers through the sleek shoulder-length cut which accentuated her high cheekbones.

'It'll take some getting used to, but it's going to be a lot easier to manage for work.'

I'd only ever known her with long hair, but she'd had it all cut off after work last night and I couldn't help thinking that removing the curtain of hair was also a statement about how far she'd come, completing her amazing transformation since moving into Hedgehog Hollow almost two years ago. She'd finished college last year and secured her job as a trainee accountant and now I hardly recognised the shy, nervy student in the woman before me. With only a few months until her twenty-first birthday, her confidence had blossomed. She was excelling at work, had been fast-tracked onto the next level of accountancy exams, and it was wonderful to see her developing friendships.

Darcie had changed too. She'd always been confident and bubbly, but she'd carried an air of loneliness which had thankfully eased as she settled into her new school and started making friends. Attending after-school clubs – something she'd never been given the opportunity to do in her old life – had made a massive difference. She went to ballet, street dancing, judo and the Cub pack run by my in-laws, Connie and Alex. Making more friends at each club, that loneliness had well and truly disappeared, and I was confident that Darcie's childhood memories would be happy and positive, having escaped from the Grimes family before they'd inflicted any lasting damage.

* * *

'Happy birthday, poppet!' Dad said, returning with Josh when I was in the lounge with Phoebe and Darcie a little later.

Dad kissed me on the cheek then drew me into one of his bear hugs. 'Can't believe my little girl is thirty-two. It seems like no time since I was in my early thirties. I'm getting old.'

'You don't look old, Grandpa Jonathan,' Darcie said, earning her a hug from Dad too. 'Not like Grandpa Terry.'

Dad laughed. 'That's good to hear because Terry's twenty-five years older than me.' He pointed to the pile of gifts in front of the log burner. 'Are those for me?'

Darcie squealed and dived for the pile of gifts. 'They're Samantha's! This one's from me,' she said, holding out a soft package wrapped in hedgehog wrapping paper.

I carefully peeled back the tape and removed a pair of black dungarees with a mother hedgehog, hoglet and wildflowers embroidered on the bib and the words 'Bublet on board'.

'Aw, they're gorgeous. Thank you, Darcie.' I stood up and held the dungarees against me.

'I asked Auntie Chloe to make them for you. She's very clever.'

'She certainly is.' Chloe had become quite the sewist since making the first batch of crafts for our Family Fun Day last year.

'I'm excited about making a Christmas wreath,' Darcie said as I folded up the dungarees.

We were going out for a meal tonight with friends and family, but a smaller group were spending the day at Crafty Hollow making Christmas wreaths with cream scones for lunch provided by Fizz's mum, Natasha.

Crafty Hollow was the crafting school Lauren and Chloe had set up together in the old stables beyond Wildflower Byre. The conversion had been complete in time for tours and demonstrations at our Family Fun Day in late June and the first few months had gone really well. Lauren and Chloe would be announcing details of their Christmas-themed workshops soon and we were getting our very own sneak preview today.

Darcie handed me another gift, then another, until the pile was gone and I was surrounded by gorgeous presents, including more clothes, scented candles, perfume, jewellery, and books.

'I'm feeling very spoilt,' I said. 'Thank you all very much. I think I'll change into my new dungarees and then we'll head down to Crafty Hollow.'

* * *

It was a beautiful autumn day, with clear cornflower-blue skies but a nip in the air holding the promise of winter. Birds chirped in the trees, and I liked to think it was a special birthday chorus for me.

Darcie blew kisses to the animals as we passed the rescue centre and giggled as she kicked her way through a trail of fallen orange and brown leaves. I still hadn't decided which season I loved the most at Hedgehog Hollow, as each brought fresh colours, new sounds and such beauty.

I stroked my hand over my bump, smiling contentedly. It was definitely a happy birthday so far.

2

SAMANTHA

Crafty Hollow could probably have opened for business sooner than June, but Chloe and Lauren had wanted to think carefully about what sort of crafts they'd offer and how they wanted to use the space. Fizz's architect friend Robbie had done such a great job designing the holiday cottages that they'd been keen to use him and what they'd created together was so impressive. The upstairs was used for material-based crafts like sewing, quilting, needle-felting, knitting and crocheting, with the ground floor devoted to bigger and messier activities such as art, upholstery and mosaic-making. On the ground floor, one side still had individual stables – beautifully retaining the building's equestrian origins – each housing the materials and equipment needed for different crafts.

Chloe and Lauren had already developed so many skills and they kept learning new ones to add to their offering. They'd also partnered with a guest art tutor. Javine Dafoe had been the Head of Art and Design at Reddfield TEC until a restructure last spring. She'd taken redundancy, just like Lauren, and ran art workshops at Crafty Hollow alongside running her own art gallery.

'Looks like everyone's here before us,' I said, recognising the various cars in the car park.

I pushed open the door and squealed as party poppers sounded and paper streamers were tossed towards me. Giant number three and two helium balloons stood on a table with a colourful balloon bouquet, along with a stack of gifts.

'You weren't meant to be getting me presents,' I gently reprimanded them.

'You deserve it,' Chloe said.

I worked my way round the group with hugs and kisses. Knowing how desperate Darcie was to get started, I suggested opening my gifts when we broke for lunch.

Chloe handed out mocktails and asked the guests to find a seat. I sat at the largest table with Mum, Auntie Louise, Hannah and Rich. Fizz, Phoebe, Beth and Natasha were on the table beside us, leaving the third one for Rosemary, Celia, Darcie and Beth.

'Good morning, ladies and gent,' Lauren called once we'd all settled.

Everyone smiled in Rich's direction, and he did a bow.

'A very warm welcome to Crafty Hollow for a special wreath-making workshop in celebration of Sam's birthday.' Lauren paused for whoops. 'Chloe and I are going to demonstrate some of the techniques you'll need today, but don't worry if you don't take it all in, as we'll come round the tables.'

'One of the many fabulous things about crafts,' Chloe said, 'is that what you create is completely unique to you. We've prepared some sample wreaths which you can copy, use for inspiration, or completely ignore.'

As Chloe spoke, Lauren held up different Christmas wreaths showing a variety of styles and colours.

'On your tables,' Chloe continued, 'you'll find the basic wreath and the equipment you need to decorate it.'

She named each item as Lauren held them up.

Lauren pointed to some tables laid down one side of the room. 'Over there, you'll find crates full of materials like artificial holly, poinsettias, pinecones and a selection of other Christmas goodies, so have a good rummage and find what speaks to you. We want you all to go home with something you love.'

'If there's something you'd like which isn't there, do ask, as we may well have it,' Chloe added. 'And if you add something to your wreath and decide it's not quite right, it's easily removed.'

It was such a delight to see Lauren and Chloe in full teaching mode. Their passion shone brightly, and I loved how they worked as a double act. I'd never have predicted that they'd form such a strong friendship and end up in business together.

We gathered round their table while they did a couple of demonstrations, sharing tips on how to attach the materials securely and lay them out to the best effect.

'Over to you,' Lauren said, smiling round the group. 'Check out the crates and, as it's only ten weeks until Christmas and we're doing Christmas crafts, I think you'll forgive us for putting on a Christmas playlist.'

I hung back with Hannah while everyone dived for the crates.

'How are you feeling?' I asked her.

She placed her hands on her baby bump and rolled her eyes. 'Enormous. I saw my midwife yesterday. I'm booked in for a C-section on Wednesday, but I'm hoping he'll put in an appearance before then.'

Hannah and Toby were expecting a boy, and three-year-old Amelia couldn't wait to have a little brother to boss about. It had been lovely being pregnant at the same time as Hannah and it was exciting to think that our children would go to school together and hopefully be the best of friends, like us.

Mum, Auntie Louise and Rich returned with a selection of

materials, so Hannah and I went to explore. As I passed Rosemary and Celia's table, it warmed my heart to see Chloe sitting with them, asking Rosemary for her ideas and handing her different materials to touch. I tuned into what she was saying as I hovered by the crates.

'This is so kind of you, my dear,' Rosemary said. 'I assumed I'd just be helping Celia.'

'Wreath-making is a great craft for the visually impaired because it's very tactile, so your fingers can do the work instead of your eyes. We can help with any really fiddly bits, but I'm certain you're going to produce something spectacular.'

Tears rushed to my eyes – pregnancy hormones making me cry at everything these days – and Hannah patted my arm and touched her heart. Chloe was like a different person these days, or rather she was consistently the lovely person I knew she could be instead of the self-centred, selfish Chloe who'd emerged far too often. Hannah had admitted recently how much she liked her now, which was great to hear. Toby and James were best friends, so Hannah hadn't been able to avoid Chloe but had really struggled with her presence at first.

I decided to make a wreath which blended Christmas and autumn with pinecones, berries, conkers, leaves and fruit. Auntie Louise and Rich were both going all-out Christmas with poinsettias, holly and berries, Mum had selected pastel pinks, greens and creams, and Hannah had chosen dried orange segments and cinnamon sticks.

My thoughts didn't usually turn to Christmas until well after my birthday, but I felt so Christmassy right now, surrounded by all the glitter and sparkle and with seasonal music playing. There was a large tree by the entrance which Lauren and Chloe had put up at the start of the month to encourage customers to think about booking Christmas workshops. Christmas bunting and fairy lights were draped across the storage stables and the whole atmosphere was warm and festive.

'Dave tells me that Orchard House is nearly finished now,' Rich said to Mum.

Mum had moved into the house in Little Tilbury last summer and had made amazing progress with the renovations. Rich's partner Dave had project managed the interior while Mum developed the extensive gardens. She'd loved her first year at agricultural college and was planning to set up her own landscape gardening business when she finished her course.

'There's just the en suite in the master bedroom to finish,' Mum said, 'and then that's all the major work done. Your Dave and his team are brilliant. I'm so thrilled with their work.'

Rich glowed with the compliment. 'I'll pass that on. Thank you.'

Lauren joined us. 'I love seeing what everyone chooses,' she said, looking at the materials we'd picked. 'They're all going to be beautiful.'

'What's your favourite craft?' Hannah asked her.

'I love them all, and I never in a million years imagined I'd say that. Who knew there was a closet crafter inside me? At a push, maybe mosaics or stained glass. There's something really special about taking what appear to be broken bits and turning them into something whole. A metaphor for life, I think.'

I was pretty sure from the wide smile and the sparkle in her eyes that she was thinking about the broken heart she'd nursed ever since her first husband walked out on her with no explanation. Now she knew what had happened, they'd become friends once more, and she'd found love with Riley. They were such a great match.

'How are you enjoying life on the farm?' Mum asked.

'It's the stuff of dreams,' Lauren said. 'I get to wake up to stunning views every day and then I come to work here and it's a different set of stunning views. I'm very lucky.'

Lauren had moved into the most gorgeous farmhouse – Briar Ridge – with Riley and his twelve-year-old son, Kai. It was a similar set-up to Hedgehog Hollow, where most of the land was rented and farmed by a neighbouring farmer, leaving the farmhouse, gardens, a meadow and an orchard for them to maintain.

Lauren chatted to us a little longer and gave us a few more tips before moving on to the next table.

The stables were alive with chatter, singing and laughter and I couldn't imagine a better way to spend my birthday.

Chloe sat down beside Darcie, who was unsurprisingly creating a pink wreath. I couldn't hear what Chloe was saying but I didn't miss the squeal of delight when Chloe handed her a sparkling unicorn to attach to it.

Fizz, who was wearing a Christmas jumper with a sequin pug in antlers on the front, was saying something to Phoebe and Natasha which had them all in fits of giggles. Fizz's girlfriend Yasmin had been invited and I couldn't help feeling guilty at how relieved I'd been when Fizz told me that Yasmin would join us for the evening meal only. I found Yasmin hard work, but Fizz's parents, Natasha and Hadrian, seemed to really like her, so I wondered if it was just me. Could I have unwittingly given off a vibe which made her feel uncomfortable in my presence – wishful thinking on my part to see Phoebe and Fizz together because, in my mind, they were infinitely better suited?

Watching Phoebe and Fizz together now couldn't be more different to seeing Fizz with Yasmin. The bubbly, laughing Fizz was the one we knew and loved but she always seemed on edge around Yasmin. Fizz sometimes joked about how refreshing it was that Yasmin didn't try to change her like her ex-girlfriend Nadine had, but I wasn't convinced that was true. Fizz's outward appearance had remained the same – bright, sparkly, unicorn-themed clothes and colourful hair, a purple ombre look being her latest – but there was a behavioural change which had surfaced a couple of months into their relationship.

An hour into our wreath-making, I went to make myself a mug of fruit tea and Rich joined me in the small kitchen.

'Have you decided what colour to paint the nursery?' he asked, pouring himself a coffee.

'No. I've narrowed it down to four colours, but I keep changing my mind on which I like best. We're getting some sample pots next weekend and I hope seeing them on the wall will help me decide.'

'It should do.' He stirred in some milk. 'I have some news for you. Dave and I have decided to move house.'

'Really? Not out of the area?'

'Definitely not. We love it here. We want somewhere bigger because we'd like to become dads.'

'Oh, my gosh! Rich! That's amazing news. But I didn't think you were interested in having children.'

'We weren't but, you know, you get a bit older and your friends start having kids and you get a different outlook on life. We haven't decided whether we want to foster, adopt or go down a surrogacy route but we've been talking about it for months and we're certain it's what we want. You can tell Josh, but we're not sharing it with anyone else just yet.'

'I'll keep quiet.' I put my drink down and hugged him. 'I'm so excited for you. You'll both be amazing dads.' I wasn't just saying that. Darcie adored them and they'd always been brilliant with Josh's young half-siblings, Archie and Lottie.

'Thank you.'

As we took our drinks back to the table, I couldn't stop smiling at the prospect of another expansion to the Hedgehog Hollow family.

There was a sudden clatter, making me jump, and a shout from Mum. Hannah was standing by her upturned chair, a pool of water on the floor.

'Guess I won't be needing that C-section on Wednesday,' she said, grimacing at me.

I put my drink down as Rich righted the chair and gently eased Hannah into it.

'Any contractions?' I asked.

'None so far. Ooh! Spoke too soon!'

She scrunched up her face and gripped the table, waiting for the sensation to pass.

I glanced at her phone in front of her. 'It's 11.11, nice and easy to remember. How about you call your midwife and I'll give Toby a ring?'

The volume of the music lowered.

'Everyone!' Chloe called. 'Why don't we give Hannah some space and go on a little tour upstairs? I can show you some of the Christmas crafts we've been preparing.'

I gave her a grateful thumbs up as everyone was ushered away.

Lauren brought a pile of towels over and dropped a couple on the floor. 'How are you feeling, Hannah?'

'Okay. Bit embarrassed doing that in front of everyone.'

We all assured her there was no need to be.

'It's a natural part of pregnancy and every woman's experience is different,' Rich said gently. 'It's a slow trickle for some and like floodgates opening for others.'

'It was a trickle with Amelia, but trust me to be floodgates this time when I'm out.'

She picked up her phone and I grabbed mine to make the call to Toby. I walked away from the table as the phone rang out, tutting as it went to voicemail.

'Hi, Toby, it's Samantha. Hannah's waters have just broken and she's started her contractions. She's on the phone to her midwife now but you might want to drive over here in case—'

A cry from Hannah stopped me mid-sentence.

'Another contraction,' Rich called to me. 'Four minutes apart.'

'Toby, scrub that,' I said. 'You *definitely* want to drive over now. Baby's on his way. Don't worry about Amelia. We'll look after her as planned.'

Rich was looking at his watch as Hannah gripped the table once more. 'You're doing great. Four minutes apart, lasting longer than sixty seconds, which means baby's going to put in an appearance a little sooner than we thought but you're a nurse, we have two former nurses here, and I'm a paramedic, so you're in very good hands. Are you comfortable with me doing an internal examination to check your cervix?'

'Yes. That's fine.'

'Okay. I'll grab my medical bag from the car, but we could do with lying you down somewhere comfortable.'

'There's a sofa in our office,' Lauren said, pointing towards the door by the kitchen.

Lauren and I linked arms with Hannah and helped her over to the office.

'Toby?' she asked.

'Voicemail, but I'll keep trying.'

Inside the office, Lauren laid a throw on the sofa. 'You might want to remove those wet leggings. Can't be comfortable.'

While Lauren helped her out of her leggings and knickers, I rang Josh in the barn and asked him to bring my largest nightshirt and more towels as quickly as possible.

Hannah was in the midst of another contraction when Rich returned.

'Lauren, can you take Hannah's pulse while I check how things are coming along?' he said, helping Hannah lie down on the sofa after her contraction passed.

I tried Toby again but he was still on voicemail, so I sent him a text and WhatsApp message in the hope he'd pick one of them up soon.

'Seven centimetres dilated,' Rich reported. 'It looks like things are moving along quickly. We're going to need to get you to hospital. Where were you—'

Another contraction stopped him mid-sentence and he held Hannah's hand as she cried out in pain.

'Three minutes,' Lauren said.

'Anything I can do to help?' Mum asked, poking her head round the door.

Rich was asking Hannah what had prompted the c-section for Amelia's birth, assessing the likelihood of her needing one for this birth, so I stepped outside.

'Yes, please. Baby's on his way very quickly. We're about to call an ambulance but there's a strong possibility of Hannah giving birth here. Can you ask Chloe to take everyone up to the farmhouse? Josh is on his way with towels. Can you watch out for him?'

'Okay. Give Hannah my love.'

Back in the office, Lauren was on the phone to the emergency operator and Hannah had changed position so that she was on all fours on the office floor. I tried Toby again but it went straight to voicemail once more, so I left another update before returning to Hannah.

'I don't think I'm going finish my wreath today,' she said ruefully, blowing her fringe out of her face.

'But you'll leave with an even more special creation,' I said, smiling at her. 'And I won't ever forget this birthday.'

3

FIZZ

We'd only been up at the farmhouse for fifteen minutes when Chloe's phone rang. Darcie was sitting on the floor, absorbed by Saturday morning children's television, but the rest of us looked expectantly at Chloe.

'It's Sammie,' she said, crossing her fingers and dipping out of the lounge.

You could have heard a pin drop as we awaited the news.

She was back a couple of minutes later and the tense atmosphere lifted at her smile.

'He's here and they're both doing well. Because he was born in the stables, they've named him Jesus.'

Phoebe and I glanced at each other, eyes wide, then Chloe burst out laughing.

'Kidding! His name's Mason George Spiers, he's 8lb 2oz and they're on their way to hospital now for a full check, but Sammie says that's just routine.'

'Did Toby make it on time?' Beth asked.

'Yes, but only just. He'd been in the middle of the supermarket with no signal and then, when he got to the till, all the messages came through so he had to abandon his trolley.'

Shortly afterwards, Josh arrived with Amelia and told us the ambulance had just arrived. Amelia seemed oblivious to the drama surrounding her brother's arrival as she settled in front of the TV with Darcie.

* * *

'Did you believe Chloe when she said they'd called the baby Jesus?' Phoebe asked me a little later as we loaded the dishwasher after a round of drinks.

'A hundred per cent. I didn't know what to say!'

'Me neither. Mason's a cute name.'

'It is. I can't believe what some people call their kids. I bumped into a lass I used to know from Young Farmers' and she's just had a girl. You'll never guess what she's called her. Peach.'

'As in the fruit?'

'Yep. Her full name's Peach Honey Ryder.'

Phoebe scrunched up her nose. 'Ew! Sounds like a paint colour or a yoghurt flavour.'

'I thought it sounded more like a porn star name.'

'Oh, my God! It does! Poor kid doesn't stand a chance.'

We were still giggling about some of the strange names people gave to their children as we left the farmhouse to walk back to Crafty Hollow. Yasmin would have hated that conversation. She didn't do jokes, banter or silliness and she definitely didn't do toilet humour.

Recently, she didn't do much humour at all. She was an artist and sculptor, working on several big commissions, and was under a lot of pressure at the moment so I'd barely seen her and, when I did, there was tension. As soon as she'd met her deadlines, things would be back to normal. Hopefully.

* * *

Mum had prepared an amazing spread for lunch. We had finger sandwiches, mini quiches, scones with jam and cream, and a selection of miniature cakes and pastries including sugared doughnuts. I challenged the guests to try to eat the doughnuts without licking their fingers or lips, which had everyone laughing, and I took photos of everyone with sugary pouts. Another thing Yasmin would have hated.

Phoebe and I helped Mum clear everything away then returned to our wreaths. I'd gone for a fairly simple design – Yasmin wouldn't appreciate anything fussy on the door – so mine was nearly finished.

'Can I make another one?' I asked Chloe. 'Obviously, I'll pay you for it.'

'Of course you can. Where are you putting them?'

'We never use the front door, so this one's for the side door into the kitchen, but I thought I'd make a second one for Yasmin's studio.'

'That's really sweet of you,' Phoebe said, smiling at me.

I smiled back, even though I wasn't sure I was doing the right thing. Yasmin's house was at the end of a row of six former farmworkers' cottages. It benefitted from an enormous garden which wrapped around the turning circle at the end of the lane and her studio was tucked away at the bottom of the garden. Originally a barn when the land was part of a farm, it had been in a state of disrepair, but Yasmin had it converted into a modern studio with a glass frontage to make best use of the light. The walls were white and she kept it minimalistic but if I didn't do anything fussy – a small wreath with muted colours – surely even she would like that.

I was halfway through making Yasmin's wreath when she messaged me on WhatsApp.

✉ From Yasmin
Behind schedule so I need to work tonight.
Please let Sam know I'm not coming

My stomach sank. Again? Especially after she'd already declined the daytime invitation.

'You're seriously making Christmas wreaths in mid-October?' she'd challenged when I invited her. 'Can't think of a worse way to spend a Saturday. You're on your own for that one.'

'You'll come along for the meal, though?'

'Do I have to? They're your friends, not mine. I don't drag you out to everything I do with my friends.'

'Yeah, but I always come when you ask. Please. It's important to me.'

She'd agreed with a sigh on the proviso that I didn't try to talk her into the day do. I should have known she was going to pull out. Yasmin never did anything she didn't want to do.

I'd told Sam that Yasmin would need to work today, so it wasn't implausible that she'd dropped out for that reason, but I wished I didn't have to deliver that news yet again. Was this how it was always going to be with us? Yasmin doing her thing with her friends and me with mine? I wasn't the sort of girlfriend who wanted to be part of every aspect of my partner's life, but surely there should be some crossover.

'Bad news?' Phoebe asked, her voice full of concern.

Mum was looking at me with a frown on her face.

I forced brightness into my tone. 'Yasmin's got a nightmare deadline and she's going to need to work tonight.'

'Oh, that's a shame,' Mum said. 'We haven't seen her in ages.'

'She's so busy at the moment, which is great for her business but not so great for the social life.'

Mum patted my arm. 'The challenges of being self-employed. You've got to take the work when it comes along.'

'I'd better let Sam know.'

What I really wanted to do was go to the toilets and cry, but I wasn't going to let it get to me this time.

'Do you want me to let the pub know?' I asked Sam after I'd given her the news.

'Thanks, but I'll do it. I was going to ring about Hannah and Toby anyway, so I'll reduce the booking by three. They won't mind. I hope she gets caught up soon. Sounds like she has a lot on.'

'She does. She's hardly ever out of her studio at the moment.' As soon as I said it, a wave of shame washed over me. She genuinely was snowed under, working very long hours, and I should be supportive of that instead of thinking badly of her for pulling out.

* * *

I picked up a bottle of Yasmin's favourite cloudy apple juice on the way home and a box of her favourite chocolates. Even though I was dead chuffed with the wreath I'd made for her, I still wasn't sure it was the right thing. Her sneer at making wreaths in mid-October kept coming back to me so I decided to leave it in my car and give it to her nearer Christmas. Or not at all. At least I knew I couldn't go wrong with apple juice and chocolates.

The outside light came on when I pulled onto the drive, but the cottage was in darkness. I lifted my bag and the larger wreath out of the car and walked towards the kitchen door, listening carefully. If Yasmin's work was going well, I could usually hear soul music drifting up from her studio, but silence wasn't good.

'Jinks?' I called, switching on the kitchen light. 'Where are you?'

Still holding my wreath, I nudged open the lounge door. My ginger cat was curled up in his bed in the darkness. Why couldn't she have left a lamp on for him?

'Hey, you,' I said, placing everything down on the armchair. 'I've missed you.'

He yawned, stretched and padded over to me for a fuss. I picked him up and he lay in my arms like a baby while I stroked his white tummy.

'Let's get you some food.'

He leapt out of my arms and paced up and down beside his food bowl, mewing at me. I emptied a pouch into it and smiled at him hoovering it up, but my smile slipped as I spotted the note from Yasmin on the worktop:

In studio. Don't disturb
Enjoy your meal

'That's me told,' I said to Jinks, scrumpling the note up and tossing it into the recycling crate.

I put her apple juice in the fridge and the chocolates on the side and started typing in a message on my phone to say I'd bought her some gifts. With a sigh, I deleted what I'd written and dropped my phone back in my bag. That would probably count as disturbing her. Best to stick to my orders.

4

SAMANTHA

⊠ From Hannah
I was hoping your birthday would be memorable
but probably not in that way! Hope everyone was
OK with all the drama. We're on our way home
now. Thanks so much for having Amelia overnight.
Sorry to be missing your meal tonight. Have an
amazing time xx

⊠ To Hannah
Probably my most memorable birthday yet and
everyone's fine. It was an honour to see Mason
come into the world and to share my birthday
with him. Enjoy your 1st night together. Hugs to
you all xx

I shrugged off my dressing gown and pulled on the dress which
Darcie had chosen this morning – a petrol blue wrap dress with
large coral flowers on it.

Josh appeared for his shower and paused by the door, smiling tenderly. 'You look incredible, Sammie.'

'Thank you. I wish my feet weren't so swollen. Do you think I can get away with wearing slippers?'

I'd had a straightforward pregnancy so far. The nausea I'd experienced during my first trimester had eased by eating little and often and always having ginger biscuits and salty snacks to hand. I'd been tired but not exhausted, so if swollen feet and ankles were all I experienced, I'd got off lightly and definitely couldn't complain.

'Hmm. As long as they're not in a clashing colour,' he said, laughing.

'What about those?' I nodded towards the enormous hedgehog-shaped slippers beside the bed which Phoebe had given me last Christmas.

'It would certainly be a style statement. I dare you!'

'Maybe I'm not quite at the fluffy slippers stage, but I think it's going to have to be flip-flops.'

I could brave bare feet tonight for the short walk to and from the jeep but the temperature was dropping and I feared I might have to attempt to wear socks with my flip-flops in the future – not easy with the toe post and definitely not stylish. Maybe the hedgehog slippers would be a better look

* * *

'... happy birthday, dear Samantha, happy birthday to you!'

It was loud and pitchy, but it made my heart happy to see so many friends and family gathered together just for me. Including children, babies and a guide dog, there were thirty of us.

The sparkler on the ice cream sundae in front of me fizzled out to cries of 'speech!' I rolled my eyes but obliged anyway.

'Thank you all for coming out tonight to celebrate my birthday. I really appreciate it. It makes me very happy to look round the table and see how much our Hedgehog Hollow family has grown...' I glanced down at my stomach, '... and continues to grow. I'd like to propose an extra-special toast to the latest addition, who clearly didn't get the memo that to be born in a stable he needed to arrive on Christmas day. To Amelia's new baby brother, Mason George Spiers.'

Everyone raised their glasses and repeated my toast.

'Enjoy your desserts,' I said.

As we finished eating, I smiled at Chloe and James seated opposite me as they attempted to clean two-year-old Samuel, who'd managed to smear ice cream across his face and hair. The pair of them seemed stronger and happier than ever. James was in complete remission and village life had done wonders for both of them. Chloe finally had the friends and social life she'd dreamed of, as well as a thriving business.

Chloe wiped her hands and passed me her phone. 'What do you think of this? Javine's just finished it and she's offering it for auction at the Christmas Fair with all proceeds going to Hedgehog Hollow.'

I looked down at the most stunning painting of a hedgehog, badger, fox, hare and owl gathered round a roaring fire. Stockings hung from the mantelpiece, which had a Christmas tree on one side and a window on the other. Peeking through the window was a deer, behind which stood a snowman.

'It's beautiful and that's so generous.'

'We've added another art workshop into the Christmas schedule – a hedgehog in a Christmas hat. I'll WhatsApp it to you when Javine sends it over.'

I couldn't wait to see it. Javine had created some stunning Christmas card designs which we'd made available at the start of the month on the online shop which Phoebe ran for me, but they'd sold out so quickly that we'd needed to get another batch printed. As well as Javine's art, we used the shop for the crafts that Lauren and Chloe made, although there was only limited stock advertised at the moment as they were building up their supplies for this year's Christmas Fair in five weeks' time. There was nothing I personally needed to do for it, as that and the June Family Fun Day were now Chloe, Lauren and Natasha's projects, leaving Fizz and me to completely focus on the part that excited us – looking after our animals.

At the end of the table, Darcie and Kai were keeping Amelia entertained with a colouring book and some crayons and she didn't seem bothered that she hadn't seen her parents all after-noon. She was my goddaughter and a regular visitor to Hedgehog Hollow, so it shouldn't be too strange for her spending the night with us.

'I'm headin' home, lass.'

I looked up at my friend, eighty-one-year-old Terry, and my stomach sank.

'Are you okay?' I asked, concerned by the paleness of his cheeks and the dark bags under his eyes.

'Aye. Just a bit tired. I've not been sleeping so well lately, and it's caught up with me.'

I stood up and hugged him. He felt thinner and his cheek was cold against mine, making my stomach sink again. He normally had a good appetite, but I'd noticed he hadn't ordered a starter or dessert and he'd only eaten half of his main course.

'I'll come and see you tomorrow, around late morning so you can have a lie-in.'

'There's no need,' he said.

'I won't take no for an answer. I'll bring some homemade soup over for your lunch.'

He gave me a weak smile. 'That'd be grand. Happy birthday, lass.'

Celia had driven him, so I said goodbye to her and Rosemary and gave Trixie, Rosemary's guide dog, a stroke before she was clipped onto her working harness. Seventy-six-year-old Rosemary had been Phoebe's neighbour when she was younger and had remained a close friend and valuable support after Phoebe's dad died. She now lived in a purpose-built bungalow in Fimberley – the same village as Terry – designed for those with reduced mobility. Earlier this year, her long-standing best friend Celia had moved in with her – a big relief for Phoebe, who had previously been worried about fiercely independent Rosemary being on her own.

Rosemary clasped my hand and murmured, 'Is Terry all right?'

'I'm not sure. What makes you ask?'

'He sounds different. Tired. Weary.'

'He just told me he hasn't been sleeping well.'

'That's what he said to me too and we both know Terry has never been a big sleeper, so I'm not buying it.'

I wasn't either. 'I'm taking some soup round tomorrow. I'll see what I can get out of him then and I'll keep you posted.'

* * *

Terry was still on my mind when Josh and I got ready for bed later that evening and I was about to ask Josh if he thought Terry looked ill, but my phone beeped with a WhatsApp notification:

✉ From Hannah
Forgot to attach a photo earlier. Mason says goodnight and happy joint birthday xx

'Aw, look!' I sat on the edge of the bed, my eyes filling with tears at the photo of a red-faced baby with his eyes tightly shut and his tiny fists clenched against his lips. Where Amelia had inherited Hannah's dark hair, it looked like Mason was going to be auburn-haired like his dad.

Josh scrambled across the bed and peered over my shoulder. 'Cute. I like the name Mason.'

'Me too. I'm glad it wasn't on our list, or I'd have been gutted.'

'So it's a boy you think we're having?' he teased.

'Could be. Or that could be a double bluff. You're not going to get it out of me.'

'Not even if I do this?' He gently massaged my shoulders.

'Ooh, that's good, but my lips remain sealed and don't you dare stop.'

'Have you enjoyed your birthday?' he asked.

'It's been the best.'

It really had been a wonderful day and such a special moment to be there for Mason's birth. I just hoped that Terry was all right.

'I'm so stuffed,' Dad said as we wandered across the car park after Sam's birthday meal. 'I might not fit behind the steering wheel.'

'Serves you right for having a sharing dessert all to yourself,' Mum responded, giving him an affectionate prod to the stomach.

'I thought you were going to share it with me.'

'I said I could probably manage a couple of spoonfuls but that was it.'

Dad turned to me. 'I can't believe you didn't help me out either.'

'Also full,' I insisted.

'Salad isn't filling.'

'It is when you have it with a double chicken burger and chips.'

We arrived at Dad's car and, after a lot of huffing and puffing, he settled behind the steering wheel.

'Sam looked lovely tonight,' I said once we'd set off.

'She did,' Mum agreed. 'Pregnancy looks fabulous on her. I got chatting to Debs and she's ever so excited about being a grandma for the first time.'

It was an obvious thing to say and Mum wasn't the sort to question me or my older brother Barney, whether directly or subtly, about the chances of her becoming a grandparent one day but, considering I was now twenty-eight and Barney was thirty, she had to be wondering. Because I was.

I gazed out of the window into the darkness, only half-listening to my parents talking about the food and the conversations they'd had that evening.

'It's such a shame Yasmin couldn't make it tonight,' Mum said as we headed into Little Tilbury. 'Do you think she'll make her deadline?'

'She should do. She works well under pressure, and she's never missed a deadline yet.'

The way Yasmin's projects came together at the eleventh hour was awesome. She could work on a painting or sculpture for days and sometimes even weeks and it would look okay and then suddenly it transformed from okay to brilliant.

'You can drop me at the end of the lane,' I told Dad. 'It'll be nice to have a blast of fresh air before bedtime.'

Appleby Lane was on the edge of the village. The two-bedroom 200-year-old stone-built cottages had small front gardens surrounded by hedgerows and, on the other side of the lane, a hedgerow ran alongside a grassy meadow. Yasmin preferred ultra-modern houses with sharp lines and lots of glass, but there weren't many of those in the Wolds villages, so she'd had to compromise on style. She regularly griped about the uneven walls, small windows and exposed beams – all the characterful elements which I loved – but she spent so little time in the cottage, I'm surprised she even noticed it.

'Give Yasmin our love,' Mum said as Dad pulled up at the lane end. 'I'm guessing she won't be joining us for Sunday lunch?'

'I doubt it.' I shuffled forward and gave them each a kiss on the cheek. 'See you at Barney's tomorrow.'

I waved and set off slowly down the lane, keeping my eye out for wildlife. A rustling to my right made me slow my pace further and I stopped completely, my heart melting as a large, rounded hedgehog emerged from the garden of number three, sniffed the air, and crossed the lane, disappearing into the meadow. My night was made!

I'd loved hedgehogs from the moment I met Gwendoline 'Hedgehog Lady' Mickleby – a friend of my grandparents – when I was a young child. A combination of seeing how she helped sick and injured hedgehogs and spending so much time at our family farm had sent me down the route of wanting to help animals too, and I couldn't imagine ever tiring of seeing them in the wild.

The gentle hoot of a long-eared owl a few paces later stopped me in my tracks once more and I squinted into the trees, but there was little chance of seeing it in the darkness tonight unless it took flight.

There was a car parked outside our cottage and I recognised it by the glow of the streetlamp as belonging to Yasmin's best friend Arianna. Hopefully Arianna had just arrived for a fleeting visit because if she'd been here all evening, I wouldn't be impressed when Yasmin had pulled out of the meal due to her workload.

The lights on the car flashed, making me jump. Arianna's girlfriend Sara-Jade opened the gate and squealed as she spotted me.

'You scared the life out of me, Fizz,' she said, clutching her heart dramatically.

'Sorry. Will you survive?' I joked.

'Just about.' Sara-Jade removed a hoodie from the back seat and pulled it over her head. 'My fault for going along with Arianna's horror films fest every time we hit October. Can't stand the things. I'm jumpy all month!'

'I can't do horror films either,' I said, feeling her pain.

I'd warmed to Sara-Jade as soon as I met her. She was warm,

enthusiastic and fun to be around. I hadn't warmed to Arianna. She'd been Yasmin's bestie since their days at art college and I got the distinct impression she tolerated my presence rather than enjoyed it.

'I was so relieved when Yasmin got in touch at the start of the week to invite us over,' Sara-Jade said. 'Arianna had a *Nightmare on Elm Street* evening planned. I've seen the films loads of times, but that Freddie Krueger still terrifies me.' She shuddered. 'Anyway, did you have a nice meal?'

'Lovely, thanks.' My voice sounded a little robotic. Had I heard her right?

As we walked across the drive together, I zoned out of her chat about horror films. Yasmin had only pulled out of Sam's meal this afternoon, but it seemed she'd been planning to let me down all week. How could she do that to me?

Arianna was in the kitchen topping up two glasses of wine when I opened the door.

'Hey, Fizzy, how was your night out with your boss's family?'

I hated being called Fizzy, especially when Arianna managed to make it sound like an insult. And why did she struggle so much with the concept of having a positive working relationship and a friendship?

'It was awesome, thanks,' I said in my brightest, bubbliest tone. 'How was your evening?'

'The best.'

With a flick of her long chestnut hair, she swept past me.

I followed Sara-Jade into the lounge, a warm smile pasted on my face. There was so much I wanted to ask Yasmin about tonight, but I wouldn't embarrass her in front of her friends. There could be any number of reasonable explanations as to why she'd cancelled on me then spent the evening with them and we could discuss that when they'd gone.

Only they didn't go. Sara-Jade said she'd had a nightmare week in her teaching role and, when she relayed the tale, Yasmin said she sounded like she could do with a drink rather than driving home, so they were invited to stay over. Another bottle of wine was opened but, not being much of a drinker, I made a hot chocolate instead.

They spent the rest of the evening reminiscing about their college days and the clubbing scene in Hull, where they'd met Sara-Jade. Always considerate, Sara-Jade did her best to include me in the conversation. I laughed with them and threw in the occasional question to try to show my interest, but it wasn't easy being the outsider in a tightly-knit group who'd known each other for fifteen years.

I didn't want to be the first to drift off to bed but, by midnight, I was flagging and had to call it a night. I hovered in the doorway, thinking Yasmin might at least roll off the sofa and kiss me goodnight, but all she did was say goodnight then launch into another anecdote. I tried not to take it personally. She wasn't one for demonstrations of affection in public, but a brief kiss or even just a hug in her lounge in front of her two best friends was hardly 'public'.

Every time I drifted off, a whoop of laughter from downstairs jolted me awake. After an hour or so, I was fed up of battling sleep, so I grabbed my phone and scrolled through the socials. Sam had uploaded photos from Crafty Hollow and the meal and tagged in her guests, thanking us for making her birthday so special. I scrolled through them, smiling. It had been a really great day and evening, as were all the get-togethers involving Sam's friends and family who'd always made me feel so welcome.

I scrolled through the comments and spotted a post from Toby, apologising for their absence this evening and attaching a photo of

Mason. My heart melted at his scrunched-up face. I adored babies and children and hoped I could be a mum one day.

Another screech of laughter drew my attention away from Mason's image and to the blank space in the bed beside me. Yasmin and I had been together for more than eighteen months now. Moving in with her had been a huge relationship step for me and I assumed it had been for her too, but I had no idea how she felt about getting married or having children. I'd lost count of the number of times I'd raised the subject only to have it changed. Perhaps we should have had those conversations before I moved in to make sure we were on the same page because, more and more often recently, I suspected we weren't, and I was beginning to wonder if we ever had been.

6

SAMANTHA

Late on Sunday morning, I pulled up on the drive outside Terry's house in Fimberley. The Victorian double-fronted detached property had originally belonged to his great-grandparents and had been passed down through the generations. With three reception rooms and six bedrooms, Terry had told me he'd thought about downsizing, but Granville House had been all he'd known and he'd never been able to bring himself to put it on the market and leave behind all those memories.

It was a little after 11 a.m. but the curtains were closed across the curved bay window in the lounge and on the matching bay of Terry's bedroom above. He was usually an early bird, up at dawn and out walking Wilbur.

Nervous butterflies fluttered in my stomach as I pressed the doorbell and a grand *ding dong* sounded in the hallway. Through the stained-glass panelling, I could see Wilbur scampering down the stairs and hear the tip-tapping of his claws on the tiled floor before he jumped up at the door. He never barked when I called round and I felt reassured by how quiet he was this morning because if there was something wrong with Terry, Wilbur would surely be barking frantically.

I waited a couple more minutes before pressing the doorbell again. Stepping back to look up to Terry's bedroom once more, relief flowed through me as I spotted the curtains twitching. Minutes later, Terry answered the door, still wearing his pyjamas and dressing gown. His white hair was dishevelled and his pallor grey.

'What time is it, lass?' His voice was husky as he ushered me inside.

'Ten past eleven.'

'It never is!'

'How are you feeling, Terry?'

He sighed and ran his fingers through his hair. 'I've been better.'

I followed him as he shuffled into the lounge in his slippers. He looked as though he was going to open the curtains, but he flopped down into his favourite armchair instead, as though the effort had been too much.

'Should I let some light in?' I asked.

The slightest incline of his head confirmed it was okay. Light flooded into the room and I noticed the coffee table was littered with partially drunk mugs of tea and plates containing half-eaten sandwiches.

'Cup of tea?' I asked.

'Aye.'

Spotting a wooden tray leaning against the coffee table, I swiftly loaded everything onto it, taking care not to make too much noise. Wilbur followed me into the kitchen and nudged at his empty water bowl. Terry must have been feeling really rough to have missed that.

'Are you thirsty?' I asked Wilbur as I rinsed out his bowl and filled it with fresh water. I hadn't even placed it on the floor before he started lapping it up. I cleaned and filled his food bowl too and he tucked in eagerly.

The kitchen was also messy, which wasn't like Terry. He prided himself on keeping a clean and tidy home. If he'd been feeling poorly for several days – as the piles of crockery indicated – it must have taken considerable strength to join us last night for my birthday meal.

I took his drink through to the lounge, but his head was lolling to one side. My stomach lurched as the scene took me back to Christmas Day nearly three years ago when I found Thomas sleeping forever in his armchair. No! Not Terry too!

I released a shaky breath when Terry twitched his nose and snored.

'Don't do that to me!' I whispered, my heart rate returning to normal as I watched the steady rise and fall of his chest.

I didn't like to wake him to shoo him back to bed, so I placed his tea on the coffee table, pulled the curtains closed, and draped a throw over him before returning to the kitchen to tidy up.

When I'd finished, Terry was still asleep. I scribbled him a note to say I was taking Wilbur for a walk round the village, as I couldn't imagine Terry feeling up to it himself.

I heard someone calling my name as I crossed the village green and turned to see Jeanette Kingston hurrying towards me. She was a community leader who'd clashed with Terry in the past, but I'd met with her to explore ways in which community leaders could help make the villages more wildlife-friendly and she'd been exceptionally supportive. We became friends, and she and Terry had buried the hatchet too when he saw how eager she was to make a difference.

'Is Terry all right?' she asked, her voice full of concern as she stroked Wilbur's ears.

'He's not very well, although I'm not sure what's wrong yet. He's asleep at the moment. When did you last see him?' Jeanette's house overlooked the village green and I knew they exchanged hellos most mornings as Terry started the day walking Wilbur round the village green around the time Jeanette left for work.

'Must have been Tuesday. He looked tired then but insisted he was fine. I called round last night but there was no answer.'

'He came out for my birthday meal but, looking at him this morning, I'm not sure how he managed it.'

'Poor Terry. Let me know if there's anything he needs. It's no problem for me to drop round with a hot meal, do some shopping and walk Wilbur. Saves you the journey.'

'That's very kind, thank you. I'll have a word with Terry and let you know.'

'And how are you doing?' Jeanette asked. 'You're looking very well.'

I rested my hand on my bump. 'Nearly twenty-nine weeks now and we're doing well, except for the swollen feet.' I pointed down to my bare feet in an old pair of Crocs – the only footwear I could still fit on my feet and safely drive wearing.

'Aw, bless you. I had that with my two but at least it was spring and summer, although I do remember a few cold, wet days, feeling frozen in flip-flops.'

I let Wilbur off his lead for a run while we chatted some more. Jeanette knew Hannah and Toby from events at Hedgehog Hollow, so I shared the great news about Mason's arrival.

'I'm going to have to go,' Jeanette said, checking her watch. 'I'm off to my daughter's for lunch, but remember what I said about Terry. It's no bother at all.'

Not wanting to leave Terry on his own for too long, I stayed out for another five minutes after Jeanette left, then called Wilbur and returned to Granville House. Terry was still asleep, but Wilbur was having none of it and gave him a great big lick across his hand, stirring him.

'Samantha?'

'I'm still here,' I said, crouching beside him. 'Do you think you can make it back up to your bed and I'll heat you up some soup for lunch?'

'Not hungry.'

'Even a few sips will do you some good.'

He eased himself slowly out of the chair and shuffled to the stairs.

'Do you need an arm?' I asked.

'I'll manage.'

It was slow going but he seemed steady enough to manage the stairs on his own, so I went into the kitchen to prepare a tray with a giant mug of tomato soup, a fresh tea and a glass of water.

Terry was propped up on a couple of pillows with Wilbur curled up beside him when I took the tray upstairs.

'Haven't walked the lad,' he said.

'I've just been out with him and he's fed and watered. Do you think you can manage a few sips of soup? It's tomato.'

'I'll try.'

He didn't take much but at least he managed some of it.

'How bad do you feel?' I asked.

'Me 'ead 'urts and I've got no energy.'

'It could be the flu. You're best to get some sleep, but how about I take Wilbur with me? Phoebe and Darcie can take him for a run round the farm when they get back from Rosemary's and Josh or I can bring him back this evening and see how you're doing.'

'Aye.'

The lack of protest at the suggestion of taking Wilbur away told me exactly how ill Terry felt.

'Have you had your flu jab yet?' I asked as he shuffled down under the covers.

'Forgot to book it.'

A bout of flu could be serious for someone of Terry's age, but he was fit and healthy otherwise, so hopefully he'd have the strength to fight it. We'd have to keep a close eye on him in the meantime.

'Why don't you stay at Hedgehog Hollow?'

'I'm good here.'

'Then can I steal a spare key?'

'Small drawer in t' kitchen.'

By the time I'd loaded the tray with more discarded mugs and glasses, Terry was already asleep.

'Wilbur, here, boy.'

The dog obediently followed me downstairs and I did the final batch of washing up before searching for the 'small drawer'. There was a wicker basket inside it full of keys, but each was clearly labelled. I took 'spare front door key', checked the back doors were locked, grabbed some dog food for Wilbur, then left Terry to rest.

As I drove back to Hedgehog Hollow with Wilbur, I tried not to think about what might happen if Terry was seriously ill. With no grandparents left on my side of the family or Josh's, Terry was like a grandfather to both of us and he saw us as the grandchildren he'd never had. He referred to Bublet as his great-grandchild and he had to be around to see our baby grow.

I woke up on Sunday morning to the sound of a car horn tooting and loud cries of 'bye'. I didn't need to look out of the window to know it was Arianna and Sara-Jade leaving. Arianna always pipped her horn when she left and I have no idea why she felt the compulsion to do that when she already had Yasmin's attention.

I checked the time on my phone – 8.54 a.m. – and lay still for a couple of minutes, listening out for the sound of Yasmin in the kitchen or coming up the stairs, but the cottage was eerily silent. I glanced out of the window and saw her heading down the garden path towards the studio. No *good morning*, then.

Jinks launched himself onto the bed and rolled around on his back while I tickled his belly.

'You know Yasmin doesn't allow pets in the bedroom,' I said to him. 'But I won't tell her if you don't. Just don't shed any fur!'

Yasmin had three cats of her own – Otis, Marvin and Etta, named after some of her favourite soul singers – but they spent their time outside or in her studio and she'd expected Jinks to do the same when we moved in. I'd expected our first night living together to be all lovely and romantic but it had been far from it. I still hadn't told anyone what really happened that night.

* * *

Seven months earlier

'I'm so excited,' I told Jinks as he sprawled across my duvet, swiping at the luggage tag dangling from my suitcase. 'You're going to love it at Yasmin's. Her garden's huge.'

Nine days ago, Yasmin and I had been out for a meal to celebrate our one-year anniversary. We'd been reminiscing about the hedgehog rescue from the drain on her drive which had brought us together when, in a rare display of affection, she reached for my hand across the table.

'I'm worried about it happening again,' she said.

'It was one of those fluke moments. It's a covered drain, so the hedgehog population should be safe.'

'I still think there's a risk and it would be safer for the hedgehog population if there was a hedgehog rescuer on hand all the time.'

I raised my eyebrows and my heart started pounding. Did she mean what I thought she meant?

'What do you think?' she asked. 'Would you like to be there all the time?'

'Are you asking me to move in with you?'

'Would you like to?'

'Seriously? I'd love to. When?'

I had a university assignment due the following week and Yasmin had a commission to finish, so we agreed to wait until the following Saturday evening. It would give me time to pack and find some tenants too.

Over the next few days, Yasmin tried to convince me to sell. The market was buoyant and Bayberry Cottage would likely sell within days, but I preferred to hang onto it as an investment. I knew a couple through Young Farmers' Club who were buying a brand-new house which wouldn't be ready until mid-December. They were keen to move out of their respective parents' homes, so I agreed an eight-month lease with them starting from the Easter holidays in mid-April.

Mum and Dad were delighted for me as they both adored Yasmin. Dad questioned whether we wouldn't be better moving into Bayberry Cottage as it was bigger but, without even having that discussion with Yasmin, I knew it was impractical because of her business. She needed her studio and kiln.

'Are you ready, Jinks?' I asked, guiding him into his carry case.

As I drove the short distance to Little Tilbury – the next village to mine – I felt as nervous as I had on my first date with Yasmin. I really hadn't expected things to last between us. I'd been smitten from the moment I met her, but she was so smart, talented and beautiful that I couldn't imagine she'd be interested in me long-term. Someone once told me I was nothing special and nobody would ever love me, and I sometimes found it hard to quieten that voice.

The past year with Yasmin had been really good. My only complaint was that I didn't get to see her as much as I'd have liked. She didn't have family in the area, but she had a large circle of friends who she saw regularly and she also frequently attended artsy events. She invited me to a gallery opening once but repeatedly warned me that I'd be bored and she'd been right. I loved her work but I knew nothing about art and felt out of place and guilty that Yasmin had to keep checking in with me when she should have been free to relax and mingle. I wasn't invited again. I hoped moving in together would mean seeing much more of each other.

I pulled onto the drive at six sharp, as agreed. I'd had a vision of her waiting for me with a glass of something special to toast the big occasion, but there was no sign of her. The cottage was locked and, although she'd given me my own key last night, it didn't feel right letting myself in without her there.

Faint music was coming from the garden, so I headed towards the studio. As I got closer, I recognised the track as one of Yasmin's favourites: Marvin Gaye's 'I Heard It Through the Grapevine'.

She was wearing a white vest-top under paint-spattered khaki dungarees, her blonde hair pulled back from her face with a maroon and white spotted bandana. It was mesmerising watching the joy on her face as she swept her paint brush across the giant canvas, or a frown creasing her forehead when she was working on a smaller section.

This particular painting was an abstract piece which depicted a story of love lost and found again. She'd enthusiastically explained how and, although I couldn't see it myself, I'd told her it was beautiful, which was the truth – I adored the red, purple and teal colour palette, even if I didn't understand the piece.

I knew better than to disturb her when she was mid-creation. I'd startled her once when she was sculpting and she'd made a mistake. Even though she claimed she wasn't annoyed with me and it had been her fault for losing track of time, I was consumed with guilt for the extra hours she'd had to put in to rectify the mistake, so I wasn't going to risk that again.

Feeling like I had little choice but to let myself in with my new key, I swallowed down the disappointment of no welcoming party and took Jinks inside.

There was no sign of Otis, Marvin or Etta, so I released Jinks from his crate.

'Should we go upstairs and see how much space Yasmin's cleared for me?' I asked him.

Jinks followed me into the master bedroom and weaved round my legs as I flung open the doors to the wardrobe on my side of the bed and tutted loudly. It was still bursting with Yasmin's clothes.

With a heavy heart, I checked the drawers. All full except the small one she'd cleared for me ages ago for spare underwear, a nightshirt and a hairbrush.

I slumped down onto the bed, willing myself not to cry. If Yasmin had been moving into Bayberry Cottage, I'd have gone out of my way to make her feel welcome. I'd have made space, bought flowers, prepared a romantic meal and I'd have been eagerly watching for her arrival so I could welcome her properly. Moving in together was a big thing and you only got one chance to get it right.

Jinks jumped up beside me and sprawled across my lap. I couldn't even muster the energy to stroke him. This wasn't how it was meant to be.

* * *

I was sitting on the floor, watching Jinks pounce on a catnip toy, a fair bit later when I finally heard the kitchen door open.

'Fizz! I'm so sorry. I lost track of time. Can you...' She stopped in the lounge doorway. 'What's going on?'

I winced at her sharp tone. She'd kept me waiting this long and this was her idea of a welcome?

'I'm playing with Jinks.' It was hard not to snap the words.

'I can see that. Why's he in the house?'

'You said it was okay for Jinks to come with me.'

'It is, but he needs to stay outside or in the studio like the others. I don't like animals in the house.'

My eyes automatically flicked to the two vivariums containing Presley the blue-tongued skink and Dionne the bearded-dragon.

'They're different,' she snapped. 'They're behind glass. They don't shed fur all over the furniture. And don't start on Percy. He doesn't come out often.'

Percy was a white rat of advancing years and I hadn't planned to mention him but, now that she had, I couldn't see why Percy was allowed to roam but Jinks wasn't.

'Do you want me to go?' I asked in a small voice, my stomach churning.

'No. Just him.'

The words were so cold and so was her expression and, in that moment, I didn't recognise her. She knew how important Jinks was to me. How could she be so dismissive? My frustration bubbled to the surface.

'If he goes,' I said, my voice strong and clear, 'so do I.'

Her eyes widened, presumably shocked that I wasn't being my usual bubbly, compliant self.

'Now you're being silly,' she said, smiling gently.

My jaw tightened and my stomach churned. If there was something I couldn't abide, it was being called silly or stupid. My ex-girlfriend Nadine used to do it all the time, belittling my love of unicorns, bright hair colours and all things sparkly and I'd never have believed that Yasmin could stoop to that level, particularly when she knew what had happened with Nadine. And somebody else had used those terms too. Far too frequently.

I reached for the cat carrier. 'Come on, Jinks, back inside,' I instructed him, fighting to keep my voice steady. 'We're not wanted here.'

'I never said that, Fizz. You're twisting my words. You're both welcome here, but he needs to stay outside or in the studio. Why is it so hard to understand that I don't want animal hair everywhere?'

With Jinks safe inside the carrier, I straightened up and raised my eyebrows at Yasmin.

'We're both welcome? Really? We confirmed six o'clock. It's now quarter past seven and you've only just appeared and what were your first words on seeing me? *What's going on? Why's he in the house?* Not exactly the happy moving-in welcome I expected. I had a quick look upstairs, by the way. Thanks for clearing some space for my stuff.'

'I've been busy!'

'I haven't just turned up out of the blue, you know. You asked me to move in with you nine days ago. Didn't you think about what that meant?'

'Of course I did!'

'Doesn't feel like it.'

We glared at each other, and my heart raced, wondering if what should be the happiest day for us had somehow become the end.

'This isn't how I imagined tonight going and I'm sure it's not what you'd hoped for either.' I kept my voice soft and steady. 'You've obviously got work to do and you're not ready for me moving in just yet. We probably should have talked about a few things, like the difference between me having a drawer for staying over and me being here permanently, and the living arrangements for Jinks. So I suggest I go back to Bayberry Cottage and we do some thinking about whether this is what we both really want.'

Tears glistened in Yasmin's eyes. 'You don't want to move in with me?'

'I still do, but not tonight,' I said gently. 'We need to talk some more. Okay?'

'That sounds like goodbye.'

'It's not goodbye. Unless that's what you want?'

'Would I have asked you to move in if I wanted to end things between us?' Yasmin cried, her cheeks reddening.

'Sorry, no. I had to check. Let's talk tomorrow, yeah? I'll come round at six. If you don't want me to, WhatsApp me.'

'See you tomorrow,' she muttered as I picked up Jinks in his carrier and moved out less than ninety minutes after I'd moved in.

* * *

Over Sunday lunch the following day at Barney's farm, Bumblebee Barn, I was too embarrassed to tell my family what had kicked off the night before. I didn't want them to think badly of Yasmin and for things to get awkward when I did eventually move in. It was just as well she was attending an art festival today and had never planned on joining us for lunch, so no suspicions were raised.

Nobody noticed my bloodshot eyes from being up half the night crying, wondering if walking out had been the right thing to do, while knowing I couldn't have stayed. For reasons unknown, Yasmin had been unprepared and in a foul mood when I'd arrived yesterday and, if it hadn't been Jinks, I was pretty sure she'd have found something else to snap at. She sometimes got like that when a commission wasn't going well, so presumably the purple and teal splodges weren't going to plan. I didn't want this important stage in our lives to be blighted by her stress over work, so it was better to talk some more and make it a happy occasion.

After we'd eaten pudding, I announced that I was going for a walk round the farm but, to pre-empt offers of company, I said I had a headache and was looking forward to some fresh air and quiet. I hated lying to my family, although I was well practised at it by now, and a little white lie about a headache was nothing.

I rested my elbows on the gate at the top field which was currently empty in preparation for the new mums and their lambs, which were due later this month and into early April. All around me were other signs of spring – buds on trees and hedges, daffodils on the verges – and I should be on cloud nine right now, but I felt down in the doldrums. Yasmin hadn't been in touch and I was trying to focus on the positive that she hadn't pulled out of tonight. Yet.

'Everything all right, sweetheart?'

I looked up at Grandma and smiled. 'Fine. The fresh air is helping my head.'

'Is it helping your heart?'

I frowned at her. 'What?'

'I drove past your cottage last night. Your car was on the drive and your bedroom light was on. Do you want to talk about it?'

I rested my elbows on the gate again. 'Yasmin and I had a fight. I didn't move in.'

'Aw, Fizz, I'm sorry. Does this mean it's over?'

'No, or at least I don't think so. It was a miscommunication thing, so I thought we'd better pause the move while we sorted it out. We're meeting tonight, unless she cancels.'

'Do you think she will?'

'I hope not but, if she does, that'll probably be the end for us.'

'And how would you feel about that?'

'Devastated.' The word came out more like a sob. 'I don't want it to be over.'

Grandma put her arm round me and rested her head against mine. 'Then make sure she knows that. If you believe she's the one and she's worth fighting for, then fight for her.'

'Thanks, Grandma.'

We stood in silence for several minutes before she straightened up and kissed my head. 'I'll leave you to it and there's no need to ask. I won't say anything to the others.'

She was right about me telling Yasmin how I felt. I was the one who'd left last night, and Yasmin could easily take that as cold feet on my part. But I didn't want to message her while she was at an event, so I'd need to bide my time.

I returned to the farmhouse.

'The fresh air has cleared my head,' I announced brightly. 'Who fancies a game of Bullshit?'

'Won't that be a bit loud?' Mum said.

'I'll be fine. Are you up for it?'

There were mumbles of 'yes', so I planted my hands on my hips and called brightly. 'I can't hear you! I said are you up for it?'

With cries of 'yes' and laughter, Barney retrieved the cards and we settled round the dining table. Bullshit was our family's favourite card game and I'd never get tired of hearing my grandparents shouting their 'bullshit' accusation when they thought someone was cheating. Laughter was guaranteed. Exactly what I needed to cover up my heartache.

* * *

I hadn't been home long when a series of photos came through on WhatsApp, bringing tears to my eyes. The first showed Yasmin's three cats sprawled out in the garden accompanied by the caption: *We prefer it out here but Jinks is welcome inside.* The second showed an empty wardrobe: *I've had a clear-out.* It was followed by a pile of clothes heaped on the bed in the spare room and the caption *Translated as I've moved some stuff!* with three 'rolling on the floor laughing' emojis. The final photo showed a bottle of Prosecco, two champagne flutes, a box of chocolates and some flowers with the message: *How last night should have looked. I'm so sorry x*

The kiss was particularly unusual for Yasmin, so I knew she was trying hard.

I drove across to her cottage a little later but didn't take my belongings or Jinks with me. The photos were great, but I needed to look Yasmin in the eye and know she genuinely was sorry and that she really did want us to move in.

'I had a horrendous day,' she said, hugging me tightly. 'I took it out on you, and I shouldn't have done.'

It all spilled out about how she'd had a run-in that morning with Nicola, a former client whose toddler had got hold of some Sharpies and had drawn on the sculpture Yasmin had made her. She'd expected Yasmin to repair it for free, or make her another one, and had turned abusive when Yasmin refused, threatening to leave negative reviews. Yasmin showed me the photos Nicola had sent her and, despite the tense situation, we couldn't help laughing at the toddler's artwork. Carnage.

'I was so riled by her that I threw myself into my work to distract me, which completely messed up my plans for our first night together,' she said. 'I was going to get you some flowers and make a meal and I was fuming with myself for letting her get to me and spoiling our big moment. I took that frustration out on you and Jinks which wasn't fair. Can you forgive me?'

'On one condition. You have to forgive yourself and let it go if we're going to make this work.'

Yasmin could be a little intense at times and was prone to letting niggles and mistakes fester, which wasn't good for her. I knew from personal experience how important it was to let go of the past and move forward.

'If that's what you want,' I added hesitantly.

'It is. I didn't ask you to move in on a whim. I want to be with you, but I've got a confession to make. Clearing the wardrobe and some drawer space never even entered my head and it should have. I want this to feel like *our* home and I do appreciate that nothing about yesterday gave off that vibe. Which brings me onto Jinks.'

She paused and lowered her eyes, and I braced myself for bad news.

'Relationships should be about compromise,' she said. 'I know how important Jinks is to you but I don't like animals having free roam of the house, so how would you feel if he moves in but he stays downstairs?'

She raised her eyes, and the uncertainty was touching.

'I think that sounds like a reasonable compromise. When can we move in?'

* * *

Present day

Jinks and I had moved in on the Friday night, but I couldn't help feeling that the moment had been lost to celebrate properly. Yasmin had made a concerted effort to give me space in her home. As well as clearing out her wardrobe and some of her drawers, I had a shelf in the bathroom cabinet and a bookshelf in the lounge, but when I suggested bringing over some of my favourite cushions, she scrunched her nose and said they wouldn't work with the colour scheme. When I mentioned putting up some of my favourite pictures, she said there wasn't space and wouldn't my walls look bare when renting out my house if I brought my pictures here? I suggested we do a swap and she laughed as though I'd made some huge joke.

I wasn't one for sweating the little things, and having my pictures and cushions around fell into the 'little things' category. After all, wouldn't we change the décor over time in line with our joint tastes?

Jinks stretched, flexed his claws, then rolled over and ran downstairs. I gave the duvet a quick once-over but couldn't see any hairs. Pulling on my dressing gown, I padded downstairs too and into the kitchen where Jinks was lapping at the water in his bowl. Yasmin had left a note for me on the kitchen table:

Studio all day. Enjoy your Sunday lunch. See you tonight

'It's nice to be wanted,' I muttered to Jinks.

I couldn't help thinking Yasmin was avoiding me. Feeling guilty for her behaviour last night? She should be! I peered out of the window in the direction of the studio, but there wasn't a clear view through the trees and shrubs.

Yasmin had made space for me in her house, but it often felt like she hadn't made space for me in her life. When I moved in, I thought we'd see more of each other, but I actually saw her less. She spent more time with Arianna, Sara-Jade and her other friends than she did with me. On the rare occasions we did go out, it was nearly always in a group. After less than seven months of living together, were we already in a rut?

8

FIZZ

When I returned from Bumblebee Barn early on Sunday evening, Yasmin was in the kitchen, slicing carrots and celery sticks into batons.

'I've been to that deli you love in Reddfield,' she said, beaming at me. 'I've got all your favourites – olives, a rustic loaf and some camembert to bake.'

'You hate going to that deli.' She always complained that it was too small and cramped and that she hated the smell.

'I know, but I wanted to spoil you.'

'Why?' A spot of food shopping wasn't enough. I needed to hear her say the words and feel that she genuinely was sorry for last night, because I wasn't convinced she was.

'I've run a bath too,' she said, completely ignoring my question. 'Off you go before it gets cold.'

She said it jokingly but there was an edge to her voice that said to me: *Go away because I don't want to talk about it.*

'I need to ask you about—'

'It can wait. Go! Bath's ready!'

Her voice was a little too high. I knew that she'd snap if I pushed her any further and we'd have yet another argument instead of calmly talking things through.

I left the kitchen and closed the door behind me. Jinks was in his bed, but he immediately toddled across to me. I picked him up and gave him a hug, his deep purrs soothing me.

'At least you're genuinely pleased to see me,' I whispered, burying my head in his fur. 'I love you so much, Jinks.'

I wanted to take him upstairs but I wasn't going to risk it with the strange mood Yasmin was in, so I gently lowered him back onto his bed and went upstairs to check out the bathroom. Yasmin had placed flameless flickering candles along the edge of the bath and on the windowsill. She hated real candles anywhere in the house but especially in the bathroom, moaning that they left sooty marks on the tiles and ignoring my protests that tiles were easily cleaned. The bubbles smelled delicious and it would have been a lovely gesture but I couldn't shake the feeling that she'd only run the bath so that I'd leave her in peace.

I sank back into the bubbles a little later, but I couldn't relax. We needed to talk and I wasn't going to be fobbed off this time. I might have been able to overlook yet another eleventh-hour cancellation, but her inviting her friends round instead was taking the piss.

* * *

'How was the bath?' Yasmin asked when I joined her in the kitchen half an hour later.

'Good, thanks. About last night...'

'Such a laugh, wasn't it? I can't believe they turned up like that, but it was just what I needed after the day I'd had. Sit down. The camembert's ready.'

'You didn't know they were coming?' I asked, fighting hard to keep the accusation out of my voice.

'No. Spontaneous visit. Can you believe that?'

No, not at all!

She dropped the box of cheese on a plate, placed it in front of me and plonked herself down.

'Before you say anything, can I just say how sorry I am for cancelling yesterday? I felt awful doing that but I was so far behind that I really needed the time to try and catch up and I thought I would manage it, but I hit early evening and I was drained. Honestly, Fizz, I had *nothing* more to give creatively so when Aria and S-J turned up unexpectedly and I told them how tired I was, they convinced me I'd be better to have the evening off and come to it fresh this morning, but I realise how bad that must have looked after I cancelled going out with you, but I promise it wasn't planned. A night off was exactly what I needed but, because I was still so far behind, I had to be up and in the studio first thing this morning. They were right to have encouraged me to have a break because I got so much more done today than I would have if I'd tried to fight my way through my creative block last night, but the thing is, it was going so well that I was in the zone and, even though I was planning to say goodbye before you left for the farm, I lost track of time, so I'm sorry we've barely seen each other.'

'That's not what your note said.'

'What?'

It was still on the side, so I grabbed it and held it up for her to see:

Studio all day. Enjoy your Sunday lunch. See you tonight

'Oh, that! I scribbled it in a rush. As if I'd not say goodbye in person. What do you take me for?'

It was best I took that as a rhetorical question.

'So you're saying Arianna and Sara-Jade's visit wasn't planned?'

'Why would it be planned when I was meant to be going out with you?' She broke the skin of her camembert with a carrot baton. 'So are we good?'

No! Far from it! I knew she wanted me to smile and say it was all right, but it wasn't, especially when she was lying to me. I already knew from Sara-Jade that they hadn't spontaneously turned up and, even if I hadn't been told that or I hadn't believed Sara-Jade, Yasmin's apology had just proved she was lying. She had a tell. It didn't matter whether the lie was small – *I swear I didn't eat the last Twix* or *There was still butter in the tub last time I used it* – or a biggie like choosing her friends over a long-arranged night out with mine, Yasmin's lies always spilled out in several long pause-free rambling sentences.

I understood that Yasmin hadn't gelled with Sam, although it wasn't for lack of trying on Sam's part. I got that none of mine or Sam's friends or family were into art and there was little else they had in common with Yasmin, but that didn't mean they were to be avoided. They were warm, welcoming people who'd always shown an interest in what she did.

Yasmin shoved her cheese-covered carrot into her mouth, making appreciative sounds as she chewed, and it was as though the subject was closed. She'd said her piece and I could either keep quiet and enjoy my food or I could call her out on her lies. But if I did that, I'd be dropping Sara-Jade in it, and I didn't want to do that when she'd always been so nice to me.

'Mmm, this is good,' Yasmin said, taking a bite from the bread. 'So how was lunch with your family?'

I wanted to challenge her so badly. I wanted to tell her how rude I thought she was for repeatedly cancelling on my friends. I wanted to ask why she listened to her friends telling her to take a break but she never listened to me. But I felt too exhausted by it all to do any of that. So I did what she wanted and I smiled and enthusiastically told her about lunch and another family game of Bullshit, keeping everything nice and civilised.

Yasmin returned to her studio after we'd eaten, leaving me to clear away. I watched a film with Jinks curled up beside me, then went to bed alone. As I lay in the darkness, I replayed our dinner conversation over and over. I hated myself for letting it go, but I couldn't bear confrontations. I'd never been able to stand up for myself, even when the other person was behaving deplorably, so I bent over backwards trying to avoid situations where anyone could take advantage. Yet somehow I was like a magnet to that type of person. Ever since I was little. Things could have been so different if I'd had that ability, that strength, that determination back then.

I shuddered and tugged the duvet more tightly round me. I wasn't going to go there tonight. I needed to focus on Yasmin instead. I still couldn't shake the feeling that, while she'd got her act together and made space for me in her house, she hadn't actually made space for me in her life, and I wasn't sure how that made me feel about her or our future together.

9

SAMANTHA

When I visited Terry on Monday night, he wasn't in a good way. On Tuesday, he'd deteriorated further. His temperature was high, his pulse weak, and there was a rattle in his chest.

'I think we need to get you to hospital,' I told him.

'No.'

'Terry, you're really ill. It's the best place for you.'

'No.'

'Please.'

'If I'm dying, I'm right where I want to be,' he whispered.

When I was a district nurse, I'd had elderly patients who frequently spoke about dying – even when their appointment with me was for something non-life-threatening like a twisted ankle or a scald – but Terry wasn't like that. For him to mention death, my worst fears were confirmed. He knew exactly how ill he was.

I swallowed down the lump in my throat. 'You can't die, Terry.'

''Appens to us all one day, lass.'

I grasped his hand. 'Well, it's not happening to you today. Get better. Do you hear me?'

But he'd drifted off to sleep once more.

His skin felt cold, so I placed his arm back under the duvet and settled into the bedside chair, watching the slow rise and fall of his chest.

A little before midnight, Josh sent me a text telling me he was outside.

'What are you doing here?' I asked, opening the front door to him.

'Relieving you.'

'I can't leave him in case...' I couldn't finish the sentence but I'd already messaged Josh with my fears, so he knew what I meant.

'I thought you might say that. I've got an overnight bag and your pregnancy pillow in the car. You're sleeping in one of the spare rooms and I'm sitting with Terry. No arguments. I'll wake you up if anything changes.'

There was no point arguing. I was shattered and really did need the sleep.

* * *

When I woke up on Wednesday after a surprisingly deep sleep, there was no improvement in Terry, but no deterioration either. Josh went to work, and I stayed until after lunch when Jeanette Kingston relieved me.

Back at Hedgehog Hollow, I felt on edge, fearing a phone call from Jeanette with bad news.

'I need to be with him,' I told Josh when he arrived home from work. 'I know Lauren's staying overnight but I'm so worried about him.'

'Promise me you'll do what we did last night and get some sleep?'

'I promise.'

* * *

Despite the circumstances, it was good to have some time on my own with Lauren. I saw her regularly but we were usually in a group or it was a snatched conversation before or after one of her workshops.

'Have you finished all the painting at Briar Ridge now?' I asked her.

'Riley and Kai did the finishing touches at the weekend so all we need is a bit of work on the garden. Your mum's going to take a look and give us a few suggestions. I could manage the garden at Chapel View, but this one's too big for me to visualise what to do with it.'

'I bet she'll come up with some great ideas,' I said, feeling a stab of pride for my mum.

'Has your dad finished putting his stamp on Chapel View? I meant to ask him on Saturday night.'

Dad had been Lauren's lodger for over two years and loved her cottage in nearby Amblestone, so he bought it from her when she moved into Briar Ridge.

'All done and it's great to see him so settled in the area. It's as though he's always lived here.'

'Like someone else I know,' she said, smiling at me. 'And your mum. And Chloe.'

I returned her smile. 'It's been a great move for all of us.'

It really had been. Everyone was settled in their new homes and jobs. All I needed was for my parents to find love again – although not with each other! I'd been concerned that recon- necting at my wedding and breaking up again might have caused a rift, but it seemed to have brought them closer together and it was heartwarming to see them enjoying each other's friendship. Their divorce was complete and Dad had been on a few dates this year.

Nothing had progressed beyond a third date, but it was good that he was getting out there again. As for Mum, she was far too busy settling into her studies, new home and finding herself to think about taking a chance on love again, but I was hopeful that it would happen, perhaps next year.

We talked in hushed tones about how things were going with Riley and Lauren's great relationship with his son, Kai.

As she crept down the stairs a little later to get us each a glass of water, I moved over to the bed and gazed down at Terry. The joy I'd just felt at Lauren's obvious love for Riley and Kai faded as I took in his grey pallor and hollow cheeks.

'You have to get better,' I whispered. 'We need you, Terry.'

* * *

Thursday morning brought hope. There was colour in Terry's cheeks and he managed to eat some porridge for breakfast.

'You had us scared,' I told him, holding his hand.

'It weren't my time. Need to meet that little 'un first.'

'And he or she wants you in their life, so you make sure you fully recover and don't do that to us again.'

'Can't guarantee it, but I'll do me best.'

'Good. I'm counting on you to reach a century.'

That drew a smile. 'How about we try for eighty-two and take it from there?'

'That's only a few weeks away.'

'It's a start.'

Yes, it was but, considering how the week had begun, it was better than expected.

The bell sounded on Friday afternoon and the children of Bentonbray Primary School spilled out of various doors into the playground. The usual laughter and chatter was extra loud with it being the last day before the half-term break. Darcie ran up to me waving several pieces of paper, presumably more drawings and paintings to add to the ever-growing art gallery in the kitchen.

'Can we see Grandpa Terry?' she asked as she hugged me. I loved how she called him that and I knew Terry was touched by it. My parents, Josh's parents, Alex, Beth, Auntie Louise and Uncle Simon had all been adopted by her as grandparents, aunties and uncles, and why not? With no biological family in her life, she deserved the love of her surrogate family and they all lavished it freely on her.

'We can,' I said, ruffling her hair. 'He's feeling a lot better and is looking forward to seeing you.'

We set off across the playground, hand in hand.

'Does that mean Wilbur's going home?' she asked. She and Phoebe had adored having a dog to play with all week.

'Not just yet, but Wilbur's in the car so he can visit Terry too.

We'll wait until Terry's feeling stronger before Wilbur moves back in with him.'

'Do you think Grandpa Terry will let Wilbur stay with us over half-term?' Darcie asked.

'Probably not for the whole week, but maybe a day or so. Terry will have missed Wilbur a lot, so I'd imagine he's desperate for his company again.'

'But we can visit Wilbur if he moves back home?'

'Definitely.'

* * *

Terry was still wearing his pyjamas and dressing gown when we arrived at Granville House, but he was downstairs, which was a good sign.

I'd warned Darcie not to hurl herself at him like she usually did as he'd still be quite weak from his illness. Terry was on the sofa, so she clambered onto the cushion beside him and snuggled up to his side.

'I've missed you, Grandpa Terry,' she said.

'I've missed you too, Princess.'

As though sensing that leaping on his master still wasn't a great idea, Wilbur rested his head on Terry's knee.

'And I've missed you too, boy,' Terry said, his voice catching with emotion.

Wilbur usually slept on Terry's bed, so his absence would have been felt strongly with Terry pretty much confined to his bedroom.

'Wilbur's missed you too,' Darcie said, 'but we've taken him on lots of walks and given him cuddles. Can he stay a bit longer?'

Terry glanced across at me.

'Darcie would love Wilbur to stay during the school holiday

next week,' I told him, 'but I've said you'll want him back because you've missed each other.'

He stroked Wilbur's head and nodded slowly. 'I'm still on t' mend, so how about he stays with you over t' weekend? Comes back 'ere on Monday?'

'Thank you!' Darcie cried, snuggling even closer to Terry. 'I love Wilbur.'

'I know you do. Our Wilbur's a grand lad.'

Seeing the three of them huddled together was almost too much to bear and I muttered something about making drinks, escaping to the kitchen before I burst into tears. It wasn't just the pregnancy hormones this time – it was the fear of how close we'd come. Hopefully Terry would make a full recovery and be around for many more years, but this had been a tough reminder of how fragile life could be and how we could never take it for granted how long someone would stay in our lives.

11

FIZZ

I'd lost count of the number of times Sam had asked me if I was all right today. I wouldn't have cared it if was just because I'd been a bit quiet, but I'd passed her the wrong meds on two occasions which could have been disastrous if we didn't have a system in place of always double-checking.

I considered myself a dedicated professional and I hated that my life outside of work was affecting my performance at the rescue centre and putting our patients at risk.

When Sam went to pick up Darcie from school and visit Terry, relief flowed through me that she wouldn't be around to witness any further displays of incompetence, but then I panicked in case I made a mistake and she wasn't there to pick up on it.

I wandered round the barn, peeking in the crates and pens and smiling at any glimpses of an animal. I'd hoped for a glimpse of a badger, but Attila was well hidden in his pen. Josh and I had rescued him from the springs of a fly-tipped mattress. The terrified creature had been somewhat aggressive – understandably so – making for a challenging and dangerous rescue, so I couldn't resist naming him after the feared leader. Since being admitted to Hedgehog Hollow, he'd been fairly docile, though, and I wondered if he'd realised we were there to help him.

Sam had been gone about an hour when a hedgehog was dropped off – an adult male covered in patches of white and grey blobs. His spines were soft and his skin was loose, indicating a very poorly hog who'd need significant rehydration. In my distracted mood, even I couldn't mess up tick removal and the injection of subcutaneous fluids to rehydrate him.

My priority was to get him warmed him up on a heat pad and get some fluids into him. Once I'd done that, I laid a fresh towel across the treatment table, prepared a small container of hand sanitiser to drop the removed ticks into, killing them off, and dug out my tick lasso. Resembling a pen, the lasso has a special loop on the end designed to remove ticks correctly, ensuring that the whole tick – mouth parts included – is removed from the hedgehog.

With Halloween only ten days away, we had a new theme for naming the hogs. The first name that popped into my mind was Krueger, but our patient had the cutest face and was far too adorable for a name like that.

'How about Casper?' I asked him. 'Some of those white ticks look like ghosts, although they're not friendly ones like Casper.'

I'd removed half the ticks and was giving Casper a breather when Phoebe arrived home from work. I still couldn't get over how different she looked with her hair cut. I'd thought her long, glossy hair was gorgeous, but the shorter style suited her even more.

'Are Samantha and Darcie still at Terry's?' she asked when we'd exchanged greetings.

'Yeah, they're staying there for tea. Terry's feeling a bit better.'

'That's a relief. I got the impression Samantha thought we might lose him.'

'I thought that too. He's made of strong stuff is our Terry.'

Phoebe peered into the box where Casper was curled up. 'What are you working on?'

'Removing a gazillion ticks from our new admission here and imagining how gutted Zayn would be that he's missing out on all the gross stuff.' I enjoyed it myself, but our volunteer Zayn loved it. Anything with blood, pus, maggots or ticks and he was all over it.

'I'll get changed and give you a hand if you like.'

Ten minutes later, Phoebe was back in jeans and a T-shirt with her hair clipped back from her forehead. Hedgehogs weren't big enough for two people to remove ticks at the same time and it was a welcome relief to swap over to ease neck and shoulder pain from being hunched over the patient.

'How's your day been?' Phoebe asked as she dropped her first tick in the container.

I was about to give my usual positive bubbly response, but Phoebe was a friend. Why lie to her?

'Not great.'

She looked up, frowning. 'What's happened? Has one of the hedgehogs died?'

'No, it's me. I've felt out of sorts all day and I've made some careless mistakes.'

'You *never* make mistakes.'

'I know, but I did today and I'm really annoyed with myself.'

'Do you know why you feel out of sorts?'

Yes. Tall, blonde and answers to the name of Yasmin.

'Just a few things to get straight in my head,' I said, shrugging. 'Nothing to worry about.'

She fixed her big blue eyes on me. 'I'm listening...'

Fobbing her off with an 'it's fine' would have been easy, but it wasn't fine, and another perspective would be welcome. If Phoebe thought I was making a mountain out of a molehill, she'd let me know that gently.

'You know how Yasmin cancelled on Sam's birthday meal last minute? When I got home, two of her friends were round...'

Phoebe continued to steadily remove the ticks, nodding and looking up occasionally as I explained everything that had happened over the weekend.

'You didn't call her out on her lie?' she asked.

'I didn't want to cause problems for Sara-Jade. She's always been kind to me.'

'So what did you say?'

'Nothing. All I could think about was how she was lying and that's been eating away at me all week. I'm questioning how many other lies she's told me and why she's doing it. Why's she so desperate to avoid my friends? Or is it me she doesn't want to spend time with?'

'Uh-uh, no way!' Phoebe dropped another tick into the jar as she vigorously shook her head. 'Not possible. *Everybody* loves Fizz time and if anyone thinks differently, I'll... I'll...' She looked around as though seeking inspiration. 'I'll set Attila the Badger and his hedgehog army on them,' she declared.

'Oh, my God!' I started giggling. 'I can just picture Attila the Badger strapping on his battle armour and all the hedgehogs and hoglets scurrying after him.'

'Gollum would be driving a tank,' she said, laughing with me.

The laugher intensified as we added in increasingly more ridiculous suggestions of what our patients might wear to battle, who the leaders would be and their battle cries as they avenged any wrongdoings towards me.

'My name is Foximus Hedgimus Stoatidius,' Phoebe announced in a deep voice, standing tall, hands on her hips, 'commander of the hedgehog armies of North Yorkshire, general of the patients of Hedgehog Hollow and loyal servant to the best person in the world, Fizz Kinsella. And vengeance will be mine...' She cleared her throat and returned to her normal voice. 'Or something like that. I think I've missed a bit!'

'Foximus Hedgimus Stoatidius? Oh, my God, Phoebe!'

It took us quite a while to compose ourselves after that. *Gladiator* was my dad's all-time favourite film. I'd only been six when it was released but I'd watched it dozens of times when I'd been old enough, recently introducing it to Phoebe on one of our film nights. I'd memorised Russell Crowe's iconic speech years ago and was impressed that Phoebe had not only learned it but she'd managed to edit it off the top of her head just now.

'I can't tell you how much you've cheered me up,' I said when we'd calmed down. 'Thank you.'

'Just returning the favour. You brighten every day for me.'

My heart skipped a beat, and I felt a little tearful. What an unexpected and gorgeous thing to say!

'Anyway,' she said, picking up the tick lasso and turning her attention back to Casper, 'back to the situation at home, has anything more been said this week?'

'I've barely seen her.' It hadn't been intentional, but I'd spent more hours than usual at Hedgehog Hollow so Sam could be with Terry. 'We're going out tonight, just the two of us for once. We're off to the cinema and a drink afterwards, so we'll see what happens then.'

'I'm off to the cinema tonight too! What are you seeing?'

I gave the name of an action blockbuster.

'No! We're seeing that too. Half seven showing?'

I nodded. 'I've already bought the tickets or we could have sat together.'

We compared bookings and Phoebe was a few rows in front. Probably just as well because I couldn't imagine Yasmin wanting to spend the evening in the company of one of my friends.

'Who are you going with?' I asked.

'Leo – the other trainee accountant from work.'

I'd never heard her mention him before and was about to ask her if it was a date when a notification on my phone drew my attention.

'You're kidding!' I muttered.

'What's up?'

I opened the WhatsApp message and scanned it just in case I'd misread the notification then held my phone up in front of Phoebe.

'Sara-Jade's a teacher and she's away on a school trip,' I said to give the message context.

✉ From Yasmin
Hey hun, Aria's lonely without S-J so I've said she can join us for drinks after the film. You don't mind, do you?

'Ooh, that's a bit off,' Phoebe said, wincing. 'She's already invited her. You can't say no without it looking like you're being awkward.'

'Exactly! So much for spending some time together at last. She's always doing stuff like this.'

Phoebe removed ticks in silence for the next few minutes while I sat at the treatment table, head in my hands, staring at Yasmin's message and fighting the urge to type in something sarcastic like: *As if I have much choice.* Sarcasm had never been my style but there'd been so many occasions recently where I'd wanted to resort to it and I didn't like that about myself. I'd sworn always to be a kind and caring person, especially in a world where there were too many who weren't.

Phoebe placed the tick lasso down with a sigh and tilted her head to one side as she studied my face. 'So, I have a question. If

Yasmin's always putting you on the spot like that, cancels plans you've made at the last minute and prioritises time with her friends over time with you, why do you stay with her?'

Epic question, spoken without judgement.

'Because I...' I slumped back against my chair, my arms dangling loosely by my sides. Yep, seriously epic question.

'I'm no expert on relationships,' Phoebe said gently, 'but I'm kind of thinking there should have been an obvious response to that question.'

I gulped. She'd nailed it! I wasn't just out of sorts because of what had happened at the weekend. It was because the weekend had very likely been the final nail in the coffin.

"There should be,' I said, my voice catching in my throat with the realisation that, if the obvious response – *because I love her* – wasn't there, the relationship probably shouldn't be there either.

'What are you going to do?'

Was it the end? It had to be because what did we have going for us to keep us together? We had separate social lives and that could be healthy in a relationship, but we barely saw each other at home either. When we were together, it never felt like we were actually 'together'. We didn't enjoy the same things or share the same sense of humour and there'd been so many niggles recently.

I ran my hands down my face. 'I think it's over.'

'Aw, Fizz. How do you feel?'

At Barney's farm after the original moving-in date, Grandma had asked me how I'd feel if it was over and I'd told her I'd be devastated. That wasn't how I felt now. She'd also told me that if Yasmin was the one, I should fight for her. Was there anything worth fighting for?

'Disappointed,' I said. 'And maybe a little surprised. I knew I was unsettled, annoyed, frustrated but I hadn't realised that it was so much more than going through a sticky patch. I've fallen out of love with her.'

'Do you know when that happened?'

'No, it just crept up on...' I shook my head as I recalled the day I moved in and the disappointment I'd felt when Yasmin wasn't there to greet me, the churning of my stomach when I went upstairs and found all the wardrobes and drawers still full of her clothes, and the disgusted look on her face as she stood in the lounge doorway staring at Jinks and asking what he was doing there. A piece of my heart walked away from her then and each time she let me down, another piece joined it and I hadn't realised until now.

'Should I have kept quiet?' Phoebe asked, her eyes wide.

'No. You asked the question I should have been asking myself and I'm glad you did.'

The barn door was flung open and Darcie ran inside with Wilbur by her side. 'Grandpa Terry says Wilbur can stay with us for the weekend but he's feeling lots better so he wants him back next week.'

'Then we'll have to spoil Wilbur this weekend with lots of walks and play,' Phoebe said, giving Darcie a hug. 'How was school?'

'Awesome. Mr Huggins gave us all some chocolates and I got a big star for my drawing of Attila the Badger.'

Phoebe glanced at me, and I knew from her grin that she was thinking about our earlier conversation, but I could only give her a weak smile in return. How had the afternoon moved from hysterical laughter about a badger and his hedgehog army into a realisation that I didn't love my girlfriend anymore?

12

FIZZ

I left work later than intended as I'd wanted to ensure Casper was tick-free. Driving towards Little Tilbury, I wavered between suggesting we cancel the cinema so Yasmin and I could talk and having what might be our last night out together before saying anything. Even as I pulled onto the drive, I was still undecided which was best.

'Not saying anything feels like lying,' I muttered to myself. 'I *will* say something. Maybe. Argh!'

Yasmin was on the phone when I stepped into the kitchen, and it was immediately obvious who she was talking to.

'... be back on Sunday. It'll fly by... Really? That is amazing. I'm so chuffed... Yeah, yeah, we can plan it tonight. Okay. See you at the pub.'

She hung up and turned to me, eyes shining. 'You'll never guess what! Aria's going to ask S-J to marry her.'

'I thought she didn't believe in marriage.' Arianna and Sara-Jade had been together for eight years, but Yasmin had told me they'd briefly split up a few years back because Sara-Jade had wanted to get married but Arianna, scarred from her own parents' battlefield of a marriage, didn't. They'd got back together after Arianna reassured Sara-Jade that she loved her and was committed to their relationship, but I'd wondered where the compromise was. Arianna got what she wanted but what about Sara-Jade? Were all relationships one-sided? Mine certainly was, with me doing all the giving and Yasmin all the taking.

'She doesn't but she knows it's what S-J really wants and she's missed her so much that it feels like the right time to ask. She needs us to help her plan a romantic proposal tonight so get yourself sorted as we've got a busy evening ahead of us.'

'Why don't we skip the cinema and you and Arianna meet on your own?' I suggested, seeing a way to wriggle out of the evening's plans and give myself some breathing space to work out what I was going to say to Yasmin.

'Nope,' she said. 'She specifically wants your input.'

'Mine? Why?'

'Because she says you're romantic and I'm not so you'll be the one with the ideas.'

I was shooed upstairs to get changed, my stomach in knots. What was worse than a night out with my girlfriend, knowing I needed to call time on my relationship? A night out planning someone else's romantic proposal to their girlfriend!

Looking back, Yasmin and I had been steadily drifting apart since I moved in. Had it been my fault? Had I unconsciously pulled away from her after the moving-in day disaster or would it have happened anyway because we weren't compatible? Or was it because of what *that* person had said about me? *You're not special, Fizzy, and nobody's ever going to love you.*

* * *

We had a thirty-minute drive to the cinema on a retail park at the other side of Reddfield. I'd been worried about blurting out how I was feeling if there was a moment's silence, but Yasmin never shut up the whole way. Did I think they'd marry quickly? Would they elope or get married locally? Would they go traditional or plan a big surprise? Would they ask her to be their bridesmaid? And even though she fired the questions at me, she didn't wait for my response, debating each query out loud herself.

By the time I pulled my Mini into the cinema car park, I'd only spoken twice – when she double-checked the time the film started and to confirm that I wanted popcorn.

As we waited in the refreshments queue a little later, I craned my neck, searching for Phoebe.

'Who are you looking for?' Yasmin snapped.

'Phoebe mentioned she had tickets for tonight too, but I can't see her. She must already have gone in.'

'Tell me we're not sitting with her.'

I winced at the edge to her tone. What had Phoebe ever done to justify that other than to be my friend?

'No. We booked separately.'

That response seemed to satisfy Yasmin as she was back to speculating about the wedding. 'I'm sure S-J will want a big white dress but, even though she never wanted the big day, I have a sneaky feeling Aria will go big too. She might add her own spin on it like a traditional style but in bright red or she'll wear sparkly Docs or... Are you listening to me?'

Her voice rose on the last statement and the couple in front of us whipped round and stared.

'Yes,' I hissed and, because I was pretty sure the next question would be to challenge me to prove that, I added, 'You were talking about Arianna wearing a bright red dress or sparkly Docs and I think you're right. I don't know her like you do but I think that, if she's decided to go for it, she'll want to make it special and she *will* want the big dress.'

Yasmin looked a little taken aback that not only had I listened but I had an opinion too. We'd reached the front of the queue and she placed our order for popcorn and drinks.

'I need the loo,' she said before payment was taken. 'Meet you outside the ladies.'

My jaw tightened. She'd offered to buy the snacks because I'd paid for the tickets but, as usual, I was left paying for both.

I settled up, balanced the drinks and popcorn and wandered down the corridor to wait outside the toilets. I watched the other cinema-goers wandering past and suddenly there Phoebe was, one arm linked through her companion's, the other wrapped round a giant sharing bucket of popcorn.

'Fizz!' she said, smiling widely.

'Hi!'

'This is Leo.'

Leo beamed at me, flashing a perfect set of white teeth. Just a tiny bit taller than Phoebe, he had dark wavy hair and mesmerising green eyes. They looked great together.

'I was hoping I'd meet you tonight,' Leo said. 'Love the hair.'

'Thank you.' I felt I should offer him a compliment in return but the only thing that sprang to mind was *your teeth are very straight* which was definitely better staying in my head.

Yasmin appearing and grabbing her refreshments from me saved me from trying to think of something else.

'She was looking for you earlier,' she said flatly, looking Phoebe up and down. Would it have killed her to say hello?

'Well, we found each other,' Phoebe said, smiling politely as she let go of Leo's arm. 'This is Leo.'

'Hi,' Yasmin said, her voice barely audible. 'Come on, Fizz, trailers will be starting.' And off she strode.

I gave Phoebe and Leo an apologetic shrug. 'Nice to meet you, Leo. Enjoy the film.'

Phoebe lightly touched my arm and I swallowed down a sob. Why was it that you could be fine about the difficult stuff but the minute somebody showed you unconditional kindness, you felt yourself crumbling?

'You've got this,' she whispered, which nearly broke me.

One of the things Yasmin and I agreed on – one of the few things now that I thought about it – was absolute silence in the cinema including during the trailers and, as they'd just started, I had about two and a half hours ahead of me to decide how to handle our break-up. If there'd been even a sliver of doubt, it had slithered away in the corridor just now with how dismissive she'd been of Phoebe and Leo.

One approach was to fake a headache, go home after the film and tackle it in the morning but that meant leaving Yasmin without a lift home and, even worse, meant sharing a bed with her tonight. It didn't feel right to do that.

I could go ahead with the night out and insist on talking when we got home. I could then sleep in the spare room or, if she kicked me out, I could go to Mum and Dad's or Barney's farm and stay there until my tenant moved out just before Christmas. Thank goodness I'd rented out my lovely cottage instead of selling it like Yasmin had wanted.

As I debated the merits of the second plan if Yasmin had too much to drink – very likely in Arianna's company – my gaze settled on Phoebe and Leo. The trailers had finished and the cinema etiquette film was playing. Leo had his face turned towards her, mouth open, trying to catch the popcorn Phoebe was throwing at him, the pair of them giggling with each attempt. Had it really only been a few hours since we'd been laughing together? I wished I could swap places with Leo right now.

She reached across and brushed her hand against his cheek, presumably removing a piece of popcorn. I imagined sitting close to Phoebe as she brushed popcorn from my cheek and butterflies stirred in my stomach. Where had that come from? My cheeks flushed and I shot a panicked look at Yasmin, but she was staring straight ahead, lost in the opening credits.

I tried to concentrate on the film, but my attention kept drifting to Phoebe and Leo. They were sitting very close together. Were they holding hands? I glanced at Yasmin again, one hand holding her popcorn while the other dipped in and out in a steady rhythm. She never took my hand in the cinema. She never took my hand at all. I was an affectionate person and I missed that connection. For all her other faults, Nadine had at least acted like she cared about me.

At one point, Phoebe jumped at something. She and Leo both laughed and he put his arm round her. I imagined I was beside Phoebe, my arm protectively round her and the butterflies stirred once more. Why? Phoebe and I were friends. Nothing more.

I stole another glance at Yasmin, who was resting on the chair arm on the other side of her, her body angled away from mine, as though eager to sit as far away from me as possible. My reaction wasn't specifically about Phoebe – it was about the affection, or the lack of it in my case.

As the film approached its climax, I still hadn't decided what I was going to say to Yasmin to end things. Every time I tried to focus on a suitable conversation opener, my thoughts strayed to Phoebe. I thought about us laughing earlier over Attila the Badger and how easily she could lift me when I felt down. She'd done that at Sam and Josh's wedding after Michael Jackson's 'Thriller' came on and Yasmin stormed off the dance floor, moaning that group dance routines were embarrassing. Why couldn't Yasmin have been more like her?

There'd been an instant attraction to Yasmin and the chemistry had sizzled between us at first. I'd been stunned that somebody as beautiful and talented as her had chosen me and I think that shock had blinded me to everything that was wrong in our relationship. We weren't the best of friends, we weren't a partnership, we weren't even on the same page most of the time. How could I have been so blind to have stuck it out for so long?

It was over and I was going to have to spit it out. When we got back to the car, I'd start with one of the classic relationship break-up lines – *Sorry, Yasmin, but this isn't working anymore* – and we'd take it from there. After that, I needed to get my act together when it came to relationships. I needed to stop being dazzled by looks and talent and focus on compatibility.

I wanted what my parents and Sam and Josh had, what my friend Robbie had with his fiancée Kate. I wanted someone who'd throw popcorn at me and hug me when a film made me jump because, despite what I'd been told long ago, I deserved it.

13

FIZZ

As soon as the credits started rolling at the end of the film, Phoebe and Leo stood up and shuffled along the row. She turned and waved at me and I waved back. Were they going out for a drink or was this the end of their evening?

Yasmin was busy tapping something into her phone and scowling. A couple of teenaged girls waited to get past, but Yasmin showed no signs of moving her bag or legs to let them. I was about to nudge her when they gave up and headed to the other end of the row. I'd never thought about it until now, but Yasmin was horrendous for being wrapped up in her own world at times. I wasn't sure whether she was deliberately inconsiderate or completely oblivious but there'd been several occasions like this in the past when I'd felt really uncomfortable. How had I not registered that we were so different and not in a good way?

With a sigh, she tossed her phone into her bag.

'Everything okay?' It seemed like a pointless question.

'Remember Nicola, that stupid woman whose daughter scribbled all over the sculpture I'd made her? One of my other clients,

Jilly, spotted Nicola slagging me off in a community group and had a go at her. Look.'

Yasmin passed me her phone and I scrolled down the screen-shots of the increasingly heated conversation between the two women. The language and the name-calling from both of them was shocking. A couple of other randoms had dived in to stir things up. One woman shared that she'd looked on Yasmin's website and believe her work resembled the content of a baby's nappy and another commented that her toddler could paint better. Why did people say things like that on social media?

I returned Yasmin's phone with a sigh. 'Nicola seriously needs to let it go. It was months ago and it was her fault for not locking away the Sharpies.'

'Did you see what those other women said about my work?'

'I did, and it's a pile of crap, excuse the pun.'

Yasmin didn't laugh. The cinema lights flicked on and my heart broke for her as she looked so sad and defeated. She'd had stacks of criticism in the past and usually managed to shrug it off, saying it went with the territory, but this seemed to have got to her.

'We'd better go,' she said, grabbing her bag and standing up. 'Yes, I know it's crap,' she said as we shuffled out of the row. 'Everyone's an art critic and everyone's two-year-old can allegedly do better. I'm more bothered about the Nicola thing. I can't get my head round why she thinks I owe her any sort of refund. She got a perfect sculpture from me, created to her brief. What happened to it after that is *her* problem and it's driving me insane that she can't see that. And why's Jilly sending me this anyway? What's she hoping to achieve?'

'I was just wondering that myself.'

We left the cinema and walked towards my car.

'I know it hurts,' I said, 'but there'll always be the Nicolas who think the world owes them a favour and who say and do questionable things. They're not worth your time and energy. You're a brilliant, talented artist and the people who count know that. Keep doing what you do and forget about the noise.'

She sighed and gave me a weak smile. 'You're right. They're not worth it and I'm *not* going to let them ruin my night out. Thanks, Fizz. You're a good friend.'

I frowned as she walked round to the passenger side. A good friend? Is that what she thought of me? Had that just been a turn of phrase or was it possible that I wasn't the only one whose feelings about our relationship had changed?

I clambered into the car beside her and closed the door, but I didn't pull on my seat belt or start the engine.

'Just now, you called me a good friend.'

'And?'

'And is that all I am to you?'

'Being friends is a good thing. Aria and S-J are friends. Most couples I know are friends.'

Her voice was overly high as she rummaged in her handbag in what looked like a clear tactic to avoid eye contact. I hadn't missed the pause before she spoke either.

'Yes, but they're also a lot more than that and—'

'Fizz, don't...' She stopped rummaging and her shoulders dropped as she held my gaze.

I ignored her plea and finished my sentence anyway. 'And I can't help thinking we're not. This isn't working and it probably hasn't been for a long time. I'm sorry.'

'So you're ending it?' she asked, her tone flat.

'I think we've grown too far apart,' I said, gently. 'Don't you?'

'Yes, but...' She looked down, chewing on her lip. 'I didn't want it to end yet. I thought we'd...' She shrugged. 'Never mind.'

What did she think? That we could work it out? That it would get better? How could it when she only saw me as a friend and I wasn't sure we were even that?

'I'm sorry,' I repeated. I wasn't sure I was, but it seemed the right thing to say in the circumstances.

I wished I'd started the engine before saying anything to Yasmin as the music would have masked the uncomfortable silence. It felt too dismissive to start it now.

'Why now?' Yasmin asked eventually. 'Is it because I pulled out of the meal on Saturday?'

'It wasn't only that. It's been coming on for a while.'

'So why didn't you say anything before now?'

'Because I didn't realise how I was feeling until today.' I raised my eyebrows at her. 'And I could ask you the same question.'

'Yeah, well, I thought we might make it to Christmas.' She shrugged again. 'Are you moving out tonight?'

'If you want me to.'

Silence. Then she shook her head. 'It's late. You can do it tomorrow,' she said in a gentler voice than I'd heard in a long time. 'The spare room's yours tonight. I changed the bedding after Aria and S-J stayed.'

'Thanks. That'd be good.'

'Do you still want to join Aria and me tonight? You're welcome to.'

I pondered on it, but it didn't feel right. I wasn't sad it had ended with Yasmin, but I wasn't elated either. Even an amicable break-up like this wasn't pleasant. Arianna was meant to be planning the next exciting stage of her life with Sara-Jade and she didn't need me ruining that by being melancholy.

'Thanks, but I'll drop you off if you don't mind and make a start on that packing.'

'Okay. Makes sense. Are we good?'

'We're good.'

I pulled the seat belt on, started the engine and reversed out of the parking space.

Yasmin was preoccupied with her phone as I drove into town, which was fine by me. There was nothing more to say at the moment. I veered between wanting to laugh and wanting to cry. It had never entered my head that Yasmin could be feeling the same way, but it now seemed so obvious. She wasn't a tactile person, even in private – not a fan of holding hands, hugging or snuggling together on the sofa watching TV – but she'd often surprised me in the early days with a moment of passion. There hadn't been any of those lately. Somehow we'd become two women who shared a house but very little else. I should never have let it get to that.

* * *

'Where do you fancy living?' I asked Jinks as he padded up and down the duvet in the spare bedroom, weaving his way round the piles of clothes and toiletries I'd dumped on the bed ready for packing. I hadn't wanted to stay in the master bedroom longer than necessary, already feeling like I was trespassing in a space that wasn't mine, not that it had ever felt like mine.

'Do you want to stay at Bumblebee Barn with your Uncle Barney or Ashrigg House with my parents?'

Jinks was no help. He just kept padding and purring.

'We could even ask my grandparents, although Granddad can be a bit grumpy, so maybe not.'

I dumped the first pile of clothes in my case. 'You'll be happy to leave, won't you, Jinks? She never made you feel welcome. Don't take it personally. She never really made me feel welcome either.'

Jinks stretched then settled into a curled-up position against the pillows and closed his eyes.

As I continued to pack my clothes, my emotions were all over the place. I hadn't woken up this morning expecting my relationship to end tonight. At what point had Yasmin realised that she wanted out? She'd said earlier that she 'didn't want it to end yet'. Yet? What did that mean? That she hoped we'd work it out or that she'd been thinking about it for ages but had wanted to string me along for a bit longer?

'No!' I cried out as a thought struck me. 'She wouldn't be so cold.'

Or would she? After I moved in, we'd had a conversation about finances. I'd had a lottery win a few years back. It hadn't been a life-changing never-need-to-work-again sum of money, but it was enough to buy Bayberry Cottage outright, buy my Mini, put me through university and give me an emergency fund. Because Yasmin had a mortgage on her cottage, I'd offered to give her most of my rental income to cover food and bills. At the time, she'd joked that she needed a new kitchen and would be able to afford one in time for Christmas thanks to me. What if that hadn't been a joke? What if her asking me to move in, the lack of passion after that point, and the sticking together despite it clearly not working had purely been driven by her desire for a kitchen re-fit?

Now that the idea had taken root, I couldn't stop it sprouting wings, especially when she'd specifically mentioned thinking we'd make it to Christmas. Mum and Dad had always warned me against being so honest about my lottery win with new people, fearful of them taking advantage. Nadine had come crawling out of the woodwork wanting to try again when she'd discovered my win, and I'd picked up some fake friends who were only after me for a few rounds of drinks, but I thought I'd been wise to the hangers-on since then. If my hunch about Yasmin was right, it seemed not.

My mind began racing through all the times I'd paid for cinema trips or meals out, a painting she'd loved, a new lamp she simply had to have, a replacement coffee machine. The list went on and on. I even regularly paid for the weekly shop and she'd repeatedly promised me she'd transfer me the cash back, but she only 'remembered' once in a blue moon and I never chased.

I tossed in more clothes, not caring how creased they'd be when I unpacked.

'I can't believe how stupid I've been,' I muttered. 'Nadine was a user; Yasmin was a user and so was...'

I gulped back the end of that sentence, a deep shiver chilling me from head to toe. I needed to stop thinking and focus on the packing.

I didn't want to stay here tonight. Zipping up the first case and dumping it on the floor, I reached for my phone. I'd go to Bumblebee Barn. Barney wouldn't bombard me with questions, so I'd have some peace and quiet to get my head around how much of a mug I'd been and what my next steps were. I was about to ring him when I remembered he was going out for his best mate's birthday so he wouldn't be home until late. I had a key, but no way was I willing to be at the farm all alone. It was irrational but I couldn't help it.

'It'll have to be Mum and Dad's,' I murmured. Hopefully they'd accept *I don't want to talk about it* tonight and we could leave the well-meaning questions until tomorrow when I didn't feel like such an idiot. I tutted to myself as I remembered they were hosting a dinner party, which just left my grandparents, but it was late and they'd already be in bed.

I plonked myself down on the bed and stroked Jinks. 'Looks like we *will* have to stay here tonight after all.'

He swished his tail and I smiled at the timely act of demonstrating his displeasure.

'No, I don't want to stay either, but I'll pack everything tonight so we can leave first thing and we won't have to return. I don't think we need to stick around and find out any answers from Yasmin, do we? We've already worked it out.'

I packed my second case then went downstairs, took a bag for life from the understairs cupboard and sought out my belongings.

After twenty minutes, I sat down heavily on an armchair and peered into the bag. Three paperbacks, one recipe book, my lunchbox and flask, a pale pink spatula, a hand blender and the Christmas wreath I'd made. Was that really it?

Tears pricked my eyes. I wasn't sad that it was over. I was sad that it had never really started. I'd lived here for nearly seven months but had barely left an imprint on the cottage or on Yasmin's life. The only difference I'd made was a boost to her bank account.

I swiped at the tears trailing down my cheeks, angry at myself for letting it get to me, especially when I'd known all along that it wasn't quite right. The day I didn't move in spoke volumes about our relationship, and I should have listened to those voices that told me it was a sign of things to come. Another valuable life lesson learned to always trust my gut instinct.

Back upstairs, I did one more scan round the master bedroom, retrieved some clothes from the laundry basket, and that was it. Not quite 11 p.m. and I was already packed and ready to leave.

'I'm going to put these in the car,' I told Jinks as I picked up one of the suitcases.

The idea of slipping away in the morning and posting the keys back through the letterbox was increasingly appealing. Yasmin and I had nothing more to say to each other. If I only had Jinks in his carrier and an overnight bag to move in the morning, I could probably slip out without waking her up. That would be better for both of us than ending things with a fight.

I loaded up the car, shaking my head at the Christmas wreath I'd made for Yasmin, still lying on the back seat. When I'd shown her the first one and she'd said, 'So that's what you spent the whole day making?' I'd known there was no way she'd appreciate hers. She hadn't thanked me for the apple juice and chocolates either. I was well out of it.

14

SAMANTHA

Darcie and I had been back from Terry's for a couple of hours when Hannah rang to say they'd be passing Hedgehog Hollow and would it be all right to drop in. Darcie was beside herself when I told her Amelia and Mason were coming. We'd have ideally seen them at some point during the week but spending so much time with Terry had made that impossible.

'Oh, my gosh! He's grown so much!' I said, taking a sleeping Mason from Hannah so she could slip her coat off.

Josh made a round of drinks and I settled onto the corner sofa with Mason, Darcie squashed up beside me, stroking his hand.

'No Phoebe tonight?' Hannah asked.

'She's gone to the cinema,' Darcie said. 'Can I hold Mason?'

I knew I wouldn't be able to keep him for long. Darcie was used to handling babies from when Lottie and Archie lived with us but she'd never held a newborn, so I explained that she'd need to support Mason's head. She grasped it immediately and we all had an 'aww' moment when he wrapped his fingers round hers.

'What do you think of your new brother?' I asked Amelia.

She pressed herself against Hannah's legs and put her arms up to be cuddled.

'She's not so sure at the moment,' Hannah said, lifting Amelia onto her lap. 'She's a bit clingy,' she added, her voice low. 'She loved the idea of a brother but isn't loving all the attention he gets.'

'Aw, bless her.'

Josh returned with mugs of tea and a hot chocolate for Darcie. 'Should I get the gifts?'

'Ooh, yes, please.' I hadn't had a chance to go gift-shopping but Phoebe worked in the centre of Reddfield so she'd been an absolute star, picking up an assortment of new baby gifts for me during her lunch break.

Josh returned with a large gift bag for Mason and a small one for Amelia.

'Amelia, why don't you see what Josh has got in that little gift bag?'

She raised her head then slid off Hannah's knee, grinning as she took the bag from Josh. Amelia was currently obsessed with dragons, so we'd bought her a soft sage green dragon, suspecting she'd feel left out when Mason was showered with gifts.

'Dragon!' she cried, dropping the bag on the floor and hugging him tightly. She hugged Josh's legs then did the same with me before clambering onto the sofa next to Darcie and cuddling against her.

Josh whipped out his phone and took a photo of the three of them.

'We'll have to get another one like this with Bublet in,' he said, showing it to me.

'There's a load of gifts in the big bag for Mason,' I said, 'but you're welcome to open them later and, if you give me a sec, I've got something for you too, Hannah.'

I retrieved her Christmas wreath from the former dining room downstairs which we now used as a library/snug.

'Chloe finished your wreath for you,' I said, holding it up for Hannah to see.

'Aw, it's gorgeous. Thank you. And sorry again for all the drama disrupting your birthday.'

'No need. It was a really special day. I mean that.'

Amelia ran up and down the lounge with her dragon, making roaring sounds. The gift had clearly done the trick in bringing her out of her shell.

'Darcie, why don't you take Amelia and her dragon up to your bedroom to play for a bit?' I suggested.

Darcie kissed Mason on the forehead before handing him over and running upstairs with Amelia.

'Well played,' Hannah said. 'I knew you'd want more cuddles.'

* * *

'It was so lovely to see Hannah tonight,' I said as I cuddled up to Josh in bed later.

'It was lovely to see Mason, you mean.'

'I didn't see you objecting to cuddles.'

'Needed to get my practice in. I can't believe we'll have one of our own soon, although hopefully it won't be such a dramatic birth.'

'I'll pass on them being born in the stables, but I wouldn't mind it being as quick as Hannah's. Mason was *not* messing around. He wanted to be out!'

I took Josh's hand and rested it on my bump as Bublet started kicking. They were usually gentler on an evening than a morning but there was no point trying to sleep until they settled.

'That's so amazing,' he said. 'What does it feel like for you?'

'At first it was a kind of fluttering sensation like butterflies but then it was more like my stomach dropping, like on a rollercoaster. Now it's like waves. It's weird because I can feel the wave before the actual kick that you can feel.'

We lay in silence for a while as Bublet kicked.

'What if Bublet arrives early?' Josh asked. 'If they were born on Christmas Day, that would only be...' He paused to do the maths, '... ten days early.'

'It's possible. First babies are more likely to be late, but you never know. Hannah and Toby had the baby born in a stable, but we could have the Christmas Day one.'

'That must be strange, spending the day in hospital instead of tucking into the turkey and chocolates.'

'Hopefully it won't happen,' I said. 'It would be a Christmas miracle, but I'd rather enjoy Christmas at home with our family and welcome the newest family member in the New Year. Do you hear that, Bublet? You stay put until next year, please.'

'How are the nerves?'

'Still bubbling away but I'm mostly excited. Not quite Darcie proportions of excitement, but getting there.'

'On a scale of sparkling unicorns, what are you?'

I laughed. 'Love it! A glittery seven, I think, but I reckon it'll go up to a shimmering eight when the nursery's ready. What about you?' I nodded towards the parenting manual on his bedside drawers. Even though I'd suggested that the advice could be conflicting, Josh wanted to feel like he was at least doing something to prepare for such a major life-change.

'About the same. Every so often I get this huge panic that I haven't a clue what I'm doing. I don't know how to be a dad, I've no idea how to raise a little person, and I worry that I'm going to make a mess of it. Do you know what calms me down? Knowing we'll be muddling through and making those mistakes together.'

'Aw, Josh. You'll be an amazing dad and it won't be because you've read a stack of books. It'll be because you love our baby and you want to do the best for it. Bublet is so lucky to have you.'

'And you.'

15

FIZZ

The creak of the door woke me up and my heart began racing as my eyes tried to adjust to the darkness. I couldn't see him, but I knew he was there. I could hear him breathing and smell the alcohol.

Go away! Please!

I was lying on my side, facing the door, and my hands gripped the duvet, pulling it more tightly round my body.

The blackout curtains were too effective and I still couldn't see him, not even a dark shape. Had I imagined it? I was beginning to think I must have been until the bed dipped as he sat down on it – a sensation that made my stomach churn and bile seep into my mouth.

Fear clawed at me, paralysing me, as I anticipated his next move, praying tonight would be one of the nights when he watched me instead. But those nights were rare.

I scrunched my eyes tightly shut, feeling sick at the feeling of warmth emanating from his body and onto my legs, despite the duvet barrier.

Leave me alone!

I could feel a scream building in my churning stomach. Any moment now, he'd place his hand over my mouth and whisper his lies. You can't scream, little Fizzy. You can't tell anyone. Nobody will believe you. They'll know it's your fault because you're stupid. They'll hate you. This is our secret. Our special thing.

Releasing a soft sigh, he leaned closer and stroked a lock of my hair back from my face and I couldn't help it. He hadn't covered my mouth this time and, despite all his warnings, I couldn't contain my fear any longer and released a loud, terrified scream.

He leapt from the bed and the room flooded with light.

'What the hell...?'

That wasn't *his* voice. This wasn't *my* bedroom.

'Yasmin?'

She was standing over me, her hands on her hips, her brows knitted. 'What's with the hysterics?'

'Why are you in here?' I demanded, my heart pounding as I tried to catch my breath.

'I got back from the pub and wanted to make sure you were okay.'

'I'm fine,' I snapped. 'Why did you sit on my bed?'

'Because I've been drinking and it was easier than standing.'

'Why did you touch me?'

'Because your hair was in your face so I moved it. For fuck's sake, Fizz. It's not a crime. I wish I hadn't bothered checking on you now. You scared me shitless.'

'You scared me too. I thought you were...' I took in her furious expression and the words died in my mouth. 'Never mind. Sorry for scaring you.'

'I should think so too. Are you packed?'

'Yes. Jinks and I will be gone first thing.'

'Okay. I'm planning a lie-in, so I probably won't see you.'

Without even saying goodbye, she closed the door. I lay back on the pillows and took a few deep breaths to try to steady my racing heart and churning stomach while I focused on when and where I was. *Spare room, Yasmin's house, twenty-eight years old and thousands of miles away from him. He can't hurt me anymore.*

Except he could.

Distance made no difference. At the back of my mind, there was always the fear that this year would be the year he decided to return to the UK for Christmas. And there was always the guilt that I'd kept my childhood promises and never told anyone, which made him a free man.

Free to hurt others like he'd hurt me.

16

SAMANTHA

On Saturday morning, I was on my way to Thomas's bench with my post-breakfast mug of tea when Fizz phoned.

'Can I ask you a huge favour?' she asked when we'd exchanged greetings. 'I know it's really short notice but is there any chance of you working today and me taking next Saturday instead?'

'That's fine. I haven't got any plans for today.'

'Really appreciate that. Thanks, Sam.'

Fizz didn't sound like her normal bubbly self. 'Is everything all right?' I asked.

'Yeah... no... sort of.' She sighed. 'I split up with Yasmin last night.'

I sat down on the bench, wishing I could reach out and hug her. She sounded so deflated. 'Aw, Fizz, I'm sorry.'

'It's fine. Mutual decision and definitely a good thing.'

'Are you okay?' She didn't sound it.

'Not sure. Mixed emotions.'

'I presume you're moving out?'

'Already done that first thing. I'm in April's Tea Parlour having breakfast and trying to decide whether to ask Barney or my parents if I can stay until my tenants move out. I'm not sure which will be least stressful – Mum worrying about me or me worrying about Barney.'

Fizz was desperate for her brother to find love but he kept choosing and dating women who were totally unsuited to farm life, so she was concerned about him nursing a perpetually broken heart.

'You could always move in here,' I said.

'I couldn't impose like that. You've already got so much on with preparing for the baby.'

'There's only the nursery to sort out and it's Josh's project for this week. All I need to do is paint colour approval. You and Jinks are more than welcome to stay here or, if you'd prefer your independence, Meadow View isn't booked until New Year.'

There was silence and I wondered if we'd been cut off.

'Fizz?'

'Still here,' she said, her voice sounding shaky. 'I'm just a bit choked up by that offer. That's really kind of you.'

'Hey, you're part of the Hedgehog Hollow family,' I said, gently. 'It's no bother at all.'

She sniffed and cleared her throat. 'Can I come back to you when my head's clearer?'

'Of course. Enjoy your breakfast and try to relax today. I'm here for you if you want to talk and the farmhouse or Meadow View are here if you want a place to stay. Take care, Fizz.'

'Thanks. I'll let you know what I decide.'

When the call ended, I took a sip of my tea and rested back against the bench. In my past relationships, I'd been the one who got dumped, but I could imagine that break-ups were still horrible even if they were mutual decisions or if you were the instigator.

I was sad for Fizz that it had ended with Yasmin, but couldn't help feeling relieved. They'd acted so differently together from all the other couples I knew. Even when James and Chloe had split up when going through an exceptionally rough patch in their first year of marriage, they'd still seemed more 'together' than Fizz and Yasmin ever had. Couples didn't need to be tactile to show how much they cared, but I'd never picked up on any affection from Yasmin towards Fizz – no adoring looks, playful banter, or proudly relayed anecdotes – and I'd always felt like Fizz deserved so much more.

Misty-Blue jumped up on the bench beside me and I swapped my mug into my left hand so I could stroke her. Luna would still be curled up on Darcie's bed.

'Will you make Jinks welcome if Fizz stays with us?' I asked Misty-Blue. 'You and Luna can show him around.'

I suspected Fizz wouldn't take me up on the offer. She had a really good relationship with her family and, even though Natasha and Hadrian would be worried about her, they weren't the sort to constantly fuss round her. Fizz fussing round Barney was more likely. Even though he was a couple of years older than her, he did seem quite immature when it came to relationships.

Another reason for not staying here was the proximity to work. It could be hard to switch off and I didn't want Fizz to feel that she couldn't relax and should be in the barn all the time. If she did accept, I'd have to lay down some ground rules to ensure she kept a balance.

I finished my tea, returned my mug to the kitchen and headed over to the barn with Misty-Blue trotting alongside me. Josh had been on hoglets duty last night.

As soon as I opened the barn door, Wilbur ran over to greet me, his claws skidding on the wooden floorboards. He gave Misty-Blue a gentle nudge with his nose and she weaved round his front paws, purring. I loved how the pair of them had instantly bonded.

Luna had been a little more wary and preferred to maintain her distance.

Josh looked up from the kitchen area where he was squeezing a teabag in a mug and gave me a huge smile.

'Tea?'

'Just had one. Did you get much sleep last night?'

He hugged me and kissed my forehead. 'A bit. This being up every few hours malarky must be good training for when Bublet arrives.'

'You'd think so, although I think Bublet might be a tad louder than the hoglets when they want feeding.'

I sat down at the treatment table with Josh.

'Did you say you were going to sort out the over-wintering this week?' he asked.

'Yes. I'll message our hogster parents shortly.'

Over time, we'd recruited an army of supporters and 'hogster parents' was our play on words with foster parents. They took different roles depending on their home and work circumstances. Some were happy to hand-feed hoglets – typically those who had difficulty sleeping and therefore weren't affected by the broken sleep – and others who were happier over-wintering. Sadly, the odds of survival are stacked against autumn juveniles because, as well as the challenge of colder weather, they don't have long to gain the weight they need to see them through hibernation. Rescue centres around the country need to 'over-winter' those at risk, providing them with food and shelter through the winter months. At Hedgehog Hollow, having hogster parents for over-wintering was invaluable for freeing us up to focus on the admissions who were sick and injured.

Some rescue centres had volunteers to take on adult hogs when they were overcrowded but we were blessed with a two-storey barn and, even with taking in additional wildlife, I couldn't imagine us ever being so full that we needed additional space.

'Can't that wait till Monday?' Josh asked. 'It's your day off.'

'Not anymore. I've swapped Saturdays with Fizz. She's split up with Yasmin.'

'Oh! Is she okay?'

Josh felt the same way about Fizz and Yasmin as I did, convinced they weren't happy together.

'She's a bit meh, I think. I don't know any details, but I know she's moved out this morning and is trying to decide where to stay. Bayberry Cottage has tenants until next month.'

'Have you said she can stay with us? Or in one of the cottages?'

I smiled at him, loving that he was on the same wavelength as me.

'Both. She's going to think about it. It sounds like she needs a bit of space today to decide what happens next.'

'Break-ups are crap and I feel bad for Fizz, but I can't say I'm not relieved. Yasmin was never right for her. When she's ready, she'll find someone who is.'

'I agree.'

'Like Phoebe,' he said, winking at me.

I gasped. 'You know? How?'

'I've got eyes! At the risk of sounding cheesy, Phoebe lights up when she's with Fizz and Fizz does the same. They're perfect for each other. Phoebe knows it, we know it, and Fizz will realise it eventually.'

I squeezed his hand across the table. 'You big softie.'

'I have my moments. So I take it Phoebe's shared her feelings with you?'

'No. Like you, I guessed it. It was last summer at our post-honeymoon barbeque. She said something poignant about relationships and she was looking across the garden at Fizz, all dewy-eyed. Phoebe didn't want me to say anything to anyone.'

'I won't say a word, Josh said. 'If it's going to happen, it'll happen naturally. Did she enjoy the film last night?'

'I haven't seen her. They're both still in bed.'

Darcie was usually exhausted by the end of each half-term and often had a lie-in on the first day of the holidays, and I suspected Phoebe was tired after her night out with Leo. Phoebe was taking Darcie to a birthday party at a soft-play centre later this morning, so she was sensible to take advantage of some peace and quiet for now.

'How about I help with the next hoglets feed, grab a few hours' kip, then relieve you so you can visit Terry?' Josh suggested. 'I know you'll only worry if you don't see him today.'

'That'd be great, thanks.'

'And because plans for today have changed, I'm thinking that we should give Phoebe a list of the paint colours we like for the nursery. I'm sure she won't mind picking up sample pots on the way home. What do you think?'

I stood up and put my arms round Josh. I hadn't needed to say a word, but he automatically knew what was on my mind by covering for Fizz and had presented a way of me seeing Terry and keeping the work on the nursery on track. Perhaps that made me predictable, but I didn't care because it also made him a partner who understood me and was eager to take away any unnecessary stress.

'I think that's a brilliant plan. Thank you.'

17

FIZZ

I settled my bill in April's Tea Parlour, including a large tip for them letting me have breakfast in the café when they were only meant to be open for pastries for the first ninety minutes of the day, and for allowing Jinks to join me. With Bayberry Cottage being just round the corner, I knew the owner April and her daughter Daisy really well. They both adored cats and were amazed that Jinks was content to sit in his carrier with the lid off instead of roaming round the café. I'd laughed and told them it was the reason he was known as Jinks the lazy cat – too much effort required to jump out of the carrier. He usually had one burst of energy each evening, going on a neighbourhood prowl, then vegged for the rest of the day.

Much as he liked it, Jinx couldn't stay in his carrier all day, so I needed to make a decision on where to stay for the next six weeks or so. What I'd said to Sam about Mum worrying about me and me worrying about Barney was true, but it wasn't a strong enough reason not to stay with either of them. There was something far stronger keeping me away.

I carried the cat carrier over to the playground on the large village green behind April's and placed it beside the swings. I removed the lid once more and Jinks sniffed the fresh air but remained on his cushion. I sat on the nearest swing and gently rocked back and forth.

'It needs to be Hedgehog Hollow,' I said to Jinks. 'The only memories there are happy ones. Well, except the epic strop Yasmin had at Sam and Josh's wedding, but we'll not let her taint that special place for us, will we?'

I'd actually cried earlier when Sam invited Jinks to stay and not as an afterthought. It took considerable strength to compose myself and continue that conversation. Sam was so kind and thoughtful and the exact opposite of Yasmin.

I still wasn't sure why Yasmin had decided to check on me last night. She'd have known I hadn't moved out because my car was still on the drive and, even inebriated, she couldn't have failed to notice my belongings inside. She wasn't the sort to be worried about how the break-up had affected me and, even if she had been, we'd established that it was a mutual decision and it had all been amicable, so she wasn't going to find me sobbing into my pillow in desperate need of comfort. The only logical explanation I kept coming back to was that she'd had a few drinks and fancied her chances before I moved out. If that was the reason, I was both disappointed and disgusted that she'd think that way. If it wasn't the reason, I had no idea what was. Either way, I was well out of there but the very act of her entering my room in the dead of night, sitting on the bed and touching me had triggered me and I'd never felt more unsettled.

I couldn't see Bayberry Cottage from the playground, which was probably just as well, as I had an urge to bang on the door and evict my tenants so I could return to the home I loved where I felt safe and secure. The place that *he* had never been and never would.

* * *

It's amazing how slowly time passes when you've got nowhere to go. I sat on the swing until the first children appeared, rushing over to Jinks and prodding him. Fearing that he might get startled and make a bolt for it – and also realising that a woman and a cat in a playground screamed *stranger danger* – I politely answered their questions and left.

I drove around for a while, but the waste of fuel felt senseless. I couldn't go anywhere with Jinks and I couldn't leave him alone in the car, fearful of the sun coming out and overheating him.

Shortly after eleven, I pulled up in the farmyard at Hedgehog Hollow and took Jinks into the barn. Sam was at the treatment table, typing into her laptop. She looked up and, moments later, had me enveloped in a warm hug.

'Can Jinks and I take you up on the offer to stay here?'

She hugged me a little tighter. 'You're more than welcome.' She stepped back and smiled at me. 'Do you want to stay in Meadow View or the farmhouse?'

'I don't want to put you to any trouble.'

'Neither option is trouble. I'd love you to stay in the farmhouse and I'm sure Phoebe and Darcie would too, but I'm thinking you might like some space and Meadow View would be best for you.'

'It probably would. I have some thinking to do. You're sure nobody's booked it?'

'They haven't and I've already blocked it out for you because I had a feeling you'd need it. It struck me that if staying with your parents or Barney had been the right choice for you, you'd already have made that decision when we spoke.'

'How is it that you know me so well and I don't think my girl-friend knew me at all?'

'Because you and I were destined to be lifelong friends and

colleagues thanks to Jinks here, and you and Yasmin were—'

'Never meant to be together?' I suggested.

'I wouldn't say that. I think she was probably what you needed at the time, but you weren't a long-term match. They say opposites attract and sometimes they do, but I don't think that's what works for you in a relationship.'

'It doesn't. I don't think we understood each other at all. I can't believe how long it took me to realise that.'

'Do you want to tell me what happened over a cuppa?'

I lifted Jinks out of his carrier and sent him off to explore the barn while Sam made the drinks. He managed half a lap before returning to his cushion for a nap.

Sam handed me a mug of tea and we sat side by side on the sofa bed.

'You didn't think Yasmin was right for me?' I asked her.

She winced. 'She didn't seem to make you happy. You weren't the bubbly Fizz we know and love when you were with her.'

'I didn't feel it.'

'I wondered whether to say something, but nobody appreciates being given advice on their relationship. If you'd ever asked me, I'd have been honest, but it wasn't my place to interfere otherwise. I hope you're not annoyed with me.'

'Never. So what went wrong? That would be pretty much everything...'

I brought her up to speed on the moving-in day that didn't happen right through to our break-up last night, leaving out the incident in the early hours.

'Mum and Dad are going to be so disappointed,' I said. 'They really liked her.'

'Only because she charmed them. If they'd known how she behaved on your original moving-in day, they'd have started seeing her differently, just like you did.'

'I shouldn't have moved in with her when the doubts surfaced.'

'You can't do that to yourself, Fizz. You loved her – or thought you did – and you moved in hoping it was an oversight and things would get better. You weren't to know that they wouldn't. I did the same thing with Harry – my boyfriend before James. Red flags everywhere but I ignored them all because I wanted to believe it was going to work. The heart wins over the head so many times.'

I smiled at her appreciatively. 'You sound like a relationship coach.'

'I practise on the hedgehogs when you're not here, but I can't seem to convince them that staying with their partner for more than procreation is the way forward.'

That tickled me. Hedgehogs were solitary creatures and hoglets were the result of one-night liaisons with a male never to be seen again. The mothers didn't stick as a family unit for long either. Once the hoglets were weaned and able to forage for themselves, they parted company.

'Feeding time,' Sam said as a familiar squeaking noise reached us. 'How about you help me feed the hoglets, then I'll get you the key to Meadow View and you can settle in?'

'You're on. Where's Phoebe and Darcie, by the way?'

'You've just missed them. Darcie's at a soft-play birthday party and then they're nipping to the retail park. They should be back by three.'

It was good that they weren't here right now. Hopefully I'd be back on form this afternoon when they returned. The break-up with Yasmin hadn't caused any real harm and, as Sam had suggested, I could put it down to experience, learn from it and move on. If only she hadn't come into my room this morning. *That* was going to stay with me. *That* had brought too many unwanted memories to the surface.

18

FIZZ

My first week living in Meadow View – my first week without Yasmin – flew past. It had been the half-term holiday and, as Phoebe had only been able to book the Thursday and Friday off work as annual leave, Darcie spent most of the start of the week with Sam and me in the barn. Her questions and chatter were a welcome distraction and even the quieter moments when she was curled up on the sofa bed watching animated films on the iPad transported me into a magical world of Disney princesses, talking dragons and happy ever afters. Safe worlds. Happy worlds. If only real life was like that.

I worked late into each evening, joking with Sam that I needed something to keep me occupied when my plans for the foreseeable future had disappeared in a puff of smoke. She tried to talk me out of it, telling me I needed a work/life balance, but there was no changing my mind.

'Just don't work too hard,' she said. 'I don't want you burning out.'

'I'm fine. Throwing myself into work is my way of adjusting to change. I did the same when I split up with Nadine.' I smiled at

her. 'That and cleaning. I was still living at home at the time and
Mum said she was going to have to start charging me for furniture
polish and anti-bac because I went through the stuff so quickly.
Meadow View is immaculate, so I can't go on a cleaning frenzy
there, so Attila the Badger and his hedgehog army get my full
attention instead.'

'Attila's hedgehog army? Have I missed something?'

I giggled my way through the story, which Sam found amusing
too.

'It's good to see you laughing,' she said. 'In fact, I'm impressed
at how positive you've been all week.'

'It's not worth getting down about it. We weren't a good match
and it needed to end. I just need that bit of work-focused time to
clear my head of it.'

'If you ever have a day where you're not feeling so bright and
you want to talk about it, I'm here for you.'

I smiled gratefully and shoed her back to the farmhouse, but
my smile slipped as soon as she'd closed the door. If I ever had a
day when I wasn't feeling so bright? I had lots of those, but I pulled
on my sparkliest clothes, smiled widely and made jokes. Fizz
Kinsella was fun and bubbly and everybody's friend. Fizz Kinsella
was also a façade. If I let that mask slip and truly let anyone in,
what would happen? *Nobody will want to be your friend if they find
out. They'll all turn against you. So sparkle and shine, little Fizzy, and
keep our secret.*

So I did.

And it was exhausting.

I knew I couldn't stay in the barn working late every evening
and had to return to Meadow View at some point. The cottage
itself wasn't a problem and I loved staying there. It was warm,
comfortable, inviting. The problem was the dark memories
swirling round in my mind when I was alone without the distrac-

tion of work. I barely gave Yasmin any headspace. *He* was the one dominating my thoughts.

Today was Sunday and I usually loved family Sunday lunches, but I really couldn't face today's. After the break-up, I'd pulled out of last week's lunch at Grandma and Granddad's house, citing a dodgy takeaway, so there was no way I could duck out of today's at the farm.

I hadn't told them about splitting up with Yasmin yet or me temporarily staying at Hedgehog Hollow and it wasn't because I was uncomfortable or embarrassed about it. It was because it had been overshadowed by the final incident and everything that triggered. I couldn't seem to separate the two things, so I feared that, if I talked about my split, I might give something away about the past.

While I showered, I rehearsed a speech. *I just wanted to let you all know that Yasmin and I broke up last weekend. It was a mutual thing and all very amicable, although we won't be staying friends because we've realised we don't have much in common. Jinks and I are staying at Hedgehog Hollow until my tenants move out of Bayberry Cottage. I'm absolutely fine, it's for the best, and I don't need or want to talk about it. Can someone pass the gravy please?*

They'd accept that, wouldn't they? If they ignored my request and asked questions, surely those would be focused on what specifically went wrong rather than the details of the break-up conversation... and anything that happened afterwards.

In an attempt to feel brighter about it all, I pulled on my sparkliest unicorn top over a pair of leggings and my favourite purple boots. I piled my purple hair onto the top of my head into my signature messy bun and added some pink sparkly clips.

I peered out of the front window to check the weather and spotted Darcie cycling up and down the path outside the holiday cottages. The sky was pale blue and cloud-free so, satisfied that there'd be no rain, I reached for my purple fluffy faux-fur jacket. I always felt like I was being hugged when I wore it, which was exactly what I needed today.

Big smile.

'Ooh, you look pretty!' Darcie said, stopping her bike when I stepped out of the cottage.

'Thank you.'

'Can I stroke your jacket?'

I held out the arm for her.

'That's so soft.'

'It's my favourite. It's like wearing a teddy bear. Are you enjoying your bike ride?'

'I like riding on hills best, but Phoebe said I needed to stay close to the farmhouse because we're going to Rosemary's soon. Are you going to Bumblebee Barn?'

'I am. Lunch with my family.'

'Blow kisses to the animals for me.'

'I will. And can you say hello to Rosemary and Trixie for me?'

'I'll give them both a cuddle from you.'

I blew Darcie a kiss as she zipped past me and down the road towards Wildflower Byre. If I could capture and bottle the genuine joy which that girl emanated, the world would be a much happier place.

* * *

'Ten-minute warning,' Mum called, heralding the usual scramble to nip to the loo, wash hands and top up drinks before moving into the dining room.

I still hadn't given them my news. In the car on the way over to Bumblebee Barn, I'd decided that the best approach was to say it while everyone was together so I wouldn't have to repeat it and we could move on. What I'd failed to think about is that we were *never* all together until we sat down to eat. The family rule was that the house hosts made lunch but, when we were at Barney's, Mum and I alternated in helping him. She'd taken that mantle today so I'd found myself acting overly interested in Dad's plans for a new drive at Ashrigg House and the intricate details of the extension one of my grandparents' neighbours was having built, even though I didn't know the neighbour and couldn't picture which house it was. All to avoid talking about me.

By the time we sat down to eat, I felt drained from thinking of questions and new small talk subjects each time a conversation topic reached exhaustion point.

Our family embraced the old Yorkshire tradition of having Yorkshire pudding as a starter, served up with onion gravy. It was my favourite part of the meal and I normally wolfed it down, but I wasn't hungry. I knew that if I left any, questions would be asked, so I forced it down, but it sat heavily on my stomach. When Mum and Barney served the main course and finally sat down, I'd announce my news and hopefully everyone would be too busy eating to ask questions.

The dishes were cleared and the main course was brought through. I smiled politely and drew on every ounce of patience I had as we went through the rigmarole of everyone filling their plates with beef and vegetables from the various tureens adorning the table and passing dishes from one end of the table to the other.

Granddad placed a final dollop of mashed potato on his plate and sat down. Time to eat. Time to tell them.

'We've got some news!' Granddad declared and I groaned inwardly as I picked up my cutlery. I might have to wait until after pudding now to make my announcement.

'I know we said we'd host Christmas dinner at our place this year, Barney, but we might need to come to the farm after all because we're going to need a bigger table. After years of begging, Melvin has finally agreed to come home. He's bringing the family over for Christmas.'

My knife and fork clattered onto my plate, flicking gravy-covered peas across the crisp white tablecloth. No! He couldn't do that!

Nobody seemed to notice as they were too busy expressing their delight and firing off questions: when, for how long, would they stay with Grandma and Granddad?

I only had one question: why?

'They haven't booked the flights yet,' Grandma said. 'Kimberly's never been to the UK so, with the girls not being school-age yet, it's the ideal chance to explore and they're trying to decide how long to stay.'

I stared at my plate of food, feeling sick, while the volume of chatter increased as my family discussed how amazing it would be to have Uncle Melvin back on home soil for the first time in sixteen years. And the speculation was rife again about why he'd walked away from the chance to take over the running of the family farm in favour of being an Arizona ranch-hand.

I knew. I'd always known.

'I wonder if I'll still recognise him,' Barney mused.

'He hadn't changed much when we went over for the wedding,' Dad said. 'Do you remember much about him? When he emigrated you'd have been...' He paused to do the maths.

Fourteen.

I'd been twelve.

And I'd recognise that monster anywhere.

* * *

'Are you still feeling poorly?' Mum asked softly as she reached for my plate at the end of the meal. 'You haven't eaten much.'

'A bit.'

'Just say if you want to get off early.'

'I might do that. Thanks, Mum.'

I hadn't actually eaten anything but thankfully my nerves had prevented me from piling my plate high like I usually did so it hadn't taken much effort to move it to one side and look like I'd made some sort of dent. Everyone had been too distracted reminiscing about *him* and speculating on the impending visit to pay any attention to me.

Pudding was served and I passed on it, despite it being my all-time favourite. No way could I stomach a stodgy steamed sponge with custard.

I might have stayed for coffee if the subject had changed, but it seemed all anyone wanted to talk about was the 'prodigal son's' visit and I couldn't cope with it any longer.

When Mum went into the kitchen to clear the dishes away and make the drinks, I followed her.

'I'm feeling a bit worse,' I said. 'I might slope off, but I don't want to make a fuss. Will you give everyone my apologies?'

'Of course, sweetheart. I hope you feel better soon.'

If only it was that simple.

I smiled weakly as I pulled on my fluffy coat. 'See you later.'

She hugged me and kissed my cheek. 'Give me a call if you need anything.'

Closing the kitchen door behind me, I forced myself to place one foot in front of the other as I walked to the car, when all I wanted to do was jump up and down screaming.

19

SAMANTHA

'Oh, you have to be kidding me!'

I looked up from my book as Josh and I relaxed in the lounge on Sunday evening, concerned at the evident frustration in Josh's voice. He was staring at his phone, his brow deeply creased.

'What's up?'

'I've got a resignation email from Alan Dinklage! I can't believe it. And he doesn't want to work his notice.' He released a frustrated growl.

'Does he say why he's leaving?'

Alan had been the veterinary practice manager for longer than Josh had been a qualified vet. He was skilful, efficient and a friend.

For the first time since I'd known Josh, the veterinary practice was fully staffed, so providing cover to the rescue centre worked smoothly. Josh's dad, Paul, had turned down the veterinary surgeon vacancy, so Josh's friend Tariq had accepted that role. Paul worked there as a veterinary nurse and his girlfriend, Beth, had returned as a part-time receptionist but a key position like practice manager being vacant with immediate effect would be a problem for us all, as cover for that role had to be the priority.

'Unexpected circumstances,' Josh muttered. 'Oh, no!' He grimaced as he handed me his phone to read.

I scanned down the message, my stomach sinking at the news that Alan's wife Moira's eyesight had been deteriorating for a while and she'd received the prognosis on Friday that it would go completely within a year. They'd spent all weekend discussing what to do and had concluded they wanted to spend time seeing as much of the world as they could while Moira was still able to.

'What a shock that must have been for them both,' I said, returning the phone.

Josh sighed. 'Massive one. I'll see if he can come in tomorrow to say goodbye and sort the paperwork. I'd better let your dad know what's happening. See if he has any contacts.'

'Ask him about Adele. She was the practice manager for the Brothers Grim and she was brilliant at her job.'

The Brothers Grim had been the perfect name for Dad's former bosses in Whitsborough Bay because they never spent any money on modernising their veterinary practice, leaving it dark, dingy and very grim.

'Did she get another job after they closed?' Josh asked.

'I think so, but I don't know any details. Dad hasn't mentioned her recently, but it doesn't mean he's not in touch with her. She's a lovely person too and she'd fit right in at your place.'

'She sounds ideal. I'll see what he says. Back later.'

Now that she was on my mind, I couldn't resist looking for Adele on LinkedIn. She'd worked for the Brothers Grim for as long as Dad. I'd helped out there when I was younger, cleaning out animal crates, and she'd always been really kind to me, which had been much appreciated because I was a bit scared of the brothers. Her two sons had been at the same senior school as me but they'd been in the years either side of mine so we'd known each other but hadn't been friends.

I found Adele but her profile didn't appear to have been updated since leaving the Brothers Grim so I had no idea if she was working now or not. She was on Facebook too but her privacy settings were good so there was no information to glean there. I'd best leave it to Dad and Josh but hopefully they could sort something fast. There was only a month left until I started my maternity leave and we could do without staffing stresses.

20

FIZZ

My back was aching so I adjusted my position on the sofa in Meadow View, thinking I should probably get up and close the blinds. I should probably put a light on too. At the moment, the only illumination came from the television which I had on a volume so low that I couldn't hear it. I had no idea what programme was on or even which channel was broadcasting. I'd switched it on when I arrived home from Bumblebee Barn in the hope of a distraction, but the noise had irritated me and I'd gradually lowered the volume as I lay on the sofa, staring into space.

A shape moving past the window made me jump and, at the next moment, there was a knock on the door. Phoebe? She'd messaged me a couple of hours ago to say she and Darcie were back from Rosemary's and did I fancy some company after Darcie had gone to bed? I was no company to anyone today so I hadn't replied, had switched my phone to silent and placed it face down on the coffee table.

There was another knock and I knew it was fruitless trying to pretend I wasn't home because whoever had passed the window had likely already seen me.

'Coming!' I called, reluctantly rolling off the sofa and stretching out my seized-up limbs.

'Mum?' I exclaimed when I opened my door. 'What are you doing here?'

'Shouldn't I be the one asking you that question?'

I moved back so she could step into the entrance hall.

'I was going to tell you this afternoon but...' I couldn't finish the sentence without giving anything away.

Mum followed me through to the kitchen area, where I switched the kettle on to boil. She delved into a shopping bag and started piling the contents on the worktop.

'Cranberry juice and paracetamol for if you really are feeling under the weather,' she said. 'Your favourite chocolates, a box of shortbread and a bottle of wine for if you're nursing a broken heart, and a syrup sponge pudding and custard because you missed out on your favourite pudding today. I know a tin and a packet aren't the same as homemade, but they're still tasty.'

I couldn't help but smile at the goodies. 'Thank you. That's really kind. You know, then?'

'I was worried about you, so I bought this lot and called round at Yasmin's with it and she told me you didn't live there anymore. You hadn't moved in with any of us and I knew you couldn't have gone back to Bayberry Cottage so Hedgehog Hollow seemed the logical choice. A quick text to Samantha confirmed it. Do you want to talk about it?'

The kettle clicked off so I took a couple of mugs out of the cupboard. 'There's not much to talk about, but plonk yourself down and I'll bring you a drink and tell you my sorry tale.' I pointed to the shortbread. 'You'd better take those with you.'

'I'm sorry I never told you about the original moving-in day disaster,' I said when I'd brought her up to speed. 'I didn't want anyone to think badly of her when we sorted it out, which I was sure we would.'

'I understand that logic completely. I remember being in my twenties and a friend of mine splitting up with her fiancé. Several of us piled in about how relieved we were because we'd never liked him and she was better off without him. Guess who got uninvited from the wedding and shunned from her life when they got back together a few days later?'

'Ew, awkward!'

'Exactly. I'm just sorry you went through that on your own.'

'Looking back, I probably should have said something. The red flags were there. You'd have spotted them even when I couldn't... or didn't want to.'

'Don't punish yourself. It's happened and it's not pleasant but you've learned from it and you won't let yourself get into that situation again.'

'That's what I thought after Nadine.'

Mum shook her head. 'Yasmin and Nadine were two very different relationships. Nadine was a control freak and, after you split up, she was only after you for your money and Yasmin was...'

'A control freak who was only after me for my money?' I suggested. 'They both had very different ways of demonstrating the behaviours but, ultimately, they were all about what *they* wanted and I *knew* that about Yasmin, deep down. I need to trust my gut more.'

'Your dad would agree with that. Shame gut instinct doesn't count for anything in policing or there'd be a lot more criminals behind bars.'

'Damn pesky evidence,' I joked, which was Dad's favourite lament.

'If it's any consolation, your dad and I never spotted any of

Yasmin's controlling behaviours and we were specifically on the watch out for that after Nadine. Yasmin was always so friendly around us.'

'Likely because she knew you'd be watching her carefully after my Nadine disaster.'

We sat in companionable silence, finishing our drinks and munching on shortbread.

'She wasn't so friendly today,' Mum said eventually.

'Really? What did she say?'

'It wasn't what she said. It was the look she gave me. It could have frozen hell over.'

'She's probably pissed off that we didn't make it to Christmas so she wasn't able to wheedle an expensive gift out of me and enough money for her new kitchen.'

'What will you do now?'

'Stay here until my tenants move out and then Jinks and I will move back into Bayberry Cottage and heave a sigh of relief that we never sold it like she wanted.'

'You won't give up on love, will you?'

I bit into another piece of shortbread and shook my head. 'I believe Miss Right is out there somewhere. I just haven't found her yet.'

As I said those words, Phoebe's face flashed into my mind. I must have looked confused or something because Mum asked if everything was okay.

'Yeah. Weird moment. Phoebe popped into my head just now.'

'Are you attracted to Phoebe?'

'No! She's my friend. I've never thought of her like that. She's not gay. Or is she? I don't know. We've never talked about it. But she was on a date with that Leo last week. Unless it wasn't a date. She never said it was...'

'You're rambling,' Mum said, her eyes twinkling at me. 'Phoebe would be a great match. Definitely not a money-grabbing controller.'

'Give over! She's just a friend. She only sees me as a friend. She's never said or done anything to...' I tailed off, searching my mind for any signs that Phoebe could possibly be attracted to me. Nearly every memory involved us laughing. We were tactile but we had been ever since her past came out and she came to Hedgehog Hollow in desperate need of love and comfort. The touches had been friendly, not flirty, hadn't they? I actually had no idea. What did I know about flirting and relationships with my track record?

'She's very pretty,' Mum ventured.

'She's stunning, but I think we're getting carried away here. Even if Phoebe is attracted to women, and more specifically attracted to me, I'm fresh out of a relationship and not a good prospect. Rebound relationships don't work.'

'The rebound relationships that don't work are when the person on the rebound is nursing a broken heart. You, Felicity Kinsella, have not had your heart broken. You've had your pride wounded and your confidence knocked but your heart is still intact because, unless I'm very much mistaken, you never gave it to Yasmin Simms.'

'That's not...' But I couldn't protest. She was right. Yasmin had never had my heart because when that initial burst of chemistry faded, there was nothing in its place except for a stubborn streak on my part to want to make it work. To prove that *he* hadn't destroyed my ability to have a normal loving relationship. To prove that I could be special to someone else.

Mum stood up and rolled her shoulders. 'I need to send out some invoices before bedtime, so I'd better get home.'

She carried our empty mugs through to the kitchen and I

followed with the box of shortbread before I polished off the rest of the biscuits.

'Everything will be all right,' she said, hugging me. 'Take some time to lick your wounds if you need to, but please don't rub sand in them.' She stepped back, laughing. 'Is that a saying or have I just made it up?'

'I'm not sure but, if it isn't a saying, it should be. Thanks for coming round tonight, Mum. I really appreciate it.'

'I'm always here for you. You can tell me anything, you know.'

I smiled and nodded. If only that were true.

After Mum left, I felt unsettled. *He* was back in my mind again and he didn't deserve the headspace. I felt guilty for ignoring Phoebe's message earlier so I picked up my phone.

✉ To Phoebe

Only just seen your message. Would love some
company. Come over whenever you're ready xx

I checked myself in my selfie setting and winced. What a state! Chunks of hair had escaped from my bun and hung limply down my back. As Grandma would say, I looked like I'd been dragged through a hedge backwards. My eyes were bloodshot, my eyeliner smudged, and my cheeks were blotchy. I wasn't normally bothered about how I looked but even I had limits. Phoebe couldn't see me like this.

I raced upstairs and into the bathroom, removed my make-up, splashed my face with cold water and quickly reapplied a fresh, subtle face. With my hair re-done and a fresh T-shirt on – bright coral with a sparkly mermaid on the front – I ran back downstairs and put a couple of lamps on. Mood lighting. Nice. I lit a scented candle, a flicker of delight in me that I could do that now without

Yasmin moaning about weird smells or sooty marks. Then I panicked and blew it out worried that it was too cosy and romantic. Phoebe was a close friend and I'd never thought about her as being anything other than that until this evening.

I pictured Phoebe and me cosied up together on her bed at Hedgehog Hollow watching films, sometimes with Darcie snuggled between us, sometimes on our own, and how her eyes sparkled with enthusiasm as we analysed the characters and plot points. I thought about all the occasions where we'd laughed hysterically together like sledging in the heavy snowfall on Darcie's first birthday at Hedgehog Hollow and sumo-wrestling in giant inflatable suits on Phoebe's birthday a week later.

Hugs, light touches and gentle smiles sprang to mind, which I'd always put down to a close friendship. Could they have been more? Was there any way Phoebe could be attracted to me?

I knew she'd never had a relationship but what I didn't know was whether she'd had any dates or who her type was. Leo? Me? Both of us? It seemed ridiculous now that we'd never talked about it. I felt I knew pretty much everything about Phoebe except that one detail that suddenly seemed very important.

My heart pounded as my phone beeped and a message from Phoebe flashed up on my screen.

✉ From Phoebe
Really sorry but I can't come now. I'm at the cinema with Leo again. Maybe one night next week? xx

Leo. She was at the cinema with Leo. I pictured them arm in arm at the cinema last Saturday night, throwing popcorn at each other, his arm round her shoulders and my heart sank to the floor.

I'd watched them, thinking I wanted that with someone, but now I realised that I wanted that with Phoebe.

I re-lit the candle and stared into the flame, trying not to picture Phoebe and Leo together but also trying not to picture Phoebe and me together. I failed abysmally at both.

21

SAMANTHA

On Tuesday morning, Fizz had a routine eye test first thing, so I was on my own in the barn when a rescue call came through.

'There's a hedgehog stuck up my drainpipe,' the woman caller said. 'Or at least I think it was a hedgehog. It's definitely a small animal and you rescue more than hedgehogs now, don't you?'

'Yes, we do. You're certain it's stuck?'

'Definitely. My dog scared it and it ran up there. I can hear it scrabbling around as though it's trying to get out but I can't reach it. My husband's taken the dog inside.'

'Okay. I've got a few tricks we can try. Where can I find you?'

I scribbled down the address in Cherry Brompton – the same village as Bloomsberry's Garden Centre, which Riley's family owned – and collected my kit. In the car, I sent a WhatsApp to Fizz before I left.

✉ To Fizz
Been called to a rescue in Cherry Brompton but suspect it'll involve an awkward lying down situation which I won't be able to do. When your

appointment ends, can you come straight to
Weeberley Hall in Cherry Brompton? xx

Cherry Brompton was a stunning village and one of the most
affluent in the area. It was full of grand old houses and pretty stone
cottages. I hadn't explored sufficiently to know which one was
Weeberley Hall, but it sounded impressive.

My sat nav took me straight to exactly what I'd envisaged – a
grand old hall set back from the road in the middle of the village.
There were two sets of wrought-iron gates through which carriages
would have swept in and out of the driveway. The age of the prop-
erty confirmed one thing for me: there'd be no plastic drainpipes
we could cut through. It would be heavy cast-iron ones, so we were
going to have to rely on our tools and some good luck.

I drove through the open gate. A woman dressed in a burgundy
gilet was standing with her back to me next to what I presumed
was the drainpipe in question.

As I heaved myself out of my jeep, she waved me over without
turning.

'Hi! I'm Samantha from Hedgehog Hollow Wildlife Rescue
Centre.'

'Thank goodness you're here,' the woman said, still not turning. 'I haven't taken my eyes off the drainpipe since I called you. It's
still up there. Listen!'

I crouched down, pushing my hair behind my ear, and could
hear scrabbling sounds.

'Ah, yes, I hear it.'

'I've tried putting my hand up there but I couldn't get it round
the bend and the hedgehog's obviously climbed further than that.
You might have a better technique if you...' She glanced at me for
the first time and her eyes widened as she clocked my stomach.
'Maybe not.'

'A colleague's on her way, but we can try a few other things first. Keep watching and we'll try food for starters. If it's just hiding up there rather than stuck, it might be tempted out.'

I tipped a pouch of wet cat food into a bowl and placed it near the bottom of the drainpipe.

'We'll step back and stay quiet,' I whispered. 'If it's hiding because it thinks there are predators out here, food and silence might be all it needs. What's your name, by the way?'

'Geraldine.'

We waited several minutes but the cat food didn't do the job. Either the hedgehog (or whatever else it might be) wasn't tantalised by chicken in jelly or it definitely was stuck and unable to get to the food.

I was debating whether to attempt to get onto the ground myself or issue some instructions to Geraldine when Fizz pulled onto the drive beside my jeep.

'That's my colleague, Fizz,' I said. 'I'll be back shortly.'

'I'm so glad you're here,' I said, joining Fizz at her car and handing her a protective boiler suit. 'Next step was me getting on the ground and I might not have got up again.'

As I explained what we were faced with, she pulled the boiler suit on.

'I'll try the hooks first,' she said, removing them from the rescue kit. They were strong but bendable pieces of metal with a circular end which could grip onto spines and help lift or drag hedgehogs from tricky situations.

'I've got contact and it feels like a hedgehog to me,' Fizz said as she lay on her side, poking the first hook up the drainpipe.

After several attempts, she managed to hook one side and moved onto the other.

'He's stuck fast,' she said. 'Slidey time.'

I passed her a bottle of quality washing up liquid which she squirted liberally round the bottom of the drainpipe. We had another homemade tool – a pastry brush strapped to a bendy pole – which Fizz used to daub the area closer to the hedgehog as we didn't want to risk squirting any liquid into the hedgehog's nose, ears or mouth.

I crossed my fingers, praying this would work.

'Yay! I can feel it moving!' Fizz cried.

I rushed forward with a towel and crouched down below the drainpipe, catching the creature as it plopped out.

'Oh, that's such a relief,' Geraldine said.

'Definitely a hedgehog,' I confirmed. 'Do you have a hose or a watering can so I can clean it off before we go?' I wanted to get the washing up liquid off it before our journey.

'You can bring it into the house. There's a sink in the utility room with one of those hose taps on it.'

'That would be perfect, thank you.'

I grabbed the carry case and left Fizz to pack our tools away while I followed Geraldine through the house. In the utility room, I handed Geraldine the towel to hold temporarily while I checked the water temperature and set the tap to a flow which would clean the hedgehog but not sandblast it.

'Right, you,' I said, lifting the hedgehog up. It hadn't even curled into a ball, so either it had hurt itself or it was too exhausted to move. 'Let's get you cleaned off.'

I gently placed it in the bottom of the Belfast sink and directed the hose towards its back. Bubbles filled the sink but so did a significant amount of mud and with each pass of the hose, the colour of the hedgehog became lighter and lighter.

'It's an albino!' Geraldine cried.

I peered more closely at its face and shook my head. 'No, it's a blonde one. They're extremely rare in the UK.'

I continued hosing it down, my heart racing with excitement.

I'd seen photos and read all about them, but I'd never seen one for real. The hedgehogs we handled all had dark brown noses but this little one had a pink nose, which was so adorable.

'Albino hedgehogs are also rare,' I told Geraldine, 'but they have white spines and red eyes. The blonde ones have dark eyes like this and, as you can see, the spines are blonde rather than white.'

'Why are they like that?'

'It's a genetic thing where the normal skin pigmentation is lacking. The official name is leucistic but most people use the term "blonde". I can't tell you how excited I am to have rescued one.'

'Do you know if it's a boy or a girl?'

'Bear with me.' I flipped the hedgehog over and gave its belly a clean. 'It's a girl.'

'Can I name her? I'm going to show my age here but the name that springs to mind is Debbie after *the* Blondie, Debbie Harry.'

'I love it! Debbie it is.' That was my mum's name too and she'd be tickled to hear she had a namesake.

I finished cleaning Debbie, and Geraldine gave me a saucer to put some cold water in for her to lap up, which she eagerly did before curling into a ball, obviously feeling much better but wanting to hide.

I gently placed her on the fresh towel in the carrier and fastened it up safely while thanking Geraldine for being so responsive in calling us. I wouldn't have wanted to miss this experience for the world.

Fizz was waiting for me by the cars. 'All cleaned up?'

'Good as new and you won't believe what we've discovered. I'm going to leave you on that cliffhanger because I don't want to disturb her again until we get back to Hedgehog Hollow, but you are going to love this so much.'

'You little tease!' she said. 'I'm getting a head start. See you there.'

Laughing as Fizz pulled off the drive, I secured the carry crate then followed her back to the farm. On my travel bucket list was a trip to Alderney in the Channel Islands. There was a thriving hedgehog population there and 60 per cent of them were estimated to be blonde. I'd watched a fascinating TV programme about it. They weren't actually native to the island, but a few pairs were taken there as pets back in the 1960s and it was believed they'd either escaped or been intentionally released and the blonde population of hedgehogs had boomed from there. And now we had our very own blonde hedgehog. What a happy day!

* * *

There was more good news when Josh arrived home from work.

'Your dad spoke to Adele today and she's very interested in the role, so she's spending the day with us tomorrow.'

'That's brilliant news! Is she working at the moment?'

'Luckily for us, no. She got another role as a practice manager after the Brothers Grim but it was a one-year maternity cover. She took some time out after that because she was going through a divorce.'

'So she's available for an immediate start?'

'Yes, if the fit's there for both of us.'

'It will be. I think you'll love her.'

'Your dad does too and, from what I've seen on her CV, I'm impressed. I'm going to interview her tomorrow and Jonathan will give her the grand tour. Fingers crossed everyone loves everyone and she can start next week.'

While Josh went over to the farmhouse to get changed, I Face-Timed Dad.

'Have you seen our Facebook page today?' I asked after we'd exchanged greetings.

'No. I've not been in long. Why?'

I'd already printed off a photo of Debbie and added it to the Happy Hog Board so I held my phone up against the photo. 'Look what we rescued today!'

'Oh, my word, is that a blonde hedgehog?'

'It certainly is. Isn't she beautiful?'

'I've always dreamed of seeing one of those. What happened to her?'

I gave him an overview and suggested he visit our Facebook page as I'd taken photos of the drainpipe and Fizz's rescue attempt and she'd taken one of Debbie before we'd gone into the house to clean her off.

'You should call her Debbie after Debbie Harry in Blondie,' Dad said.

'Great minds! The finder has already named her that.'

'Your mum'll be chuffed. Do you think Debbie will still be with you when she gets back from holiday?'

Mum was currently island-hopping in the Canary Islands with Auntie Louise and a couple of friends of theirs who'd just turned sixty.

'Probably not. I reckon she'll be ready for release at the end of the week. I'll put some photos on our WhatsApp group so you can both see them. Anyway, subject change, I hear Adele's coming to the practice tomorrow.'

'Yes! I'm trying not to get ahead of myself but she'll be fantastic at the job, she'll fit right in, and it would be great to work with her again.'

'Josh says she's divorced now. What happened?'

'It's apparently been on the rocks for a long time with Steve. When the Brothers Grim made us redundant, he was really unsupportive, telling her she should have demanded more redundancy pay. He pushed her into the first job that came up, which wasn't right for her. She left after a fortnight but the only job she could find was for maternity cover. Steve had a right go at her for walking away from a permanent job into a temporary one. She'd supported him through a couple of redundancies and career changes but he wasn't prepared to do the same for her, which helped her realise she didn't like him very much.'

'He sounds like an idiot.'

'I only met him a few times but I can't say I was impressed. She sounds like she's in a good place now and she's excited about our practice.

'What about the commute? It wasn't long before you found it a trek.'

'Apparently the family home's on the market and neither of her sons live in Whitsborough Bay anymore, so moving is an option.'

'Could be the perfect solution all round. Hope it goes well tomorrow.'

'Me too.' He held up his crossed fingers as a buzzer sounded in the background. 'That's my tea ready so I'll say goodnight and probably see you tomorrow evening because I have to meet Debbie!'

After the call ended, I clicked into the WhatsApp group I'd set up with Mum and Dad which we mainly used for me sharing photos and added a photo of her namesake. Mum responded with the smiling emoji with heart-shaped eyes followed by a message:

✉ From Mum
She's unbelievably cute and it's made my day
that we share names. Thanks so much for sending
the pics. We'll have a cocktail in her honour
tonight. Hugs xx

I smiled contentedly at the message. It had taken a long time but what a joy it was that we now had a relationship where we exchanged messages with genuine affection, signed off with kisses. It was strange thinking how close we'd come to severing ties forever.

Mum was so different now. I often found myself looking at her as she smiled or laughed, struggling to compute that warm and friendly person with the moody, snappy woman I'd known before. If we hadn't both found the strength to let go of the past, I'd have missed out on so much.

The past wasn't forgotten but, for me, the desire to have a future which included my mum was too strong to let me hold her permanently accountable for her past behaviour and I felt empowered that I'd made that choice. Some toxic influences need to be cut out of our lives completely, but my decision had been that Mum wasn't one of those and I'd already been rewarded a hundred-fold for taking that stance. Bublet and any future children that came along would be too.

22

FIZZ

Josh arrived home from work and Sam went over to the farmhouse with him, leaving me to give Debbie an antiseptic bath. I'd poured a small amount of water mixed with the tiniest amount of antiseptic into the bottom of a washing up bowl which she was now paddling through, pausing every so often with her nose sniffing the air. Although Sam had cleaned the wounds on admission, this would help heal the ones on her feet which had been particularly caked in mud. We still had no idea where she might have been to get so dirty.

'You're home on time today,' I said, surprised to see Phoebe. Tuesday was Cubs' night for Darcie. With Connie and Alex running the pack, they collected her from school, made her a meal and dropped her home after Cubs. Phoebe therefore usually worked late to get ahead, show her commitment and hopefully build up some goodwill in case she ever needed to rush off to a school emergency.

'I *was* planning to work late but I spotted the cutest photos on Facebook earlier. Is this her?'

'This is Debbie, our leucistic hedgehog who I'm honoured to have rescued.'

'Leucistic? Get you with your posh language!' Phoebe joked.

As she leaned across the treatment table for a closer look, I breathed in a whiff of her perfume – a fresh aqua scent which stirred the butterflies in my stomach.

How many times had we huddled together like this? She'd never had this effect on me but now I couldn't stop thinking of Phoebe as more than a friend.

I gathered myself together and focused on explaining the purpose of the bath.

'Looks like she's enjoying it,' Phoebe said, moving closer and making my heart race even faster.

'She definitely is. How was work?'

'Good. Leo and I have been assigned a special project to work on together, which should be fun. Well, not to most people but to accountancy geeks like us, it's fun.'

Leo. It had to be a project with Leo.

It was the ideal prompt for asking how her cinema trip on Sunday night had gone but I was reluctant to do so because I didn't want to hear that it had gone well. Although what sort of friend would I be if I didn't pose the question?

'How was the film on Sunday?' I forced my voice to sound jolly but kept my head down, pretending to be absorbed in watching Debbie. It would be enough to hear the positivity in her tone without seeing *awesome date* written all over her face too.

'The film was pants. It was so bad that it was actually funny, but I think Leo and I were the only ones who thought that. At one point, we were wetting ourselves laughing and this man on the row in front turned round and told us to shush or he'd have us kicked out.'

'One to avoid, then,' I said.

'You'd have found it funny too,' she said softly.

Something about her tone made me look up. Had that been affection in her voice? Or was I imagining that because I wanted to hear it?

'Leo's such a good laugh,' she gushed, her eyes sparkling, and my heart sank. Maybe I was overthinking the softness in her voice.

I lifted Debbie out of the bowl and wrapped her in a towel to dry her off while Phoebe told me something 'hilarious' that Leo had done at work which was probably one of those *you had to be there* anecdotes but I smiled politely, not wanting to hurt her feelings.

'He sounds great,' I said.

'Oh, he is. But he's—'

Whatever she was about to say was interrupted by the rescue centre phone ringing.

* * *

'We must be close,' I said to Josh, my breath hanging in the freezing night air as we crunched along the frosty woodland path. 'That bloke who called must be frozen without his coat.'

The call had been from a man called Daz – a dog walker who'd found a badger trapped in a snare while on his evening walk. He'd read somewhere that placing a coat over an injured animal's head would help reduce stress so told me he'd carefully placed his over the badger's head. That was correct and was exactly what we'd have requested of him if possible – keeping the animal warm as well as reducing stress – but Josh and I had scraped a sheet of frost off Josh's windscreen before leaving Hedgehog Hollow, so I hoped Daz had some thick layers on or that the shelter of the trees provided some respite from the cold.

'Over there!' Josh said just as I spotted a flash of the light in the distance.

Daz had presumably seen our torch beams as his light began moving back and forth as though he was waving at us.

We veered off to the right, pushing the wheelbarrow containing the large rescue crate, and soon came across a tall man with a brown and white Jack Russell Terrier which was straining at the lead. The dog barked as we approached but settled as soon as Daz issued a command.

'You must be frozen,' I said to him, noting that he was only wearing a short-sleeved T-shirt, straining across his chest muscles.

'I don't feel the cold much.' He flexed his biceps, as though that proved his resilience to minus temperatures.

'Where's the badger?' Josh asked, his tone all business-like, clearly as unimpressed as me by the random display of testosterone.

'Over there. The bugger tried to bite me!'

I bit back the urge to ask, 'Did you flex your muscles at him too?'

There was a wire fence nearby and, against one of the fence posts, our torch beams picked out a dark coat and the back half of a large badger.

'Damn! I was hoping it would be a free-running snare,' Josh muttered as he shone his beam round the badger.

Free-running snares are a legal type of snare for trapping animals or birds. If functioning properly, the wire loop should relax once the trapped creature stops struggling, in theory avoiding severe injury or death. As far as I was concerned, it was simply the lesser of two evils compared to the illegal type – self-locking snares that tighten as the animal fights and which cause horrific suffering.

My heart sank as the torchlight picked up blood round the badger's back legs where the snare had tightened. If there were any positives out of such a pitiful sight, it was that the wounds looked fresh and the badger had likely only been trapped this evening, so we hopefully weren't too late.

Even though the natural instinct was always to cut an animal free from a trap, we needed to be careful as that could cause further damage depending on what the trap was restricting.

We could see the badger breathing but Josh wanted to quickly check he had no injuries to his face. He pulled on a pair of thick gloves and I held a fleecy blanket at the ready as he slowly lifted Daz's coat. Badgers have sharp teeth and can give an extremely nasty bite, especially when feeling threatened, so should only ever be handled carefully by an expert.

Content that there was no injury to the badger's top half, we made the swap and I returned Daz's coat to him.

'We've got it from here,' I said, 'but thank you so much for calling us and for lending the badger your coat. It was exactly what was needed.'

I expected him to pull his coat straight on, but he draped it over one arm.

'Daz to the rescue,' he said, flexing his muscles once more.

'Yes, thank you,' I said, stifling a giggle. Admittedly, he'd played a valuable part, but I suspected it was the Jack Russell that had actually found the badger.

'What's your name?' he asked, his voice all seductive.

'It's Fizz. I need to get back to Josh. Thanks again.'

I scuttled off before he could say anything else.

'I've taken some photos and a video,' Josh said. 'Can you hold the badger still while I cut the trap free?'

The photos and video were essential to educate the public on the devastating impact of snares and what to do if they found a trapped animal, as well as being evidence. In the case of an illegal trap like this, we needed to alert the police.

I did as Josh asked while he cut the trap away from the fence. Ridiculously, if the trap was a properly set legal free-running one, we could be in trouble for removing it, but we were 'safe' to remove an illegal one. We'd removed plenty of free-running ones, though. Our number one priority was always to the trapped wildlife and the prevention of further risk.

For some reason, it always surprised me how big and heavy badgers were and it always felt strange handling one after being so used to dealing with tiny, light hedgehogs. Keeping it covered in the blanket, we transferred the badger and trap into the crate, placed the blanket over the crate to minimise stress, and set off back through the woods.

'We'll go straight to the practice as we might need to do an X-ray on those legs,' Josh said once we'd secured the crate and wheelbarrow in his jeep.

'Do you think it's a boar?' I asked when we set off. A boar is a male badger.

'From the size of it, I'm pretty sure it is. If it's a sow, we're outside the usual gestation window, luckily.'

Badgers' cubs are typically born from mid-January to mid-March after a gestation period of six to eight weeks. It isn't unknown for cubs to be born in December, but it's extremely rare. I hoped our rescue badger wasn't a female rarity because there could be tragic repercussions for a pregnant female from the distress of being trapped like that.

I peered out of the window at the dark shapes of hedges and trees as we travelled down the country lanes towards the veterinary practice. The external damage on that badger hadn't looked as bad as some of our rescues but, on the inside, there could be a different story. Just like mine. I'd been trapped too. Externally, nothing showed because I didn't let it. Internally, a battle raged.

23

SAMANTHA

Around mid-afternoon on Thursday, I made myself a mug of tea and wandered over to the large floor-level pens housing Attila the Badger and our newest admission, Bonaparte the Badger, who'd been admitted two days ago. Attila was hidden from view but one of Bonaparte's rear paws was sticking out from under the bedding.

Bonaparte had been Fizz's idea. We followed themes for naming our hedgehogs but were still on 'anything goes' with naming the other wildlife. As Attila was named after a famous historical leader, she'd suggested Napoleon or Bonaparte and we both liked the alliteration of the surname best. He was also smaller than Attila, so the name worked well.

Josh had contacted the police about the illegal trap and I'd informed the local badger group who liked to keep track of any rescues. If it had been babies' season and Bonaparte had been a lactating sow instead, I'd have needed their help in locating the sett so we could rescue the cubs too.

Bonaparte was doing well. His wounds were deep but there was no nerve damage and, thankfully, no bones were broken, so we'd return him to where he'd been found as soon as he was fully healed. Attila was nearly ready and Josh was thinking about Friday for his release.

Debbie, our blonde hedgehog, would be ready for release by the end of the week too. Her faeces samples had been clear of parasites. An abundance of ticks usually pointed to a weak hedgehog with something else going on but, with Debbie not carrying many of them, I'd thought it possible her samples would be clear. The cuts were all superficial and she was a really good weight – hence getting wedged in the drainpipe – so there was no need to detain her for long, much as we all loved having her here.

We tried not to have favourites, but some patients captured our hearts and, as well as being so beautiful and rare, Debbie had turned out to be quite a character. Yesterday morning, I'd had a panicked moment when I couldn't find her in her crate. It should be impossible for hedgehogs to escape from their crates but I wondered if she'd somehow done a Houdini act on us. Then I spotted her lying on top of her nesting box, camouflaged against the pale fleece cover. Clearly she had a penchant for climbing! I changed the fleece to a bright orange one for easier spotting next time.

I was on my own today as Fizz had a day off, although she wasn't strictly switching off from work. She was having lunch with her architect friend, Robbie. As well as being a brilliant architect, he was also a talented illustrator and had produced the 'hedgicorn' design – a hedgehog with a unicorn horn – along with a range of other hedgehog designs which we'd had printed onto T-shirts. They were another valuable income stream for the rescue centre and Fizz wanted to talk to him today about adding additional wildlife to the range.

The pair of us had been in fits of giggles yesterday trying to merge unicorn with other animal names. We decided that 'foxicorn' worked, we weren't so convinced by 'badgicorn' and it all fell apart when Fizz attempted a serious face while suggesting 'goosi-corn'. After that, it was any animal we could think of, whether we rescued them or not.

I returned to my laptop, chuckling to myself at some of my favourite suggestions – 'armadillicorn', 'velocirapticorn', 'mega-lodonicorn' and 'narwhalicorn'. The latter had caused further hysteria as we debated whether it would have two horns.

I'd only just logged onto my emails when my phone rang and Jeanette Kingston's name flashed up on the screen.

'Hi, Jeanette,' I said.

'Samantha, I'm sorry to call you when you're working...'

My smile evaporated at the seriousness of her tone.

'Everything all right?' I asked.

'It's Terry. I didn't see him with Wilbur this morning, so I've just called round and, as there was no answer, I let myself in. He's not in a good way.'

I released the breath I'd been holding. 'How bad?'

'I think he's got the flu again. Perhaps it never went. He's in his bed and says he has no energy. I'm heating up some soup for him.'

'Thank you. I'll get there as soon as I can.'

'No rush. I can stay with him for a couple of hours, but I've got a speaking commitment this evening that I can't change.'

'Two hours would be helpful. One of us can stay with him tonight. You're not concerned enough for an ambulance?'

'Oh, no. Apologies if I scared you. He's poorly but he's lucid. He just needs plenty of rest. You know what he's like. The moment he felt better last time, he was up and about walking Wilbur. I don't think he'd given himself a chance to recover.'

'I agree. Hopefully he'll listen to the advice this time. I'll text you later when I've made some arrangements.'

I released a heavy sigh when I disconnected. It was almost certainly a relapse. I'd told him he needed longer to rest – we all had – but he could be exceptionally stubborn. I wondered if he'd always been like that or whether spending his adulthood as a single man with only himself to answer to had made him more fiercely independent and set in his ways.

Half an hour later, I texted Jeanette to confirm that Josh would meet me at Terry's on the way back from work and we were going to try again to persuade him to come to Hedgehog Hollow as it would make it easier to look after him and Wilbur. If he refused, one of us would stay with him overnight, but I was hopeful he'd see sense. He'd said that he felt bad having me running around after him last time, especially when I was pregnant, so that might work in my favour.

I needed a lift and music was the best way to do that. I selected my favourite feel-good playlist on my phone – one I often used when we'd lost a patient – and stuck my EarPods in. Closing my eyes, I soaked up the rousing chorus of the first song, and felt uplifted as I returned to my emails.

A little later, I stretched and closed my laptop then nipped to the loo. An Abba track had been playing but the toilets were out of range and the music cut out before I reached them.

I was humming the track to myself when I emerged from the toilets and stopped dead. Debbie was in the middle of the floor.

'How did you get out? Did I not shut your crate properly?'

I bent down to scoop her up and did a double-take at another three hedgehogs approaching us. It was possible although highly improbable that I hadn't closed one crate properly, but there was no way I'd failed to close four.

I looked towards the hedgehog shelves and the hairs on the back of my neck stood up and my heart pounded. Several of the crate doors were wide open, including some at height. If any of those hedgehogs made a bid for freedom, they wouldn't survive the fall.

I hurriedly placed Debbie back in her crate and shut the door then quickly slammed all the others closed. One of the hedgehogs on the floor had curled up into a ball so I scooped up the other two and placed them in an empty crate on the side before grabbing the balled one and placing it with them. I needed to work out who they were before I put them back in their beds.

Somebody had been in the barn and had done that deliberately. Who'd do such a thing? Several names sprang to mind, but they were all in prison.

'Hello?' I called glancing anxiously down the barn. Darkness was falling and the far end was bathed in shadows. 'Anyone there?'

I crept closer to the treatment table. 'Hello?'

A gust of wind rattled the window, making my heart race even faster. A door creaked and my breath caught in my throat.

Reaching the table, still staring into the shadows, I removed my EarPods. They hadn't reconnected to the music and they should have. I felt around for my phone, even though the lack of music screamed to me that it wasn't there. My fingers brushed against the edge of my laptop and my heart thudded faster as I glanced down at the table. I knew exactly where I'd left my phone and, as I'd feared, it was gone.

'Looking for something?'

My head shot up and a scream caught in my throat as I recognised the lanky form of the man blocking the barn door, holding up my phone. Connor Grimes, the younger of Tina's two sons. The thug who'd vandalised the barn, broken the window, terrorised Misty-Blue, and split my cheek open by pelting a box of eggs at me.

The one who'd brought on my PTSD.

'What are...?' I couldn't get the rest of the words out. He was meant to be behind bars. They all were.

His hair was shaved into a buzz cut and he had two slits in his left eyebrow. His dark eyes bored into me and, as he took a couple of steps closer, I instinctively wrapped my arms across my stomach.

His eyes widened and he released a sinister laugh. 'You're up the duff? Fucking sick. Two for the price of one.'

It was only then that I noticed the knife in his other hand.

I slowly backed away towards the end of the barn, never taking my eyes from him as he swaggered closer, humming to himself as though this was some sort of game. It probably was to a sick mind like his.

There was an emergency exit at the back of the building. I fumbled with the panic bar, but the door held fast.

'Oh, no! Is it jammed?' he called in a scary sing-song voice. 'Shocker!'

I felt sick as I struggled to catch my breath. Panic welled up inside me and I willed myself not to succumb to a panic attack, a PTSD episode or to pass out.

'What do you want?' I cried, my voice shaking.

'You *know* what I want. This is our family's farm. You didn't even know Gwen.'

I edged along the wall towards the toilets. If I could get inside and lock the door...

'Her name was Gwendoline!' I snapped. 'And yes, I did! But you didn't. You didn't know Thomas either.'

'That wanker? He owed us money.'

'He owed you nothing.' I'd read the begging letters. I knew that every generation of the Grimes family had tried to bleed the Micklebys dry.

'Stop moving!' he yelled. 'Do you think I'm fucking stupid?'

He lunged towards me, arm outstretched as he waved the knife. 'Move back! Now!'

Gulping, I shuffled a few paces in the other direction.

Behind Connor, the security light illuminated the farmyard

and brightened the doorway. Dark shadows passed across the glass. I needed to keep Connor distracted but I couldn't argue with him about the farm in case it made him even angrier.

'Did you escape?'

He laughed again. 'Released on good behaviour. Thought they'd have let you know and there'd be cops crawling all over this place.'

There should have been. Hopefully there now were and my eyes hadn't been playing tricks on me.

'But we're all alone and there's no bugger here to hear you scream.'

He was so close, I could smell the heady mix of alcohol and weed, making my stomach churn.

'Where's that dumb bitch, Phoebe?'

He showered me with spit as he spoke.

'I don't know. I haven't seen her since the trial.'

He lunged at me with his left hand and grasped me roughly at the throat, slamming my head back against the door. Stars sparkled in front of my eyes as he squeezed.

'Don't lie to me!'

With his right hand, he pressed the tip of the knife at my neck and I winced as it punctured the skin. This was it. He wasn't messing about. He wanted me dead.

'Police! Drop your weapon!'

There was a buzzing sound and Connor's grip on my neck released. The knife clattered to the floor as his body jerked. And then it all went black.

24

FIZZ

'Fizz Pops!'

'Robster!'

Robbie stretched his arms out to me and kissed me on both cheeks. 'This has to be the longest gap so far.'

'I think it might be,' I agreed, 'but you have had a good excuse this year.'

Robbie and his fiancée Kate had become first-time parents in January and I'd been to their house to see the new baby back then but this had been our first get-together since. We'd met when we were both thirteen and he joined the Young Farmers' Club after his family moved to the area from South Wales. We had the sort of friendship where we might not see each other or even speak for months but, when we did get together, it was like we'd only seen each other yesterday. He was by far the most reliable of my long-standing friends. I had a group of three female friends who were lovely but extremely flaky. If Robbie said we'd meet up, he'd stick to that commitment.

'How's baby Arlo?' I asked when we'd settled at our table in The Fox and Badger in North Emmerby.

'He's getting so big. Did we make it against the law for new parents to bore their friends with baby photos?'

I laughed, recalling a conversation with him after one of Kate's friends had insisted on showing them about 500 baby photos. He'd wanted my dad to arrest her for theft of an evening of his life.

'Bit different when it's your own baby?' I asked.

'It's like a compulsion. I promise just a few pics and only because you've asked, but you have permission to throw your drink over me if I turn into a baby bore.'

'Let's make a deal. I'll coo over photos of Arlo if you go gushy over the latest wildlife admissions.'

We placed our lunch order and spent a pleasurable half an hour scrolling through photos while waiting for our food to arrive.

'We've been here over an hour now and you haven't mentioned Yasmin once,' Robbie observed when we'd finished eating. 'Does that mean...?'

I was always going to tell him today, but I hadn't wanted to start on a downer.

'It's over.'

'Whose decision?'

'Mutual.'

'When?'

'It'll be a fortnight on Saturday.'

'Chances of you getting back together are...?'

'Minus numbers.'

Robbie raised his glass towards me. 'In that case, congratulations on your escape. I'm very relieved for you.'

I grimaced. 'You didn't like her either?'

He shuddered in response.

'What was it about her?' I asked. 'Genuine question. All my friends seem to have disliked her.'

'I only met her a couple of times so I'm probably being unfair, but do you remember that lass who came to Young Farmers' briefly whose constant stories about the fuel system on her quad bike made us want to gouge our eyeballs out with a teaspoon?'

'Oh, my God! That's how Yasmin made you feel?'

'It wasn't just me. Kate knew her and that Arianna lass at college and they weren't nice to her.'

I'd forgotten about Kate saying she'd been at college with them. She hadn't added the part about not liking them but had obviously been trying to be diplomatic.

'Is there a future Mrs Fizz Pops on the scene?'

'No. There's nobody.'

He narrowed his eyes at me. 'Felicity Kinsella, how very dare you! After fifteen years of friendship, do you really think I don't know when you're fibbing? Who is she and will I need my teaspoons?'

He propped his elbows on the table and rested his head on his hands, staring at me. There was no way he'd allow me to fob him off.

'It's Phoebe, if you must know, but nothing's happened.'

'Phoebe? Nice. You have my approval. I can safely pack away the teaspoons. So why hasn't anything happened?'

'Because she's been seeing this lad from work, Leo, and I don't know if they're friends or a couple. I don't actually know if she's attracted to women.'

'What? How? You've been besties for a couple of years. How can you not know?'

'It's never cropped up in any of our conversations and I don't know how to go about finding out. After two years, I can hardly suddenly blurt out *do you fancy women?* in the middle of removing ticks from a hedgehog.'

He rubbed his fingers over his chin. 'Remind me again what your dad does for a living?'

'You know what he does! He's a police serg... oh, I see. You're hilarious.'

'Seriously, Fizz, there are ways of finding out these things without blurting out blunt questions, although I don't see the harm in you asking straight out if this Leo is her boyfriend. If you know she's been going out with him, asking if they're dating is a natural question from a friend and she probably thinks it's a bit weird that you haven't asked it.'

I hadn't thought of it like that, but he raised a good point. 'What else?'

'You could ask her who'd be on her list.'

'What list?'

'The top five celebrities she'd have a pass to sleep with even if she was in a relationship. We watched it on a *Friends* re-run once.'

'Oh, yeah! That's actually genius.'

'Should I be offended that you look so surprised?'

'Sorry. You have been known to have your moments. I'm going to do that. Not sure when, but I'll definitely ask her.'

'I'd maybe ask about Leo being her boyfriend first, though, as that's going to answer the question for you. Unless she's bi or pansexual or... maybe try both.'

The next couple of hours passed in constant chatter, banter and laughter. We discussed more designs for the T-shirts and, after I told him the story about Attila the Badger and his hedgehog army, he said he was inspired to draw that for me. I couldn't wait to see it. All too soon, it was time to part company.

'Let's not leave it so long next time,' Robbie said, hugging me in the car park.

'Send my love to Kate and Arlo.'

'I will. I've got an idea. Let's put a date in the diary for our next meet-up in the New Year.'

'We never do that.'

'New Year, new things. You can come to our house for dinner.'

'We never do that either.'

'That's because you've never had a girlfriend I'd want to spend time with, but I like Phoebe and I know Kate will too. Let's say the first Saturday in February. If you and Phoebe aren't a couple by then, we'll be having words. Unless she's straight, of course, in which case I will forgive you.'

'Very kind of you. Okay. First Saturday in February it is.'

We hugged again. When he stepped back, Robbie kept his hands on my arms and studied my face for a moment.

'I know we muck about and take the piss out of each other, but you know I'm here for you if there's anything else you ever want to talk about – anything serious. I *can* be serious, you know.'

My heart started to thump. 'I know you can be,' I said, trying to sound casual. 'You were when I came out. I couldn't have done it without you.'

'It's just that... I don't know. When we were first mates, I was certain you were hiding something but then you came out, so I assumed that was it. But coming out wasn't a big thing for you. You knew who you were and have always been comfortable with it, so I started wondering if you were hiding something else. Every so often, you'd get this haunted look and I haven't seen it in years, but I saw it again today.'

I stiffened. 'I don't know what you're talking about.'

'I think you do.'

I felt panic welling inside me. I wasn't ready to do this. Not today. Not in a pub car park. Not when we'd had such an awesome afternoon and I'd been able to push *him* to the deepest recesses of my mind.

'I genuinely have no idea what you're talking about,' I insisted, my voice way too high and squeaky. 'Open book, me.'

Robbie's eyes searched mine and I wavered between wanting

him to let it go and wanting him to push that bit more until I cracked.

'My mistake,' he said, smiling as he removed his hands from my arms. 'But you know where I am if you ever want to talk about anything. I know I've got Kate and Arlo but, before they came along, it was Fizz Pops and Robster against the world. That's never changed.'

25

As I drove over the final incline on Hedgehog Hollow's farm track after my afternoon with Robbie, I slowed down, heart thumping at the sight of four police cars parked at peculiar angles in the farm-yard, blue lights flashing.

'Oh, my God!' I whispered.

Swallowing my fear, I floored the accelerator and jumped out of my car at the edge of the farmyard.

'Dad!'

'Fizz!'

'What's happened?' I cried, running towards him.

He led me back to my car. 'Connor Grimes was released from prison this morning.'

'What? Why?'

'Don't get me started.'

'Did he come here?'

'Yes, and he cornered Samantha in the barn, but she's okay.'

'Shit! Where is she?'

'She's gone to Reddfield Hospital with Josh to get checked over.'

I clapped my hand across my mouth, feeling sick. 'He hurt her again?'

I'd been at the barn with Sam when he first assaulted her – the night I met her, two and a half years ago, after Jinks found a hoglet in my garden – and I'd seen how badly that and the arson attack by his brother and cousin had affected her. I couldn't bear that she'd experienced yet another attack from that sick, twisted family.

'Yes, but not badly,' Dad reassured me. 'He had a knife. He nicked her neck with it and she has some bruising but honestly, Fizz, she's all right. She's safe and we've got him.'

'Phoebe and Darcie?'

'They're both safe at Rosemary's.'

I sank back against the side of my Mini, feeling weak with relief. I don't know what I'd have done if anything had happened to that group of people I cared so much about.

'If he had a knife, do you think he was going to...' I couldn't say the rest of the words. Connor's brother Cody and cousin Brynn were already serving time for burning down the original Hedgehog Hollow, nearly killing Sam when she went in to rescue the hedgehogs but, since Connor's return to prison, his mum and auntie had also been sent down for a multitude of drugs-related offences, violence and neglect. In Connor's disturbed mind, all of that would be Sam's fault and she'd have to pay. Possibly with her life.

'That would be speculation,' Dad said. 'It's best not to think that way. We caught him, Samantha and her family are safe, a dangerous man has been taken off the streets and somebody's going to be in big trouble for not giving me advance warning of Connor's release.'

We turned in the direction of some more flashing blue lights.

'There's the holiday bus to transport him back to his luxury accommodation,' Dad said as the custody van approached.

'I hope they throw away the key this time,' I said.

'I know. Me too. Your mum's been trying to call you, by the way, to make sure you were safe.'

'Sorry. I've been out with Robbie, so I had my phone on silent. I'll call her now. Am I okay to go to the cottage?'

'Yes, but wait until we've done the transfer. I wouldn't put it past him to lunge or spit at you, delightful individual that he is.'

The van backed up to the police car where they were holding Connor. After an exchange of words between the police officers, Connor was bundled out of the back of the car and into the van. He glanced across at Dad and me, his face illuminated by a mix of the security lighting in the farmyard and blue lights.

'Why's he smiling?' I asked, disgusted by his smug expression.

'Because he thinks he's a hero. Back in a minute.'

Dad went to speak with the officers from the van then sent it away.

'You can go to the cottage now and ring your mum,' he said, returning to me. 'I'll be over when we're done here.'

'I can't believe he came back here. I thought it was finally over for Sam and Josh.'

'It's never really over for the victims of crime. The closest to closure they can get is when the perpetrators are behind bars paying for their crimes. The rest of that family already have long sentences to serve and, if there's any justice in the world, Connor will serve a long one too now.'

As soon as I was inside Meadow View, I phoned Mum to reassure her I was fine. Dad joined me afterwards for a cup of tea and was keen to check I was okay following this and my break-up. The break-up seemed insignificant compared to what Sam had been through this afternoon.

'We'll see you for Sunday lunch this weekend, yes?' he asked as I saw him to the door.

'Yeah. Sorry about the last couple of weekends.'

'I understand, but please never feel you can't tell us anything. I know that sometimes things can feel embarrassing or uncomfortable but we're your parents and we love you very much, so we'll be there for you with an understanding hug no matter what's going on in your life.'

'Thank you. Hopefully I won't have any more nightmare girlfriends, but I'll seek your counsel if I do.'

He stepped outside. 'Remember we're getting the drive flagged. The builders are starting the digging tomorrow, so you'll have to park on the road on Sunday.'

'Thanks for the warning.'

A little later, I sat cross-legged on an armchair, my hands clasped round a fresh mug of tea. Dad's words rang in my ears: *The closest to closure they can get is when the perpetrators are behind bars paying for their crimes*. Would I feel closure if *he* paid for his? Was I strong enough to talk about it after all this time?

Robbie's face swam into my mind and his earnest expression in the car park earlier. Had he really guessed? Could I tell him? Finally say those words out loud after sixteen years of silence? And if I managed that, could I find the strength to tell my parents? Dad had just said they'd be there for me no matter what was going on. He and Mum would be tested to the limit on that if I opened up to them.

26

SAMANTHA

'They're here,' Josh said, watching the farm track from the lounge window on Friday morning.

'Come on, Princess Darcie,' Phoebe said, reaching out her hand. 'We'll watch a film in the snug while Sergeant Kinsella speaks to Samantha.'

Darcie, cuddled up to me on the sofa, showed no sign of moving. The pair of them had stayed at Rosemary's last night. After assuring Darcie that there was nothing to worry about, Phoebe had explained that Connor had been released early from prison, had come to the farm looking for trouble and had given me a big shock so I needed a bit of peace and quiet with Josh to get over it. Darcie had accepted that but had been up first thing this morning, desperate to come home and give me a hug.

Connor was actually Darcie's uncle but none of us used that title, at Darcie's request. She barely spoke about her biological family but, if they were mentioned, the titles were dropped and she even called Jenny by her first name instead of Nanna.

I wished we could protect her from yesterday's violence. I'd toyed with wearing a scarf to hide the hand-shaped bruises and the wound on my neck but it would only have led to questions, so I left my neck exposed. Darcie burst into tears as soon as she saw me and she hadn't left my side since.

I stroked her hair back from her face and gave her a gentle squeeze. 'I'm all right, Princess, but I really need you to go with Phoebe so I can speak to Sergeant Kinsella. Can you do that for me?'

She squeezed me back then slipped off the sofa, took Phoebe's hand and followed her out of the room.

I looked at Josh, tears pooling in my eyes.

'She's strong and resilient,' he said, gently. 'It's the shock and we both know she'll bounce back within a couple of days. I'm more worried about you and our baby.'

I stroked my hand over my bump. When I blacked out in the barn, I'd slid down the wall rather than landing on my stomach and, although my backside and the base of my spine were throbbing, a scan had confirmed that all was well and Bublet wasn't in any distress. Josh and I had both wept with relief.

Hadrian passed the window with PC Sunning, who'd attended on previous Grimes-related crimes. Josh caught my hand on his way to the door and gave it a gentle squeeze. As he welcomed them and invited them inside, I rearranged a couple of cushions and the soft throw.

'How are you feeling?' Hadrian asked as soon as they entered the lounge. He looked worse than I did, with bags under his eyes and dark stubble.

'Like I've done five rounds in a boxing ring, but I'm okay.'

Josh sat beside me while Hadrian and PC Sunning took an armchair each.

'I can't tell you how sorry I am,' Hadrian said.

'It's not your fault they didn't contact you, so please don't waste any of your time feeling guilty. I'd rather you spend that time making sure he gets put away for a very long time.'

'Oh, he will.'

'Good. Do you need me to go over my statement again?'

'Only if you're up to it,' PC Sunning said, whipping out his notepad. 'Sometimes additional details come to mind after the initial shock.'

'I'm fine to do it. Anything to help strengthen the case against him.'

* * *

'I want to go to the barn,' I told Josh after Hadrian and PC Sunning left.

'The doctor said you need to rest for a few days.'

'And I will but, for the sake of my mental health, I also need to go back to where it happened and be with the animals for a while. I don't want the barn to become a place I fear and, if I leave it until next week, I know I'll find it harder to return.'

The four of us took a very slow walk across to the rescue centre after lunch. Fizz was working today. I hadn't seen her yet, but Josh had called round at Meadow View last night when we returned from hospital to make sure she was okay, as we knew from Hadrian that she'd arrived back at Hedgehog Hollow before Connor was taken away.

My heart thudded as I approached the barn and I clung onto Josh's arm a little more tightly but willed myself not to slow my steps any further or hesitate by the door in case Darcie latched onto my apprehension.

Fizz looked up from the treatment table and pushed her chair back, her eyes fixed on mine. I knew her instinct would be to rush at me with a hug and, much as I'd have welcomed it, I knew it would set me off crying again. I didn't want Darcie to see that.

'Morning!' I declared brightly. 'Have you got a new patient to show Darcie?'

'I have indeed!' she said, picking up on my signal and staying where she was. 'Come and meet Pumpkin, Darcie. She's the cutest.'

Darcie looked up at me as though seeking permission to leave my side. 'Go on. I'll be over shortly.'

With a smile, Darcie ran down the barn to Fizz and Phoebe followed her.

'How are you feeling?' Josh whispered when they'd huddled over the table with Fizz.

'My heart's racing and I've got goose bumps, but I need to do this. This is *my* rescue centre and I'm damned if I'm letting him scare me away from it.'

27

SAMANTHA

I spent the rest of the half-term break with my feet up, reading and watching films with Darcie and Phoebe, but when they returned to school and work on Monday, it was time for me to return to work too.

I'd made an appointment to see my counsellor, Lydia, first thing which, coupled with Friday's visit to the barn, helped alleviate any anxiety. Fizz's presence helped too but I felt strong enough to have returned on my own if I'd needed to.

Visiting the barn on Friday had also been the best thing for Darcie. It hadn't taken long before Fizz – or, more specifically, new arrival Pumpkin – had her laughing. Pumpkin, an adult female, had been found lying on someone's lawn during the day with several cuts across her face. We had no way of knowing how she'd got them but my guess was from a discarded food can. If the lid was still partially attached, she'd have sustained cuts like that while trying to lick out food remnants. She was in good health otherwise and had thankfully been spotted and brought in while the cuts were fresh and before the flies got to them.

Across the weekend, Darcie had returned to her normal bouncy self, exactly as Josh had predicted.

* * *

By Thursday, a week on from Connor's attack, it felt like everything was back to normal and almost as though nothing had happened. My angry purple bruises had faded to yellow and brown, and my cut had healed. Connor had been sent straight back to prison for breaking the terms of his parole yet again – something he'd done the previous time he assaulted me – and was awaiting sentencing for the latest attack. He'd stolen a trials bike to get to Hedgehog Hollow and had been carrying a large quantity of drugs, so they also had him on theft and possession with intent to supply.

With winter approaching, the shorter days were not helping my pregnancy fatigue. It was only 3 p.m. but it felt more like seven. Fizz had been called out to rescue a hedgehog from a garden pond. The elderly lady who'd called it in used a walker and feared she'd end up joining the hedgehog if she attempted to retrieve it herself. It would hopefully be a straightforward rescue with a child's fishing net, so Fizz had gone alone and had taken a hedgehog ramp with her so that any hedgehogs in a similar predicament would be able to find their way out.

I'd never been a big coffee drinker pre-pregnancy and I'd cut it out completely since, but what I wouldn't give for a huge injection of caffeine right now to keep me awake. The next best thing was a spot of fresh air, so I bundled myself up warm, locked up the barn and went round to Thomas's bench.

We were in plus temperatures but there was a strong, icy wind making it feel much colder. I looked over towards the meadow, the silhouettes of dark grasses and winter buds swaying in the wind. There was so much to tell Thomas but, in my exhausted state, I couldn't find any words. Sitting in the wind with an empty head was enough for now.

I managed about ten minutes before my feet were too cold. My latest footwear solution was two pairs of men's socks and a pair of men's sliders. Stylish! Shivering, I returned to the barn and removed my outer layers.

My phone beeped with a notification on the WhatsApp group for Mum, Dad and me:

✉ From Mum
On the train from York so nearly home. The
Canaries were wonderful although I think I might
have gained at least 2 stone! Sammie — I've had
some more ideas for the secret garden but would
love some input on them. Bit short notice but,
if you have no plans for Sunday lunch, I'd love
it if you can both come over to mine, with Josh,
Phoebe and Darcie too, of course xx

I hesitated before replying. I'd asked everyone who might be in touch with Mum or Auntie Louise not to mention anything about Terry being ill again or Connor Grimes's attack. There was nothing they could do about either situation, so why put a dampener on the first big holiday either of them had been on for years?

I decided to go for a generic response and let Mum settle back in before I called her tomorrow with an update on the bad stuff.

✉ To Mum
Welcome back! Look forward to hearing all about
it. Thanks for the lunch invite. I'll speak to
Josh when he's home from work and come back to
you xx

Terry had picked up a little yesterday but was still very weak and he found it a struggle to do anything more than move from his bed to the bathroom and back. It had been his eighty-second birthday on Tuesday and, despite several visitors, he'd barely noticed the day. There was still a pile of unopened cards and gifts in the corner of his bedroom.

Connie and Alex would be staying with Terry tonight and Lauren was taking the shift tomorrow night – our second attempt at releasing Debbie and Attila. The original plan to release them last Friday had needed to go on hold thanks to the latest Grimes drama and Terry taking ill once more. We'd hated having to keep them in the rescue centre longer than necessary, but it was down to bodies, or lack of them. With Terry to look after – who had, as expected, insisted on staying at home but had allowed us to take Wilbur again – and a surge in admissions of autumn juveniles, we were struggling. The positive was that Josh had been extremely impressed with Adele during her interview last week and the feeling had been mutual after her tour, so she'd started as practice manager on Monday. This meant the practice wasn't a key staff member short and could be a little more flexible with cover for the rescue centre... not that that helped with supporting Terry. I was very much reliant on family for that, especially when I was still meant to be taking it easy after the attack.

Tomorrow night, the new plan was for Josh to man the rescue centre while Fizz and I drove to Cherry Brompton to release Debbie in the gardens at Weeberley Hall and, when we returned, Josh, Zayn and a couple of members of the badger club were going to release Attila in the woods where he'd been found. Organising for the right people to be in the right place at the right time had been like planning a military operation.

We didn't see much of Zayn these days. He'd graduated from his animal care course at Reddfield TEC in July last year and had started training as an RSPCA inspector. He still volunteered at Hedgehog Hollow when possible but he often had to work weekends and evenings, so I was looking forward to a catch-up with him between the two releases.

The fresh air only managed to liven me up for about twenty minutes and my eyelids were soon heavy once more. I walked a couple of laps of the barn, eating a banana to try to give me an energy boost before returning to some work.

I'd no sooner opened my laptop when the barn door burst open and Mum came running towards me, arms outstretched.

'I've just spoken to your dad. Are you okay?'

The concerned look on her face and in her voice broke me and I rushed into her arms, crying. The tears were as much about her reaction as they were about the drama. A couple of years ago, I could never have imagined we'd become this close.

'Why can't that family leave you alone?' she whispered, stroking my back.

'Because they're bad, deluded people.' I stepped back and wiped my tears. 'You look well.'

'Never mind me! Are you all right? Baby? Josh? Everyone?'

'We're fine.' I led her over to the sofa bed and lowered myself onto it with an oof. 'It was terrifying at the time, but the police were amazing.'

'When your dad called, I was beside myself. I got the taxi driver to bring me straight here,' she said. 'My suitcase is in the middle of the farmyard.'

'You might want to go and retrieve that before someone drives into it and your dirty undies are strewn all over the yard. And pop the kettle on as you go.'

A few minutes later, Mum was back with a suitcase-related disaster averted.

'Did Dad tell you Terry's poorly again?' I asked after she handed me a mug of tea.

'Ah, no, is he? He only mentioned you. How bad this time?'

I updated her on Terry and what had happened with Connor and finished on the more cheery subject of our wildlife release plans for tonight. I also gave her a peek at Debbie, although she could only see one side through her bedding as we never disturbed the hedgehogs unless it was for medication, feeding or cleaning.

'And now it's your turn to tell me about your holiday,' I said when we returned to the sofa bed.

She wafted her hand. 'It seems trivial to talk about my holiday after what you've been through.'

'Believe me, after the week we've had, trivial is welcome. Spill it all.'

She started hesitantly, checking I really wanted to hear it, but my eager nods must have finally convinced her as she whipped out her phone and scrolled through her photo reel, taking me through their fortnight.

'That was brilliant,' I said when she'd finished. 'I felt like I was there.'

'Maybe we could have a holiday together one year? A mum and daughter weekend away, or I could join you and Josh on a family holiday as the live-in babysitter. Just a thought.'

I clasped her hand in mine, tears spilling down my cheeks. 'I'd love that. Yes, please. And you wouldn't just be the babysitter.'

'Oh, what are we like?' she asked, dabbing at her eyes.

Josh returned from work at that point. 'Has something else happened?' he asked, looking from me to Mum and back again.

'No, thankfully. We're just having a moment.' I heaved myself up to give him a hug.

Gramps's phrase – *the fragrance stays in the hand that gives the rose* –

was so apt for my relationship with Mum. I'd kept trying, I'd shown her kindness, I'd encouraged her to seek help and now I got to enjoy the sort of relationship many mothers and daughters aspired to reach. We were friends. We understood each other. We cared. It would have been easier to walk away but I chose to stay and now I reaped the rewards. And I couldn't wait to see those secret garden designs.

28

FIZZ

Nothing beats the feeling of releasing a healed animal back into its natural habitat. It's awesome! Every release gives me a buzz but, for me, there's something special about releasing hedgehogs. It's a combination of having worked solely with them for so long before we expanded the rescue centre, knowing how vulnerable, and totally and utterly adorable they are. I defy anyone to get to know hedgehogs and not to fall in love with them.

Debbie's release tonight would be extra special. Sam and I were returning her to Weeberley Hall where she'd been found. It was a hedgehog paradise with sprawling grounds, a copse and several wild areas – perfect for foraging and nesting and also for movement, as the grounds were surrounded by hedgerows, providing easy access to open fields at the back and other gardens either side.

It was early on Friday evening when Sam drove us to Weeberley Hall. Alongside the usual elation, we'd admitted we were both sad to be saying goodbye. It was possible neither of us would see her or another blonde hedgehog ever again and she'd been such a cheeky, playful character who'd have left a lasting impact on us even if she hadn't been blonde.

'I wish I could have released her at Hedgehog Hollow,' Sam lamented. 'At least there'd have been an outside chance of us spotting her again.'

'Me too.'

Sam's garden was full of hedgehog houses and feeding stations and we'd spotted or caught on CCTV several hedgehogs with distinctive markings who we recognised as previous patients. But the general rule of animal rescue was to try to release the animal where it was found, or nearby, unless there was a reason for being unable to do so like it being found by a busy road or where there was a known predator.

Geraldine was waiting for us on the driveway of Weeberley Hall, illuminated in the darkness by a couple of Victorian lampposts.

'I've been looking forward to this all day,' she gushed, peering into the carry crate. 'Thank you so much for bringing her back here.'

'It's a pleasure,' Sam said. 'I'm sorry about the delay.'

'Goodness, don't apologise. I saw the write-up in *Wolds Weekly* yesterday. Shocking. Are you all right?'

'I am now,' she said brightly, 'and I'm very excited about tonight's release.'

It was obvious to me that Sam didn't want to go over the details again – understandably so – and, if Geraldine had read the paper, she already knew them anyway.

Geraldine smiled. 'In that case, let's crack on with it. Follow me, ladies.'

We followed her down a pathway along the side of the house and into the garden.

'I've got a couple of feeding stations in the copse,' she said. 'Would it be a good plan to release Debbie there?'

'Perfect,' Sam and I said together.

'You've created something really special for them here,' Sam told Geraldine as she drew our attention to several hedgehog houses and feeding stations nestling between the trees.

Sam gently placed the carry crate onto the ground near one of the feeding stations but didn't open it. We liked to give the hedgehog a few moments to settle from the journey, unfurl, and sniff the air.

'I've become a bit obsessed with hedgehogs since the rescue,' Geraldine said. 'I've been looking back over all your social media posts. So many wonderful photos and helpful tips. I'm quite in awe of what you do and wanted to do my bit too. My husband loves pottering in his workshop, so he knocked together the hedgehog houses and feeding stations from your guidance. He was delighted at the information about keeping areas of the garden wild because he hates gardening and that gives him the perfect excuse not to fuss so much over the lawn. There are other houses and stations around the garden and he's created a couple of log piles too to attract the beetles and other creepy crawlies.'

'What you've done is awesome,' I said. 'If you have friends with gardens, please do spread the word.'

Sam asked Geraldine if she'd like to do the honours and explained how to release the door to the carry crate.

Debbie had already unfurled and she shuffled half out of the crate, her pink nose in the air, sniffing out the various scents. She'd already been fed at Hedgehog Hollow but our little blonde hedgehog was a good eater, so my money was on her heading straight for Geraldine's food rather than running off. Sure enough, with one final sniff, she scurried out of the crate and straight to the nearest bowl of food, her eager slurps and lip smacks making us all smile.

'We'll leave her to dine in peace,' Sam whispered, retrieving the crate and indicating for us all to move away.

We watched Debbie for a few minutes in silence – from us, not her – then left the garden.

'That was delightful,' Geraldine gushed. 'Thank you for giving me the opportunity to be part of it.'

Sam didn't respond and I suspected she was feeling as choked up as me at saying goodbye to Debbie. She was one hedgehog whose pawprints would remain on our hearts forever.

* * *

Zayn had arrived when we returned to Hedgehog Hollow, so it was hugs all round and a catch-up with him. I was so proud of him for following his dreams and becoming an RSPCA inspector. He seemed to have really matured since he started working there.

It was time to say goodbye to Attila too. Phoebe and Darcie joined us and Darcie blew Attila a kiss as Josh pushed the wheelbarrow containing his crate out of the barn to load into his jeep.

'Fizz, do you think Bonaparte will miss Attila?' Darcie asked, slipping her hand into mine and pressing herself against my side.

'I'm sure he will. They've probably been having a right gossip between their pens.'

Darcie giggled at that. 'I'll keep visiting Bonaparte and talking to him so he's not too lonely.'

'Maybe you could draw a picture of them both and put it on the Happy Hog Board.'

'Ooh, yeah!' Darcie released my hand and ran over to the cupboard where we kept the paper and pens.

'Not so fast,' Phoebe called. 'Fizz means at the weekend. It's late and way past your bedtime, so it's back to the farmhouse now.'

'Will you tell me a story about Attila and Bonaparte?'

Phoebe smiled at her. 'I think I can manage that, but only if you're super speedy getting ready for bed, and that means brushing your teeth properly, not tickling them! Say goodnight to Fizz and Samantha.'

Grandma used to say that same thing about not tickling my teeth when I stayed at Bumblebee Barn as a little girl, so it was funny to hear it from a different generation.

With goodnight hugs dished out, Darcie skipped out of the barn and Sam and I smiled at each other.

'She's so good with Darcie,' I said.

'It's a joy to see. Never thought I'd pick up so many parenting tips from a twenty-year-old.'

Sam yawned and stretched. She looked drained and in desperate need of an evening off.

'Why don't you go over to the farmhouse, put a film on and relax?' I suggested. 'I'm fine here.'

It was a sign of how done in she was that she didn't argue. She simply threw me a grateful smile, nodded, reached for her coat and left with a little wave.

Josh and Zayn returned an hour later with news of a successful badger release. Zayn needed to head off as he had an early start in the morning and I sent Josh over to the farmhouse to enjoy what was left of the evening with Sam.

At half ten, I was about ready to call it a night when the barn door opened and my heart leapt as I spotted Phoebe in the doorway with her hands on her hips.

'Why are you still here?' she asked.

'Why are you here?' I responded, laughing.

She closed the door and came over to the treatment table.

'Because I saw the light was still on and wanted to check you were okay. The past week's been crazy. I feel like I've barely seen you.'

'Fingers crossed it'll calm down now.'

She slipped onto one of the chairs and there was a moment's silence. I couldn't randomly ask who was on her 'list', but would this be a good opportunity to ask her about Leo? Phoebe spoke before I had a chance to form a question.

'I wanted to ask you something.' She bit her lip as though she was nervous and my heart raced. There was only one thing she could be nervous about.

But it wasn't that.

'Do you think Darcie's okay?' she asked. 'Samantha and Josh seem to think she's bounced back but I can't decide if she's putting on a front because she doesn't want to worry them.'

Putting on a front? My special talent!

'She was subdued at first last Friday, which is completely understandable,' I said, 'but, when she was laughing at Pumpkin trying to escape, I think it was genuine. Has she said or done something to worry you?'

'No. It's probably just me being overprotective. We've had so long without the Grimes lot in our lives and it's been amazing seeing her so settled and happy here. I don't want that tosser bringing back any bad memories.'

I placed my hand gently on her arm. 'I honestly think she's doing great. She's an awesome person who oozes positivity who had a little shock but has picked herself up again. The key thing to remember is that she didn't see Connor. She wasn't here when it happened, so it's not her personal experience. She's upset that Sam was hurt, as we all are, but she didn't experience the attack herself. She has the empathy but she doesn't have the memories, so it's going to be much easier for her to brush herself down and move on.'

Tears pooled in Phoebe's eyes and she took a deep shuddery breath. 'Thank you. I needed to hear that. Tell you what, this parenting thing can feel pretty overwhelming sometimes and I'm scared of messing up.'

'Messing up is part of the process but, from what I've seen, you haven't messed up anything. Keep doing you because you're awesome.'

She wiped her eyes and smiled gratefully. 'I'd better get to bed and so had you. Have you got much left to do?'

'A couple of emails to finish. Five minutes max.'

I thought she might say she'd wait. Walking out together would give me a chance to ask about Leo, but she stood up.

'Okay. I'll let you get finished. Sleep well.'

And then she was gone.

I finished the emails and shut the laptop with a sigh. I pictured Phoebe walking me to Meadow View, standing on the doorstep in the moonlight, leaning closer... I stopped that train of thought. I was getting carried away imagining more than friendship and I needed to push those thoughts firmly out of my head before I fell too deeply.

I only hoped it wasn't too late for that.

I was on the Saturday shift at Hedgehog Hollow when Sam dropped by shortly before noon.

'I'm heading over to Terry's for lunch,' she said. 'I'll be back by teatime.'

'Did you relax and watch a film last night?'

She smiled. 'I did, thanks. I went to bed and watched one of my favourite romcoms and it worked a treat. Connor was out of my mind and I had the best night's sleep I've had in weeks.'

'I'm so pleased to hear that. And what's the news on Terry this morning?'

'Lauren tells me he ate some soup last night and some porridge this morning and there's some colour in his cheeks, so we're hoping he's through the worst, but we're not counting our chickens after last time.'

'Send him my love.'

'I will do. Is everything okay here?'

I nodded. 'All good. A cyclist brought in an autumn juvenile which he found in the middle of a forest track. She was icy cold, but I've warmed her and fed her and she seems to be doing okay. Unfortunately there were two others – presumably siblings - found nearby and they'd already gone. I've started a new theme – the weather – so I've called her Rain because the cyclist said it bucketed it down just after he found her.'

'That's sweet. Just as well he found her before she got drenched. Hope she's okay. Give Josh a shout if you need any help. He's on call so he'll let you know if he has to go out.'

An hour later, my stomach was rumbling and I was thinking about nipping back to the cottage to make a sandwich when Phoebe arrived with a plate full of cheese toasties.

'Thanks for the reassurance last night,' she said as we sat on the sofa bed eating them. 'I really appreciated it.'

'You're welcome. Where's Darcie today?'

'She's on a trip with Cubs, so I dropped her off at Connie and Alex's earlier. It'll do her good to have a fun day out.'

'How are you coping with it all?' I asked gently. 'I should have asked last night.'

'I'm okay. That thing you said about empathy versus memories was helpful for me too. I think it's easier to cope with knowing he's back behind bars. Even though I wish Sam hadn't had to go through any of it, there's some comfort in knowing Connor will pay. Not everyone gets that closure.'

Phoebe's expression was wistful.

'Are you thinking about your mum?' I asked.

She nodded. 'I can't help it. I start thinking about justice or lack of it and it takes me right back to her hit and run. I sometimes have this little fantasy about the case being re-opened and, thanks to advances in forensics, they finally find the driver. The first time I watched *Gladiator* with you, that big speech Maximus makes about vengeance got me right here...' she thumped her fist against her heart, '... because I understood where he was coming from. We've joked about how I can recite the entire speech, but do you know why? Because I've stood in front of the mirror and pretended I'm in front of my mum's killer and I've made that speech to him. Obviously not those *exact* words, but do you get what I'm saying?'

'I do.' More than she could know because I'd also imagined giving that speech to *him*.

'I don't know if it would make any difference to me if they did find him now. It's not like it would bring Mum back.' She sank her head back against the back of the sofa bed and closed her eyes for a moment. 'I wish I'd known her. I wish Dad had talked about her more.'

'What *do* you know about her?'

'Hardly anything.' She opened her eyes and rolled her head so she could look at me. 'Dad said she was a walking contradiction. Her favourite colour was orange, but she couldn't stand the smell of oranges, she ate tomato ketchup with everything but hated tomatoes, she wasn't fond of reading but loved making up stories, she often wore make-up around the house but would go out barefaced because she hated any expectation for women to always look their best in public.'

I could hear the warmth in her voice as she shared what little she'd learned.

'I'm sure there were other things he told me, but I can't remember them now.'

'She sounds awesome. Strong-minded, like someone else I know.'

Phoebe held my gaze, a gentle smile on her lips, and I longed to touch her cheek, to brush my lips against hers.

'I need to focus on something different,' she said, sitting up straight and brushing a couple of crumbs off her hoodie. 'I might nip into Reddfield and start my Christmas shopping while Darcie's out. Do you need anything from town?'

'No, I'm good, thanks. I'll see you later.'

She picked up the empty plate. 'Thanks for listening.'

'Here for you if you want to talk again.'

With a smile, she walked towards the door then stopped.

'Actually, it *would* make a difference if they caught him. Maybe not to me, but it would mean he couldn't hurt anyone else. See you later.'

I remained where I was for several minutes with her final comment ringing in my ears. *He couldn't hurt anyone else.* It had always been my worst fear. What if I hadn't been the only one? What if my silence had paved the way for him to hurt others? What if he was still hurting them?

I was jolted from my troubled thoughts by the ringing of the rescue centre line.

'Hello, Hedgehog Hollow resc—'

'I've got a hedgehog in a bad way,' a woman interrupted. 'I don't know what to do. I don't drive.' She sounded as though she was crying.

'Okay, I'm here to help,' I said calmly. 'What's wrong with it?'

'I thought it was a ball they were kicking but one of them said something about spikes and I realised what it was. Who does that?'

My stomach dropped to the floor. 'They were kicking the hedgehog?'

'Yes. A bunch of teens on the playing fields. They ran off laughing when I shouted at them. What's wrong with people?'

'Where's the hedgehog now?'

'In my kitchen on a towel. It's bleeding but it's still breathing.'

'Give me your address and I'll come straight over. It's going to be in shock and it needs to stay warm. Keep it wrapped in towels but try not to move it. I'll be there as soon as I can.'

* * *

Josh floored the accelerator along the farm track and drove as fast as it was safe to do so along the country lanes towards Bentonbray. Fortunately it was one of the villages closest to us.

'The little bastards,' he said, his voice deep and guttural. 'If I get my hands on them, I'll kick their arses round the bloody playing field.'

I was just as angry as him. I'd heard about cases like this or where kids daubed hedgehogs with paint or even set fire to them 'for a laugh', but we'd never been called out to one. I'd hoped we never would be.

After alerting Josh, I'd rung Dad and they were sending a patrol car to the playing fields too to get a statement from the caller and search for the youths, although it was likely they were long gone.

We pulled up on the road outside the address I'd been given. If the hedgehog was still breathing – and I prayed it was – then we were taking it straight to the practice for X-rays to assess what damage there was and whether there was anything we'd be able to do to save it. Josh had already told me to prepare for the worst.

The door opened and a middle-aged woman rushed out, cradling a bundle of towels.

'It's still breathing,' she said. 'Do you think you'll be able to save it?'

'We'll do our best,' I assured her. 'The police will be here shortly. Thank you.'

I held our precious cargo on my knee and fought back the tears. I needed to stay strong and focused.

* * *

Josh put his arms out and drew me into his embrace some time later.

'The odds were never in our favour,' he said, his voice shaking with emotion.

Euthanising animals was part of what we did and it was never easy, but they were typically old, ill or badly injured and it was the kindest thing to do. Having to euthanise an animal which had been brutally murdered – there were no other words for it – was incomprehensible. The tears had started as soon as we placed her under the X-ray and what those brutes had done to her was revealed. Broken jaw, several other broken bones, a ruptured eye... the list went on. How she'd made it as far as the operating table, I'd never know. She'd clearly been a fighter, but her tiny body could not have fought such extensive damage.

'Why did they do it?' I cried. 'What could possibly be going on in their heads to think it's okay to kick a hedgehog like it's a football?'

'I have no idea. I can't comprehend cruelty to animals. It makes me sick to the stomach.'

I glanced at her broken body lying on the operating table. We didn't usually name the hedgehogs who came to us already sleeping or who died immediately but I felt compelled to give her a name.

'We'll call her Rainbow,' I whispered. 'Because she's crossed...' I couldn't finish the sentence. She shouldn't have had to cross the rainbow bridge.

'It's a good name.'

We pulled apart and I wiped my cheeks with the backs of my hands.

'Let me finish up here and I'll get you home,' Josh said gently. 'Do you want to wait in reception?'

'No. I'll help. But can I do the equipment and you see to Rainbow?'

Josh removed Rainbow immediately and I was so grateful to him for trying to reduce my distress in that way. Shame out of sight didn't mean out of mind. I'd see her for a long time to come.

* * *

I was in a dark mood when we returned to Hedgehog Hollow. Sam's car was in the farmyard, so she was obviously back. Josh challenged whether I wouldn't prefer to have some company, but I really wanted to be alone with my anger.

I pushed open the door at Meadow View, stormed into the lounge, tossed my bag into the corner and released a frustrated screech.

Dad phoned a few minutes later. The youths had been long gone and Rainbow's rescuer hadn't been much help with descriptions – four average-sized youths wearing dark hoodies – which was understandable in the stressful situation, but unbelievably frustrating.

I wasn't a big drinker and I never drank on my own, but that bottle of wine Mum had brought round for my broken heart was in the fridge. My heart was well and truly broken right now, so I poured myself a large glass.

I hadn't eaten since my lunchtime toasties and the wine on an empty stomach went straight to my head. Wobbling a little, I poured a second glass, desperate to numb the pain. And the fear.

'To the yobs who murder hedgehogs!' I held up my glass and took a large gulp.

'To the arseholes who mow down innocent women on zebra crossings and never get caught.' Another gulp.

'Where's the justice in the world? Why do they all get away with it?' The rest of the glass.

By the time I reached the end of the bottle, I was a mess, ricocheting from laughing hysterically to sobbing. It wasn't just about Rainbow or Phoebe's mother. This was about me.

'To the sick bastards who prey on children.' I raised my empty glass, tipped the final drops into my mouth and slammed it down onto the coffee table far too hard. The glass broke in my hand, a shard slicing my palm.

I rushed to the sink and thrust my hand under the cold water. It wasn't deep, but it was long and painful. I needed help. I needed someone to talk to.

Wrapping a tea towel round my cut hand, I stumbled back into the lounge and reached for my phone. There was only one person I could call...

'You were right about me having another secret,' I cried when the call connected. 'I need to tell you what it is. Can you come over to Hedgehog Hollow?'

* * *

'Bloody hell, Fizz Pops, what are you doing drinking on your own?' Robbie's Welsh accent was stronger than usual as he scolded me.

'I didn't plan to. It just happened.'

He led me into the kitchen to run my hand under the tap again. 'Let's get this hand sorted then you can tell me about it. Do you have a first aid kit?'

'Bathroom. Under the sink.'

'Okay. Back in a moment. Don't move.'

I wasn't sure I could even if I wanted to. I'd felt the need to be further inebriated if I was going to finally tell somebody the truth, so it had seemed like a good idea to down a couple of miniature bottles of vodka that I'd had kicking around for ages from a train journey. They'd taken hold and my legs didn't seem to want to work anymore.

Robbie returned with some antiseptic spray and a bandage, and he poured me a pint of water to drink while he patched me up.

'Drink the rest of that while I pick up the broken glass,' he said when he'd finished. 'Every last drop.'

'Yes, Dad.'

I closed my eyes to the clink of the broken glass as Robbie dropped it into the recycling crate. Finding comfort in drink was the one thing I'd sworn I'd never do and look where it had got me the one time I succumbed.

I'd downed most of my water when Robbie returned to me, so he topped it up, poured himself one and led me into the lounge.

'Your secret?' he prompted when we sat down at either end of the sofa.

It was harder to say the words than I'd imagined, even with all the alcohol taking the edge off.

'What do you think it is?' I asked eventually.

'Ah-ah, we're not doing that, Fizz. You need to say it yourself because that's going to be your first step in dealing with it.'

I gulped and lowered my eyes. 'Something bad happened to me when I was younger. Somebody *did* something bad to me. And he kept doing it.' The words sounded distant and alien, as though somebody else was saying them.

'How old were you?'

'Six when it started, twelve when it ended.'

'Shit! I'm so sorry, Fizz. Who was it?'

I dropped my head to my chest and had to force the words out.

'My Uncle Melvin,' I whispered. 'My mum's younger brother.'

'Shitting hell. What a bastard!' Robbie tilted my chin up. 'Listen to me very carefully. You have nothing to be ashamed of.

You have nothing to be embarrassed about. *He* did this to you. *He* is the monster.'

He lightly rubbed his thumb across my cheek, catching one of my tears.

'I didn't know it was wrong at first,' I said, the words spilling out between sobs. 'All I knew was I didn't like it. He said he loved me and what we had was really special, but I had to keep it secret because if I told anyone, they wouldn't believe me and they'd send me away.'

'Oh, Fizz.' Robbie adjusted his position and pulled me into his hug. 'And you've kept that secret all these years?'

'He emigrated and I thought it was over. Every year, my family would go on about how much they wanted him to come back for Christmas and I'd hold my breath, dreading the news that he was, but he never came. But this Christmas, he's coming back and they're all so excited and I... I can't see him. I can't be in the same room as him. I can't bear the thought of even being in the same country as him.'

'You have to tell your parents.'

'What if they don't believe me?'

'That's *his* voice in your head, not yours. Why wouldn't they believe you?'

'Because they think he's great.'

'He doesn't sound very great to me. He sounds like a dirty paedophile who preyed on an innocent young girl, and I think your parents would want to know about that and see that he pays. I know mine...'

He tailed off and looked away.

I gasped. 'It happened to you?'

His jaw tightened. 'It's not about me. This is about you.'

'But if you've been through it, you'll understand more than anyone.'

Robbie held my gaze, chewing his lip as though weighing up whether to re-focus me once more. 'Sod it. If it helps you... His name was Mr Pritchard, and he was a neighbour of ours in Wales. He was a retired teacher and my parents paid him to give me extra maths tuition when I started senior school and he was a brilliant tutor. At first.'

There was so much emphasis on those last two words and I didn't need him to give me any details.

'Oh, my God! Robbie! I'm so sorry.'

'It turned out I wasn't the only one. He'd left a massive trail of damage across the years. Probably hundreds. I testified along with a handful of others and it was enough to put him behind bars for the rest of his life. When it was over, Mum, Dad and I all decided we needed a fresh start and that's how we ended up moving here.'

'That's awful.'

'It is and so is what happened to you. You *have* to tell your parents. They'll believe you.'

'Did your parents?'

'Slightly different scenario for me. I'd become withdrawn and stopped going to swimming and judo and I played truant a few times. In my mind, if my tutor could do that to me, any of my teachers at school or at my after-school clubs could too. Dad isn't daft. My change in behaviour didn't come long after my tuition started so he asked around and heard a few things he didn't like so it was actually my parents who confronted me about it rather than me having to tell them.'

I shook my head, my heart breaking for him. 'I had no idea.'

'And I had no idea about you. Like I said at the pub, I did get this occasional sense that something was haunting you and I even thought about abuse at one point, but you were so different to how I'd been – so bright and bubbly instead of withdrawn – so I convinced myself it couldn't be that. I suppose I didn't want to think someone had done something so horrific to my best friend. I should have trusted my instincts.'

'I'm not sure I'd have confessed even if you'd asked me. How did it feel to get him put away?'

'I'm not gonna lie. It wasn't as good as I expected. I was relieved it was over and he'd been sentenced but I had – still have – so many questions. How could he have been allowed to get away with it for so long with so many young boys? He was in a position of trust. He...' Robbie broke off and took a deep breath. 'Your uncle was in a position of trust too. He's someone who should have kept you safe, not someone you needed to be kept safe from. Do you think he did anything to your brother?'

'No. Barney was really close to him and he's dead excited about having his "brilliant Uncle Mel" back for Christmas. He wouldn't be like that if he'd been through what I've been through.'

'You can say the word, you know.'

I lowered my eyes and Robbie tilted my chin upwards again. 'Your Uncle Melvin is an abuser. He abused you. He might have abused others. He's a paedophile, Fizz. A sick, child abusing piece of scum and you owe it to yourself to make him accountable for that.'

'He's got two little girls himself now.'

'Then you need to protect them from him, along with any other little girls or boys who take his fancy. And you need to protect yourself. When you tell your parents, I can't say that the memories and the hurt will miraculously disappear because they won't, but you'll be more at peace with yourself. I can come with you if you want.'

The thought of not doing it alone – with having a friend by my side who'd been through it himself – gave me strength. Fizz Pops and Robster against the world.

'I'm going to Mum and Dad's for Sunday lunch tomorrow. We could go early. Would Kate mind me stealing you again?'

'She'll be fine. I've already told her I'm staying in your spare room tonight. She'll understand. So do you want to tell me more now that Pandora's Box has been opened?'

The tears started to flow again. 'Yes, please.'

'I'm listening. Take your time.'

30

FIZZ

Light flooded into the bedroom, yanking me from my slumber.

'My head,' I muttered, pressing my hand to my forehead as I tried to sink beneath the duvet.

'There's fresh water and two paracetamol next to you,' Robbie said, 'and a strong coffee in the kitchen.'

'Close the curtains. It's too bright.'

'Stop whining! Today is the day you claim your life back.'

He crouched beside the bed and tucked my duvet under my chin so he could see me.

'Hangover aside, how are you feeling now that you've told me? And please don't say embarrassed.'

'I was a drunk mess last night.'

'This is true, and it wasn't pretty. You're allowed to be embarrassed about that but not about what you told me. How does it feel to have finally said it out loud?'

'Weird. It's been a secret for so long that it feels like telling you happened in a dream. I'm glad it was you I told, but I'm sorry you've been through it too.'

'It was quite the confessional last night,' Robbie said gently.

'Look, I know it's hard talking about it and I know you can only face it when you're ready, but I'm fairly certain you're ready to tell your parents and have your abuser face the consequences, aren't you? You wouldn't have told me if you weren't.'

I sighed. 'Yes, I'm ready. But I'm so scared.'

'What's worse? The fear of telling your parents and starting down the road to justice or letting him get away with it forever?'

I slowly eased the duvet down. 'I'll go for a shower.'

'I'm glad you said that. I think you're sweating eau de alcohol. It's a bit whiffy in here.'

'Charming as ever,' I said, managing a smile despite everything. 'What time is it?'

He screwed his nose up. 'Nearly ten. Sorry. I slept through the alarm.'

The family always congregated at noon ready for a 1 p.m. lunch, so the plan Robbie and I had come up with last night had been to go to Mum and Dad's for nine, giving us plenty of time to talk and for them to cancel lunch for the rest of the family if they felt that was appropriate. But Robbie and I had been up well into the early hours talking about our connected experiences, so an early start had clearly been too ambitious.

'Do we have enough time this morning?' I asked him.

'Ah-ah, no delaying. Have a *quick* shower, down that coffee, and we'll go.'

* * *

It was almost eleven when we arrived in Amblestone. Because my parents' drive was being dug up, I pulled into the car park by the chapel and Robbie parked beside me.

The service was underway and I tuned into the singing of a hymn which I recognised from my school days – 'Lord of All Hopefulness'. The lyrics drifted out to me – a line about praying for strength – and I glanced up at Robbie.

'You've got this!' He took my hand in his.

'I feel sick.'

'That's the bottle of wine and two miniature vodkas talking,' he quipped, the humour helping calm me.

'Let's get this over with,' I muttered, crossing the road.

I kept my head down as we walked down the main street, playing over and over in my mind how I was going to open up the conversation with my parents. All too soon, we reached their house. Robbie hugged me to his side.

'You can do this,' he whispered, 'and I'm right here with you.'

We walked across some wooden boards the builders had placed over the dug-out driveway and headed down the side of the house to enter via the kitchen.

Mum was standing at the sink peeling vegetables and the kettle was bubbling on the side.

'Fizz!' she exclaimed, pausing her peeling. 'And Robbie! Are you joining us for lunch?'

'Erm...' He glanced at me. 'Probably not.'

'Well, you're very welcome. The more the merrier.' She resumed her work on the carrots. 'We've actually—'

Dad bursting into the kitchen interrupted her.

'Robbie! Haven't seen you in ages.' He strode over and enthusiastically shook Robbie's hand and went to hug me but stopped, evidently noticing my serious expression.

'Is everything okay?'

'I need to tell you both something.'

Mum turned round from this sink. 'Can it wait because we've —' Her smile slipped too. She dropped the peeler into the sink and reached for a tea towel to wipe her hands on, her eyes fixed on mine. The kettle clicked off and the only noise was the fan on the oven which I could barely hear over the pounding of my heart.

'Fizz? What's going on?' She took a step closer to me.

I glanced at Robbie, and he nodded.

'I need to... There's something... I haven't been...'

Robbie squeezed my hand.

'When I was younger, a lot younger, something bad...' It was so much harder saying this sober. 'Somebody hurt me, and I didn't tell anyone.'

Mum's face was blank. 'You're not making any sense, sweetie. Who hurt you?'

'Someone I knew.'

'Someone from school?' she asked. 'A bully?'

'No. Not a bully. Well, yes, but not in that way. He did things I didn't want him to do and I was scared and he told me I couldn't say anything but he might have done it to other people and I told Robbie last night and he says I have to tell you and you'll believe me and you have to because I'm not lying and...'

Tears spilled down my cheeks and I was shaking. I longed for Robbie to take over but at the same time, I knew he wouldn't. This had to come from me.

'Take a few deep breaths, Fizz,' Dad said gently. 'What are you trying to tell us?'

The words were all scrambled in my mind, and I couldn't seem to pull them together into a coherent sentence.

'Uncle Melvin's a paedophile!' I shouted, exasperation getting the better of me.

It wasn't the soft easing in I'd planned but it was out there now. I'd finally said it. I gulped as I glanced from one shocked expression to the other.

Mum gasped. 'What?'

The colour had drained from Dad's face.

'He abused me! I was six the first time and it didn't stop until he went to the States.' I've no idea why I felt the need to continue shouting, but I couldn't seem to lower my voice.

The tea towel dropped to the floor by Mum's feet and she clapped her hand across her mouth, looking wide-eyed at me then Dad.

'Fizz, sweetheart,' Dad said. 'Melvin—'

'I'm not making it up!' I cried. 'He did it when I stayed at the farm or when he babysat me here. And then it was any time he saw me and... You have to believe me!'

'I do,' Dad said, 'but Melvin and his family are—'

The door from the lounge was flung open and Granddad stood in the doorway, his face bright red, his body rigid.

'What the bloody hell are you saying about my son?' he yelled.

'Shit!' Robbie hissed, placing a protective arm round my shoulders.

'Frank, go back in the lounge,' Dad said in his calm, professional sergeant's tone. 'We need to speak to Fizz.'

'Like hell I will! Did you hear what she said?'

'Yes, and we need to talk to Fizz about it.'

'And you expect us just to sit there making small talk with Melvin and Kimberly while you do that?'

'They're here?' I cried, my stomach in knots as I pressed myself closer to Robbie. How were they here? Last I heard, they hadn't booked any flights yet and I'd been praying they never would.

'Yes, they're here!' Granddad shouted. 'It was meant to be a surprise. They heard every word. We all did.' He jabbed his finger towards me. 'We've always accepted you without question, young lady, putting up with your ridiculous hair colours and your girl-friends, but this is an outrage. He's my son! What sort of a sick joke is this?'

'Enough!' Dad didn't need to shout. The authoritative tone of his voice was sufficient to silence Granddad. 'You do *not* speak to my daughter like that.'

'I didn't know they were here,' I implored Granddad. 'The drive...'

I couldn't bear the way he was looking at me, his eyes boring through me, his expression full of loathing. We'd never been as close as Grandma and I were, but I'd put that down to me spending more time with Grandma as a child because he'd been busy managing the farm. To hear him say he'd been 'putting up' with my sexuality and my appearance was devastating. They weren't things to 'put up with'. They were me! Did that mean he hated me? And he'd used 'we'. Had Grandma been 'putting up' with me too?

'I can't do this,' I muttered, diving for the door.

'That's right! Throw the grenade in and run away, leaving everyone else to clean up your mess. That's typical of you.'

'Dad!' Mum cried.

I couldn't stay and hear any more from Granddad and I couldn't be in the same house as *him*.

'I'm sorry.' I looked from Dad to Granddad to Mum. 'Come on, Robbie.'

'She's not lying,' Robbie said, his voice strong and confident. 'You shouldn't need proof but—'

'Leave it!' I hissed, pushing the door open.

He ignored me. 'Look under the floorboards in her old bedroom.'

'You can't have any proof,' Granddad shouted, 'because my son has done nothing wrong. He's a good boy.'

I slammed the door closed, closing off Mum and Dad crying out my name.

'Fizz, I...' Robbie began, but my heart was pounding and my stomach was heaving and I was going to be sick.

I sprinted over the wooden boards on the drive, panicking, hoping my stomach would ease but the combination of last night's alcohol, the nerves, the fear of *him* being in such close proximity and the horrific confrontation just now got the better of me.

'It's all right,' Robbie said, by my side in seconds and stroking my back as I emptied the contents of my stomach over a drain. 'Let it all up.'

I wiped my mouth with the back of my shaking hand.

'I didn't see Granddad's car. If I'd known they were here...'

'He's upset. He'll come round.'

'Kimberly and the kids...'

'You weren't to know.' Robbie gently placed a hand on each of my shoulders and looked me square in the face. 'None of this is your fault. You must keep telling yourself that. It's not ideal that your grandparents and the paedo's family were there, but they'd have found out eventually.'

'Fizz!' Dad appeared at the end of the drive, looking either way.

'Thank God you're still here,' he said, rushing over to us and pulling me into his embrace.

'I'm so sorry, Dad,' I whispered.

'You have nothing to be sorry for. Nothing at all. But we need to talk. Where do you—'

He was interrupted by shouts from the house and suddenly Uncle Melvin sprinted down the road in the opposite direction to us. I froze to the spot, barely able to breathe. Sixteen years had passed but, to me, he looked exactly the same. Tall, dark, menacing, the shadow in my doorway, the demon in my nightmares.

'You disgusting, lying, worthless piece of shit!' Kimberly screamed, running after him. 'Is that why we left Wyoming? New job opportunity, you said!'

Melvin leapt into Granddad's car and took off at speed, almost losing the back end as the wheels spun.

'You're dead to me!' Kimberly yelled after him, but Melvin and Granddad's car were already gone.

She broke down, sinking onto the pavement, pounding her hands on the tarmac, anguished sobs pouring from her.

'You weren't to know they were there,' Robbie repeated, slipping his arm round my waist.

Dad ran to Kimberley and managed to ease her to her feet. She was like a rag doll, flagging against him as he led her back towards the house. My heart broke for an innocent woman whose world had just collapsed around her.

Dad indicated with an incline of his head that I should follow them inside, but I hesitated on the pavement. I couldn't face Kimberley or her girls, my grandparents, my own parents. I wanted to run away and hide, turn the clock back to last night and not get drunk. Keep a lid on Pandora's Box.

'Fizz?' Robbie said. 'Are we going back inside?'

'I can't,' I whispered. 'That poor woman. Oh, God, what have I done?'

'You did nothing. This is all on him. *All* of it.'

'I shouldn't have told you. I should have kept quiet. The only person my secret was hurting was me.'

'That's bullshit and you know it. Do you know what I heard just now? I heard her suggesting there've been others. You couldn't do anything to stop them – *his* fault, not yours – but you're stopping him now. What you did today might have saved his own daughters. What you did today was incredible, and do you know why? Because you're an incredible woman. Always have been and always will be and I'm so proud to be your friend.' His voice cracked with emotion.

I threw myself at him and we stood there in the middle of the pavement, holding each other tightly, our friendship stronger than ever.

'You should probably get back to Kate,' I said to Robbie, reluctantly letting him go. 'I've got to face the music and it's probably best I do that alone.'

'Will you be all right?'

'*He's* gone and Dad's here. I think I'm safe.'

'Your granddad?'

'I've got to face him sometime.'

Robbie hugged me again and I thanked him for being a rock and helping me.

'Final words of wisdom,' he said when he pulled away. 'I found these really helpful myself. You're not a *victim* of abuse. You're a *survivor* of abuse. You, Fizz Pops, are a strong, remarkable woman. He's a weak, disgusting, pathetic excuse for a man. Even his wife thinks so.'

As I approached the kitchen door, I could hear Granddad's raised voice and both children crying. The desire to flee was still strong but, as I'd said to Robbie just now, I had to face Granddad and the rest of them at some point. Now was as good a moment as any.

I eased open the door. Mum was at the kitchen table with her arm round my sobbing grandma.

'Fizz!' She rushed over to me and threw her arms round me and relief washed through me that I hadn't lost Mum. Hopefully I hadn't lost my grandparents either, but only time would tell.

31

SAMANTHA

Josh, Phoebe, Darcie, Dad and I all joined Mum at Orchard House for Sunday lunch. Wilbur had been invited too and he was now lying by my feet, full of roast chicken, while Phoebe and Darcie did the washing up.

'Sammie tells me Adele's working at the practice now,' Mum said.

'Yes,' Dad said. 'She started on Monday.'

'And already settling in and doing a great job,' Josh added.

Mum smiled. 'That's good to hear. It'll be years since I last saw her, but I liked Adele. How's her family, Jonathan? I presume the boys have left home.'

'Yeah, they're both married with kids. Ferdie's in Leeds and Jacob's in Claybridge and, between them, they have four boys and a girl.'

'Aw, how lovely. And Steve's well?'

'They're divorced.'

'Oh. Is she okay about it?'

'Best thing that could have happened to her, she says.'

'That's good, then. I always thought she could do better than him. Too moody for my liking.' She laughed and rolled her eyes. 'That's like the pot calling the kettle black, isn't it? She was probably thinking the same about you and me, as in you could do better than me.'

There was no bitterness in her voice, and it was great that she and Dad had got to a place where they could laugh about it.

'I'd love to see Adele again,' I said. 'Do you think she'd like to come to the Christmas Fair on Saturday, Dad?'

'I can ask her. I'm sure she'd love to come if she's free. We had lunch together on Friday and she was asking after you and wanted to know all about the rescue centre. I don't know if you'll remember, but she's got a thing about hares, so if you ever rescue a hare, she says you have to let her know.'

'Will do. No hares at the moment. We have a rabbit but I'm guessing that won't cut it.'

'Close but not the same. I'll ring her later and ask her about Saturday.'

'You could ask her out for dinner afterwards,' Mum suggested, her eyes twinkling at Dad. 'You're both single now and you've always got on well.'

'We're just friends!'

'My face doesn't light up like that when I talk about my friends,' Mum said teasingly.

Dad's cheeks were bright pink and it was sweet to see him all flustered as he topped up his tea from the pot on the table. It seemed Mum had called it.

'She's an employee,' he said.

Josh held his hands up. 'Doesn't bother me. She's a good match for you.'

'Not you too!' Dad cried. He turned his gaze to me. 'I suppose you think I should ask Adele out?'

'I thought nothing of the sort until now, but I think you might be a little bit smitten.'

Dad glanced guiltily in Mum's direction, and she laughed.

'Jonathan Wishaw, our time has passed. We tried again and it didn't work and now we're friends. I have no claim over you and, selfishly, I'd really like to see you happy and settled with someone new so I can rest easy knowing I haven't completely screwed you up for life.'

'Aw, Debs, you know you haven't,' he said, gently.

'Then at least think about it. Not that you need it, but you have my approval to go for it with Adele or whoever you take a shine to. You deserve to find love again.'

'So do you. And as you've started the after-dinner conversation about my love life, it's only fair that the spotlight is turned on you. Did anyone catch your eye in the Canaries?'

'A holiday romance?' Mum burst out laughing. 'You have to be joking. It was a girls' holiday and it stayed that way. As for back here, I've been asked out a couple of times over the past year, but I've turned them down.'

'Not ready?' I asked.

'It was probably that for the first one. The second one wasn't right for me, but I'm not averse to the idea for the right person.'

'Pleased to hear it.' Dad smiled affectionately at her and it touched my heart that they could discuss this with each other and that they could both see a future with other people.

I sensed it was time for a subject change. 'You said you had some ideas for the secret garden,' I said to Mum.

'Oh, yes! We need the girls for this. Shoes and coats on and we'll head down to the garden.'

* * *

Mum had only discovered Orchard House's secret garden by looking at the plans and realising there was a patch of land she couldn't see when standing out the back of the house. It was entered through two offset hedges which had overgrown and entwined but Mum had cut them back and, over the past year, had cleared a stack of rubble and waste that had been dumped in the garden. This was the first time Darcie had seen it.

'Oooh!' Darcie exclaimed, eyes flicking round the large space. 'Can I go on the swing?'

I winced. 'It might not be usable.'

'It's in a better state than we thought,' Mum said. 'It needs a new seat and some rust treatment but it's solid. I've been on it, so it'll definitely take Darcie.'

'Will you push me?' Darcie asked Phoebe, sprinting over to the swing before waiting for an answer.

'So you're keeping it?' Josh asked Mum as we watched Darcie grinning while Phoebe pushed her.

'Yes, and I've designed the garden around it. Hold this end.'

Josh took one end of the rolled-up plan as Mum unfurled it.

'Mum! It's incredible.'

The drawing itself was beautiful, showcasing Mum's talent with watercolours, but her plans were spectacular too. I'd known she was going to make it child-friendly, but I hadn't been expecting the whole garden to be for children.

'I had too many ideas,' she said, as though reading my thoughts, 'so I decided to do them all. It'll give Darcie, Bublet and any other grandchildren who come along a safe place to play but it'll also showcase to clients what I can do.'

The garden flowed seamlessly from grassy to paved to decked areas, with trails leading through doors, gates and willow tunnels, round raised flower beds and over wooden bridges. There was a 'dining' area with a mini wooden kitchen and colourful toadstool seats set round a larger toadstool table. A 'sleeping' area housed a wooden tepee and a small shepherd's hut. The swing remained central with a mound nearby for a small slide, and a sandpit.

'I want to make it work for toddlers and older children,' she said, 'which is why I want your input and Darcie's.'

'It's amazing,' Josh said, 'but you do realise you'll have a constant stream of children here?'

Mum looked at me and gave me a gentle smile. 'I've got a lot of making up to do.'

'Aw, Mum,' I said. 'We've parked that now. No more guilt. Please only do this if it's what *you* want, not to make up for lost time with me.'

'It *is* what I want. I've already got more garden than I need, which will keep me busy for years to come. I made the decision to buy the house before I even knew this space existed, so this was an unexpected bonus. A secret garden deserves to be a magical place, so that's what I'm going to create.'

We spent the rest of the afternoon discussing Mum's plans, Darcie's delight at being chosen to play Mary in a traditional school nativity, and the Christmas Fair next weekend.

Dad left at the same time as us and headed home with a promise to give Adele a ring about the Christmas Fair. The rest of us called into Terry's for a quick hello and I was relieved to see him looking a lot better, although I think the sight of his faithful companion helped.

'Do you want Wilbur to stay now?' I asked.

I glanced at Darcie's shocked expression and Terry must have noted it too.

'I think a couple more days at t' farm,' he said, 'but then I need me boy back. I miss him too much. Is that all right, young Darcie?'

She nodded solemnly. 'He misses you too, Grandpa Terry.'

On the journey back to Hedgehog Hollow, the conversation

returned to Darcie's role as Mary and getting hold of a costume. At Phoebe's suggestion, Darcie called Chloe on the hands-free and asked if there was any chance of her knocking together a simple one.

'I'd be honoured,' Chloe said.

'Can it be pink?' Darcie asked.

'If it's a traditional nativity, it'll need to be blue,' Chloe said, and I laughed as Darcie screwed her face up.

'I wish you could see Darcie's face right now,' I told Chloe.

'Is it the same expression as when you try to feed her cauliflower?'

'Exactly that!'

'We'll do something fabulous with it just for you, Darcie,' Chloe said. 'A bit of bling. Subtle, but definitely bling.'

Darcie was happy with that and spent the rest of the journey speculating on what subtle bling might look like, most of her suggestions being all about bling and nothing to do with subtlety.

But as we drove over the final ridge towards Hedgehog Hollow, the laughter in the car faded. I recognised Hadrian's car parked in the farmyard alongside a marked police car.

'Oh, God, what now?' Josh murmured.

32

FIZZ

When I went back inside Ashrigg House, Granddad was spitting feathers and I feared he might keel over at any moment.

'He stole my car!' he shouted at Dad, barely glancing in my direction.

That car was Granddad's pride and joy, and it was a family joke that nobody, not even Grandma, was allowed to drive it in case they scratched it.

'He just grabbed the keys off the sideboard and legged it. What's he playing at?'

It wasn't the time to explain to Granddad that his son's past had finally caught up with him and he was hoping to escape from it. Or to point out the absurdity of him being more concerned about Melvin taking his car – repairable if there was any damage – than the other irreparable crimes he'd committed.

Dad went upstairs to call the police station to report the abuse and the theft but, once he'd done that, he had to step away from it all due to the obvious conflict of interests.

Barney arrived and Mum steered him into the garden to explain what had kicked off. Minutes later, he rushed back into the kitchen and grabbed me in a bear hug. I knew what would be going through his mind, even though he didn't vocalise it. He'd have wished it had been him instead of me. He'd have wished he could have protected his little sister. Nobody should have to make wishes like that.

Even though I mainly stayed in the kitchen, out of Granddad's way, my presence in the house was clearly agitating him and, although Kimberly hadn't so much as looked in my direction while she tried to comfort her little girls, there was a risk that she'd turn on me, so I needed to go. Mum assured us that she and Barney could handle things so, after the tightest hug ever, Dad and I left and he followed me back to Meadow View to keep me company until an officer came to take my statement.

When the specialist support officer arrived, Dad waited in his car to give us some space and to ensure there was no risk of him being seen as trying to influence any part of the investigation.

'Samantha and the others have just arrived back from her mum's,' Dad said, returning to Meadow View after the officer left. 'They were panicking about the police car, but I've assured them it's nothing to do with the Grimes family and that one of my colleagues needed to take a statement from you about a completely unrelated incident.'

'Good. Thanks. I *will* tell them. Just not yet.'

'Do you want to talk to me about it?'

'I don't think I have it in me to go through it again and I'm not sure you really want to hear the details. It might be too hard for you.'

He ran his hand through his hair, blinking rapidly. 'We should have protected you.'

'Don't do that to yourself, Dad. It's not like he was some random stranger you invited into our home. He was your brother-in-law. Why wouldn't you trust him? I did.'

We sat in silence for a while. I still felt like I was in a dream but at least it was the start of a nightmare for *him*.

'Can I ask you a question?' Dad said eventually. 'It's not about the details. It's about Melvin moving to the USA. It seemed to come out of nowhere. Did you have anything to do with that?'

'Yes. I was at the farm one weekend, mucking out the stables. I wasn't expecting him to be there, so I thought I was safe, but I had this sudden sensation of being watched and I turned round and there he was, leering at me.' I shuddered at the memory. 'I don't know why it happened that day, but I finally snapped. I told him that I wasn't going to keep our secret any longer. He laughed and spurted out the usual about nobody believing me, but I told him I'd set up a video camera and recorded him the last time he'd come into my bedroom and that if he didn't leave the country for good, I'd show you.'

'He believed you?'

'Of course not. But I really had set up a video camera. He drove me home and insisted on seeing it then destroyed the tape, laughing at me for giving him my evidence. But I laughed back and told him I had another five recordings and he had a week to book himself a one-way ticket to the other side of the world or I'd destroy him.'

'Oh, Fizz, the courage that must have taken. You still have the evidence?'

'With my diaries. I started keeping one when I was nine or ten. I'm not sure why. Maybe deep down I knew that one day I'd need dates and details. It helped me. Writing it all down was like taking it out of my mind and into a book which I could close.'

'I wonder why he came back, knowing you could blow the whistle at any point.'

'I've wondered that ever since Granddad announced it. I've no idea how he had the nerve to show up for lunch today, knowing I'd be there. What did he think was going to happen? Did he think I'd sit there and smile politely, eager to hear all about his life in America?'

'I wouldn't like to speculate what's going on in his sick mind.'

* * *

A couple of hours later, Mum arrived and Dad let her in.

'I've just spoken to my mum,' she blurted out, as soon as she entered the lounge. 'They found Melvin and he's been arrested. They're interviewing him at the station now.'

I sank back against the sofa cushions, shaking with relief. Arrested. This was it. I'd taken control, I'd broken my silence and this was the start of the healing and recovery process.

Mum sat beside me and cuddled me like she used to when I was a little girl.

'How's Grandma doing?' I asked after a few minutes.

'In shock. We all are. Your granddad's gone down to the police station. Kimberly and the girls are with Mum. The police have just taken her statement.'

'Let's hope he confesses to everything. How's Kimberly?'

'Very subdued.'

It couldn't be easy for her, being in a strange country with people she barely knew. The wedding was the only time she'd seen my grandparents and parents face to face and she'd have barely known them from that.

'She didn't want to talk about it,' Mum added. 'All she'd say was that they'd moved on a couple of times after murmurs of untoward behaviour and she'd believed Melvin when he protested his innocence. Hearing you earlier woke her up.'

'I wonder what she'll do now.'

'I don't know and, awful as it sounds, I don't really care. The only person I care about is you. As far as I'm concerned, I no longer have a brother. Melvin Dodds can rot in hell.'

Dad slipped onto the sofa beside her and took her hand.

'There can never and will never be an excuse for abuse,' she said, tears pooling in her eyes. 'Never.'

33

SAMANTHA

'How are you feeling today?' I asked Fizz when she arrived at the barn for work on Tuesday.

Yesterday morning, she'd explained why the police car had been at the farm on Sunday and my heart broke for her. What a shock! It was a no-brainer when she asked if it would be okay to have the day off to spend some time with her family. I'd offered her the whole week, but she'd wanted to return to normality, refusing to let that man disrupt her life any more than he already had.

'Tough day,' she said, 'but my family know everything now and we've got a pact that none of them are allowed to feel any guilt for not knowing what I was going through. The only guilty party is *him*.'

'Any news from the police station?'

'They're still holding him. It's going to be complicated with some stuff over here and some stuff in the States. I personally don't care where he gets tried. I just want him to be put away so he can't hurt anyone else.'

'Did you see your grandma?'

'No. Kimberly and the girls are still with her. They've got

nowhere else to go. She spoke to Mum and she asked after me, so that's a start. I feel awful saying it, but I haven't the energy to try and support her through it as well.'

'The only one you need to focus on right now is you, Fizz. Did you manage to sleep?'

'Surprisingly well. I know it's not over yet, but I feel like a weight's been lifted.' She filled the kettle and switched it to boil. 'Anything good happen here yesterday? And I mean good. If we lost any patients, you can save that bombshell for tomorrow.'

'No losses, but three new admissions. We've got a pair of autumn juveniles – a girl called Storm and a boy called Crunch.'

'Crunch? Let me guess – Darcie named him!'

I smiled. 'Whatever would give you that idea? She spotted the weather theme and said frost crunches. It's cute.'

'It is. And the third admission?'

'You're going to love this. We've released one large badger and gained an even bigger animal. Come and look.'

Fizz followed me over to our largest pen where our patient was lying on a bed of straw.

'Oh. My. God. Our first deer!'

'Young male roe deer hit by a moped,' I said. 'He's got a broken leg but it's a clean fracture and Josh is confident he'll make a full recovery and be bounding across the fields again soon.'

'What's he called?'

'It's six weeks till Christmas and Darcie named him, so...'

'Rudolph,' Fizz said, chuckling. 'That's made me happy. Not that he was run over, obviously, but to see him up close. Absolutely gorgeous. Lovely to meet you, Rudolph.'

Fizz made the drinks and had no sooner sat down than we had a call to a hedgehog tangled in some fruit netting on an allotment, so Fizz went to retrieve it. Not long after she'd gone, Chloe and Lauren called in.

'Look what Riley's loaned us from the garden centre,' Lauren said.

She and Chloe both whipped green and red elf outfits from behind their backs.

'Oh, my word. For Saturday?'

Lauren nodded. 'They don't open their grotto until next weekend so, as long as I get them cleaned, we can use them at the Christmas Fair. The downside is they're not huge so that rules out Riley and James, and Kai is far too cool to be seen dead in one.'

Dad was already roped in as our Santa and Josh was Santa Paws – our Mickleby the hedgehog mascot wearing a Santa hat and a stack of tinsel.

'I'd offer, but what a shame,' I said with mock sarcasm, pointing to my bump, which definitely wouldn't fit into one of the outfits.

'Would Phoebe wear one?' Chloe asked.

'She probably would and I'm sure we have enough volunteers to cover her stall.' I bit my lip, thinking. 'The costume would swamp Darcie, and Fizz is looking after the demonstrations.'

'We've drawn a blank too,' Lauren said, hanging both outfits up on the coat rack. 'You don't have to use them, but they're here if you want them or even just one of them. We'd better go and do the final prep for our class.'

'Good luck. What is it today?' With everything going on, I'd lost track of which classes were running when at Crafty Hollow.

'Christmas mosaics,' Chloe said with a wave as they both left the barn.

* * *

'I'm up for it,' Phoebe said when she arrived home from work and saw the elf costumes. 'And I know exactly who to ask. Give me five minutes.'

She stepped outside with her phone and returned a few minutes later.

'Leo's in. He was going to come anyway and he's loving the idea of having a role.'

'What a star. I'm looking forward to meeting him after hearing so much about him.'

'You'll love him. He's such a great guy.'

'Does Fizz know the two of you are just friends?'

'Yeah, of course. They met at the cinema and I told her he was a mate. Why do you ask?'

'No reason. Just wondering.'

'Speaking of wondering, did you find out what the police car was here for on Sunday? I haven't seen Fizz. I sent her a message asking if she's free one night this week, but she hasn't replied.'

'I'm sure she'll reply when she has a minute.'

'Do you know if she's in now? I might nip round.'

'She's gone to Robbie and Kate's tonight.'

'I thought she'd only just seen Robbie.' Phoebe shrugged. 'I'll hopefully catch her tomorrow.'

With a wave, she left for the farmhouse. I was surprised that Fizz hadn't responded to Phoebe's message when they were so close, although she had a lot on her mind. Hopefully they'd be able to catch up in the next few days. Phoebe's abuse hadn't been sexual, but it had still been abuse, so she'd had an insight into the sort of trauma Fizz had experienced and would hopefully be able to help her heal. But it was up to Fizz if she wanted to share it with Phoebe. It wasn't my place to say anything.

34

FIZZ

Robbie and Kate invited me to their house for tea on Tuesday with a promise that we didn't have to talk about anything serious unless I wanted to. I considered declining but what was the alternative? Being alone with my troubled thoughts? I'd spent all day on Monday with my parents and Barney had joined us in the evening. It had been a heavy day so some light relief was needed, and I knew Robbie would bring that so I accepted and drove across after work so I could see Arlo before his bedtime.

He was sitting on a playmat when I arrived, banging two wooden blocks together and giggling. I settled on the floor beside him and played for a while, eager to be lost in a world of innocent child's play. After tea, I helped Robbie bathe him and get him ready for bed. I even gave him his night-time bottle. Holding a warm, snuggly baby in my arms with his hand round my finger lifted the darkness and healed part of my broken heart.

After Kate settled him in his cot, she and Robbie regaled me with stories of explosive nappies, being peed on mid-change and various other parenting moments that had my sides aching with laughter. It was exactly what I needed.

As I prepared to leave, Robbie presented me with a red, long-sleeved T-shirt with his 'hedgicorn' wearing a Christmas hat on it, poised for a kiss under the mistletoe.

'Thought you might like to wear this for the Christmas Fair on Saturday,' he said.

'Oh, my God! It's amazing! Thank you.'

He handed me a bag. 'I made one for Samantha, Phoebe and Darcie too. Didn't think they'd be Josh's thing.'

'Robster! That's too generous. How much do I owe you?'

'Absolutely nothing. They're gifts.'

'You all deserve to be spoilt,' Kate added.

I hugged them both.

'Thank you for tonight and for everything over the weekend. You've both been amazing.'

'You're welcome,' Kate said, 'but I'm not sure I was much help.'

'You loaned me your husband when I needed a friend. Not everyone would be that understanding.'

'You've been there for him over the years, so it was the least I could do.' Kate's eyes sparkled and she sounded quite choked up. 'He's probably never told you this, but you helped him through a dark time when he moved up here.'

I glanced at Robbie, frowning. 'But I didn't know what had happened in Wales.'

He smiled gently. 'You didn't need to. You got me through it by being you. I know you've talked about putting on a front to hide things, but I don't fully accept that. You are naturally warm and friendly. That's not a front. That's you.'

'Stop it,' I joked, blinking back the tears. 'You're going to set me off again.'

'I agree with him,' Kate said. 'Keep being you because Fizz Kinsella is a truly special person and we both love her very much.'

I gave them another hug each then waved goodbye and drove down the street. I made it round the corner then had to park as I couldn't see through my tears. *You're not special, Fizzy. Nobody will ever love you but me.* He was wrong. So very wrong.

* * *

Back home at Meadow View a little later, I dug out my phone and re-read the message that Phoebe had sent on Sunday evening.

⊠ From Phoebe
Spotted the police car on Sunday and your dad said you were giving a statement for something. Hope everything's OK. Feel like we haven't had a proper catch-up in ages. I need to work late on my project with Leo tomorrow night but are you free any night from Tuesday onwards? x

I hadn't known how to respond. I wanted to tell Phoebe about *him* but letting so many people into my long-held secret was feeling overwhelming. I knew how understanding and empathetic Phoebe would be and I was scared that, in my vulnerable state, I'd do something stupid like try to kiss her.

She had to be wondering why I hadn't replied. It wasn't fair of me to avoid her, so I typed in a response.

⊠ To Phoebe
Sorry for the delay in replying. It's been a difficult week. How about Thursday night after Darcie's gone to bed? x

That still didn't give me much time to get my feelings in check, but it was better than suggesting tomorrow.

* * *

By 8 p.m. on Thursday evening, I'd bitten all my nails down to the quick. Pacing up and down in the lounge, I took several deep breaths as I tried to quell the nausea. It wasn't telling someone else that was difficult. It was telling Phoebe. She'd understand after the physical, verbal and emotional abuse she'd suffered at the hands of the Grimes family, but would she be hurt that I hadn't shared that I'd also been abused? Would she think I hadn't trusted her enough? I'd wanted to say it so many times, but the words never came.

Ten minutes later, Phoebe arrived. I took another deep, shaky breath before pasting a smile on my face as I opened the door.

'These are for you.' She handed me a stunning bouquet full of deep red, russet and cream flowers.

'They're gorgeous. Thank you. I'll see if I can find a vase.'

She grinned as she produced a cream ceramic vase from behind her back. 'Also for you.'

Tears pricked my eyes at the thoughtfulness as I thanked her and ushered her in from the cold November evening.

Phoebe grabbed a couple of soft drinks from the fridge while I put the flowers in the vase and carried them through to the lounge.

'I've been worried about you,' she said softly. 'You said it's been a difficult week. Are you okay?'

I plonked myself down beside her on the sofa and sighed. 'Not really. I've got something to tell you. It's connected to the police car being here.'

My hands were shaking, and I had to put my can of drink down before I spilled it.

'Take your time,' Phoebe said, lightly touching my leg. 'Whatever it is, I'm here for you.'

Her gentle words gave me the strength to go on.

'You know how you had to keep quiet about what the Grimes family were doing to you? I know first-hand how that feels and I'm sorry I couldn't tell you that at the time, but I wasn't ready to share my secret until now. That statement I gave to the police on Sunday was about my uncle and how he sexually abused me for six years.'

Phoebe's mouth dropped open, and tears rushed to her eyes.

'Oh, Fizz! Oh, my God!'

She held her arms out and I gratefully fell into her embrace, the tears flowing once more.

'Is this your mum's brother who lives in the States?' she asked when my sobs eased.

'Yes. Melvin. He emigrated when I was twelve because I threatened to tell...'

I told her everything that had happened since Granddad's 'exciting' news that Melvin and his family were coming home for Christmas before going back to the start and explaining how the abuse had affected me. Phoebe shared more tragic details from her time under Tina Grimes's roof. We cried, we hugged, and we understood each other.

It was after 2 a.m. when fatigue overcame us both and we had to call it a night.

'You're not alone in any of this,' she assured me as we said goodbye at the door. 'If you want to talk some more or if you want to do something completely unconnected, I'm here for you every step of the way.'

She kissed me on the cheek and I closed my eyes at the touch of her warm lips.

'Good night, Fizz.'

'Good night, Phoebe. And thank you.'

She blew me a kiss then ran off into the darkness.

I closed and locked the door and rested my back against it. I had no idea if we'd ever be more than friends but, for now, friendship was enough. Friendship and understanding was what I needed. Another piece of my broken heart slotted back into place.

35

FIZZ

After a heavy week, Saturday's Christmas Fair was perfect timing for some much-needed lightness. The focus of the Christmas event was on fundraising, so we didn't run talks like we did on the June Family Fun Day but, never ones to miss out on an opportunity to educate, we'd set up the information boards on one side of Wild-flower Byre. The equipment we used had been laid out across a couple of tables with soft toy animals to act as our patients and I was looking after that section, giving demonstrations and answering questions to anyone interested.

I pulled on Robbie's Christmas hedgicorn T-shirt, swept my hair into a pair of messy buns and added an over-the-top Christ-massy headband.

I'd felt really positive all day yesterday – if a little tired after staying up so late with Phoebe – and immersing myself in the Christmas spirit today would help maintain that.

I still hadn't seen my grandparents all week, but I'd heard through Mum that Kimberly had returned to the USA with her little girls and would be staying with her family. I hoped they were as supportive and understanding as my parents had been because she'd need that support network around her.

* * *

By lunchtime, Wildflower Byre was packed with visitors. There were fairy lights everywhere and several Christmas trees, each one decorated in homage to an animal we rescued. Baubles matched that animal's colour, there were photos of past and current rescues hanging from the branches, and there were handmade decorations which could be removed and purchased from the craft stall Chloe and Lauren were running.

Christmas music was playing, although I could barely hear it over the chatter. Every so often, a whiff of something delicious travelled into the byre from the food stalls set up in Fun Field, tantalising my tastebuds. Sam was relieving me at 1 p.m. so I could grab something to eat and have a wander round. It felt so good to be immersing myself in such a happy atmosphere.

I'd had a steady flow of visitors, but the biggest attraction was definitely Santa Claus, Santa Paws and the two elves who'd had a sizeable queue since we opened. Every time I had a quiet moment, my eyes were drawn to Phoebe and Leo. From what I could see, they were a great double act, making the waiting children and parents laugh. They were very tactile, just like they'd been when I saw them in the cinema, playfully shoving each other and stealing each other's hats.

'He's not her boyfriend.'

I glanced down at Darcie. 'Where did you spring from?'

'I was helping on the candy cart and I saw you looking at Phoebe and Leo and you looked sad.'

'I'm not sad, Princess.'

It wasn't right to question an eight-year-old, but I couldn't help myself. 'Are you sure Leo's not her boyfriend? They look very close.'

'I'm sure. Phoebe told me. Leo has a boyfriend and he's lonely because his boyfriend's working in another country until Christmas and they used to go to the cinema every week so Phoebe's his cinema buddy but she says she'll still take me because Leo probably likes different films to me.'

The sudden regular cinema trips all made sense now.

'Anyway,' Darcie added, 'Phoebe loves you.'

'What?'

'She loves you. She thinks you're really pretty and she wants to kiss you.'

My heart leapt. 'She told you that?'

No answer.

'Darcie? Did she actually say those words?'

Darcie wrinkled her nose. 'She did say you're really pretty but she didn't say she wanted to kiss you. But I know she does because she talks about you all the time and she looks at you all gooey.'

'People talk about their friends all the time. It doesn't mean they're in love with them.'

'Then why did she do that heart thing?'

'What heart thing?'

'She drew a heart in her notebook and it had your name and hers in it and I know she wants a girlfriend and not a boyfriend because she told me she only likes boys as friends and girls as more than friends.'

I longed to continue the conversation, but a family had appeared wanting my attention and it wasn't fair to interrogate Darcie. She skipped back to the candy cart while I answered their questions but, as I explained how we fed hoglets, I couldn't stop smiling. I wasn't sure about the wanting to kiss me or the gooey looks bit, but Phoebe wouldn't have written our names together in a heart if she didn't feel something for me. And Darcie had confirmed one thing: Phoebe was interested in women and there was no way Darcie would have come out with that if they hadn't had that conversation.

When the family left, I looked over to Phoebe and she turned in my direction and gave me the warmest smile, making my insides liquify. I wasn't ready to dive into a relationship just yet, but I would be one day and it would finally be with somebody who knew me, understood me and loved me for who I was. Hopefully that person would be Phoebe.

Despite everything, it might just be a happy Christmas after all.

36

SAMANTHA

It was tipping it down as I pulled into a parking space at my local doctor's surgery on Wednesday morning, the week after the Christmas Fair.

I was early so I stayed in the jeep, hoping the rain would ease, and scrolled through the WhatsApp feed with my parents, smiling at the message Dad had sent first thing which had made me punch the air with happiness.

✉ From Dad
OK, so you called it, Debs! I took Adele out for a drink after the Christmas Fair and there was something there. We went out for a meal last night & I'm cooking for her on Friday. I'm not saying we're an item, but there's a possibility. Thanks for the push x

It had been great seeing Adele on Saturday. Over hot chocolate and a catch-up, I hadn't missed the lingering glances and the obvious chemistry between her and Dad, so I was thrilled he'd gone for it and asked her out.

As the windows steamed up, I sang softly along to the music on the radio.

'Thirty-four weeks today,' I said, stroking my bump. 'Not long until we meet you.'

I still felt exhausted from the Christmas Fair and, conscious that I could easily drift off to sleep in the warm car, I decided to brave the elements.

I had a big baby bump now so exiting the jeep while simultaneously attempting to put up a golf brolly wasn't particularly graceful, but I managed to stay mostly dry, unlike some of the other patients in the waiting room who looked to be drenched through.

'Samantha Alderson?' my midwife Tammy called a little later. A curvaceous woman in her late-fifties, I'd warmed to her immediately. She had what I considered to be the perfect balance between being friendly and chatty alongside efficiency and professionalism. Appointments usually ran on time and I always left feeling listened to, reassured, and informed.

I heaved myself up and followed her down the corridor into her consulting room.

'Happy thirty-four weeks!' Tammy gushed when we settled into our chairs. 'How are you feeling?'

'Big and tired.'

'Aw, bless you. I hate to say it but there's more of that to come, but the gift at the end will be more than worth it. How are the swollen feet?'

I pointed to my ankle-length wellington boots. 'Extra wide, two sizes bigger than I normally wear, and I can only put them on using a shoehorn, but they're better than flip-flops, especially in this weather.'

'They're very pretty.'

'Thank you.' The only ones I'd been able to find were a navy-blue base covered in red, yellow and pale blue flowers. They clashed with lots of my clothes but they were comfortable, so I didn't care.

'Is baby still moving regularly?' Tammy asked.

'Yes. Still mornings and evenings mostly.'

'And is there anything you're concerned about?'

'Not at the moment.'

'Brilliant. Well, do shout up if you think of anything, no matter how minor it seems.' She entered a couple of notes into her computer then focused her attention back to me. 'Today, we'll talk about recognising active labour, pain management and your birth plan but, before we go onto that, let's do a few checks. Roll up your sleeve, please.'

Tammy took my blood pressure and shared the figures with me.

'It's particularly high today,' she said. 'Have you had a busy morning or a rush to get here?'

'Neither.'

She gave me a reassuring smile. 'Not to worry. We'll measure the size of your uterus and check your urine sample then take your blood pressure again. Pop your urine sample on the desk then hop on the bed for me and lift your top up, please.'

The uterus measurement, known as fundal height, gave guidance on the baby's length and weight to make sure the baby was developing as expected. At my stage in pregnancy, the length in centimetres should be the same as the number of weeks pregnant, give or take two centimetres.

'Thirty-two centimetres,' Tammy declared when she'd completed her measurement. 'That's the bottom of the range but still normal. You get yourself sorted and I'll test your urine.'

I pulled my top back into place and half-rolled, half-lowered myself down from the bed.

'I've tested your urine and there's protein in it,' Tammy said when I joined her at the desk.

My stomach sank. 'Pre-eclampsia?'

The exact cause of pre-eclampsia remains a medical uncertainty, but it is believed to be caused by the placenta not properly developing as a result of a problem with the blood vessels supplying it. An effective placenta with a large and constant supply of blood from the mother to the baby is essential for the baby's growth, and problems with the placenta would mean a disruption to that blood supply. Although most cases of pre-eclampsia are mild, there is a risk of fits known as 'eclampsia' which are life-threatening for the baby and the mother, so medical practitioners take any indications very seriously.

'Yes, but it's common and most of the time, it's only mild.' Tammy gave me a reassuring smile, but it didn't stop the nervous butterflies.

'Any headaches, vision problems, pain below the ribs or vomiting?' she asked, listing what I recognised as potential further symptoms of pre-eclampsia.

'Nothing like that.'

'Have your feet become more swollen since the last time I saw you?'

'Yes.'

'What about your hands or face?'

'I haven't noticed any swelling on my face, but my hands are a bit swollen.' I held them out for her to see. 'I've had to stop wearing my rings.'

Tammy took my blood pressure again and the readings were a little higher than before. She typed the details into her computer as my heart thumped. Even though I knew I'd need a blood test to confirm pre-eclampsia, the combination of protein in my urine, high blood pressure and swollen limbs all pointed to me having it. And even though I knew most cases were mild, there was always that fear of being the exception.

'If it was just the protein in the urine,' Tammy said, her tone warm and reassuring, 'I'd take some blood now and we'd take it from there but, with the high blood pressure and the swelling, I'd rather admit you to hospital for closer monitoring. Please try not to feel anxious about it.'

'Easier said than done.'

She placed her hand over mine and gave it a gentle squeeze. 'I know. I had pre-eclampsia with both of mine and it's scary getting the diagnosis but, as I say, it's usually mild. They typically like to monitor things overnight, so you'll need to pack a bag. How long do you think you'll need to get packed and get there?'

I did a swift calculation in my head of time to get home, pack, and have Josh drive me through to Whitsborough Bay. Hopefully he wasn't in surgery and would be able to leave work.

'Maybe an hour and a half.'

'Okay. You get home and get packed and I'll make the arrangements, but please don't worry yourself and don't rush unnecessarily. This isn't a blue light situation.'

That last sentence made me feel so much better. I called Josh's mobile via my jeep's Bluetooth on the way back to Hedgehog Hollow and caught him between appointments. He said to give him ten minutes to speak to Dad and Tariq about moving some of his patients around and then he'd come home.

Arriving back at Hedgehog Hollow, I gave the news to Fizz and checked she was okay to hold the fort alone before going to the farmhouse.

It didn't take me long to throw a few things into my overnight bag but then I stupidly searched online for the implications of pre-eclampsia. I knew the basics from my nursing training, but I wasn't a midwife, so I didn't know the finer details including the risks. Ignorance would have been better.

It all got on top of me as we drew closer to the hospital and I started to panic. Josh had to pull onto a side road and hug me until the worst of it passed. So much for Tammy telling me not to be anxious.

* * *

Josh squeezed my hand as he sat down in the chair beside my hospital bed an hour later.

'How are you holding up?'

'Still nervous, but at least I'm in the right place for help.'

The staff at the hospital had been so kind, repeatedly reassuring me that I was likely to have a mild case and that monitoring was key to ensuring it didn't progress beyond that.

'Do you think they'll keep you in for more than one night?' Josh asked.

'I'm not sure. It'll depend on what the blood test reveals.'

'Hopefully you'll be home in the morning.'

I hoped so too but, when the consultant did her rounds later, it didn't sound like I'd be going home any time soon.

'I'm Lynne Hayes,' she said. 'I can confirm the presence of protein in your blood and that you do have pre-eclampsia. Accompanied by the swelling of your hands and feet and the high blood pressure, we want to keep a close eye on things, so we'd like to keep you here.'

'For how long?'

'I can't say for definite. There's no cure for pre-eclampsia – just close monitoring – so it's not going to suddenly go away. It'll be present until the baby's born and, depending on what happens with your protein levels and your blood pressure, it may be that we need to induce.'

'Induce? When? I'm only thirty-four weeks.'

Babies born before thirty-seven weeks were classed as premature and, although there was a high survival rate for babies born at my stage of pregnancy, it was still terrifying.

'We'd prefer to pass thirty-seven weeks,' Lynne said.

'So Sammie will be here until the baby's born?' Josh asked. I could hear the surprise in his tone.

'I'd work on that being a possibility,' Lynne said, clearly unwilling to fully commit.

Josh caught my eye and I grimaced. At least three weeks in hospital and maybe longer as they'd want to induce as late as they possibly could. What about the rescue centre? I'd arranged maternity cover from the practice commencing the first full week in December, but that was a week and a half away. Josh would need to provide further cover for me, but he'd also need cover for himself as he'd be travelling to and from hospital to see me.

What about Phoebe and Darcie? We'd taken care to ensure that Phoebe was the mother figure for Darcie, but Josh and I had been very much a part of their lives, like parents to Phoebe and grandparents to Darcie, despite the lack of generational age-gaps. I was certain they'd manage just fine without me, but would I manage without them?

'I appreciate there's a lot to take in,' Lynne said. 'We're going to do another ultrasound scan to check your baby's growth more accurately. One of my colleagues will be along later to give you an approximate time so you can increase your fluid intake to get the best reading. Do you have any immediate questions for me?'

Stacks, but nothing that she could answer without a crystal ball or a time machine.

'Not at the moment, thank you.'

Tears burned my eyes as Lynne left.

'It'll be all right,' Josh said, standing up and hugging me to his chest. 'Bublet will be fine and, with constant monitoring, they'll pick up on any problems.'

'I know it's the best place for me,' I said when I lay back against my pillows, tears under control, 'but being stuck in hospital isn't how I imagined spending my maternity leave. When's thirty-seven weeks? I can't think straight.'

Josh dug out his phone and checked the calendar. 'Three weeks today takes us to 14 December.'

'They'll want to wait as long as possible after that point to induce, if that's what they need to do, which could realistically mean I'm in here until just before Christmas. I'm not going to be around to put the tree up or write cards. I haven't done any Christmas shopping yet. Why didn't I think of that before?'

'You weren't to know this would happen. Phoebe and Darcie will help with the tree, so don't worry about that. We can write the cards too or I can bring them in for you if you prefer. As for the presents, I can brave the shops on my own this year or we can shop online. I know you prefer to shop local, but I think we can make an exception this year. Everything can be sorted.'

I felt a little calmer. Josh bringing me the cards to write was a good idea because boredom was likely to hit me hard and if I was bored, I'd worry. I hadn't had a full-blown PTSD episode in well over a year, but I'd come close when Connor attacked me and I'd had a panic attack in the car coming over. Stress wasn't good for the baby, so it was important for me to remain as calm as possible.

I took hold of Josh's hand. 'If they do keep me in until Bublet's born, I'm not expecting you to visit every day.'

'Sammie, I can't leave you here on your own.'

'Yes, you can. If Hedgehog Hollow was ten minutes away, I'd think differently, but it's not. It's nearly a two-hour round trip and you're going to be needed at home and at the rescue centre. We can sort out some sort of visit schedule so I don't get lonely, but it's not practical for you to be here every day. You'll be exhausted before Bublet arrives.'

'The downside of living in the middle of the countryside,' Josh said, rolling his eyes at me.

'But think of all those positives. Could there be a better place to raise our family?'

He raised my hand to his lips and lightly kissed it. 'No. It's perfect.' He sighed. 'I don't like it, but I get it. At least you have your Auntie Louise and Uncle Simon on the doorstep.'

They lived on the hospital side of Whitsborough Bay so were very handy for visiting.

Josh went to the shop to get us a couple of soft drinks while I prepared him an email of what to bring me for a longer stay including my laptop, a notepad and pens, and some books to read. I used to be a voracious reader but had struggled for reading time since setting up Hedgehog Hollow. Now was my chance to catch up on all the reads that Chloe had highly recommended and the books I'd been given for my birthday. I'd probably get through a paperback every couple of days.

I'd put my phone on silent, but a text flashed up on the screen.

✉ From Dad
Any news? Sending all my love xx

✉ To Dad
Blood test confirmed pre-eclampsia & I'm going for a scan later. Likely to be in hospital until baby's born & they may induce after 37 weeks

✉ From Dad

Let me know what you need from me and when it's
good to visit. You're in the best place for care
and attention. Stay strong. Hugs xx

✉ To Dad
I'll text when I've had my scan and I'll let
everyone else know at that point xx

I didn't anticipate that the ultrasound scan would reveal anything to be concerned about, especially when Bublet was active and Tammy had said my fundal height measurement was in the 'normal' range, but I didn't want to tempt fate by sending out an *I'm in hospital but all's well* message then have to follow it up with *Ignore previous message. There's been a complication...*

I shuddered, unable to bear thinking about it. I had to believe that everything was fine. This wasn't the way I'd anticipated spending the last six weeks of my pregnancy but, as I'd learned over the past couple of years, very little in life did go to plan and you just had to roll with it. Whatever the scan revealed, we'd get through it.

37

FIZZ

The week following the Christmas Fair was a very strange one. I felt lighter having unburdened my secret, but I was heartbroken that it had raised a barrier between my grandparents and me. I was excited by Darcie's declaration that Leo was just a friend of Phoebe's and that Phoebe really loved me, but I felt anxious that it wasn't the right time for me to be entertaining any romantic thoughts. And I was worried about Sam.

I had no idea what pre-eclampsia was, so I'd been online. I was glad Josh had emphasised that it was mild because it all sounded pretty scary to me. He'd said that Sam was very calm about it and was taking it in her stride, but I imagined her being like a swan, all serene on the surface while her legs paddled frantically. She'd be worried about the baby and she'd be worried about the rescue centre. I knew she wouldn't want to be cut off from it completely, so I'd proposed to Josh that I send her photos every few days of our recovered patients along with any super-cute new admissions who weren't high-risk. I wouldn't mention any losses. Josh liked that idea.

It was late November and we were now well past having newborn hoglets needing hand-rearing, so nobody needed to stay overnight at the rescue centre. Even though I was tempted to stay and continue working – especially with Sam not being around – I forced myself to close down the laptop at 6 p.m. on Friday night. It wasn't healthy for me to keep avoiding downtime so that I didn't have to think about what was going on with *him*.

Before retiring to Meadow View for the evening, I needed to put fresh food and water in the feeding stations in the garden. I'd finished doing that and was standing in the garden with the empty water jug in one hand and some empty cat food pouches in the other. I closed my eyes for a moment, the promise of frost making me feel awake.

Suddenly I had the sensation that someone was watching me and the hairs on the back of my neck stood up.

'Hello?' I called. 'Is anyone there?'

I lowered the pouches and jug to the floor and slowly removed my phone from my coat pocket.

'Hello?'

Was that someone crunching on the gravel?

I dialled 999 and held my thumb over the green button, ready to connect the call.

I'd never felt vulnerable at Hedgehog Hollow before and I'd been alone here on numerous occasions, but now I felt how remote it was.

'Melvin?' I shouted. 'Is that you? I'm not scared of you, you know!'

'Who's Melvin?' Darcie asked, running across the garden towards me in her judo uniform.

It took me a moment to gather myself enough to answer. 'Nobody. How was judo?'

'Wicked. I'm doing another grading next year.'

'That's brilliant news. Where's Phoebe?'

'Getting something out the car but I saw you and she said I could come and say hello.'

'Let's go and find her.' I retrieved the jug and empty food packets and walked with Darcie into the farmyard.

'Are you all right?' Phoebe asked, frowning at me.

Darcie was bouncing round the farmyard, pausing every so often to do a judo move.

'Fine. I felt someone watching me and thought it was *him* but it was only Darcie.'

Phoebe reached for my hand, sending butterflies stirring. 'You're bound to be jumpy. Why don't you come over to the house with us? I've copped out and picked up takeaway pizza for tea and there's way too much for two.'

'Thank you. I'll ditch this lot and be right over.'

She squeezed my hand then released it. 'He's not here, Fizz. You're safe.'

I nodded, feeling a surge of strength. No, *he* wasn't here and I was and I wasn't going to become a victim. As Robbie said, I was a survivor of abuse and that's how I was going to behave.

* * *

Sitting at the kitchen table in the farmhouse, tucking into pizza that evening with Phoebe and Darcie lifted my spirits and in the midst of it, more good news came in a text from Dad.

✉ From Dad
The woman in Bentonbray who stopped those youths kicking the hedgehog has seen them in the

village again, taken photos & we've got an iden-
tification. My team are on it x

At last! Rainbow deserved some justice and hopefully it would
be served.

38

SAMANTHA

I'd missed Phoebe and Darcie so much across the week. FaceTime just didn't cut it and visiting time after lunch on Saturday couldn't come soon enough for me. Visitor numbers were limited so they were only staying for the first thirty minutes, with Fizz bringing Terry over for the second and Josh taking the evening slot.

Fizz had said half an hour would probably be enough for Terry as he remained devoid of energy. I'd rather he wasn't coming at all for that exact reason, but there'd been no talking him out of it. He'd admitted he didn't feel well enough to drive but had threatened to catch a bus if nobody was willing to bring him, so we'd had to concede. The thought of him catching three or four buses each way was worse than the thought of him driving himself.

I was at the far end of a ward with six beds but, when all the patients had their curtains pulled back like now, I could see the nurses' station. My heart leapt as I spotted Phoebe speaking to one of the midwives, with Darcie bouncing up and down beside her. Moments later, Darcie ran down the ward, beaming at me.

'Careful!' Phoebe called after her. 'Mind the baby.'

I'd feared Darcie might launch herself straight onto the bed, but she slowed down at Phoebe's words and stopped alongside me, flinging her arms round my neck instead.

'I've missed you, Princess,' I said.

'I've missed you too.'

Phoebe joined us and hugged me. 'How are you feeling?'

'I'm feeling fine and Bublet's doing well, but my blood pressure says otherwise. The boredom's the hardest part.'

'We've brought you some presents which might solve that,' Phoebe said.

Darcie zipped open the holdall which Phoebe had placed on one of the chairs and passed me a photo frame.

'They miss you too,' she said.

I laughed at the gorgeous picture of Misty-Blue, Luna and Jinks on Thomas's bench.

'You have no idea how long it took to get them all on the bench at the same time,' Phoebe said, laughter in her voice. 'Jinks the lazy cat was happy to curl up and stay there, but the other two wanted to be stroked or to play. This is the result of a last-ditch bribery attempt with catnip and treats.'

'I love it, thank you.' I placed it on my bedside cabinet.

'We've been shopping,' Phoebe said, 'but before you tell me I shouldn't have spent all my wages on you, everyone who signed the card clubbed in.'

I opened the oversized card and glanced at the stacks of messages, feeling a little choked up by how many people had contributed to the gifts.

'So many names! I think I'd better read this after visiting hour or I won't get to talk to you two.'

The gifts were so thoughtful. There was a pack of two wood-land-themed nighties, some fluffy badger bed socks and a soft hedgehog fleece blanket in case I felt a little chilly. There were items to keep me entertained – paperbacks, puzzle books, an adult colouring book, felt tip pens, a small hedgehog cross stitch kit and a beautiful notebook with a sparkly fox on the front – and practical items to make me comfortable like a back scratcher, lip balm, sleep mask, and ear plugs.

'Some posh toiletries,' Phoebe said, placing a pretty toilet bag on my lap. 'All suitable for pregnant women.'

'Some sweets,' Darcie added, passing me a carrier bag containing bars of chocolate and boiled sweets. 'And this!'

The final item she passed me was a soft ivory unicorn with a pink horn, tail and ears.

'She's magical and she'll look after you and Bublet while you're in hospital. Everyone needs a unicorn.'

'I agree. She's gorgeous, Darcie, and she's going to be great company. We can snuggle under my lovely new blanket together and watch films on my tablet. Thank you both for organising this. These are all amazing.'

Phoebe packed everything back into the holdall to give us some room while Darcie clambered onto the bed beside me so she could give me a proper cuddle.

'How are the nativity rehearsals going?' I asked her.

'Mr Huggins says I'm a brilliant Mary, but he says the shepherds have to carry soft sheep and not unicorns like I wanted.'

'Well, if it's a proper *traditional* nativity, I don't think the Bible mentions unicorns at the birth of Jesus, so he has a good point.'

'Auntie Chloe's finished my costume.'

'You've got to see her in it,' Phoebe said, handing me her phone.

'Oh, Darcie, you look incredible.'

Chloe had surpassed herself. The dress and matching head-dress appeared to be made from a mottled cream material. She'd introduced some subtle bling as promised by sewing gold trim onto the blue cape, which she'd attached to the dress to keep it in place. A blue and gold ribbon was fastened round the waist and the headdress.

'I wanted to wear the sandals from your wedding,' Darcie said, 'but they're too small now.'

'We found a pair that fit in the bags from Mrs Kingston's granddaughters,' Phoebe said. 'They look brand new.'

When Darcie and Phoebe had moved in with us, Jeanette Kingston's daughter had kindly donated several binbags and boxes full of pre-loved clothes and toys from her own two daughters who were two and four years older than Darcie. Some items had fit at the time and others had been put aside for growing into, so it was great that there'd been a pair of sandals in there.

'We have good news,' Phoebe said. 'Mr Huggins has given special permission to video the nativity for you. We have to sign something to say it won't be uploaded onto the socials.'

'That's brilliant.' The nativity was scheduled for a week on Thursday and I'd just have hit thirty-six weeks at that point, so it was unlikely I'd be induced by then. I'd hoped that, because the head teacher knew me from school visits and I had DBS clearance, they'd make an exception to the no-video rule. I really didn't want to miss Darcie in a lead role.

The thirty minutes with them was up way too soon.

'Say goodbye, Darcie,' Phoebe said, glancing down the ward. 'Grandpa Terry and Fizz have just arrived, and Terry will need to sit down.'

'I'll come back one evening during the week,' Phoebe said when Darcie had hugged me. 'I'll see what works best with Josh and let you know.'

'Can I come?' Darcie asked.

'It'll be too late for you, but we'll come back together next weekend.'

As they left, I watched Terry shuffling towards us, clinging onto

Fizz's arm, and my stomach turned over. Terry had never looked his age but that second bout of flu had definitely taken its toll. Seeing him up and about now, he looked more like a man in his nineties than his early eighties. I busied myself straightening the covers, feeling too sad to watch him struggling.

Fizz helped settle him into the chair beside her.

'Great to see you both,' I declared a little too brightly.

'Aw, lass, I'm sorry you're stuck in 'ere,' Terry said, his voice quiet and raspy.

He started coughing and Fizz poured him a cup of water from the jug on my overbed trolley. His hands shook as he sipped it and I glanced at Fizz, who clamped her lips together and slowly shook her head. She was clearly worried too and unsure how to address it.

'It's not so bad,' I said, focusing my attention back on Terry. 'Phoebe and Darcie have given me loads of lovely presents to keep me occupied. Thank you both for contributing.'

'Our pleasure,' Fizz said. 'So how are you feeling?'

Fizz and I tried to keep Terry involved in our small talk about the weather, the rescue centre and hospital life, but he appeared confused and distant. Nobody mentioned the elephant in the room, but we couldn't ignore its presence. Terry wasn't a well man at all. His skin was grey, his eyes watery and pale, and he seemed to be struggling to keep his eyes open.

After fifteen long minutes, he struggled to his feet. 'I need the little boys' room.'

'Do you want my arm?' Fizz asked, but he waved his hand in response and shuffled slowly down the ward.

I watched him, my heart in my mouth, terrified that he might fall at any moment.

'How was he coming over?' I asked Fizz.

'He slept most of the way. I'm worried.'

'Me too. How did the house look?'

'I didn't go in, but I will do when I drop him home.'

'He needs to see a doctor.'

She sighed deeply. 'I said that too, but he's adamant he's all right.'

'He's not all right. Could you hear that rattle in his chest when he was coughing?'

Five minutes passed and Terry hadn't returned. Six. Then seven.

I craned my neck to look towards the nurses' station. There were two bathrooms there and I presumed Terry would have used one of those as the public toilets were near reception and that was quite a trek which I couldn't imagine he'd have attempted on his own.

'We need to look for him,' Fizz said, reading my thoughts.

I lowered my legs off the bed, eased my feet into my wide mule slippers and shuffled down the ward beside Fizz.

One of the midwives at the nurses' station – Emma – looked up from the computer but her smile slipped. 'Everything all right?'

'My visitor went to the toilet and hasn't returned,' I said, feeling sick. 'He doesn't look well, and we're worried about him.'

Emma looked towards Fizz. 'Is it the elderly man who came in with you?'

'Yes.'

'I saw him go into that bathroom...' she pointed to the nearest one, '... and I haven't noticed him coming out.'

We followed her to the bathroom door, which was showing 'engaged'.

'What's his name?'

'Terry,' I said.

Emma knocked on the door and we all listened for a moment. Silence.

She knocked again. 'Terry? Are you in there?'

No response.

She knocked even louder. 'Terry, if you're in there or if anyone else is in there, please speak now as we're coming in.'

She gave it a few moments then inserted something into the lock and pushed open the door.

I clapped my hand over my mouth. Terry was lying motionless on the bathroom floor, a trickle of blood running down his forehead.

Emma shouted for a colleague and Fizz gently pulled me to one side as a team of medical professionals surrounded the bathroom. I looked on helplessly, clinging onto Fizz, terrified we'd lost him.

'He's breathing but his pulse is weak,' Emma told us.

I gulped back my fear and tried to remain calm as he was lifted onto a stretcher and rushed out of the room.

'Sit down, Samantha.' Emma eased me into a chair behind the nurses' station.

'Sip this.' A cup of water was pressed into my hand, and I took a few sips of the cool liquid.

'What happened?' I asked.

'We don't know yet,' Emma said, gently.

'The blood?'

'There was blood on the side of the bath too, so it's likely he hit his head on there as he fell. Can you give me some details so I can pass them on?'

I gave her Terry's full name, address, date of birth and told her about his recent two bouts of flu.

'Do you know if he has any pre-existing health conditions?'

'Nothing that I'm aware of, but that doesn't mean he hasn't. He doesn't like making a fuss.'

'Let me pass on these details,' Emma said, 'and can I suggest you return to your bed and get some rest, Samantha? Visiting time is over, but your friend is welcome to stay with you until we have news about Terry.'

'Thanks, Emma.'

Feeling a little unsteady on my feet after the ordeal, I slipped my arm through Fizz's as we returned to my bed.

'I shouldn't have brought him,' she said, her voice shaky as she sank down onto the chair.

'You know he'd have gone through with his threat if you hadn't and, let's face it, he couldn't have been in a better place to collapse than hospital.'

'I suppose. Do you think it's the flu again?'

'It could be. Or it could be that, in his weakened state, he's picked up pneumonia. We'll find out soon enough.'

Feeling shivery, I snuggled down under the covers, then suddenly sat up again.

'I'd better let Josh know. He'll need to collect Wilbur.'

Josh was on duty in the rescue centre, but his phone went to voicemail so presumably he was mid-treatment or speaking to someone. He could even have been called out to a rescue. I left him a message and sent him a text too, reminding him where I kept Terry's key.

Fizz looked broken, hunched down in the chair, her fluffy teal jumper pulled up over her chin. I wanted to assure her that everything would be all right and that Terry would make a full recovery after proper treatment, but I had a horrible feeling I'd be lying. I kept thinking about that rattle on his chest when he'd coughed earlier. Pneumonia could be mild and it could be fought off, but Terry's immune system would be so low from the flu and it wouldn't surprise me if there was an underlying health condition he'd never mentioned.

I rolled onto my side and curved my pregnancy pillow

round me.

'Are you okay?' I asked Fizz.

'I'm not sure. That was tough to see.'

'I know. When it's someone you know and love, it hits hard. All we can do is wait.'

'You look shattered,' she said.

'I feel it.'

'Then have a nap. I'll be fine here. I've got my phone.'

I pointed to the holdall Phoebe had brought. 'There's some books and puzzles in that bag if you want anything.'

I hugged my pillow and soon drifted off.

* * *

'I thought we were never going to rouse you,' Fizz said when I opened my eyes to see who was nudging me.

'How long have I been asleep?'

'A couple of hours.'

I rubbed my sleepy eyes. 'How's Terry?'

'He has pneumonia,' Emma said. I hadn't noticed her standing at the foot of the bed.

'I thought he might have. How bad is it?'

'He's had a chest X-ray and it's developed into pleurisy.'

Fizz gasped at the same time as I whispered, 'No!' Animals could contract pleurisy so I knew she knew what it was – when the thin linings between the lungs and ribcage become inflamed – and how dangerous it could be if not treated in time.

'They've started him on antibiotics and anti-inflammatories,' Emma continued. 'We won't know the full details until his blood-work comes back. Were you aware he has diabetes?'

'No. Can we see him?'

'He's asleep at the moment but they'll let us know when he's awake again and you can visit him then. He's given us permission to talk to you about his condition and treatment. Are you related?'

'Not genetically, but he's like family to us.'

Emma took my blood pressure – still high – and confirmed that Fizz could stay with me until Terry woke up, as long as we weren't disturbing the other patients.

'I know she said they need the bloods back to make a full assessment,' Fizz said when Emma was out of earshot, 'but pleurisy's bad, isn't it?'

'It can be.'

'Could he die?'

'I hope not, but it's a possibility.'

39

FIZZ

I knew I could rely on Sam to be honest with me, although I already knew the answer to that question before she answered it. My maternal grandparents were both alive and well, but my paternal grandparents were gone. I didn't remember Grandma Kinsella as she'd died when I was four, but I'd been eleven when Granddad Kinsella fell ill. He'd had a cough that he'd been unable to shake off for months, but he wouldn't go and see a doctor 'just for a cough'. He finally conceded to an appointment when he started coughing up blood. By then it was too late. The colour of Terry's skin earlier had reminded me of the last time I'd seen Granddad. 'Death warmed up,' I'd heard Dad say to Mum and I remembered thinking what a strange saying that was because he looked anything but warm. I understood what it meant now, and I feared for what that meant for Terry.

Sam drifted off to sleep again and I fished one of the paperbacks out of her holdall. After reading the same page over and over and still not registering the name of the main character, I returned the book to the bag and pulled out my phone. There was a WhatsApp message for me:

✉ From Phoebe
Josh has just arrived home with Wilbur. He
couldn't give details cos I'm with Darcie but he
says Terry isn't well. What's happened?

✉ To Phoebe
He looked really ill and he collapsed in the
toilets. Pneumonia has developed into pleurisy
which is bad although we won't know how bad
until his bloods come back. Sam's asleep —
drained by it all — and we're waiting for Terry
to wake up again so we can see him. The midwife
has said I can stay with Sam until then. Can you
check on Jinks & give him his tea? x

✉ From Phoebe
That's awful! No wonder Josh looked so worried.
We'll sort Jinks out. Are you OK? x

I replied with three crying emojis to which Phoebe responded with a broken heart and a kiss.

I laid my phone on the bedside cabinet and smiled at the photo of the three cats on Thomas's bench. Sam was sleeping peacefully, her nose occasionally twitching, and I couldn't help thinking about the circle of life. Here she was about to bring a new life into the world and, in another part of the hospital, Terry might be about to leave us. I really hoped it wasn't too late for him and he still had several years in him yet and, if we weren't blessed with that much time, that he'd be able to see Sam and Josh's baby. He was looking forward to the birth nearly as much as they were. It would be cruel if he didn't get to hold that little baby in his arms.

* * *

It was early evening when we were told that Terry was awake and we could visit. Sam had already had her evening meal and I'd nibbled my way through half a baguette from the shop in the lobby.

'I wonder if he'll be awake for long,' I said to Sam as we took the lift down one floor.

'Probably not.'

We found Terry's ward and checked in with the staff at the nurses' station. He was in the first bed on the left, wearing a hospital gown and attached to a drip. His skin was so pale against the white bedding, it appeared almost translucent. His eyes were closed but they flickered open as we approached.

'You gave us a scare earlier, Terry,' Sam said as she sat down beside his bed.

'Sorry, lass. Didn't mean to.'

'How are you feeling?' I asked.

'Like a pincushion. All this fuss over nowt.'

Sam placed her hand over his drip-free one. 'It's not fuss. It's about trying to make you better.'

'Wilbur?'

'Josh has taken him to Hedgehog Hollow. He's been for a long walk with Phoebe and Darcie and he's doing well. Josh is on his way here with an overnight bag for you. You'll be able to put a fresh pair of pyjamas on instead of that gown.'

'That'll be grand.'

'If there's anything else you need, I can bring it in tomorrow,' I offered.

'I'll be goin' home tomorrow.'

Sam and I exchanged surprised glances.

'They've told you that?' she asked.

'No, but they can't keep me 'ere when I don't wanna be 'ere.'

Sam squeezed his hand. 'I understand that. I don't want to be here either, but sometimes we have to accept that hospital's the best place for us. I wish you weren't here because I wish you weren't poorly but, seeing as we're both in hospital at the same time, we can keep each other company.'

'I want to die in me own bed.'

'Who said anything about dying?' Sam somehow managed to sound jovial when her heart, like mine, had to be breaking. I couldn't speak for the lump in my throat and my eyes were burning with the effort of keeping my tears at bay.

'I'm not long for this world,' Terry murmured. 'I can 'ear Gwendoline callin' me.'

He looked away towards the window at the end of ward, a gentle smile on his lips, as though he could see her ghost. The tears I'd tried to hold back spilled down my cheeks and I heard a little whimper beside me and saw Sam wiping at hers.

Terry's breathing was laboured. Was that the pleurisy or was there something else he wasn't telling us? Grandma Dodds – my mum's mum – believed that older people instinctively knew the difference between being ill and dying. She'd nursed her mother-in-law through illness, sitting up with her every night for several weeks. One night, her mother-in-law insisted that Granddad – her own son – sat with her to give Grandma a break. Grandma was exhausted so didn't debate it and when she kissed my great-grandmother goodnight, the response was, 'Goodbye and thank you for everything.' She passed away peacefully in the early hours with her son by her side and Grandma was convinced she'd known it was the end and wanted to be with her own flesh and blood for that final night.

'Tell us more about Gwendoline,' Sam said softly.

There was a pause before Terry looked back at us both.

'She were an angel. Everyone loved 'er. She'd walk into a room and light it with 'er smile and she were so kind...'

* * *

Sam, Josh and I sat in the deserted hospital lobby a couple of hours later with hot chocolates from the vending machine, feeling the need for something sweet after the news we'd just heard. Lung cancer. They were taking Terry for a CT scan tomorrow which would give them more details than the X-ray could, but the prognosis wasn't good. They couldn't consider radiotherapy or chemotherapy because of the pneumonia and pleurisy and, even if they could have, Terry had vehemently declared that he wasn't interested in treatment.

'Do you think he's serious about wanting to die at home?' I asked eventually.

It was clear from the conversation we'd had with one of the nurses earlier that, even if Terry had consented to treatment, it would buy him time rather than cure him.

'Yes.' Sam released a deep, shaky breath. 'We'll have to wait for the results of his CT scan tomorrow so we know where we are with the cancer, but he won't be forced to stay in hospital against his will. If we can find a way to manage his pain at home, we will. It depends how long he has left.'

Even though she didn't spell it out, I knew she was fearful we were talking weeks or even days and she'd therefore be unable to take on the caring role she'd otherwise have willingly stepped into.

'I'll help,' I said. 'If he goes home while you're still here, I'll do whatever I can to support.'

Sam nodded, tears clouding her eyes. It had been an emotional afternoon for us all and I wasn't surprised she couldn't speak.

'We'll work something out with the rescue centre,' Josh said.

'I'll bring some locums into the practice if we need to. Someone who cares about Terry will be with him all the time.' His voice cracked and I saw tears glistening in his eyes too.

He pushed his chair back and held out his hands to help Sam to her feet. 'We'd better get you back to your bed before they send out a search party.'

'Will you be okay driving home?' Sam asked me.

'Yeah, I'll be fine.'

'Text me when you get there.'

'Yes, Mum,' I joked, bringing a flicker of a smile to her lips.

I hugged them both goodbye and dropped our empty cups in the recycling before stepping out into the cold night air. The temperature had massively dropped and the ground glistened with frost. Hopefully the gritters had been out or it was going to be a very slow drive home. Although, even if they had been out, it was going to feel like a long, slow drive knowing what I now knew.

40

SAMANTHA

December had arrived and there was a feeling of excitement on my ward in anticipation of Christmas. A tinsel-strewn artificial tree stood by the nurses' station and there were garlands hanging from the walls. It was so pretty but I'd never felt less festive, fearful that we'd be spending Christmas Day without a wonderful man.

I'd settled into a routine of going down to see Terry around mid-morning, even though every visit broke my heart. Sometimes he lay staring into space, barely noticing my presence. Other times he spoke to me, but I wasn't convinced he knew who I was. He struggled to catch his breath and his words were mumbled. The parts I caught were always the same – how excited he was about seeing Gwendoline again that night and how he'd decided to tell her he loved her. It seemed his mind had taken him back to a moment in the past where that had been his intention. I knew his love was unrequited, but I didn't know whether he'd discovered that by telling Gwendoline how he felt, by gut feeling, or by Thomas arriving on the scene.

There was no more talk about going home and he didn't even ask after Wilbur, which reinforced my belief that his mind was elsewhere. Every day, I held his hand and told him I loved him. On Monday, he'd smiled at me and said, 'I love you too, my Snow White.' In that moment, he clearly believed I was Gwendoline, and I wasn't going to correct him.

He'd had other visitors – Josh, Fizz and Phoebe, Lauren and Connie, and Jeanette Kingston – but they all reported the same: mumbled conversations about Gwendoline.

Last night, I'm not sure what made me do it, but I felt compelled to visit him again. He was quieter, more thoughtful, staring at a spot on the ceiling.

'I'm tired,' he whispered.

'I know you are,' I said, drawing his cold hand to my lips so I could gently kiss it. 'It's been a tough few months.'

'I've 'ad a good life. Wouldn't change a thing. I couldn't 'ave made 'er 'appy like he did.'

'Thomas?'

'Aye. He were a gem. Sparkled together, they did, like you and Josh.'

I sat up straighter. He knew who I was!

'I was very lucky.'

'You 'ad some help.' He looked up to the ceiling. 'They watch over you, you know.'

I pushed down the lump in my throat and tried to keep my voice steady. 'I know they do, Terry. I feel them in the meadow where I scattered Thomas's ashes and where he scattered Gwendoline's.'

'Scatter mine there too. Thomas says it's all right. Will you do that for me?'

'Terry, don't talk like that.'

'Promise.'

'I promise, but *you* have to promise me to try to get better. I need you to meet your godchild.' I hadn't discussed it with Josh, but I wanted to give Terry something to live for.

'Godchild? That's grand, that is.'

'So you'll stick around?' I asked, desperation in my voice.

'I can't, lass. It's time.'

He looked up at the ceiling once more and I imagined him seeing Thomas and Gwendoline beckoning to him.

'I thought she were the best thing in my life,' he murmured before focusing his eyes back on me, 'but it were you. Thank you, Sammie. You made it all worthwhile.'

He closed his eyes and I thought for a moment that I'd lost him. Tears streamed down my cheeks and soaked into my nightie, but his breathing remained slow and steady. He was still with us. For now.

* * *

On Friday morning, I awoke shortly before 6 a.m. with a sense of dread in my gut. I immediately checked my phone to see whether there were any messages from Josh, who was also named as Terry's next of kin.

Pulling on my dressing gown, I shuffled to the nurses' station. Emma was on the night shift and looked up from her coffee and paperwork.

'You're up early, Samantha. Everything all right?'

'I'm not sure. I've got this horrible feeling. Has there been any news about Terry?'

'Not that I've heard. Why don't you get yourself back to bed, I'll finish this – ten minutes at the most – and I'll phone down to his ward?'

'That'd be great. Thank you.'

I'd only just settled back into bed when Emma walked towards me, the grave expression on her face confirming my worst fears.

'They've just rung. I'm so sorry. Terry passed away about an hour ago.'

I covered my face with my hands and dipped my head to my chest. I heard the swish of the curtains being pulled round the bed.

'They told me his heart failed,' Emma said, her voice soft and gentle, 'but he'd signed a DNR, so they couldn't do anything.'

Terry had asked to sign a DNR – do not resuscitate order – on the day he was admitted and I'd seen no point in trying to talk him out of it. As a former nurse, I was all about the patient's choices, even though they didn't always align with what friends or family might hope for.

I nodded to indicate that I'd heard what Emma said.

'I should have been with him,' I whispered.

She gently touched my arm. 'You weren't to know when it would happen and do you know what I believe? There's lots of talk about being with a dying loved one at the end and I understand why that feels right for some people, but I personally believe there are others who'd prefer not to put us through that pain, so they slip away quietly when we're least expecting it.'

I raised my head and studied her sympathetic expression through my tears.

'What would Terry have wanted for you?' she asked gently.

'To spare me.'

'And you've seen him every day since he was admitted, haven't you? I'm sure that meant the world to him. I'll leave you to your thoughts. I'm sorry again for your loss.'

My loss, but Gwendoline and Thomas's gain. I wasn't a religious person, but I genuinely believed that death wasn't the end and that we were reunited in some way with those we'd loved and lost.

'Look after him,' I whispered.

I reached for the soft unicorn which Darcie had given me and lay back down on my bed, pressed against my pregnancy pillow, hugging it tightly.

* * *

As soon as the breakfast service began and there was enough hustle and bustle on the ward for me not to be disturbing anyone, I FaceTimed Josh. He'd be at the practice already, but I wanted to catch him before any patients arrived.

'I've got bad news,' I said after we'd exchanged greetings. My voice cracked and the tears flowed once more. 'It's Terry.'

'Oh, no! He hasn't!'

'Earlier this morning. Heart failure.'

Josh gulped and blinked a few times, clearly battling with trying to be strong for me while devastated himself for our loss.

'Oh, Sammie, I wish I could be there with you.'

'I'm okay. Well, I'm not, but it is what it is. I can't believe he's gone.'

'Do you know what time he died?'

'About five. Why?'

'I think Wilbur knew. He was really restless around five. I could hear him pacing downstairs so I went to check on him. He was in the hallway and suddenly he stopped pacing, held out his paw and bowed his head before settling down on the floor. It was the strangest thing.'

'Like Terry came to say goodbye,' I whispered, picturing the scene. 'Where is he now?'

'Right here. I brought him to work with me because he seemed listless this morning and I wanted to keep an eye on him.'

'Give him a hug from me. He's had a tough few weeks too.'

Josh moved the phone so I could see Wilbur laid by his feet, his head resting on his paws. My heart broke for him losing his beloved master. We all loved him at Hedgehog Hollow, but it wasn't the same as the bond he'd shared with Terry. How could you tell a dog that he'd never see his owner again?

'I'd better let you go,' I said when Josh's face appeared on the screen once more. 'I need to let Fizz know. I wish I could do it face to face.'

'She'll understand and I'll make sure she's all right tonight. I'll tell your dad. Anyone else you want me to contact?'

We agreed that it made sense for me to tell everyone else because Josh had work to do but for him to sort out the funeral arrangements, as it would be harder for me to do that from hospital.

Today was going to be a long and difficult one. Terry had kept himself to himself before we met him, only regularly spending time with his sister until she died, but he'd touched so many hearts over the last couple of years. I hoped I'd be able to attend his funeral to pay my final respects, but I feared it wouldn't be possible. At least I'd had the opportunity to tell him how much he meant to me this week. I'd be forever grateful for that.

41

FIZZ

It was Darcie's nativity play six days after Terry died. With Sam unable to attend in person, Darcie wanted me to join Phoebe and Josh in the audience.

Perched on a small, rock-hard chair in the school hall among the buzz of chatter from excited parents and grandparents, I felt festive for the first time since the Christmas Fair nearly three weeks ago. An enormous Christmas tree at one side of the stage was strewn with colourful paper chains and hand-crafted decorations, there were more paperchains draped across three of the walls and the other wall was devoted to several Christmassy scenes, the different skill levels in each giving a clue as to which year groups might have attempted them.

I hadn't done any Christmas shopping yet and there was nothing up in Meadow View to suggest Christmas was two and a half weeks away, although the farmhouse hadn't been decorated either. Josh had planned to put the tree up with Phoebe and Darcie last Saturday, but it hadn't felt appropriate with losing Terry the day before. He'd been conscious of spoiling the magic of Christmas for Darcie so had asked if they wanted to do it on

Sunday instead, but Darcie suggested this evening after her nativity play and had asked me to help. I felt honoured to be included.

'I can't believe how nervous I am,' Phoebe whispered as the music stopped and the hall lights dimmed.

'Me too,' I whispered back. But my nerves weren't just for Darcie. Being in such close proximity to Phoebe had my heart racing. Every so often, her leg brushed against mine, making the butterflies soar. Her left hand was resting on her thigh, right beside mine, and it felt like it would be the most natural thing in the world to entwine my fingers with hers. I sat on my hands and had to keep reminding myself to focus on the play.

There'd never been any doubt that Darcie would steal the show. She delivered every line confidently and clearly with a huge smile on her face throughout. I felt like a proud parent myself, so Phoebe had to be bursting with pride.

* * *

Darcie was buzzing from her performance and her excitement was infectious as we decorated the Christmas tree back at the farmhouse. Even Wilbur got caught up in it and it was so good to see him running round the lounge with Darcie, chasing a felt bauble, showing some enthusiasm for the first time since Terry's death.

Phoebe streamed a Christmas playlist on her phone and we sang along to an eclectic mix of Christmas songs from the past fifty years. There were playful arguments over bauble placement and a debate as to whether tinsel was tacky and should have forever remained in the eighties. Darcie won that one, having been the one to talk Josh into buying the stuff in the first place.

'It's certainly colourful,' I said, stepping back to see the finished tree.

'It looks like an explosion in a fireworks factory,' Phoebe said, laughing.

Darcie did a pirouette in front of it. 'Fireworks are pretty and so's the tree. Do you think Samantha will like it, Josh?'

We all turned to look at him expectantly and my heart went out to him as tears sparkled in his eyes. This must be so hard for him, preparing for such a special time of the year without Sam by his side, knowing how much she loved Christmas.

He gulped and cleared his throat. 'She's going to love it. Why don't you take a video of it and we can send it to her with your nativity play? Then she can feel like she's here with us.'

His voice cracked and Darcie hurled herself at him, wrapping her arms round his waist. If anyone needed a hug at that moment, it was Josh, and Darcie had obviously sensed that. Phoebe and I exchanged *aww* looks and those butterflies took flight once more.

'Are you finished with these boxes now?' Josh asked a little later.

Phoebe's gaze swept round the room. 'I don't think there's room for anything else, so I'd say yes.'

'One last look!' Darcie rummaged in the boxes of decorations, mumbling to herself as she moved various items aside. She stopped and pulled something out.

'Ooh! This is so cute!'

We both looked at the item in her hand – soft velour mistletoe with smiling faces and feet on the two berries.

'What is it?' she asked.

'Mistletoe,' Phoebe said. 'You hold it over someone's head and give them a kiss.'

Darcie immediately ran up to Josh and held it over him. He kissed her on the cheek and she giggled, running up to Phoebe and me for the same.

'Now you!' she announced, holding it over Josh's head so that Phoebe and I could kiss him on the cheek.

She gave me a mischievous look and I knew what was coming next. My heart pounded as she held the soft decoration over my head.

'Phoebe, you need to kiss Fizz now.'

The music seemed to soften and the world slow down as Phoebe's eyes met mine. My heart pounded as she moved closer. I could hear her breathing, smell her aqua perfume blended with the fruity smell of her shampoo, feel her gentle touch on my arms.

Time seemed to stop as her lips touched the lower part of my cheek, brushing so close to the side of my mouth. Soft. Lingering. Leaving me longing for more.

She stepped away, her twinkling eyes still fixed on mine and in that one kiss and one look, I felt certain that Darcie was right and Phoebe did feel the same way as me.

As I settled down to sleep later that evening, I replayed that kiss and that look over and over. The ball was in my court but, with so much going on right now, I didn't want to rush it and ruin it. If... when... Phoebe and I kissed properly for the first time, it would be special and memorable.

42

SAMANTHA

On the Wednesday after Darcie's star turn in the nativity, which I'd watched with tears in my eyes, I reached the key milestone of thirty-seven weeks in my pregnancy – the point beyond which Bublet would no longer be considered premature – but it was also the day we said our final goodbye to Terry. Every moment of elation about Bublet was swept aside by a wave of sadness about Terry.

Unbeknown to us, Terry had appointed Jeanette Kingston as the executor of his will during his first bout of flu and had shared his wishes with her for his funeral, most of which were typical Terry: no fuss, no hymns or prayers, cremation anywhere convenient to us, donations in lieu of flowers to the rescue centre, and no black clothes. I was particularly touched by his request that we wear wildflowers to honour Thomas and Gwendoline.

I'd decided to go full-out on the wildflower theme and had ordered a pink-blush maternity dress online covered in tiny flowers. It was very summery, so I'd accompanied it with a belted cardigan.

'You look beautiful,' Josh said when he collected me from the ward.

'I'm not sure about the wellies,' I said, rolling my eyes at him.

'They've got wildflowers on them. Terry would love them.'

I smiled gratefully. 'This is true.'

Because Terry hadn't been bothered about venue, Josh had booked Whitsborough Bay crematorium due to its location right by the hospital. It meant most of the mourners needed to travel, but nobody objected when that meant that I could attend.

My blood pressure had remained high in my three weeks at hospital so far, there was still protein in my urine and inducing labour was a strong possibility, especially now that we'd reached thirty-seven weeks. I'd been given permission to attend the funeral but needed to return to the hospital after the service rather than continuing to the pub. I'd get my chance to fully celebrate Terry's life with our friends and family when we scattered his ashes in the meadow at Hedgehog Hollow.

Lauren and Chloe had made wildflower corsages for everyone, and Josh had mine in his jeep.

'It's beautiful,' I said as I pinned it to my cardigan.

'Ready?' he asked, starting the engine.

'As I'll ever be.'

Terry had no family, but he'd been adopted by mine and Josh's, and it warmed my heart to see all our relatives and friends who'd grown to know and love Terry over the past few years mingling outside the crematorium, alongside Jeanette Kingston and several other villagers who'd befriended him.

The frontage was beautiful. A fountain sprayed water into a pond full of goldfish which was surrounded by tubs of shrubs. There were stone and wooden benches separated by raised flower beds and trees, giving privacy to attendees who needed it.

I was touched to see all the women wearing floral clothes and many of the men sporting floral ties. Rosemary's guide dog, Trixie, had a corsage attached to her harness. Wilbur – for whom Josh had secured special permission to attend – wore a floral bandana round his neck.

'We should have looked for a floral tie for you,' I said to Josh.

He whipped off his suit jacket, revealing the back of his waistcoat covered in embroidered daisies.

'Aw, you're going to set me off again.'

Josh pulled his jacket back on and drew me into a hug. 'You've got this.'

I'd wanted to say a few words to pay tribute to Terry, but I was concerned I wouldn't be able to get through it, especially when my emotions were even more heightened than usual because of Bublet. My consultant had strongly advised against it, not wanting me to get worked up and unnecessarily escalate my already high blood pressure. There was no way I was going to put myself or Bublet at risk, but Josh offered to read an eulogy I'd written about how loved Terry had been and his devotion to all animals.

The funeral celebrant invited us to move inside and take our seats. The front row had been reserved for Josh, me, Phoebe, Fizz and Wilbur. Although Phoebe had kept Darcie informed about Terry's illness and told her when he'd died, she'd decided not to take her out of school to attend the funeral so close to Christmas. She'd involve her in the scattering of his ashes instead.

One of the hardest parts of funerals for me was looking at the coffin, knowing that the body of someone I loved was inside and I'd never see them again. I reluctantly looked towards Terry's, a lump in my throat. He'd wanted to be as environmentally friendly as possible and had chosen a seagrass coffin, which somehow looked less intimidating than the usual wooden style.

'Good morning, everyone,' the celebrant announced, looking round the room. 'We have been blessed with beautiful blue skies on this December day as we celebrate the life of Terrence Blake Shepherd, known to you as Terry, although I do appreciate that the skies may feel dark and grey as we say goodbye to someone we love...'

* * *

It had been a beautiful service and Josh was amazing reading out my eulogy.

'How are you holding up, my dear?' Rosemary asked when we moved outside.

'I've been better. You?'

'He was a good friend and, even though our time together was short, I feel blessed to have met him.'

'It's a good turnout,' Celia said. 'Terry would have been stunned to see so many.'

'I really hope he realised how much he was loved,' I said, the words catching in my throat.

Rosemary slipped her hand through my arm. 'Oh, my dear, he certainly did. Especially by you and Josh.'

'And it was reciprocal,' Celia added, such warmth to her tone. 'He once told us that the best day of his life was the day Wilbur found that hedgehog tangled in the goalpost netting because that was the day he met you.'

'Arwen,' I said, remembering it well. 'She was the first of many that Wilbur the hedgehog sniffer and Terry rescued.'

Rosemary patted my arm. 'He rescued hedgehogs, but you rescued him. I do believe rescuing the lonely might be one of your special talents. Come along, Celia, I'm parched so let's get to this pub and hope they'll make an old lady a nice cup of tea.'

'We'll look forward to seeing you soon with that new baby of yours,' Celia said, giving me a hug. 'Take care.'

I wished I could go with them, but I actually felt drained and ready to return to the hospital. Hopefully there'd be news today from my consultant. Perhaps in the week we said goodbye to Terry, we'd say hello to Bublet.

43

SAMANTHA

Over the days following Terry's funeral, my blood pressure continued to rise and every time my consultant, Lynne, did her rounds, there were conversations about inducing labour but no firm date for doing so.

After breakfast on Sunday morning, Lynne joined Emma as she took my blood pressure.

'I'm not happy with it,' Lynne said, shaking her head at the readings. 'It's time to induce. Are you ready to meet your baby?'

My heart soared. 'Definitely.' Bublet gave me a resounding kick and I placed my hand on my stomach, smiling. 'And I think they're ready to meet me too.'

Now that we'd passed the thirty-seven-week mark, my anxiety about being induced early had dissipated. If the professionals were happy with Bublet's development, I was happy to go for it.

Half an hour later, I'd packed up my belongings and was settled into a smaller ward with four beds, although they were all empty. A midwife who I hadn't met before explained that they'd insert a pessary, which should bring on contractions.

'I'd recommend you get as much rest as possible,' she said. 'It could take up to twenty-four hours for the pessary to take effect and, if it doesn't, you might need a second one.'

When she'd gone, I decided to take advantage of the ward being empty and FaceTimed Josh to explain what was happening.

'Should I come over?' he asked.

'From what I've been told, it's not a speedy process. I'd suggest you keep your phone handy, but I don't think anything's going to happen until tonight at the earliest and probably more likely tomorrow.'

'How are you feeling?'

'A bit nervous but excited too. It's weird being in an empty ward but I don't imagine it'll stay this way for long.'

'Do you think you'll manage to get some sleep?'

I shrugged. 'I'm going to try while there's nobody here. Could be a long night tonight.'

'Okay. Let me know if anything changes, otherwise take care and I'll see you after work tonight and bring the baby bag and car seat with me. I love you.'

'I love you too.'

We blew each other kisses then I disconnected the call. This was it! Three weeks of constant monitoring while being pretty much confined to a hospital bed was drawing to an end and, all being well, I'd be taking home our baby in the next couple of days for their first Christmas. I couldn't wait to meet them. The past couple of months had been full of anguish and sadness and this baby would bring joy and happiness when we needed it more than ever.

I'd had several more scans while in hospital and I'd been asked if I wanted to know the sex of the baby. I'd said no, so the sonographer had taken care not to reveal anything on the screen which could give it away. It felt a little weird knowing that they knew and

I didn't, but I'd gone this far without knowing so I wasn't going to cave at the last moment.

* * *

When Josh arrived that evening, there was no sign of labour starting. Frustratingly, two other expectant mothers had joined me and things had moved much faster for them and they'd already both been transferred to the delivery suite.

I'd been online, looking at the process of being induced, and there was something called a membrane or cervical sweep which could induce labour. When one of the midwives came in to do another check on my blood pressure, I asked her about that, but she shook her head.

'The delivery suite is full so it's a good thing that you're not progressing just yet. Your blood pressure has gone down a little, so we'll be keeping you here and we'll give you another pessary tomorrow and possibly the sweep then.'

She glanced at Josh. 'Are you Dad? You're welcome to stay here, but we can't offer you a bed. You might want to go home and get some valuable rest and come back tomorrow. Mum's going to need your support and you can't give it if you're exhausted.'

With a knowing raise of her eyebrows, she left the room.

'I think I just got told off,' Josh said, biting his lip.

'I think you just did.'

'I'd rather not drive back to Hedgehog Hollow and get a call in the early hours. Do you think your Auntie Louise and Uncle Simon would let me stay at theirs?'

'Only one way to find out.' I picked up my phone.

* * *

I needed a second pessary but that did the trick and I was taken to the delivery suite mid-afternoon the following day. A midwife made a cervical sweep to break my waters and the anaesthetist gave me an epidural. All credit to women who wanted a natural birth, but I didn't do pain. Because the epidural meant I couldn't feel the contractions, a belt was placed round my abdomen and a clip attached to Bublet's head to constantly monitor the contractions and the baby's heart rate.

Josh sat beside my bed while a team of midwives and consultants bustled in and out, making regular checks and asking questions. The hours passed and nothing seemed to be happening, although I knew that was normal and Hannah's speedy delivery of Mason had been unusual.

By late evening, I was feeling sleepy.

'Are you going to tell me what you think we're having?' Josh asked, stroking my hair back from my face.

'No way. Not after keeping it quiet all these months. You'll find out soon. Or I hope you will. Hurry up, Bublet.'

A few minutes later, I started shaking.

'I'm so cold,' I whispered to Josh, goose bumps covering my arms.

Ally, the midwife who was leading the birth, appeared by my side and checked my temperature. 'Temperature's fine. We'll grab you another blanket.'

It didn't do the trick. I was still shaking.

'I feel sick,' I said, a wave of nausea taking hold.

Ally was back with a container and Josh held my hair back as I vomited.

'Looks like we're close,' another midwife said, looking up from the bottom of the bed. 'We'll just clean you up.'

I didn't want to know why they needed to clean me up.

Vomiting and bowel movements were the less-discussed aspects of giving birth.

'This is so undignified,' I said, looking helplessly at Josh.

'It's the miracle of birth,' he responded, smiling gently. 'I'm so proud of you and I love you so much.'

'We're fully dilated...' called Ally. 'Are you ready, Mum and Dad?'

'Nearly there!' she said a little later. 'One last big push!'

Thanks to my epidural, I could barely feel a thing, but I willed my muscles to push down.

'Woah!' Josh cried as a red bundle shot across the bed, only just caught by one of the midwives.

There was a flurry of activity at the foot of the bed and nobody spoke.

'What's happening?' I asked, panic enveloping me.

'The clip's tangled in his hair,' said Ally. 'Just need to untangle it. Nothing to worry about.'

'It's a boy!' I whispered to Josh, and he smiled tenderly and kissed my hand.

Ally carried him to a side table but my elation at the safe arrival of our baby was cut short. I watched in horror as she scooped a finger round his mouth and rubbed a towel over his head. Another midwife ran a towel over his tiny body.

'Is he all right?' I cried.

'He's a bit blue. Bear with us.'

'Blue,' Josh whispered, clutching onto my hand.

I held my breath. After more than three weeks in hospital being so closely monitored, losing our baby boy could *not* be the outcome. That would be too cruel.

'Ally?' Josh asked. Only one word, but it was filled with panic.

Another colleague joined them and there was lots of mumbling as they worked on our baby.

'Josh,' I whispered. 'Is he...?' A sob came out instead of that last word.

Josh just stared at me, eyes wide, face ashen.

'Waaahhhh!'

I've never heard such a beautiful sound. I sank back against the pillows, taking deep, comforting breaths. Beside me, Josh wiped his tears away.

'That's better,' Ally said, turning and smiling at us. 'He just wanted to make his entrance a little more dramatic. Let me weigh him, then you can have cuddles. Do you have a name for him?'

Josh and I looked at each other and smiled.

'Thomas,' we said together. There really could have been no other name for a boy.

'Aw, that's lovely. Right, young Thomas, let's get you on the scales.'

I brushed some strands of damp hair away from my face and Josh dabbed my forehead with a towel then lightly pressed his lips against mine.

'Thank you,' he whispered. 'So are you going to tell me now?'

'I was convinced it was a boy.'

'Here's your son,' Ally said, placing the tiny baby in my arms, 'but I'm afraid we're going to need to take him away from you shortly. Nothing to worry about, but he's a little smaller than we'd expected. He's 4lb 11oz so we need to take him to the SCBU – the Special Care Baby Unit – in case he needs a little extra help.'

That fear was back as I looked down at the scrunched-up face among the folds of towel, my heart already overflowing with love for this tiny little being. 'Is he in danger?'

'Oh, no, everything should be fine. It's just his weight. He might need some extra help taking on a feed before he can go home.'

'The mark on his head?' I asked, seeing a purple welt in among the thick dark hair.

'It's where the clip was tangled, but that'll disappear. He's got a fine head of hair on him.'

'Go with him when they take him,' I whispered to Josh, unable to bear the thought of our baby coming into the world and immediately being whisked away from both his parents.

Ally must have had exceptional hearing. 'Dad's very welcome to accompany Thomas to the SCBU,' she said brightly. 'You can carry him if you want. One of the team will head over there with you now while we get that placenta delivered, Samantha.'

I carefully handed Thomas over to Josh. He was all dewy-eyed as he kissed our baby's head for the first time.

'Hi, Thomas,' he said, his voice thick with emotion. 'I'm your daddy. I'm going to take care of you and make sure nothing bad ever happens to you.'

Tears trickled down my cheeks and I brushed them aside.

'I'll be back as soon as I can,' he said.

'Just make sure Thomas is okay for me.'

'He'll be fine,' Ally said. 'It really is just a precaution. Five ounces heavier and we'd be talking arrangements for going home.'

Josh returned to the delivery room after I'd delivered the placenta and had a few stitches.

'Is he all right?' I asked, reaching for his hand.

'He's doing fine, but they've had to put a tube up his nose and into his stomach so they can feed him. He's had some formula.'

'Oh! But I wanted to feed him.'

'I know you did. I told them that and the midwife says we can go there when you're ready and you can try, but he might not be hungry or awake.'

I tried my hardest not to look disappointed but obviously didn't succeed.

Josh gently stroked my cheek. 'I'm so sorry, Sammie. I know it's not what either of us planned, but he's here and he's healthy. He's just a bit on the small side and we're going to need to make a few adjustments.'

I nodded, not trusting myself to speak in case the tears started again. Nothing about the latter part of my pregnancy was how I'd imagined, but Josh was right. For a terrifying moment earlier, I thought we'd lost him. Missing out on some skin to skin contact and the first feed seemed trivial in comparison to what I thought had happened then.

I'd lost all track of time and I glanced at the large clock on the wall. It was quarter to one in the morning.

'What time was he born? Late last night or early this morning?'

'I've no idea,' Josh said. 'How weird is that? We don't know his birthday!'

A healthcare assistant appeared with a wheelchair.

'I understand we're going via the SCBU,' she said.

'Yes, but we have a question first. Do you know when Thomas was born? We didn't look at the time, so we don't know if it was yesterday or today.'

'A Sagittarius either way,' she said smiling. 'Let me see what I can find out.'

She was back a few minutes later. 'I understand there was a bit of a dramatic arrival and nobody wrote down the exact time in the kerfuffle but Ally says definitely yesterday – 19 December – and a pretty good estimate of quarter to midnight.'

'Thank you.'

'Pleasure. Let's get you on your way. You're not going to be able to feel your legs properly for some time, so it'll feel a little weird moving into the chair, but we'll make sure you're secure before we set off.'

* * *

'It's not working.'

I looked up at the young midwife on the SCBU. Thomas had been awake when we arrived but showed no interest in latching on for a feed, no matter what I tried.

'Don't worry about it,' she said. 'Express some milk with the machine next door and we'll feed Thomas that when he wakes up again later. We can keep trying. I'll get you a bottle while you change his nappy.'

I pushed aside the disappointment once more. He'd still be getting my breast milk even if he wasn't getting it directly from me. But it wasn't how I'd planned it.

I looked round Panda Ward. It was a small room with several chairs round the edge, some soft and others hard plastic. Painted a warm lemon colour, decals of adorable, illustrated pandas among trees and flowers adorned the walls.

Two premature babies – a boy and a girl – were sleeping in enclosed incubators on the right-hand side of the room and Thomas's open crib was on the left. It was strange looking at the other babies, as they were actually bigger than Thomas but, being premature, were in need of greater care.

The baby clothes we'd bought were far too big, so he was dressed in a sleepsuit belonging to the SCBU and a pale blue hand-knitted cardigan. The nappies we had also swamped him, so we'd needed to use the SCBU's stock.

Josh passed me a fresh nappy and I swiftly changed Thomas, relieved that I knew how to do that: one thing I wasn't failing at.

I kissed Thomas's forehead and Josh did the same then I placed him back in his crib, trying not to feel concerned by all the wires. We'd been told that there was a heat mat and a breathing alarm but, coupled with the tube up his nose, it all looked scary and intimidating.

'We haven't taken any photos of him,' Josh said, taking his phone out of his pocket.

Another precious moment missed.

'You look tearful,' he said when he'd taken a few photos of Thomas.

'I feel like I want to curl up in a ball and sob my heart out. I'm so grateful that he's not poorly, but it's... I can't even think of a word for it.'

'It's all a bit shit,' Josh suggested, giving me a weak smile as he crouched down beside my wheelchair. 'I'm frustrated and disappointed too, but we'll get him some clothes that fit and we'll take loads more photos and we'll find a way through this together. We've got a baby boy, Sammie. We're a pair of baddass animal-rescuers and baby baddass here has joined the clan. His start in life might not have been as we'd hoped, but has anything in our life so far been what we planned? And hasn't it all turned out even better?'

As Josh held me tightly, that urge to curl up in a ball and sob faded away. It would be fine. Thomas would need a few days of help, but we'd be home for Christmas and could write off the last few weeks and focus on our future together as a happy family.

44

SAMANTHA

I was discharged later that morning and given two options – stay with Thomas during the day but leave the night feeds to the SCBU staff or pay to stay in a private room and take on all the feeds myself under the guidance of the staff there.

I could have stayed with Auntie Louise and Uncle Simon which would have been easier than driving to and from Hedgehog Hollow each day, but I was still anxious to give the breastfeeding a go, so I chose the hospital room. It was small and basic – a single bed, desk, chair, some clothes hooks, a chest of drawers and an en suite wet room containing a toilet, sink and shower – but it was my private space and it was convenient.

Darcie's school had broken up for the Christmas holidays on Friday and Phoebe's employers had kindly allowed her to extend her Christmas break so they were going to be Thomas's first visitors this afternoon. Connie and Alex were due a little later and, this evening, we were expecting Paul and Beth, then my parents. We wanted our immediate family to see Thomas first.

I left Josh trying to get an hour's nap on my bed before the visits started and went to Panda Ward. Sitting on my own by

Thomas's crib, I felt like a spare part. All I wanted to do was pick him up and cuddle him, but I'd been advised to leave him in his crib unless I was feeding or changing him. It seemed so unnatural.

A tall blonde midwife, probably in her early forties, came onto the ward. 'You have a beautiful son. I could gaze at him all day.' Her smile was radiant.

I smiled back at her. 'Me too, but I'd rather cuddle him.'

'Aw, I know it's hard, but you'll have him home before you know it and all the time in the world for cuddles. I'm Ivanka.'

'Samantha.'

'Lovely to meet you, Samantha. If you have any questions, fire away. I know that being in here is not how any parent would want to start life with their newborn but if there's anything I can do to make the time easier, please let me know.'

Her warmth and genuine concern made me a little tearful and I didn't trust myself to speak, so I smiled and nodded.

Not long afterwards, Josh appeared. 'I can't switch off,' he said, sitting beside me and gazing adoringly at our son. 'I'd rather be with you two.'

I rested my head on his shoulder. 'This having a baby thing is exhausting. I feel really spaced right now.'

'Me too.'

'We haven't given Thomas a middle name,' he said a few minutes later. 'Do you have any preferences?'

'Not really. I didn't think much beyond Thomas. What about you?'

'How would you feel about using Terry's middle name? I don't think Thomas Terry sounds right but I like Thomas Blake Alderson.'

'Aw, Josh, that's so lovely.' I glanced down at our tiny boy. 'It suits him.'

* * *

Ten minutes before Phoebe and Darcie were due, I wandered over to the nurses' station. An older woman with short greying hair and a name badge that said 'Brenda' was typing something into the computer. She didn't even look up to acknowledge me. I waited a moment while she shuffled some papers, eyes still down. Had she even noticed me? I cleared my throat and eventually she raised her head.

'Yes?'

'Erm... we're expecting a couple of visitors. I wanted to let you know their names so you can buzz them in.'

She picked up a clipboard and pen. 'Names.'

'Phoebe Corbyn and Darcie Flynn.'

'Adults or children?'

'Phoebe's an adult and Darcie's a child.'

'And what relation is Darcie to your baby?'

'She isn't. It's complicated.'

Brenda looked up at me, an expression on her face that clearly said: *don't even think about trying to explain it to me because I couldn't be less interested.*

'So she's not a sibling?' she said.

'No.'

'Then she can't come in. Only children who are siblings are permitted on SCBU. Sorry.'

I've never heard the word 'sorry' uttered with less feeling.

'But she's as good as a sibling,' I objected. 'She lives with us.'

'Rules are rules. I don't make them.'

The desk phone rang and she picked it up, a signal to me that I was dismissed.

I shuffled back into Panda Ward, feeling completely deflated.

'She says Darcie's not allowed in because she's not Thomas's sister,' I managed to force out before bursting into tears as a combination of fatigue, hormones and stress overcame me.

Josh was by my side immediately with a reassuring hug. 'I've never heard anything so ridiculous.'

'She was really rude.'

'What difference would it make whether Darcie's a sibling or not?' he said. 'I get restricting the number of visitors and not having hordes of children running around but we're talking about one eight-year-old. We'll ask someone else.'

I straightened up and dried my tears, frustrated with myself for letting Brenda get to me. I understood that places had rules but the way she'd dealt with the situation had made me feel so belittled.

'When you were trying to sleep, I saw a different midwife earlier – Ivanka – and she was lovely. I might see if I can find her.'

Josh's phone vibrated. 'That's them. They've just parked.'

I went off in search of Ivanka and found her on Koala Ward, sanitising an empty incubator.

'Can I ask you something?'

She stopped what she was doing and gave me her full attention. 'Fire away.'

'We're expecting a couple of visitors and one of them's a child. I mentioned it to one of the other midwives and she said she can't come in because she's not Thomas's sister, but she's as good as. She lives with us.'

'One child, you say?'

'Yeah, just the one.'

'I can't see a problem with that. When are they expected?'

'Any minute now.'

'Okay, I'll come to the front and buzz them in.'

'Thank you.' I hesitated for a moment. 'Will that cause problems with the other midwife?'

'Don't you worry about that. We do have rules, but there are always exceptions.'

What a difference in attitude to Brenda. I had no idea how long Thomas would need to stay on the unit, but I hoped I'd have a lot of interaction with Ivanka during that time and very little with Brenda.

She accompanied me to the door. Phoebe was approaching along the corridor with Darcie skipping beside her holding a helium 'It's a Boy' balloon.

'What beautiful girls,' Ivanka said to me as she unlocked the door and held it open for them.

It was so good to see them both that I nearly lost it again as we exchanged hugs.

'He's so tiny,' Darcie cried as they approached Thomas's crib. 'Can I touch him?'

'You can hold his hand if you want.'

Darcie wrapped her hand round Thomas's. 'His hands are so dinky!'

She crouched down beside the crib. 'Hi, Thomas, I'm your big sister Darcie and I'm going to look after you so hurry up and get heavy so you can come home.'

Phoebe lightly stroked his dark hair. 'We've been dying to meet you, so listen to your sister and eat lots. We want you at Hedgehog Hollow.'

Josh put his arm round me and hugged me to his side as I bit back the tears at such a beautiful scene. How lucky we were to have Phoebe and Darcie – the only positive thing to have come from having the Grimes family in our lives, but what a positive.

* * *

Connie and Alex arrived shortly after Phoebe and Darcie left.

'Oh, my goodness,' Connie said, pressing her fingers to her lips as she peered into Thomas's crib at her first grandchild. 'What a little poppet. He looks just like you, Josh.'

'You think so?' Josh asked.

'Definitely. And we've brought the photos to prove it. I'll show you them in a moment.'

'I wish we could let you pick him up,' I said.

We'd warned everyone that they wouldn't be able to hold Thomas and had also asked that they save any gifts until we were home as there wasn't anywhere to store them.

'We'll have plenty of time for cuddles when he comes home,' Connie said, slipping her arm round my shoulders and hugging me to her side. 'How are you finding it?'

'It doesn't feel right but, as you say, it shouldn't be long till he's home.'

Connie and Alex had offered to look after Archie and Lottie in the evening so Paul and Beth could visit. Their timing was perfect for a feed, so they both got a chance to cuddle Thomas after we'd changed his nappy.

'My first grandchild,' Paul said, his eyes glistening as he held Thomas in his arms. 'He's perfect.'

Even though he didn't say it, I knew what he'd be thinking – if it hadn't been for that stem cell donor, he might not have been around to meet Thomas. I could see that Beth was choked up too and I gave her a gentle squeeze.

By the time they left and Mum and Dad arrived, I felt drained but it was worth it to see the delight on their faces. Thomas was asleep again but Mum cried and Dad looked like he was close to tears.

'He's so precious,' Mum said, stroking his soft cheek. 'I'm your nanna, Thomas. I'm looking forward to getting to know you. You're a lucky boy, you know, because you have the best parents in the world.' She looked up at Dad and smiled through her tears. 'And the best granddad.'

That set me off again and a tear did escape down Dad's cheek at that point.

'Debs! What are you doing to us all?' he joked, wiping his face.

'Just telling it how it is.'

'And you'll be a great nanna,' Dad said, smiling fondly at her.

There were hugs all round and I counted my blessings. What a special moment to have both my parents in a room together, happy in each other's company and in mine.

45

SAMANTHA

It was pouring with rain the following day and the gloomy weather matched my mood. Brenda was on the day shift once more. I'd said a bright 'good morning' to her, not wanting any bad vibes between us, but she'd blanked me. I'd have loved to give her the benefit of the doubt and conclude that she hadn't heard me, but my greeting had been loud and she'd been the only one around.

I went to get a drink of water a little later and returned to Panda Ward at the end of an altercation between Brenda and the mum of the premature baby girl. I didn't catch what it was about, but the atmosphere was frosty as Brenda stormed out of the room with the mum shooting her daggers and muttering under her breath before she stormed out herself.

She'd not been gone long when Josh arrived with a bag packed with tiny baby nappies and clothes. Everything seemed unbelievably small, but when I held some of the items against Thomas, it seemed some would still be too big.

'Look what I found,' Josh said, holding up a soft velour reindeer onesie with felt antlers and a red nose on the hood. 'And these...' He fished out a pair of reindeer booties. 'I thought he could wear them on Christmas Day.'

'They're so cute.'

'And I got you this.' He pulled a small pre-decorated desktop tree out of another bag and flicked a switch, illuminating the colourful LED lights. 'I know there's not much space, but I thought this would make your room a little more festive.'

It was so thoughtful of him but as I looked from the tree to the outfit to Thomas, the tears started flowing once more.

'What if he's still in here on Christmas Day?'

Josh put the tree down, gathered me into his arms and kissed the top of my head. 'Hopefully he won't be but, if he is, we'll be here with him and we'll do Christmas when he's home. And I can think of someone who'll love the idea of having two Christmas days.'

I clung more tightly to Josh. Yes, Darcie would love it and Thomas would know nothing about it. I was the one making an issue, but I couldn't help it after so long away from home. I ached for Hedgehog Hollow.

46

FIZZ

I drove Chloe to Whitsborough Bay General on Wednesday evening to meet baby Thomas for the first time. It was by far the most time I'd spent alone in Chloe's company, but the journey whizzed by with me telling her about the rescue centre's latest admissions and her talking about the recent classes at Crafty Hollow.

As we approached the outskirts of Whitsborough Bay, she fell silent and stared out of the window, nibbling on her nails.

'Are you okay?' I asked as I drove across town towards the hospital.

'Yeah, just thinking. I can't wait to meet Thomas but new babies...' She sighed. 'They always make me think about Ava.'

Chloe had found herself alone and pregnant at sixteen and had kept it secret. Sam's mum had guessed but Chloe had convinced her to keep the secret, saying she'd arranged for the baby to be adopted. She hadn't. She had the baby when she was seventeen but abandoned her in hospital. The truth had come out two and a half years ago when she left James and stayed at Hedgehog Hollow, struggling with post-natal depression after having Samuel. The police hadn't charged her, and she'd been reassured that Ava had been adopted and was happy.

'She'd be, what, fourteen now?' I asked.

'Yeah. Four more years and she might come looking for me.'

'Why four more?'

'She'll be eighteen then. Legally, that's when she has the right to request information about me.'

'What if she tries before then?'

'How could she?'

'Through social media. It all depends whether her adoptive parents have told her anything about you. A girl I knew at Young Farmers' was adopted and she knew her birth mum's name so she tracked her down on Facebook.'

Chloe was silent once more and I wondered if I should have said anything. I continued driving and it was only when I pulled into the hospital car park that she spoke again.

'What happened to your friend?'

'From what I remember, they exchanged a few messages and met up a couple of times, but I don't think they stayed in touch. She was curious about her background and a couple of meetings satisfied that.'

I pulled into a space and we got out.

'That's interesting,' Chloe said. 'I'd never thought about it.'

'I don't want to give you any false hope.'

She shook her head. 'It's okay. You haven't. James and I have talked about it a lot. If Ava makes contact, that's great and I'll answer her questions or meet her or whatever she wants but I don't have any expectations. I made a decision to give her up and she has a new family now. She's built a life without me in it and I'm good with that. All I've ever wanted is for her to be happy.'

* * *

Thomas was as teeny and adorably squidgy as I'd expected.

'Aw, Sam,' I said. 'He's delicious.'

'Thank you. We think so.'

She looked at Josh adoringly and my heart melted. I wanted that. I wanted this. Someone to love. A family.

'I know you said no gifts yet,' Chloe said, 'but I knitted this and thought you might be able to use it in here.'

She handed over a gorgeous soft lemon blanket with a hedgehog family embroidered on it.

'Aw, that's beautiful,' Sam said. 'Thank you.'

'And would you mind if I give him this too?'

She removed a Peter Rabbit comforter from her bag.

'Of course I don't,' Sam said, her voice soft.

Chloe laid the comforter beside Thomas and stroked his hair back from his face.

'I gave one of these to my Samuel and one to Ava,' she said to him. 'It's kind of a tradition now.'

As Sam hugged Chloe, I swallowed the lump in my throat. I loved their friendship – or rather, I loved how it was now. Chloe had come a long way in the time I'd known her. She said she was okay whether Ava made contact or not, but I suspected she hoped she would – if only so she could say she was sorry. I hoped she got that chance.

47

SAMANTHA

A couple of days later, I flicked my eyes open. What was that sound? And where was I?

It took a moment to orientate myself. That had to be the deepest sleep I'd had since being admitted to hospital.

I stumbled out of bed and lifted the intercom phone off the wall.

'Hello?'

'It's Brenda on SCBU. Did you sleep in? Your baby needs feeding.'

The line went dead before I could respond and I replaced the handset on the wall, feeling thoroughly chastised. Brenda. Why did it have to be her on duty tonight?

I pulled on my dressing gown and slippers and padded down the corridor to the SCBU, cursing myself for having slept through my alarm. I was meant to be up every four hours to feed Thomas, but I'd clearly been too deeply asleep when the 2 a.m. alarm sounded and had either slept through it or stopped it without realising. Brenda was bound to make further sarcastic comments.

I could hear Thomas's cries – like a mewling cat – as soon as I was buzzed through.

Brenda looked up from the desk and raised her eyebrows at me. She didn't say anything, but I could hear the unspoken words: *in your own time.*

'Sorry. I needed the loo.'

I hated myself for apologising to her and for the alarming number of times I'd done that this week. Ivanka was lovely – warm, gentle and encouraging, very much like all the other midwives I'd encountered during my prolonged stay – but Brenda was cut from different cloth. She gave off a *I hate new mothers and babies* vibe and her various facial expressions spoke a language of their own – one that only contained negative words.

I removed the breast milk I'd expressed earlier from the fridge in the unit's kitchenette but settled into the nursing chair with Thomas first in the hope that he might latch on himself. I wasn't an expert but I'd helped plenty of breastfeeding mums during my nursing years and I'd learned a lot from Hannah when she'd helped Chloe with her struggles to feed Samuel, so I wasn't a novice either.

Nothing worked and Thomas's cries grew louder. His cheeks reddened and his fists and feet flailed angrily and I felt like such a failure that tears of frustration poured down my cheeks.

'What are you crying for?'

I'd been concentrating so hard that I hadn't noticed Brenda entering the ward. I stiffened.

'Well?' she demanded.

I wanted to turn round and scream 'Piss off!' at her but she might be able to help me and that was more important.

'Can you help me feed him?' I asked, trying to keep the anger with her out of my tone because there was no way she'd help me if she knew what I really thought of her and her angry eyebrows and flashing eyes.

'Do you have any problem expressing milk?'

'No. I've got loads.'

'Then you're not the problem. He is. He's too small and, right now, he's desperate for milk. What do you think the tube's for?'

With a tut, she left the room. As I sorted Thomas's tube feed, I mentally prepared a strongly worded complaint letter. I was an emotional wreck at the moment and I'd do myself more damage than good if I tried to verbally spar with Brenda in this state, but she wasn't getting away with it. In the SCBU, they were dealing with some of the most emotionally vulnerable new mothers and I'd seen her interact with enough of them this week to know it wasn't just something against me. Nursing and midwifery were vocations and you needed to be a certain type of person. Either Brenda had never been the right sort of person, she'd become bored or jaded over time, or something was going on in her personal life that she was bringing into work. In her position, none of those scenarios were acceptable and something needed doing about it.

Thomas's cries ceased as the milk reached his stomach.

'I'm sorry, sweetheart,' I whispered to him as I finished the feed. 'Mummy'll keep trying.'

I changed his nappy then cuddled his tiny form against my chest as I wandered round the room. The two larger premature babies were sound asleep in their incubators. I'd spoken to both mums, who'd accepted that their babies wouldn't be home until well into the New Year, and they'd both asked whether Thomas would be home for Christmas. I still didn't know and it was eating away at me. It was Christmas Eve tomorrow, so time was running out.

There was a Christmas tree and decorations up in the lobby

but nothing festive on Panda Ward, unless you counted the six strands of lamenta which Fizz had tied round Thomas's balloon when she'd visited. I'd been asked if I had any objections to Christmas decorations on the ward because the staff were mindful that some mothers might feel they were inappropriate. I'd have been grateful for the festive cheer and the mum of the baby boy told me she'd agreed, but presumably the mum of the premature girl had said no because the room hadn't been decorated.

I laid Thomas back in his crib, covered him with the knitted blanket from Chloe and adjusted the Peter Rabbit comforter so it was by his hand.

'Goodnight, sweetie,' I whispered, kissing my fingers and placing them on his soft cheek. 'I'll see you again in a few hours.'

Ivanka was at the nurses' desk as I left the room and my heart leapt. I could ask her about Christmas, but I was a few paces away when an alarm sounded and she raced off.

'Do you need something?' Brenda asked, stepping out of the kitchenette with a mug of coffee.

'Er, no, I...'

'You're standing by the desk so clearly there's something on your mind. Out with it.'

'I wondered whether there's any chance of Thomas coming home for Christmas.'

'It's Christmas on Sunday.'

'I know that.'

'Which means you only have today and tomorrow.'

'I know that too. He's put on enough weight so what I'd like to know now is what needs to happen for him to be home for Christmas?'

'He needs to wake up on his own, demand a feed and take it on his own, not through his nose. We don't care if it's breast or bottle, but he's not leaving here until that happens at least twice. So if I were you, I'd plan on spending Christmas in hospital.'

I was so angry with her smug response that I could feel my whole body shaking. The only thing that stopped me venting was fear of waking up the babies on the unit who'd already had a tricky start in life and didn't need their valuable sleep disturbing.

Holding my head high, I turned and strode towards the door.

'You're welcome,' she called, aggression in her tone.

Had she really expected me to thank her? The information was helpful, but the delivery had been diabolical.

I was still shaking when I returned to my room and sank down onto my bed, my head full of how I could have – and probably should have – retaliated to Brenda. Nobody had a right to speak to another person in the condescending, sarcastic way she regularly used. Her attitude reminded me of how Mum used to behave towards me. She'd acknowledged the reason, sought help and we'd made our peace. Although her behaviour had been appalling, there had been a reason why she'd struggled to connect with me. Brenda didn't have that excuse. I was a stranger to her, as were the other new mums on the unit, and there could be no possible reason for treating us with such disdain. She wasn't going to get away with it.

I re-set my alarm for 6.15 a.m. although my mind was so active now that there was no way I was going to get back to sleep.

The overhead light was too harsh, so I switched it off in favour of the bedside one which emitted a warmer glow. I also flicked on the miniature Christmas tree lights and sat back on the bed, staring at the bulbs. What I wouldn't give to be at home for Christmas. It was hard to believe it was only two days away. Whitsborough Bay General had been my home for exactly one month today and I'd missed out on all the Christmas preparation which I usually loved. Even though Josh had tried his hardest to include me in things – filming Darcie's nativity play, filming the decorations at home and in the rescue centre, a couple of evenings of buying gifts online with me in lieu of our usual shopping trips to Reddfield and York – it wasn't the same and I felt weary with disappointment.

The reindeer outfit Josh had bought for Thomas was neatly folded on the desk next to the tree. It would be too big for him, but he was going to look adorable in it. When Josh had first given me it, I'd had a vision of us waking up together in Hedgehog Hollow on Christmas morning and me dressing Thomas in that outfit, but that had faded with the fear we might be still in hospital. From what Brenda had said, it would take a Christmas miracle for Thomas to be home on Christmas Day, so it would be back to Josh's plan of celebrating our family Christmas on Boxing Day, 27 December, 28 December... however long it took.

My stomach sank at the thought of waking up alone in this single room on Christmas morning. Three years ago, I'd woken up alone in the spare room at Rich and Dave's cottage. They were away for Christmas, and I was ostracised from most of my family thanks to the altercation at Chloe and James's wedding. Dad had offered to spend Christmas Day with me, but his relationship with Mum was already challenging and I hadn't wanted to make things worse. I'd never felt so lost and lonely as I did at that moment and I'd hoped never to feel that way again. But from a day which started with despair was born one of the best days ever and I wouldn't have traded that time with Thomas Mickleby for all the world. So if I did wake up on Christmas morning alone all alone in this room, I'd make the most of it. If Thomas came home after Christmas, so be it.

48

SAMANTHA

It was Christmas Eve and, despite the circumstances, I did feel a fizz of excitement in my stomach as I scurried along the corridor to the SCBU for Thomas's 6 a.m. feed. Four hours earlier, I'd had to abort breastfeeding yet again and resort to a tube feed, but I felt hopeful that today I'd get the first part of my Christmas miracle and he'd finally feed from me.

Brenda buzzed me in and I decided to throw everything at it.

'Happy Christmas Eve!' I declared warmly, beaming at her.

'For some, perhaps,' she said, not even raising her eyes from the computer screen.

Was it Christmas that was the problem for her? Could her partner have left her around Christmas or might she have experienced a bereavement at this time of year? Either scenario – or any other reason for disliking Christmas – was very sad but she still had no right to bring it into work and drag everyone else down with her snide remarks and bitterness.

Determined not to let her bring me down today, I strode purposely into Panda Ward and stopped short. We had a new addition. A tiny baby girl was lying in an open crib on the same side of the room as Thomas, with the same set-up of wires and the tube up the nose as him.

'Hello, baby girl,' I whispered, peering into the crib as I passed to get to Thomas. She was an absolute beauty with a crown of golden hair and pouting red lips.

'What's your name?' The chart hooked on the end of the crib had 'BABY JONES' written on it.

'Baby no-name at the moment.'

I looked up at the young woman who'd entered the ward, sipping on a cup of water. With long dark wavy hair pushed back from her face with a couple of pink slides, and rosy cheeks, she barely looked old enough to be a mum and I suddenly felt very old.

'We were going to call her Jade,' she continued, 'but I don't think she looks like a Jade. Is he yours?' She pointed at Thomas's crib.

'Yes, this is Thomas, born late on Monday.'

'Did you come up with any names for girls? I'm out of ideas.'

'We did, but do you know what name springs to mind when I look at her? Aurora. With those red lips and that golden hair, I was just thinking how much she looks like Sleeping Beauty.'

'Aurora? That's so pretty.' She gazed down at the baby, smiling tenderly. 'It really suits her. She has my boyfriend's hair colour. I'll have to see what he thinks but it's now number one on my list. Thank you.'

'You're welcome. I'm Samantha, by the way.'

'Esme.'

'I'm guessing she's not premature but she weighs less than 5lb?'

Esme nodded. 'Thirty-eight weeks but 4lb 9oz, so I guess this is where we'll be spending Christmas.'

'Thomas was two ounces heavier and it looks like we'll be here for Christmas too.'

Her eyes glistened with tears as she glanced across at the two babies in the incubators. 'I keep telling myself that we're very lucky but it's all a bit overwhelming, although the whole thing has been. I didn't know I was pregnant until the end of last month. I'm in my final year at university and I knew I'd put some weight on but I thought it was from my pre-exam stress eating. Very unexpected Christmas gift.'

I wanted to ask more questions, but I was conscious of Brenda staring at us and wouldn't have put it past her to storm into Panda Ward and demand to know why I was neglecting my baby.

'I need to feed Thomas,' I said.

'Oh, of course! Do you want me to leave the room?'

'Gosh, no, but you're not going to pick up any tips from me, I'm afraid. Thomas and I are still struggling with feeds and...' my eyes automatically flicked in Brenda's direction, '... not getting much help with it.'

Esme had obviously caught my glance. 'She's scary, isn't she? Reminds me of my PE teacher from school who I swear hated children and sport.'

'I'd like to say she gets better once you get to know her, but she doesn't. Ivanka's lovely. All the other staff are. If you have questions, try to ask anyone but Brenda.'

I couldn't get Thomas to latch on, so I decided to try something different – dripping the expressed milk onto my finger and wiping it across his mouth – but several attempts only soaked us both in milk so it had to be the tube again and a fresh change of clothes all round.

* * *

Even though I probably didn't have much milk on me, I felt covered in it, so I showered and washed my hair before returning to the SCBU.

Ivanka was behind the desk this time and her greeting was so different to Brenda's. 'Good morning, Samantha. Christmas is nearly here!'

'Are you working tomorrow?' I asked her.

'Yes. I'm finishing the nightshift shortly and I'll be back in at eight in the morning, but I only have a half shift tomorrow. We'll open presents with the kids before work then we'll have a late Christmas dinner when I get home. All I miss is the squabbling and the cooking. Big win for me, I think!'

'I think you might have Christmas sussed,' I said, smiling at her.

But my smile slipped when I entered Panda Ward. Brenda was standing beside Esme, arms folded, shaking her head.

A flustered-looking Esme was attempting a particularly smelly nappy change but managing to smear the mess all over her baby instead of wiping it clear.

'You're doing it all wrong,' Brenda said, laughter in her tone. I swear she chuckled as she walked past me.

Esme burst into tears and I rushed to her side, placing a reassuring arm round her shoulder.

'The first time I changed a baby's nappy, I ended up with poo in the ends of my hair and I didn't notice until someone asked me if I had chocolate on my blouse.'

Esme laughed through her tears. 'That's gross.'

'Yep. Would you like some help?'

'Love some.'

I pulled a wipe from the open packet beside her. 'Give your fingers a wipe as a starting point. You can wash your hands later, but this'll mean you're not transferring any back onto Aurora... sorry, I think of her as that already.'

Esme smiled. 'Me too. My boyfriend might not have much choice.'

It would have been easy to take over but Esme wouldn't learn from that, so I guided her through how to fold the wipes to get maximum use from each one. Some new parents were intuitive about things like this but, for others, it wasn't obvious and I hated the way so many new mums felt embarrassed to ask about the basics, as though they should be born with the natural instinct to know what to do.

Esme beamed at me when she picked up a clean Aurora for a cuddle. 'Thank you so much. Can I keep you?'

'My family might object but I'm happy to help where I can while Thomas is still here.'

Behind her, I spotted Brenda heading into the kitchenette with a mug. Now was my chance.

'Excuse me for a minute,' I said to Esme.

Brenda was adding milk to a mug of tea when I stepped through the door.

'Do you have five minutes?' I asked. 'I'd like to ask you a question.'

There was only half an hour until her shift ended so she couldn't hit me with an excuse of being on a break.

She rolled her eyes at me. 'I've already told you what's needed if you want to be home for Christmas and watching your performance this morning, that's not gonna happen.'

I took a deep breath and stood a little taller. I hated confrontation and sometimes that translated to others as not standing up for myself, but I chose that approach in order to keep the peace. However, how Brenda behaved was wrong and she needed calling out on it.

'First of all, don't roll your eyes at me,' I said, keeping my voice steady and my eyes fixed on hers. 'You're a grown woman – not a petulant teenager struggling with authority figures – and I'm not your mother or your teacher, although I do hope you'll learn something from our conversation today.'

Her eyes widened and her mouth opened but I held my finger up to silence her.

'Secondly, my question is nothing to do with Thomas. I'd like to know why you treated Esme in such a way to make her cry just now.'

'She cried because she couldn't change a nappy? Typical over-emotional clueless new mum.'

'She didn't cry because she couldn't change a nappy. She cried because she's only twenty-one, she didn't know she was pregnant until recently, she's in her final year at university and needs to rethink the future she planned out, she's been up all night and the baby she wasn't expecting needs some special care. She cried because she's lost, alone and vulnerable and when she reached out to the one person who should have been able to give her some empathy and support, she got sarcastic comments and was made to feel like a toddler, so I go back to my original question: why did you treat her like that?'

She flashed her eyes at me and I anticipated a mouthful of abuse but she abandoned her drink on the side and shoved past me.

'I'm not having this conversation.'

The door slammed but I wasn't done yet. I followed her to the nurses' desk where she shuffled through some paperwork and pretended to ignore me.

'Okay, so you don't want to talk about Esme. That's fine. How about we talk about how you've spoken to me instead?'

'I've no idea what you're talking about. Go back to your baby. We're done.'

Ivanka joined us, frowning as she glanced from Brenda to me and back again. 'Is everything all right?'

'Not really,' I said. 'I was curious to know why Brenda speaks to mums the way she does. The women on this unit are typically scared, emotional and vulnerable and they need support and empathy, which I've personally had in spades from you, Ivanka, and all your other colleagues, but not from Brenda. I've just seen Brenda belittle Esme and make her cry and she's made me cry on several occasions too. I don't imagine we're the only ones. I genuinely want to understand why somebody in a caring vocation such as midwifery hasn't demonstrated any caring behaviours during my time on the unit. I also want to highlight the emotional distress that this has caused to me and others and politely request that the behaviour changes.'

Brenda continued to shuffle her paperwork, but a deep flush had spread up her neck.

'Thank you for the feedback, Samantha,' Ivanka said. 'Could you give us a minute?'

I returned to Panda Ward, where Esme was tucking Aurora back into her crib.

'Did you say something to Brenda?' she asked.

'You're not the only one who she's made cry, so I wanted to have a quiet word, but she didn't want to listen.'

'You're braver than me.'

'I'm not good at conflict but I couldn't let it continue. This should be a safe space where it's okay for a woman to say they don't know how to change a nappy, fasten the poppers on a sleep-suit or even how to hold a baby. It shouldn't be a place where we're ridiculed and made to feel like failures.'

'Is that how she made you feel?'

'Several times, and it's not right.'

I plonked myself down on the chair beside Thomas's crib. I'd needed to address it, but had I handled the situation in the right way? Would it have been less messy to make a formal complaint? Possibly, but that seemed so anonymous and probably would have had less impact. If a patient from my nursing days had had issues with me, my preference would have been for them to calmly raise the concern directly with me so we could try to find a resolution. It wasn't my fault that Brenda had refused to engage in the conversation and Ivanka had been dragged into it.

A few minutes later, there were raised voices, then Brenda stormed past the window with her coat on.

'Do you think she's been sacked?' Esme asked, eyes wide.

'No. They'd have to follow a formal process, but it could have been suggested she leave her shift a little early. Or she could have stormed out.'

'Losing your job on Christmas Eve would be a shocker.'

Yes, it would, and I'd hate to be the cause of that, but I couldn't not say anything. I didn't know Brenda or what was going on in her life, but she didn't know the mums on the SCBU either because she never took the time to get to know them. She wandered round with an air of superiority, judging everyone for being emotional or, as she evidently saw it, incompetent. She'd made me feel like a failure and I'd really struggled to deal with that, but I had Josh and my family rallying around me and I'd be home soon and away from her forever. But what about a single mum or one with an unsupportive partner? What about someone who was completely alone and scared who already felt like a failure? What if Brenda's words and sneers convinced them they really were the worthless person their darkest days told them they were and they decided their baby would be better off without them? It was an extreme worst-case scenario, but it could absolutely happen and I felt a duty of care to stop it before it got to that point. Bullies could not be allowed to thrive.

Ivanka appeared ten minutes later. 'Could I have a word in private?' she asked.

'I'll grab some fresh air,' Esme said, wincing at me as she left the room.

'I'm sorry if I've caused any trouble,' I said when Esme had gone.

'You did nothing wrong. Grab a seat.'

We sat on the chairs round the edge of the ward.

'It's me who's sorry,' Ivanka said. 'I hadn't realised things had got so bad with Brenda. You were right to raise the issue. I'm her supervisor, so I *will* address it but there's a formal complaint process I can direct you to if you want.'

'I hoped talking to her would make a difference but she didn't want to listen, so I don't see that I have a choice.'

Ivanka nodded. 'I'll get you a leaflet. You probably won't believe this from what you've seen, but she's one of the best midwives I've ever worked with.'

'Really? To me, she seems like a woman who hates her job, mums and babies.'

'It's not the job. Well, it is, but it's complicated.' She glanced past me towards the nurses' station and lowered her voice. 'This is completely confidential and it mustn't get back to Brenda, but I think you have a right to know what's going on. Brenda loves babies – you need to if you're going to do this job – but her daughter recently lost twins. One was stillborn and the other only lived for a few hours.'

'Oh, no! That's horrendous.'

'Brenda asked to be transferred off the delivery suite – too difficult – but it seems like she's struggling here too.'

An alarm sounded and Ivanka excused herself and rushed off the ward.

What an awful thing for Brenda's daughter to go through and I could imagine how hard it would be for Brenda to be surrounded by babies so soon after losing her grandchildren, but why take it out on us? It was possible that she viewed us as whiny and ungrateful when her daughter would have relished the opportunity to have her babies under the care of SCBU instead of losing them, but that wasn't fair on us. We were nothing to do with what had happened to her daughter. I hope she was able to access some help in coming to terms with her loss and in understanding the impact her grief was having on others.

49

FIZZ

'Darcie's asleep at last,' Phoebe said, sinking down onto the sofa beside me in the lounge at Hedgehog Hollow.

'I thought she was going to try to push on till midnight, not that she's far off.' There were only twenty minutes left of Christmas Eve.

'She's normally so good with bedtime but she's unsettled by Samantha and Josh not being here, knowing she'll wake up on Christmas morning and they won't be back.'

It was certainly going to be a different Christmas for us all. Mum and Dad had been really supportive of why I'd chosen to spend Christmas Day at Hedgehog Hollow rather than at Bumblebee Barn with my family. Even though I'd massively emphasised my desire to support the unusual Christmas Day for my friends, I knew that they knew I was also giving Grandma and Granddad the space they so obviously needed. I could only imagine the hurt, guilt and confusion they were experiencing now that the truth was out. Who wanted to accept that their own son was capable of such atrocities?

'Are you tired?' I asked when Phoebe rested her head back against the sofa and closed her eyes.

'Yes, but I don't want to go to bed yet. I love it down here with the log burner on and the tree lights twinkling.' She opened her eyes and gave me a cheeky wink. 'I might stay up and watch out for Santa.'

'How much longer do you think Darcie will believe?' I asked.

'I'm not convinced she *does* believe.'

'You think she's pretending? She's very convincing if she is.'

'When Hayley was around, she'd do her best with gifts and with building up the Christmas excitement, but Darcie was too young to remember it. For Tina and Jenny, Christmas wasn't a time for kids. It was an excuse to eat, drink and laze around even more than usual. Darcie would get a couple of small presents from Jenny, always accompanied with a big fuss about how they were from her hard-earned money and not from Santa. Hard-earned money from her drug-dealing! So with no gifts from Santa, why would she believe?'

'That's so sad. My parents used to make such a fuss about Christmas when we were kids and they were so sad when I stopped believing in Santa.'

'Which is how it should be. When we had our first Christmas here, Samantha and Josh asked Darcie if she was excited about Santa coming and I think she saw that as a chance to capture the magic she'd never had so she said yes and she's now getting to experience what a child should experience.'

Phoebe and I had done our best to make today magical for Darcie. This morning we'd made some Christmas crafts and, during the afternoon, we'd watched Christmas films and decorated a gingerbread house. Earlier this evening, Darcie had pushed a *Santa stop here* sign into the soil in one of the large plant pots outside the farmhouse front door and hung Santa's magic key by the door.

I looked towards the tray which Darcie had lovingly prepared with a drink of milk, a mince pie and some carrots for the reindeers. We hadn't dared touch it in case Darcie came downstairs yet again.

Josh couldn't bear the thought of Sam waking up alone on Christmas Day, so he was staying in her room at the hospital tonight, neither of them bothered about having to share a single bed. The plan was for him to stay with Sam and Thomas until late morning then come back to Hedgehog Hollow for Christmas dinner with us and Jonathan.

I was staying overnight in the farmhouse so that, when Darcie woke up, there'd be two of us to come downstairs with her while she opened her gifts from Santa Claus, Phoebe and me. Sam and Josh's presents, along with those from their families, were being saved for a bigger family feast after Thomas came home. Phoebe hadn't experienced any problems selling a 'one-off super special double Christmas' to Darcie.

Phoebe and I sat in silence for several minutes, watching the flames flicker in the log burner. Jinks was asleep to the side of it, curled up against her new best friend, Wilbur.

It had been a difficult couple of months, but I knew I'd done the right thing and my grandparents would find their peace with it one day. The secret had been too great a burden for me, and I'd never felt more myself since the day I told my parents. Robbie had been right – it turned out that the friendly bubbly person I showed the world was the real me and it felt even easier and more natural to be that person now that I no longer had a secret casting a shadow over me.

'Do you still think about them and what they did to you?' I asked Phoebe.

'Sometimes. I might see or hear something that triggers a memory and occasionally I have a bad dream but, most of the time, they don't feature in my life. They took so much from my past; I refuse to let them take any part of my future. What they did to me hasn't made me who I am today. I'm who I am in spite of what they did to me. Why? Are you thinking about him?'

'Less about him – he doesn't deserve any space in my head – and more about my grandparents. It'll be the first Christmas Day ever that I haven't spent with them.'

'They'll come round. They just need time. I bet they'll miss you like crazy tomorrow.'

'I'll miss them too, although, even if I'd kept my secret and everyone had remained in blissful ignorance about the monster in the family, I'd still have chosen to spend Christmas Day with you tomorrow.'

She laughed lightly. 'Only because you get to have a double Christmas dinner by joining in our one-off super special double Christmas.'

I held her gaze, my heart thumping. 'No. Because I get to spend the day with you.'

She bit her lip as she held eye contact and I could imagine her wondering what that meant.

'I know we're not doing the proper gift exchange until Sam's back, but there's something I wanted to give you while we're on our own.'

I reached behind my cushion for her gift.

'It's squidgy,' she said, taking it from me and squeezing it. She carefully peeled back the sticky tape, opened the parcel and gasped.

'You remembered!'

She ran her fingers along the velvety dark hair and across the satin dress on the soft Snow White doll, shaking her head, tears glistening in her eyes.

'Aw, Fizz, I must have told you that story just after we moved in. That's nearly two years ago!'

'I wanted to get you something meaningful and I thought about your lost doll.'

Her mum had given her a soft toy Snow White shortly after she was born and, because she'd died in a hit and run while Phoebe was still a baby, the doll had become Phoebe's most treasured possession. Her dad used to call her Snow White because of her raven hair and pale skin so the doll had connections to both parents, but it had 'mysteriously' disappeared from her bedroom a year after he married Tina Grimes. I loved that Terry had also called Gwendoline his Snow White. Even though Phoebe had never met her, it felt like they had a connection through that.

'You look even more like Snow White with your shorter hair,' I said.

'This is the best, kindest, most thoughtful gift that anyone's ever given me. Thank you so much for remembering.'

'The story touched me and so did another story about your parents.'

'The one about how they got together?' she suggested, pushing the wrapping paper to one side and cuddling the doll to her chest. 'I've thought about that a lot recently. I love that Dad never gave up. He loved Mum but, because she was with someone else, they could only be friends. He was so convinced they were right for each other that he waited for her without saying a word about how he felt until she realised they should be together.'

'It's very romantic,' I said. 'It must be hard seeing someone you love with someone else.'

'It is, especially when you know that person isn't right for them, and you wake up every day hoping today will be the day when they realise it for themselves.'

I was certain she wasn't talking about her parents anymore but about her feelings for me instead. The log burner crackled and so did the electricity between us.

'You know what my favourite part of that story is?' I asked, my voice coming out all husky. 'When your mum's fiancé asked her what she wanted for Christmas and she realised that the only thing she really wanted was your dad.'

'She took her time, though.'

'Sometimes it's difficult to see what's right in front of you.'

I held her gaze then reached behind the cushion again, removed the happy mistletoe soft toy Darcie had hung on the Christmas tree and rested it in the palm of my hand.

'It might not be a huge bunch of mistletoe like the one your parents had but it's still pretty special and, when we put the tree up and Darcie made everyone kiss, I don't think we did justice to it.'

Phoebe's eyes sparkled. 'Well, it was a bit difficult with Darcie and Josh in the room.'

'There's nobody here now and I've realised that what I want for Christmas is right in front of me.' I shuffled a little closer and held the mistletoe out in front of me. 'I'm hoping I'm not too late.'

Phoebe edged closer to me. 'I'd say your timing's perfect.'

As our lips met, the happy mistletoe slipped from my fingers and I ran my fingers into her hair, every nerve ending fizzing with passion as she eagerly responded to my kiss.

'Sorry I took so long,' I murmured, my eyes searching hers as we broke apart.

'I'd have waited for as long as it took,' she whispered.

And then her lips were on mine again. I closed my eyes and for the first time, *he* didn't haunt my mind. It was all Phoebe – how it was meant to be.

50

SAMANTHA

'It's just gone midnight,' Josh said, as I snuggled against his chest on top of the single bed in my hospital room. 'Happy Christmas!'

'Happy Christmas to you!'

I melted into his tender kiss, my heart racing at his touch, but the intercom buzzed.

'Perfect timing,' I muttered, reluctantly heaving myself off the bed. 'Hello?'

'It's Libby on the SCBU. Little Thomas is awake and demanding a feed. And I mean *wide* awake.' Unlike Brenda, there was laughter in her voice. I'd only met Libby for the first time last night but she'd been really friendly and interested to hear how things were progressing with Thomas and what I had or hadn't tried to get him to move away from his tube-feeding.

'Really? Okay, I'll be right there.'

I replaced the receiver and pressed my fingers to my lips. 'Our baby's wide awake and hungry. You know what this means.'

Josh sat upright, his eyes shining. 'Christmas miracle?'

'Let's hope so.'

We pulled on our shoes and set off along the corridor,

hand in hand. Libby had suggested leaving longer between feeds to see whether that might encourage Thomas to be more responsive. I'd added another thirty minutes, but there'd been no change until now. I didn't want to get my hopes up, but it did feel like it was time things started working for us.

Libby buzzed us in. She was on the phone but she gave a big thumbs up in our direction.

The other three babies on Panda Ward were in the land of nod but Thomas was crying louder than I'd ever heard. He'd kicked his blanket off and was sucking on his fist, which I hoped was a good sign.

Josh grabbed my expressed milk from the fridge while I picked Thomas up and hugged him.

'Happy Christmas, little one,' I said as we moved over to the nursing chair.

Thomas was more squirmy than usual but that also gave me hope as more active surely signalled more awake and more chance of latching on. His fists continued to flail as he squawked and then he fell silent as he relaxed against me.

'He's doing it, Josh! He's feeding.'

Tears of joy rained down my cheeks. It was such a special moment, not just because he was finally feeding from me, but because it meant that we'd taken that next step to being discharged.

A little later, Josh and I stood by Thomas's crib, arms round each other, as he slept again.

'He needs to do that one more time?' Josh asked.

'At least one more time and we can go home and finally start our family life together.'

We both crossed our fingers and held them out in front of us.

'I've got a small gift for you,' Josh said. 'I was going to wait until we got home so you could put it on the tree, but I thought you might like it now.'

He opened the storage cupboard next to the crib and removed a small square box from under the nappies.

I lifted the lid and removed a round bauble with a beautiful robin painted on it, its deep orange breast puffed out on a snowy branch.

'It's lovely. Thank you.'

'Turn it round,' he said.

My breath caught in my throat. On the back of the bauble was the message: *Robins appear when loved ones are near.* Josh knew the story of how I'd seen two robins outside the window on Christmas Day three years ago at the point Thomas would have taken his final breath and how I thought of them as Thomas and Gwendoline visiting me.

'Oh, Josh!'

'I thought that next time you see a robin, it might be Terry saying hello.'

I dangled the bauble in front of me, nodding. 'It's perfect.'

51

FIZZ

'Have you seen the time?' I said to Phoebe.

She propped herself up on her elbow and squinted at the wall clock. 'Half four! Where's the time gone?'

She caught my eye and we smiled at each other. It was amazing how quickly time could whizz by when you were finally with the right person.

'What time do you reckon Darcie will be up?' I asked.

'About six.'

'There's no point going to bed for ninety minutes, is there?'

'No point at all,' Phoebe agreed. 'We'll probably only wake her up if we go upstairs anyway.'

'Hmm, what could we do for the next ninety minutes?'

She glanced at the tray for Santa. 'Oh, no! We're not Santa-ready!'

'Oops! You fill the stocking, I'll sort the tray, then let's see if we can find that happy mistletoe again.'

She cupped my face and lightly kissed my lips. 'I don't think we need that happy mistletoe anymore. It's already worked its magic.'

* * *

'Has he been?' Darcie shouted from upstairs.

Phoebe and I smiled at each other. Six o'clock, exactly as she'd predicted.

'You'll have to come in here and find out,' Phoebe called.

Wilbur stretched and jumped onto the sofa between Phoebe and me as Darcie burst into the lounge with Misty-Blue and Luna. Jinks looked up, yawned, and settled down again.

Darcie launched herself onto the sofa too.

'Haven't you been to bed?' she asked, frowning at us, obviously spotting we were wearing the same clothes as yesterday.

'We wanted to meet Santa to tell him what a good girl you've been,' Phoebe said, 'but we fell asleep down here and missed him.'

'He left you a note,' I added.

Darcie scrambled off the sofa and grabbed the note from the tray. 'Hello Darcie,' she read, 'Mrs Claus and I hear you're having a one-off super special double Christmas this year. We can't leave you double the presents, but we do send you twice as much love. Stay good. Santa. And he's put ten kisses. That's loads.'

'You'd better check your stocking,' Phoebe said.

Chloe had made Darcie's stocking this year to Darcie's design, so it was covered in unicorns and exceptionally sparkly. She'd draped it over one of the armchairs and Phoebe had filled it with small gifts and sweets, piling some larger gifts around it.

The sounds of paper tearing and excited squeals filled the room with each gift Darcie unwrapped. Phoebe took my hand and squeezed it. It wasn't the Christmas either of us had planned but it was magical in its own way.

And it had brought us together. It was early days, but Phoebe and I already knew each other so well and were the best of friends – something lacking in my relationships with Nadine and Yasmin. It seemed amazing that Phoebe had secretly been in love with me for nearly two years and I hadn't had a clue, but I don't think our time had been then. We'd both needed the past two years to grow first and our time was now. I could imagine so many Christmases and birthdays to come with the three of us happy together in our small unicorn-loving family unit, which was part of a bigger, loving found family.

* * *

'It's Santa!' Darcie squealed, pointing outside.

Phoebe and I looked towards the window, bemused.

'Ho! Ho! Ho! Merry Christmas!' Santa cried.

We followed Darcie as she rushed to the front door.

'Santa!'

He was wearing such a big white bushy beard that it took me a moment to work out who it was but the moment I saw those warm brown twinkling eyes, I recognised Jonathan.

'Young Darcie Flynn!' he boomed in a deep voice. 'I got partway home and decided that because you've been so good this year and haven't complained about Christmas being different, I had to come back and deliver one more gift for you.'

He lifted a hessian sack off his shoulder and passed a large gift to Darcie.

'Aw, thank you, Santa!' She rushed at him with a hug and almost dislodged his beard, but Jonathan managed to catch it just in time.

'And because Phoebe and Fizz have also been so good, I've brought them a little something too.'

We both thanked him for the gifts and insisted he stay for a couple of minutes while we took photos. I wasn't sure whether

Sam and Josh knew what he'd been planning, but they had to see him in his awesome outfit.

'My Christmas dinner is calling me so I must be off,' he declared, rubbing his padded belly.

With another 'Ho! Ho! Ho!' and further hugs, he ran back towards the farmyard, waving.

Not wanting to spoil the illusion of 'Santa' going to Jonathan's car or into the barn to change, I swiftly closed the door and we ushered Darcie into the lounge to open the gifts. In Darcie's package was a unicorn-shaped cushion and a necklace with a white and pink unicorn on it. Phoebe and I both had a unicorn necklace but in the most stunning origami style. Phoebe fastened Darcie's round her neck and I held my breath as she fastened mine, my heart racing as her fingers lightly brushed the tendrils of hair.

Five minutes later, Jonathan arrived with more bags of gifts.

'You've just missed Santa!' Darcie announced.

'Oh, no! Bad timing or what?'

As she scrolled through Phoebe's phone to show him the photos, I discreetly removed some white hairs from his collar and gave him a subtle thumbs up.

* * *

'What's Adele doing today?' I asked Jonathan as we peeled the vegetables in the kitchen a little later.

'She's spending the morning with her oldest son and his family and the afternoon with the youngest and praying for the day to end.'

I already knew from him that Adele was very close to her family, but her sons hadn't stopped fussing round her since the divorce and she was finding it stifling.

'Has she told them about you two yet?'

'Not yet. Taking the job with us and putting the family home on the market ruffled enough feathers and she can't face the drama of letting them know she's seeing someone too. They're very protective, although it's nice that they care. I'm happy for her to tell them what she wants when she wants. We both know it's not some crazy post-divorce mid-life crisis or whatever they'd believe it to be.'

I smiled at him as I scraped the carrots off the chopping board and into the pan. 'You really like her, don't you?'

'She's the best thing that's happened to me in a long time.' His eyes sparkled and it was obvious to me that this was a man deeply in love.

'What about you, Fizz? Will you dip your toe in the water again in the New Year?'

'No need. The deed is done.' How amazing to be able to say that.

'Really? Who?'

'I wondered if you'd already worked it out.' I ran my fingers over the unicorn necklace. 'After all, Santa gave us matching necklaces.'

'You and Phoebe? Oh, I'm made up for you both. That deserves a hug.'

'And it's about bloody time too,' he added when we pulled apart.

'You knew?'

He picked up a potato and started peeling. 'We *all* knew.'

'Who's all of you?'

Jonathan started counting them off on his fingers. 'Josh, Paul and Beth, Connie and Alex, Lauren and Riley. Even Kai knew, although he seems to have some sixth sense for these things because he was the one who outed Riley's feelings for Lauren.'

'I can't believe it! Why didn't anybody say anything?'

'Because, most of the time, outside interference doesn't work. If you were meant to be together, it would happen when the time was right. Like with Adele and me. We've worked together for a couple of decades and there was never anything between us other than friendship. A couple of years apart and two divorces later and it all fell into place. Timing's everything.'

My shoulders slumped. 'Sometimes it is. The timing of my big reveal about *him* wasn't so great.'

Jonathan laid his peeler down and wiped his hands on a cloth. 'You weren't to know everyone was there and, if you ask me, I think your timing was impeccable because it got his wife to spill the beans. He's going to answer for what he did now. That might not have happened if he'd still been in the States or even if he'd been here and she hadn't overheard. The power's shifted. He can't hurt you now, but *you* can hurt that bastard so hard, and we'll all be with you to support you through it. Even your grandparents. It just might take them a little longer to come round.'

'It's snowing!' Darcie squealed, running into the kitchen, followed by Phoebe.

Jonathan and I both turned towards the window. Fat flakes of snow were tumbling to the ground and, after several days without rain, were settling.

'Can I go out in it?' she asked.

'I think we all should,' Phoebe said.

'Vegetable duty for me,' Jonathan said, picking up his peeler, 'but be my guest.'

By the time the three of us were bundled up warm in our coats, scarves, hats, gloves and wellies, the ground was covered in a blanket of white and the flakes were falling faster and heavier.

Darcie held her arms out to the side and ran along the path towards the farmyard. As we followed her, Phoebe stuck her tongue out and caught a flake on it, laughing. I did the same then tilted my head back, closed my eyes and let the snow fall onto my face, the delicious coldness making me feel alive.

We reached the farmyard and laughed at Darcie running round in circles, making tracks in the fresh snow. She bent down and next minute a snowball flew in our direction. It fell short but she wasn't going to let that deter her, coming a little closer to pelt another one which hit Phoebe on the arm.

'Ooh! That's war!' Phoebe cried, tossing a snowball in Darcie's direction and missing by a mile.

Chaos ensued, with a three-way snowball fight full of laughter and squeals. While Darcie had me cornered, Phoebe scooped up an armful of snow, dropped it into the hood of my coat and flicked my hood up, showering me in snow.

'It's freezing!' I cried, racing after her as the snow slid down my face and back.

She squealed and tried to hide behind my Mini. I chased her round the car, changing direction every time she got too far ahead. When it was obvious I wasn't going to catch her, I gave an almighty shove at the snow piling up on the roof, covering her.

Squealing, she gave chase again, but we could barely breathe for laughing too much.

'I surrender!' she cried, shaking off the remnants of the mini avalanche.

She held her gloved hand out to me and I was about to shake it when a pile of snow landed on my head. Darcie!

I slicked my wet hair back then raised my hands. 'I surrender too. Well played.'

Phoebe brushed some hair from my face and my heart raced as I gazed into her deep blue eyes. In that magical, romantic moment with the snow tumbling down, she kissed me, and I knew I'd finally found true love.

Everything I'd always dreamed of in a perfect relationship, I had with Phoebe – my best friend and confidante. We made each other laugh and could talk incessantly about anything and everything, mundane or serious. We shared similar interests and the same outlook on life and I could see a long, happy future for us.

A cheer from Darcie broke us apart. She was bouncing up and down nearby with her fingers joined together in a heart shape.

'There's something we need to tell you,' Phoebe said, beckoning Darcie over.

'You love each other!' Darcie cried. 'You're girlfriends now?'

'Yes, we are,' Phoebe said. 'Are you okay with that?'

Darcie flung herself at us, hugging us both. 'I got my Christmas wish. I asked Santa if Fizz could be my mummy too and he gave me exactly what I wanted.'

I looked at Phoebe and, from the tears sparkling in her eyes, she was clearly as choked up as me. This Christmas was truly the gift that kept on giving.

* * *

Christmas dinner was almost ready. We just needed our final guest. Josh had texted Phoebe to say he'd be back at about 2 p.m. and hoped we didn't mind having lunch a little late. More time to eat chocolates!

She warned him that it had been snowing and to take care. Enough snow had fallen to fill in our footprints from earlier but not enough to cut us off. The farm looked so beautiful swathed in its glistening cloak.

Josh passed the lounge window at about ten to two and waved at us. Darcie squealed and ran to the door with Wilbur. The rest of us followed.

'Merry Christmas!' he called, flinging open the door.

Jonathan closed the door while Josh dished out hugs.

'How's Sammie and Thomas?' Jonathan asked.

'Why don't you ask them yourself?' Josh opened the door and my heart melted at the sight of Sam standing on the doorstep, cradling a sleeping Thomas.

'We got our Christmas miracle,' she said, beaming at us. 'He's home.'

52

SAMANTHA

Walking through the front door at Hedgehog Hollow on Christmas Day with my son in my arms was a special moment I'll never forget. The past month had been the longest of my life, full of tears, loneliness, frustration and grief but now we were home and we could finally start our life together as a family.

'I've missed you all so much,' I said. 'Happy Christmas!'

Josh took Thomas from me and I gave long, tight hugs to Dad, Phoebe, Darcie and Fizz and stroked Wilbur, Misty-Blue and Luna.

In the lounge, I sat on the sofa and removed Thomas's blankets and coat.

'Aw, he's a reindeer!' Darcie gushed, plonking herself down beside me. 'So cute.'

As planned, I'd dressed him in the reindeer outfit and booties Josh had bought for him and he looked as adorable as I'd expected. Late this morning, Ivanka had checked on his progress feeding.

'We have another SCBU rule,' she'd said, smiling down at Thomas. 'Strictly no animals, but it seems a little reindeer has found its way onto Panda Ward. There's nothing else for it.' She winked at me. 'I'm going to have to send him home.'

I'd cried and hugged her, so relieved to finally have that wonderful news.

'Can I cuddle him?' Darcie asked, bringing my thoughts back to the present.

I wanted – needed – some time to hold him myself and enjoy being with him in my own home, but how could I say that without sounding selfish?

Dad evidently picked up on my hesitation. 'Food's nearly ready, so why don't you all wash your hands and help me in the kitchen? We'll give Sammie and Josh a moment to settle in and everyone can have some Thomas time after we've eaten.'

I gave him a grateful smile and mouthed 'thanks' as they bundled out of the room.

Josh sat beside me and stroked Thomas's cheek. 'Welcome home, little one. At last!'

I closed my eyes for a moment and breathed in the scent of home. A pine-scented candle mingled with the delicious aroma of Christmas dinner.

'It's so good to have you back,' Josh said, his voice all choked with emotion.

'It's so good to be back.'

I gazed round the room at the fire in the log burner, the beautifully decorated tree with colourful twinkling lights, the discarded wrapping paper surrounding the opened gifts, the piles under the tree yet to be opened, and the snow still cascading outside. What a perfect Christmas Day.

* * *

While Thomas slept in the lounge, Christmas dinner was loud, lively and wonderful. We held our crackers in a loop round the table and attempted to pull them at the same time with varying degrees of success. Seeing everyone in their colourful paper hats transported me back to Christmas three years ago, laughing as Thomas wore six of them. My life had been so different back then.

'What have you all been doing this morning?' I asked as we tucked into our dinner.

'Santa came,' Darcie declared. 'Not just last night. He came this morning with extra gifts.'

'We've got photos to show you later,' Phoebe said, giving a sideways glance to Dad when Darcie wasn't looking. If I'd interpreted that correctly and Dad had dressed up, I couldn't wait to see the evidence. What a star.

'I'm sorry we missed him,' I said to Darcie. 'Did you get some nice presents?'

'Lots, but the best one was a new mummy.'

'A new mummy?'

'We've got some news,' Phoebe said. 'Fizz and I are seeing each other.'

I clapped my hand to my heart. 'Aw, I'm so thrilled for you both.'

'Me too,' Josh said. 'That's brilliant news.'

The updates continued across the meal – what Darcie had for Christmas, Dad's plans to see Adele, the latest admissions to the rescue centre – and it almost felt like I'd never been away. But there was a notable absence round the table.

The plates were cleared away and I checked everyone had a drink.

'Happy Christmas, everyone!' I said, raising my glass. 'I'm so relieved and grateful to be back home with you all today to make this toast to a wonderful man. To Terry, gone but never forgotten.'

'To Terry,' they echoed.

'As always, I say thanks to Thomas and Gwendoline Mickleby, without whom most of us would never have met. I'm forever grateful to them for bringing you all into my life.'

I paused for the toast.

'And finally, to the newest addition to the family – our very own Christmas miracle, Thomas Blake Alderson, home at last.'

53

FIZZ

By 7 p.m., I could barely keep my eyes open and, although I'd been told I was welcome to stay at the farmhouse for as long as I wanted or even sleep over again, it was time for me and Jinks to return to Meadow View. Sam and Josh needed some space and they probably wanted some time alone with Thomas too. He'd been round everyone for cuddles several times across the afternoon.

I hadn't discussed it with Sam and Josh yet, but my thoughts were to stay in the holiday cottage until the New Year to give them time to settle into some sort of routine with baby Thomas and be on hand for the rescue centre. After that, I needed to move back into Bayberry Cottage and form a routine of my own. My tenants had moved into their newbuild, so my home was waiting for me.

'It's been an awesome day,' I said, stretching as I stood up. 'But I am beyond shattered, so I'll say goodnight to you all now.'

Phoebe slipped her arm through mine as we crunched across the snow, which sparkled in the moonlight. It was so calm and still that we both stopped for a moment, listening to the silence, our breath hanging in the air.

'It's magical,' I whispered.

'It is. And do you know what else is magical?'

Her lips met mine in the most tender, heart-melting kiss. And to add even more magic to the perfect kiss at the end of a perfect day, gentle flakes of snow kissed our faces.

We drew apart, looking up at the snow-laden sky, laughing.

'A kiss so magical, it can summon the snow,' I said, taking Phoebe's hand.

We continued towards Meadow View.

'I wish today didn't have to end,' I said, 'but staying up all night has wiped me out.'

'Me too. There were a couple of points this afternoon where I felt myself going. It was worth the lack of sleep, though.' She nudged me playfully. 'And the two-year wait.'

'The best things come to those who wait.'

She squeezed my hand. 'They certainly do.'

We reached Meadow View and I unlocked the door and pushed it a little way open.

'I'd invite you in but...'

'I know. My bed's calling too so I'll go, but not without telling you that this has been my best Christmas ever, thanks to you.'

'Right back at you. I'm sorry it took me so long to realise.'

She placed a finger across my lips and shook her head. 'I was joking earlier. It happened when it was meant to happen. Good night, Fizz.'

'Good night, Phoebe.'

Our kiss was brief but tender and I closed the door with a sleepy smile on my face. What a day, filled with love and laughter, snow, and the Christmas miracle of baby Thomas coming home. I was going to relax and enjoy all that was good in my life and remember what Jonathan said about timing. When Grandma and Granddad were ready, we'd talk and we'd find a way through the pain together.

I'd only just changed into my PJs when there was a knock on the door.

'Phoebe,' I whispered, smiling.

'Couldn't stay away from...' I began as I flung open the front door. 'Grandma!'

She looked furtively around, as though checking she wasn't being watched. 'Can I come in?'

I stepped back and closed the door behind me before following her through to the lounge.

'Do you want a drink?'

'I'm not staying long and you're clearly on your way to bed.'

'Do you want to sit down?'

'Erm...' She looked round the room and I thought she was deciding where to sit, but she shook her head. 'No, I'd rather stand.'

'If you've come to have a go at me, I'm too tired to—'

'I haven't.' She held her hands up in surrender. 'I promise I come in peace.'

I waited for her to speak but she just stood there, wringing her hands. Feeling lightheaded with exhaustion, I perched against one of the chair arms.

'Does Granddad know you're here?' I asked.

'No.'

That didn't surprise me from his reaction.

'So why are you here?' I said the words gently. I wasn't angry with her, but I was weary and lacked the energy for either an argument or a deep and meaningful conversation.

Her hands steadied and she finally looked at me. 'I just wanted to tell you that we do believe you – both of us. You don't have a cruel bone in your body, and we know you would never make up something so vile, especially about a family member. But it's really hard to believe that the little boy we raised to love animals and respect people could do something so wicked and depraved.'

'Hard to believe?' I raised my eyebrows at her and sighed. 'But you just said you believe me.'

'Oh, sweetheart, we do. Bad choice of word on my part. I should have said it's really hard to *accept* that our little boy could do such a thing and that...' a tear trickled down her cheek, '... and that it was happening right under our nose to our beautiful grand-daughter and we had no idea. We failed our son and we failed you.'

At that moment, Grandma looked old and frail, and I felt the full weight of her guilt.

'You didn't fail either of us,' I said. 'You didn't make him what he became. He did that all on his own. And you didn't fail me. It was his secret and it was mine and we both kept it well.'

'Can you ever forgive us?'

'You and Granddad? Seriously? There's *nothing* to forgive. Him? *Never!* Abuse is unforgiveable.'

'I agree. And I didn't mean Melvin – just your granddad and me.'

'You've done nothing wrong and you can't carry the guilt for what *he* did. Don't let it destroy you. Don't let him claim two more victims.'

Grandma pressed her fingers to her lips as she studied my face. 'I remember you so vividly as a little girl helping out at the farm, feeding the lambs, chasing the ducklings. Year after year, we watched you grow and you were always smiling. How did you manage that?'

'I became Fizz. Felicity was the little girl he abused. Fizz was the quirky kid full of confidence who chatted to herself and had no secrets.'

'Oh, sweetheart.'

'Weird thing is that the kids at school didn't like Fizz. They thought she was a bit weird and avoided her. Then you shared the secret to friendship – always to be kind. *He* wasn't kind and I wanted to be nothing like him, so I went out of my way to be kind and caring towards everyone. Remember that saying about the rose – the one you got from Gwendoline?'

'The fragrance stays in the hand that gives the rose,' she said. Samantha's Gramps had used it too and we'd realised it had come from Gwendoline who'd been a mutual friend of both sets of grandparents.

'I believed that if I kept being kind to others – being a really good person – he'd stop. But the only thing that stopped him was distance. The day he emigrated was the best day of my life. You and Mum came back from the airport in tears and you sat in the kitchen talking about how much you'd miss him and how you hoped he'd come back home to visit soon. All I wanted to do was cartwheel round the farmyard singing because, for me, it was finally over. Except it never was. He was gone but the memories of what he did were in here.' I tapped my temple.

Grandma slowly lowered herself onto the nearest chair, shaking her head. She was likely reliving that day he left – at the time, one of the saddest days of her life.

'You kept being kind to others, even after he emigrated,' she said eventually. 'You still are.'

I knew where she was going with that. Plucking at straws. Desperate to put a positive spin on it, wanting so badly to draw some good from such a dire situation, to convince herself he wasn't through and through evil.

'I was and still am kind to others because that's who I am, but please don't ever give *him* even the teensiest morsel of credit for shaping me into who I am today. I'm this person because of me, because of you and Granddad, because of my parents and Barney.'

Phoebe's words from the early hours of this morning came back to me, so perfect for my situation too, and I thought about what Kate had told me about how much I'd helped Robbie, even though I hadn't known his history.

'I'm who I am today in spite of what *he* did. *He* tried to destroy me, but you and the rest of my family gave me so much strength, even though you didn't know it at the time.'

She looked at me, her eyes red and sorrowful. 'I'm so sorry. We should have known. We should have protected you.'

'No. *He* shouldn't have abused me and now he has to face up to the repercussions of what he did to me and goodness knows how many others. It's time for me to give that rose again – the thorny end. I know it's going to be painful for you and Granddad and I understand why, but I hope you can both understand why I have to testify.'

She rose slowly with her arms outstretched. 'We do.'

I stumbled into her embrace. There were tough times ahead and relationships would be fraught, but we'd get through it together. Grandma braving the snow and coming here tonight was the first step and my very own Christmas miracle.

54

SAMANTHA

'Are you sure it's the right decision?' I asked Josh over breakfast on Boxing Day. 'You don't think your parents will want to see Thomas today?'

We'd messaged family and friends yesterday to confirm that Thomas was home and that we'd be hosting Christmas Day Version Two on 27 December. The plan was to have a quiet day at Hedgehog Hollow today, but I was mindful that Dad had seen Thomas yesterday and the rest of the grandparents wouldn't see him again until tomorrow.

'I'm sure they will,' he said, 'but they won't have a problem with waiting until tomorrow. It's not like they haven't seen him already. And it's not a competition about who sees him the most and who gets the most cuddles. I think the girls – especially Darcie – would appreciate some time with us and particularly with you before we have another house full.'

'Has she been okay?' I asked. When she'd visited us in hospital, she'd been her usually bubbly, bouncy self, but she'd also seemed a little clingy.

'Hard to say when I've been here so little myself. There's been a lot happening and at such a busy time of year. We've barely been around, there's a new baby, and we've lost Terry. She's bound to have been affected.'

'Morning!' Phoebe trilled as she headed for the fridge and removed a carton of fresh orange juice.

'How was Thomas's first night?' she asked as she filled a glass.

'He was good as gold,' I said. 'Did you hear him crying at all?'

'I was out like a light. Serves me right for pulling an all-nighter with Fizz.'

She poured herself a bowl of cereal and joined us at the table.

'We were just talking about Darcie,' Josh said, 'and wondering how she's been with all the upheaval, especially Terry's death. She seemed on good form yesterday, but most children are on Christmas Day.'

'She's found it tough not having you both here, but she knew it was short term and things would be back to normal soon and she's been dying for Thomas to come home. She adored Archie and Lottie but, as far as she's concerned, Thomas is her little brother. As for Terry, she understands death better than most kids her age because of the rescue centre, although Terry was her first human loss. She cried the night I told her but I'm pretty sure she hasn't cried since then. I think having Wilbur here has helped.'

I looked down at the spaniel lying across my feet under the table. 'How's Wilbur been?'

'He was subdued at first, but he perked up when we put the tree up.'

'He still has his moments where I swear he's looking for Terry,' Josh said. 'It's so difficult for pets. You can't explain it to them. One minute their devoted owner is there, next minute they're gone. The positive for Wilbur is that he's so familiar with the farm and all of us. It'll take time to fully adjust, but he'll get there.'

* * *

'Welcome to Hedgehog Hollow Wildlife Rescue Centre,' I said to Thomas as Josh and I stepped into the barn after breakfast. 'This is a very special place to us all.'

I'd been eager to visit the barn to immerse myself in the world of wildlife once more as well as showing Thomas his new home, not that he was aware of any of it with being sound asleep in my arms.

I'd bundled him up in the most adorably cute snowsuit – mint green with cream cuffs, cream reindeer antlers and reindeer pockets – which Dad had given us yesterday.

'Hi, Thomas,' Fizz said, wandering over to us. She'd volunteered to see to our patients, allowing us to make the most of our first morning at home with Thomas.

'Thanks so much for doing the morning shift,' I said.

'It's a pleasure and the least I could do after everything you've done for me.' She handed me the key to Meadow View. 'I can't thank you enough for letting me stay.'

'You're welcome to stay longer.'

'It's tempting, but it's time to take Jinks home. Would you like to meet our new patients?'

'I'd love to.'

* * *

When we left the barn a little later, Darcie and Phoebe were in the field at the front of the farmhouse, rolling out the balls for a snowman.

'It's just like Darcie's first birthday here,' Josh said, putting his arm round me. 'Can you believe that was nearly two years ago?'

'I know! I can't believe she'll be nine and Phoebe'll be twenty-one next month. We'll have to sort out some parties.'

'Your social committee – Chloe, Lauren and Natasha – are already on it.'

I cuddled Thomas more closely to me and rested my head on Josh's shoulder, watching Phoebe and Darcie. Despite the chilly day, I felt nothing but warmth flowing through me. It had been a tough month, but the heartache lessened by seeing all my favourite people so happy.

When Sam and Josh left the barn with baby Thomas, I filled the kettle and smiled as I spotted Phoebe and Darcie in the distance making a snowman. Phoebe had messaged me to say she'd join me afterwards.

I'd woken up early this morning, feeling rested after a deep sleep. Grandma's visit last night had lightened my worries. *He* had already tried to take too much from me, and it was a relief that losing my grandparents would not be another casualty of his depravity.

It hadn't taken long to pack up my belongings ready for my return to Bayberry Cottage – still the same car load I'd moved out of Yasmin's house. It would be good to return to my own home, but I was sad about leaving Hedgehog Hollow. I'd always known it was a special place but living here and waking up to those views every morning had been magical. My bedroom back home looked out onto another cottage – pretty but not a patch on a wildflower meadow and rolling countryside.

All the holiday cottages were booked over New Year, but Sam had told me yesterday that I was welcome to move back into

Meadow View afterwards and stay until February half-term when it was booked again, but it would only mean delaying the inevitable. It was better to leave now, right at the start of my relationship with Phoebe, because settling into a routine where I lived a few minutes' walk away from her would be harder to break.

It was amazing to think I'd only been living here for two months but absolutely everything in my world had changed during that time and, even though some of it had been horrendous, it had all been worth it. It was time to start properly living. Without fear.

Outside, I'd removed my Christmas wreath from the hook on the front door and smiled at it. The day I made it, I'd had no idea what lay ahead. The wreath symbolised endings and beginnings. It symbolised life.

I hung up the replacement wreath which Sam had given me, then closed and locked the door, feeling quite choked up to be leaving the cottage which had been my safe haven during some of my darkest days.

* * *

'Who fancies a little visit to the beauty spa?' I asked Gollum around mid-morning after I'd cleaned the crates, put out fresh food and water, and issued medication.

Gollum had been one of the earliest admissions around the time the rescue centre opened. He had a horrendous case of mange and his spines began falling out. They never grew back so he couldn't survive in the wild as he had no way to protect himself. He now spent much of the year 'outside' in Hedgehog Dell – a purpose-built fully-enclosed soft release area next to the barn where injured hedgehogs could build their strength and hoglets could learn to forage in an environment that mirrored their natural habitat but from which they couldn't escape. It also worked as an interim setting for those who'd been with us for quite some time, allowing them to acclimatise and remember what being a hedgehog in the wild meant before full release.

Some rescue centres believed that, if an animal couldn't survive in the wild, it was only right and fair to euthanise, and I did completely understand that school of thought, but there were always exceptions and Sam, Josh, Jonathan and I all believed that Gollum was one of those. There was no way any of us could justify putting him to sleep when he was perfectly healthy and we had a way to give him some quality of life.

We'd faced a dilemma with another admission – a male called Fiesta (from our car model phase) who'd lost a limb. He could walk without it but, every so often, an abscess developed around his stump so releasing him wasn't an option. We'd debated Fiesta joining Gollum as a permanent resident in Hedgehog Dell, but he needed repeat treatment which had to be painful and distressing for him. It was a sad day when we concluded that the kindest thing for Fiesta was to say goodbye.

'You love that, don't you?' I asked Gollum as I rubbed baby oil into his back.

'Is somebody having a massage?' Phoebe asked, joining me at the treatment table. Her eyes were sparkling and her cheeks were rosy from the cold.

'He is and he's loving it. How was the snowman?'

'Josh is finishing it with Darcie. I was getting cold and I could tell he was dying to join in, so I left them to it. I wanted to see you. Did you get packed last night or did you do it this morning?'

'This morning, because I had a visitor last night...'

Phoebe and I had just about finished discussing Grandma's visit and I was putting Gollum back in his crate when the barn door opened and Darcie ran inside with Wilbur.

'Are you two going to get married?' Darcie asked me.

'Erm... we... I...'

'We've only just got together,' Phoebe said, playfully poking Darcie in the ribs. 'I know your game. You want another bridesmaid dress, don't you?'

'Can I be your bridesmaid?' Darcie's whole face lit up. 'Please, Phoebe! Please, Fizz!'

'We're not getting married,' I said, but the words didn't ring true. 'Well, not yet, anyway. Maybe one day.'

Phoebe gazed into my eyes, smiling tenderly. 'I'll hold you to that.'

56

SAMANTHA

'Merry Christmas, version two,' Josh said as we stirred with Thomas's cries the following morning.

'Merry Christmas, again,' I said, brushing my lips against his before rolling out of bed to lift Thomas out of his cot. 'And Merry Christmas to you too, little one.'

'Are you ready to face the invasion?' Josh asked as I fed Thomas.

'I think so. At least I don't have to prepare any food.'

We'd invited Mum, Dad, Connie and Alex, Paul and Beth and the children for lunch and they'd all said they'd bring food with them, which was probably just as well as I'm not sure when we'd have had the opportunity to go shopping.

Our extended family were joining us after lunch along with several friends – Hannah, Toby and their children, Natasha and Hadrian, Jeanette Kingston, Josh's best friends Lewis and Danny, Tariq and his girlfriend.

We had a couple of absences – Rich and Dave couldn't come as they'd gone abroad for the New Year but were looking forward to seeing Thomas for the first time on their return and, of course,

Terry wouldn't be here, and his presence would very much be missed.

* * *

By late morning, the farmhouse was alive with laughter, chatter and the occasional baby cry. Wrapping paper was strewn everywhere as Christmas presents were exchanged and Thomas was bombarded with gorgeous gifts.

After being in hospital for so long with limited company and quiet most of the time, it all became a bit overwhelming by the time lunch was finished, and I wasn't sure how I was going to cope with the increase in numbers across the afternoon. It was great to see everyone but, with hindsight, we probably shouldn't have been quite so ambitious.

'You look like you could use five minutes,' Josh whispered to me as everyone moved into the lounge after lunch and we remained in the kitchen on tea and coffee duty. With playing no part in preparing the meal, we'd insisted on at least making the drinks.

'It's lovely but, after so long in hospital, I'm finding the noise a bit overpowering.'

'Why don't you take some time out and have your tea on Thomas's bench? I bet you're dying to have a chat with him.'

'I am, actually.' I slipped my arms round Josh's neck and kissed him. 'Thanks for always understanding.'

I pulled on my scarf, coat and wellies, slipped out through the boot room and raced along the back of the house, hoping everyone was too preoccupied with the drinks distribution to notice me.

There hadn't been any further snow so the paths and the farm-yard were now clear, but the lawn and fields were still covered in a thin blanket. The fading light had turned the sky to a cool shade of peach giving an ethereal appearance.

The salt Josh had sprinkled on the patio crunched beneath my feet. I paused by Thomas's bench but it looked a little damp, so I crossed the lawn and stopped at the edge of the meadow, my hands cupped round my mug for warmth.

'How has it been three years since I last saw you, Thomas?' I asked. 'What did you think of us naming our baby after you? As if any other name would have been right. Tell you what, it's going to get confusing when we talk about Thomas's bench. He'll think it's his.' I smiled. 'I guess it is. If it hadn't been for you and everything you gave me, he wouldn't exist.'

I blinked back the tears and sipped on my tea. Movement to one side caught my attention. A robin rested on the fence post on my left and puffed out its deep orange breast. It looked up at me, cocked its head to one side then the other, then released the most beautiful song. It felt like I was being serenaded.

I thought of the message on the bauble Josh had given me: *Robins appear when loved ones are near.* Perhaps it was Thomas, thanking me for naming our baby after him.

'Is that you, Thomas?' I asked, keeping my voice low for fear of scaring the robin away. I placed the mug carefully on the fence post to my right.

'I've fulfilled another wish for you – children at Hedgehog Hollow.'

Another robin hopped onto the fence with a chirp and the two birds looked at each other.

'Gwendoline?'

Despite the warmth of my layers, goose bumps broke out all over my arms, swiftly followed by a feeling of calm flowing through me from head to toe.

'I have a favour to ask of you both,' I said. 'Will you look after Terry for me?'

The robins looked at each other and chirped. My breath caught moments later as a third robin swooped down and settled between them.

'Terry,' I whispered, tears flowing. 'It's good to see you. Wilbur's with us and he's happy. You've nothing to worry about. Rest in peace, my friend.'

For the briefest of moments, all three birds looked up at me and there was silence. Then, with a chirp, they took off one by one.

'Goodbye,' I whispered. 'And thank you.'

I rested my arms on the fence, breathing in the cold, fresh air. A few minutes later, I heard the crunch of snow behind me.

'I thought you might need your hat,' Josh said, holding it out. 'It's a bit nippy.'

'Thank you.' I pulled it on.

'And I thought you might need these.' He handed me a packet of tissues.

'You know me far too well.'

I wiped my cheeks and blew my nose.

'I saw three robins. One at a time, they sat on this stretch of fence and looked right at me.'

'Terry's with friends,' he whispered, slipping his arm round my waist.

I rested my head against his shoulder as we stood by the meadow in the fading light. Off to my right, I could see the barn and beyond that the silhouetted shape of the wedding gazebo.

'We've created something really special here, haven't we?' I said to Josh. 'It blows my mind sometimes thinking about all those animals we've saved.'

'And the humans we've saved too. And the life we've created, even if he didn't have the most ideal start.'

The past three years raced through my mind. 'The friendships we've made,' I added. 'The businesses we've set up, the memories we've helped create through those with weddings, parties and holidays.'

'The businesses others have set up,' he added, alluding to Crafty Hollow. 'It's amazing what we've done here, especially when the farm and everything on it was so dilapidated. Even the hosepipe was full of holes.'

I laughed, recalling one of our early encounters when he caught me trying to clean the plastic crates Gwendoline had bought for the rescue centre and managing to drench myself instead.

'Just think that none of it would have happened if it hadn't been for one amazing couple's dream,' he said.

'We'd better get back inside and see who our son's charming,' I said. 'It's a bit cold, though. I could do with a kiss to warm me up. What do you say?'

'The baddass wildlife saviour's wish is my command.'

57

SAMANTHA

Six months later

✉ From Chloe
HOT TIP: The summer event of the year — the
annual Hedgehog Hollow Wildlife Rescue Centre
Family Fun Day — promises to be the biggest and
best yet. Hosted by the sparkling unicorn of
best friends, it's the place to be seen. But the
question on everybody's lips is: Who is the
mystery man who Auntie Debs is bringing? We're
in Wildflower Byre when you're ready and it's
looking amazing xx

✉ To Chloe
On my way down now and I've no idea who Mum's
bringing but can't wait to find out xx

I chuckled to myself as I placed my phone back in my tunic pocket
and wandered down towards our former dairy shed. It was

amazing to think that it was now two and a half years since we'd held our first event in there – a New Year's Eve party to see whether it would work as a venue for our wedding reception – but the months were flying by. The rescue centre had celebrated its third birthday at the start of last month and we were about to host our fourth annual Family Fun Day.

Chloe, Lauren and Natasha had given me strict instructions to stay away from Wildflower Byre for the past fortnight to give them time to create 'the magic', which suited me just fine. The events were definitely their thing, and I was more than happy to leave them to it so I could focus on the animals and baby Thomas.

I'd taken six months full-time maternity leave, although I'd been unable to resist dipping into the rescue centre on a fairly regular basis to help out. I couldn't switch off from the animals completely and the opportunity for some adult company during the day had been very welcome.

At the start of this month, I'd returned to work on a part-time basis which, so far, really did feel like the best of both worlds – work and company plus quality time with Thomas. Connie and Mum had been eager to have Thomas for a day each, both completely besotted with their new grandson.

Chloe met me at the door to Wildflower Byre and insisted on doing the usual eyes closed dramatic reveal shenanigans I'd experienced so many times before. I shuffled forward while she covered my eyes.

'I'm removing my hands. One... two... three... open your eyes!'

After seeing what they'd created for the many weddings, parties and events we'd held in Wildflower Byre, I was expecting something impressive – especially after they'd had a fortnight to prepare – but this was beyond anything I'd ever imagined.

Colourful paper lanterns dangled from the beams and trusses with cut-outs of wildlife on them, but it was the artwork on the walls that took my breath away. As part of the refurbishment of the byre before our wedding, Dave and his team had plaster-boarded and skimmed the walls to soften the industrial look. They'd been painted a soft cream, but now...

Feeling as though I was in a dream, I drifted alongside the left-hand wall, my heart thumping. The three of them followed me and I imagined they were anxious for a verdict, but none of them wanted to be the first to speak for fear of breaking the spell.

'It's the story of Hedgehog Hollow,' I said eventually, my voice catching in my throat as I gazed at the mural.

Lauren took my hand and squeezed it. 'Right from the start with Thomas and Gwendoline.'

'There's a lot to take in,' Natasha said. 'We'll continue setting up over here. Take your time.'

I nodded as my eyes flicked across the various scenes. I'd known a little about Thomas and Gwendoline's story, but had recently discovered so much more thanks to an unexpected discovery at Terry's house. He'd left his estate to the rescue centre, just as he'd always said he would, but he left Granville House specifically to Josh and me, which had been a surprise. There were several generations' worth of belongings in the six-bedroom prop-erty, so it had taken some time and the expertise of an antiques expert to clear the house. There'd been some valuable items, most of which had gone to an auction in aid of the rescue centre, but we'd kept a couple of timeless pieces which felt very 'Terry'.

The most precious find for us hadn't been the antiques but an old wooden chest full of diaries, photos, letters and drawings from Terry's school days and beyond. I'd have hesitated as to whether it was an invasion of his privacy to look through his belongings – just as I'd done when I'd first inherited Hedgehog Hollow and found a box full of Thomas and Gwendoline's letters and papers – but Terry had been prepared for this day because an envelope with my name on rested on the top and the note inside was most unexpected:

> *To the healer of hedgehogs and broken hearts.*
> *If you're reading this, we've said our final goodbye and, in case I*
> *didn't get to tell you in person, I want you to know that having*
> *you and Josh and your wonderful family and friends in my life*
> *has been one of the two best things that has happened to me.*
> *The other thing, as you know, was being blessed with knowing*
> *Gwendoline. I shared some of our story with you but here's the*
> *rest. I loved the emails you wrote me from your honeymoon.*
> *You're a good writer. Perhaps you can tell our story one day.*
> *Thanks for healing my broken heart.*
> *Terry x*

I wasn't going to turn down the invitation to explore his story when it was entwined with my own. I hadn't made it through everything yet, but I'd shared with the others what I'd learned about the origins of Hedgehog Hollow and now they'd captured it on the walls of Wildflower Byre.

Whimsical silhouettes depicted the characters and everyone had their own distinct colour, providing a key for the story which started from Terry and Gwendoline's school days when she cut maths to rescue a bird in the playground.

The planning that must have gone into the storyboard was phenomenal. They'd captured everything, including when I'd met Gwendoline – the hedgehog lady – as a young child when she'd released hedgehogs at my grandparents' house, Meadowcroft. They had Fizz as a younger child meeting Gwendoline at Bumblebee Barn, the purchase of Hedgehog Hollow, the sowing of the wildflower meadow, the preparations for opening the rescue centre, then Gwendoline's untimely death.

Like a family tree, the branches of mine and Josh's stories weaved into Thomas's and Hedgehog Hollow was born again with me finding Thomas collapsed on Chloe and James's wedding day. The story of my friendship with Thomas was accompanied by a rose and the words: *the fragrance stays in the hand that gives the rose.*

They'd painted all the pivotal moments in my relationship with Josh – meeting, getting engaged, Phoebe and Darcie joining the family, our wedding, honeymoon, the birth of Thomas and so much more. The mural ended at Christmas with my silhouette beside three robins on a fence alongside the caption: *Robins appear when loved ones are near.*

So many memories and pivotal moments, so beautifully and sensitively captured. I hadn't realised I was crying until I reached the end, pressed my hand to my heart and discovered my tunic was wet.

'We wanted to show you it last night,' Chloe said, putting her arm round me, 'but it wasn't quite finished. Sorry for making you cry today.'

'It's fine. I doubt it'll be the last time I cry today. Blummin' pregnancy hormones.'

Chloe gasped and I realised too late what I'd just said.

'You're pregnant?' she whispered.

'Ssh! It was meant to be a secret until the barbeque tonight.' We'd been for the dating scan yesterday and, as we'd already invited family and friends to stay for a post-event barbeque to thank them for their help in setting up and clearing away afterwards, we'd decided to wait until tonight to announce the news.

'My lips are sealed. Oh, my God! I'm so excited for you.'

'What do you think?' Lauren asked as she and Natasha joined me.

'It's... I don't... Honestly, there aren't words. It's the best thing I've ever seen. Whose idea was it?'

'Your mum's,' Chloe said. 'I won't steal her thunder by telling you how she came up with the idea because it's a lovely story. You can ask her yourself later.'

'Javine came up with the concept and the style,' Lauren said. 'We got Josh on board and once we'd all agreed on which scenes to include, Javine drew the entire thing and we all had a hand in painting it.'

'And when she says all, she really means that,' Natasha added. 'Pretty much everyone who loves you has done some of the colouring in, some with lesser degrees of success than others. I'm sure they'll all point out their masterpieces.'

'Young Thomas has even had a go,' Lauren said.

'I spotted the handprint and wondered if that was his.'

Chloe smiled. 'Yes, but he finger-painted some of the spines on the hedgehogs and a few blades of grass too. His finger may have been strongly guided but it's still his work, right?'

Just when I didn't think it could be any more incredible, they'd just escalated it again. To think that all my friends and family including my six-month-old son had played their part was so special.

'I can't thank you all enough. This is unbelievable.'

Natasha pointed to the empty stretch of wall. 'You'll notice there's plenty of space for the story to continue.'

Chloe caught my eye and winked, and I had to fight hard to resist the urge to stroke my hand over my very small baby bump.

* * *

'I don't think I'll ever get bored of seeing you in that outfit,' I said to Josh after I'd helped him into Mickleby's oversized feet and Darcie helped pull on his paws.

'What do you think of Daddy?' I asked Thomas as I lifted him out of his bouncer.

He looked a little uncertain at first as I stroked his hand against Mickleby's soft spines, but then he laughed and bounced in my arms.

'Was that the seal of approval?' Josh asked, his voice muffled through the giant head.

'It certainly was. Ready to go?'

Darcie and I took an arm each and helped him into the hall, then I strapped Thomas into his pushchair outside before helping Mickleby over the threshold.

'When's your mum's special guest expected?' Josh asked as he plodded across the farmyard.

'About two o'clock, so she's on the craft stall with Lauren for the moment.'

'And she hasn't said who he is?'

'No. I think she's worried that if she tells us anything, she'll jinx it and he won't show up. It's a big thing for her to start a new relationship.'

'Has Nanna Debs got a boyfriend?' Darcie asked.

'We're not sure. We think so.'

'But he could be a business partner,' Josh said. 'We don't know so it's best not to speculate.'

'I hope it's a boyfriend,' Darcie said, 'especially now that Adele's moving in with Grandpa Jonathan.'

I could picture Josh rolling his eyes beneath Mickleby's head. After being the instigator for Phoebe and Fizz getting together, Darcie seemed to have become the self-appointed family match-maker and relationship counsellor but with good cause. She'd reeled off a stack of resolutions at New Year, nearly all of which were things she hoped for other people rather than plans she had for herself, and one of those had been for Rich and Dave to tie the knot. I'd never have called that one, but they'd gone to New York for New Year and had surprised us all by returning married. They'd always proclaimed that they didn't need a wedding ring to prove they were devoted to each other but now that they wanted to start a family, they'd decided to make their relationship official. They'd also fallen in love with Granville House, making for a hassle-free sale and the peace of mind that Terry's beloved family home would go to a deserving family who'd love it as much as he had.

'You weren't meant to have heard that about Adele moving in,' I said, focusing my attention back on Darcie. 'He hasn't asked her yet.'

'But he's going to and she's going to say yes because she loves him, although I think he should ask her to marry him too.'

Mickleby the hedgehog definitely sniggered at that.

As we reached Wildflower Byre, I spotted Geraldine from Weeberley Hall who'd found Debbie, our blonde hedgehog.

'Samantha!' she called, heading in our direction. 'Have you got a moment? There's something I have to show you.'

'Let me get Mickleby inside then I'm all yours.'

As soon as I'd handed our mascot over to Hannah and Toby who were running the meet and greet once again, I moved to one side with Geraldine and gently rocked Thomas's pushchair.

'You're going to love this,' she said. 'We got CCTV installed in the garden and look what it picked up last week.'

I watched the black and white footage on the screen and my heart leapt as a light-coloured hedgehog shuffled over to one of the feeding stations.

'That must be Debbie!'

Four hoglets appeared on the screen seconds later, two dark and two light.

'Oh, my gosh! Debbie's a mum!'

'My husband and I were so thrilled when we saw it.'

'That has made my day. Do you think you could email me it?'

'I'm technically incompetent but I'll get my husband to do it tomorrow.'

Geraldine spotted someone she knew so she headed off and I went in search of Mum, who was running the cake stall at the other end of the barn with Jeanette Kingston.

I greeted them both and complimented Mum on how lovely she looked in a colourful summer dress – such a contrast to the drab dark colours she used to wear.

'I love the mural,' I said. 'Chloe says it was your idea and there's a story behind it.'

'There is, but I need to show you something when I tell it, so I'll have to explain later.'

'I can look after the stall for a bit,' Jeanette said. 'You take a break, Debs.'

Thanking her, Mum removed a bag from under the table and we wandered over to the wedding gazebo with Thomas, away from the noise, and sat on the steps.

Mum removed a large journal from the bag. 'A few months ago, I had my sketchpad out. I wasn't sure what I was going to draw but my pencils took on a life of their own and I ended up drawing this little dark-haired girl blowing bubbles in a garden. When I looked more closely, I recognised the garden as being how we had ours when you were little, and I realised the little girl was you.'

She opened the journal, revealing the image she'd just described.

'Oh, Mum, it's beautiful.'

'After that, every time I sat down to draw with no plan, I found I'd drawn either you or you and Chloe together.'

I flicked through a few more pages, revealing pencil drawings and watercolour images from my childhood. I recognised some of the clothes.

'It was quite a trip down Memory Lane,' she continued, 'but it did me the world of good. I had so much anger and negativity attached to the past, particularly for how I treated you, and this was like revisiting your childhood with fresh eyes.'

'So how did you go from this to the mural?'

Mum flicked forward a few pages. 'Because I was finding it so therapeutic, I decided to go back to the start and create the story of your life, full of the positivity you've always radiated.'

The watercolour storyboard was a different style to the Hedgehog Hollow one but the principle was the same, with key moments in my childhood and each figure having its own colour. The most touching part was that there was a heart in every image – on an item of clothing, the shape of a shrub, a balloon held in the air – and I felt the love emanating from every single page.

'So that's where the Hedgehog Hollow mural idea was formed,' Mum said, her voice heavy with emotion. 'I'd like to hang onto it for now and keep adding to it, but it's yours.'

I flicked through some more pages, my heart bursting with happiness at how far Mum had come to enable her to create something like this full of positive memories and love.

'I'll treasure this forever,' I said, closing the book and running my hand over the daisy on the front cover. 'You're so talented and this is so beautiful and special. Thank you.'

'It's me who needs to thank you. You never gave up on me, even though I gave you plenty of reasons to, and everything that's happening in my life today – my college course, Orchard House, my friendship with your dad, better relationships with friends and family and the new man in my life – has all been because of you.'

I placed the journal gently to one side and hugged her tightly.

'You have to give yourself credit too,' I said when we separated.

'You wanted to change, and you braved the past to do so.'

Thomas released one of his mewls but smacked his lips and remained asleep.

'I could have missed out on this,' Mum said, gazing adoringly at her grandson.

Suddenly it didn't feel right letting everyone know our baby news at the same time. Our parents, Phoebe and Darcie should hear it first, especially when I'd already inadvertently leaked it to Chloe this morning.

'And his brother or sister,' I said.

Mum whipped her head round, her eyes wide. 'Are you...?'

I grinned. 'Due on New Year's Eve.'

'That's wonderful news!' She hugged me again. 'Just as well we left some space on the wall of Wildflower Byre.'

We headed back towards the cake stall.

'So this man we're meeting is a romantic partner, not a business partner?' I asked.

She blushed. 'Yes.'

'Why won't you tell us anything about him?'

'Because...' She sighed and shrugged. 'Because I can't quite believe it's real and I'm afraid to say too much and find it's all a dream.'

'Aw, that's so sweet. I bet he feels the same way about you.'

We said a temporary goodbye and I did my rounds with Thomas. Dad, Uncle Simon and James were running the barbeque as usual in Fun Field and Wilbur was patiently waiting for 'dropped' sausages. I pictured Terry there last year and swallowed down the ready lump in my throat. It had taken a couple of months, but Wilbur's melancholy had lifted and he was a happy, content dog again. I think it had helped having me on maternity leave so he got a lot of attention from me during the day and, on evenings and weekends, there were so many willing volunteers to walk him or play with him. I'm sure that, like the rest of us, there was a Terry-shaped hole in his heart, but he'd found a new forever home and would never be short of love here.

Adele was helping out on the tombola near the barbeque and I loved catching the adoring looks between her and Dad. They were so good together and I was sure she'd say yes to moving in with him. I suspected she spent most nights there anyway.

* * *

I'd been over to the farmhouse to feed Thomas and was on my way back to Wildflower Byre when I spotted Mum in the wedding gazebo with a man. He was tall and slim with grey hair and glasses, but I couldn't see much more from the distance.

They were facing each other and he was holding both her hands while he spoke to her. He cupped her face and tilted it towards his for a kiss and then they embraced. Everything about the way he touched her was so tender and I already knew I was going to adore him.

As they pulled apart and left the gazebo, there was no point me pretending I hadn't noticed them, so I waved in their direction.

'I wasn't spying on you both,' I called. 'I've just been feeding Thomas.'

The man was wearing jeans and a short-sleeved grey shirt and, as he came closer, I could see that he was older than Mum, possibly by about a decade. I wondered if that was another reason she'd kept quiet, worried we might have an opinion on the age gap. Ten years wasn't much and what difference did any age gap make when a couple made each other happy?

'This is Jeremy,' Mum said when they reached me. 'Jeremy, this is my daughter Samantha and my grandson Thomas.'

Jeremy thrust out his hand and shook mine enthusiastically.

'I've been looking forward to meeting you so much, Samantha. What a stunning place you have here.'

'Thank you. And I've been looking forward to meeting you too.'

His smile was so warm, as were his soft grey eyes, making first impressions extremely positive. Laughter lines round his mouth and below his eyes suggested someone who smiled a lot. The glasses were black-framed and on trend and he had a short beard on his chin and stubble across his jaw.

Jeremy peered into the pushchair. 'What a handsome young man. Six months, did you say Debs?'

Mum nodded. 'Just over. He was born six days before Christmas.'

We set off towards Wildflower Byre and I smiled to myself as Jeremy took Mum's hand and they exchanged adoring looks.

'So, Jeremy, how did you two meet?' I asked, dying to know their story.

'I've always lived in York but I wanted a quieter life in the countryside when I retired. I moved to the area at the start of the year and wanted to explore all the villages. Sandy, my cockapoo, and I visited Little Tilbury a few months back. We came across your mum's house, paused to look at the stunning front garden and managed to scare the life out of your mum, who was behind the hedge clearing leaves.'

'Jeremy's a keen gardener too,' Mum said. 'So we got chatting and I showed him what I'd been doing out the back too. He asked for my take on what to do with his somewhat overgrown garden, so we've been working on that together and things developed from there.'

'Your mother's an amazing woman,' Jeremy said.

Tears filled my eyes as they exchanged another adoring look. It had finally happened. Both of my parents had found love for a second time, and I couldn't be happier for them.

'Thanks for listening and for those great questions,' I said, 'and thank you for supporting Hedgehog Hollow by being here today. Your help really does make a difference.'

I gave an impromptu bow as the audience applauded before they dispersed around Wildflower Byre.

It was late afternoon and there were still plenty of people around, but the crowd had definitely thinned. I removed my headset, having now completed the last talk of the day, and smiled at Grandma.

'That was wonderful, sweetheart,' she said, giving me a hug. 'I'm so proud of you.'

She held me a little longer and tighter than necessary and I knew what that meant – that it wasn't just the talk that made her proud. My relationship with Grandma was back on track but there was still tension with Granddad. Sunday lunch as a family was only monthly now and I didn't always attend.

Grandma had told me that Granddad not only believed me but he also thought I'd done the right thing – if perhaps in the wrong way – but his struggle was with himself. He believed he'd failed

Melvin and me and he found it hard to look me in the eye. The only thing that was going to change that was time and a lot of patience. I had both, but Granddad wasn't getting any younger and the situation had taken its toll on him with a series of mini strokes. He'd recovered but his speech and movements were slower, and I feared that he wasn't going to be with us for much longer. I hoped he could forgive himself before it was too late, but I wasn't going to feel any guilt. This was all on Melvin.

The criminal proceedings against Melvin were still ongoing – lengthy and complex due to crimes committed in the UK and USA – but he was on remand in the UK for now. Even though he was being held on a special wing for vulnerable prisoners who'd struggle to survive amongst the regular inmates – those most likely to harm themselves or be harmed by others – he'd been hospitalised twice already. I wondered if he'd make it as far as his trial. I tried not to give him any headspace, but sometimes I wondered whether he felt the same fear that I'd felt as a child, knowing someone was watching, waiting, coming to get him. Karma.

Melvin had told me that nobody would ever love me. Phoebe and I had talked about whether those words had had a greater impact on me than I'd realised at the time. On some subconscious level, had I been drawn to Nadine and Yasmin because I'd known they would never really love me, proving him right? Not anymore.

Robbie and Kate had held me to our date of the first Saturday in February for dinner at their house and he was so smug for having called it about Phoebe. He'd also kept his promise to draw Attila the Badger and his hedgehog army and presented us with a framed sketch and a T-shirt each. It was such a special gift because that hedgehog army discussion day was the day that marked the end of my old life and the start of my new one, revealing my secret and finally letting in real love.

Phoebe and I met up with Robbie and Kate every month now

and we were looking forward to the arrival of their second child – another boy – in August. Robbie claimed they were going to call him Attila. Just as well Kate was the sensible one.

'Have you seen Phoebe and Darcie?' I asked Grandma, linking arms with her as we headed out of Wildflower Byre.

'I saw them before your talk, walking that giant hedgehog back to the farmhouse.'

'Poor Josh ends up being in that costume longer and longer each time, bless him.'

'Samantha was blessed the day she found him,' Grandma said. 'Just like you were when you found Phoebe.'

I blinked back the sudden tears. 'Aw, Grandma, that's lovely. Thank you.'

She sighed. 'I know I don't like to talk about that day but there's something I need to say about it and it's not about Melvin, so don't worry. It only came back to me recently, but I remember your granddad saying something about us putting up with your girl-friends and your colourful hair. That's not true. He was angry and he was lashing out.'

'He wouldn't have said it if it wasn't how he felt.'

She patted my hand. 'He's old-fashioned. He doesn't under-stand how things are these days. I know that's a poor excuse, but he loves you and he *does* accept you, no matter what he said. Neither of us have ever had an issue with you having girlfriends. Except Yasmin. We never really liked that one.'

That made me laugh. Had anyone liked her?

'As for your hair, your granddad has always loved your bright colours and admired you for being you, not being swayed what others might think, so I don't know why he said that. The pink was always his favourite, although I think your new colour might trump it.'

I'd gone for unicorn hair – streaks of purple, lilac, cerise, pale pink and blue – and was wearing it down for a change.

'Then I might have to come over tomorrow to show him it,' I said.

'He'd like that,' she said, squeezing my arm in a way that told me she'd like that too.

We were getting there one day at a time. I sometimes had to remind myself that I'd had years to come to terms with what had happened, but this was all new and raw for my family.

'Oh, here comes Phoebe,' Grandma said, looking towards Fun Field. 'I'd best be heading home now so I'll see you tomorrow, sweetheart.'

I waved her off and went to join Phoebe.

She welcomed me with a kiss – something Yasmin would never have done.

'Last talk done?'

'All finished,' I said. 'Now for a bit of time with my two favourite people in the whole world.'

SAMANTHA

When Connie and Alex got married, I'd looked round my family and friends and thought about how much had changed for so many of them in the four months between my wedding and theirs. I'd also hoped that a few others – Dad, Mum, Phoebe and Fizz – would find their happy ever afters.

It was now nearly two years since Connie and Alex had said 'I do' and I was looking round the same faces as they congratulated Josh and me on the news of our second baby and thinking about how many more significant changes there'd been since then. We'd had our very own Christmas miracle and there was a New Year baby on the way, Dad had unexpectedly found love with Adele who he'd known for over two decades and Mum had discovered it with her new friend Jeremy.

Rich and Dave were married and settled in Granville House, working on the next chapter of their lives together, and Chloe and James were stronger than ever. Running Crafty Hollow with Lauren had been the making of her.

Lauren and Riley were a happy family unit with Kai and there was, of course, my favourite family unit – Phoebe, Fizz and Darcie.

What a joy it had been to see Phoebe and Fizz's relationship grow and how they'd kept Darcie at the centre of their world.

I slipped away from the celebrations a little later. In the wedding gazebo, I trailed my finger across the wooden hedgehog carvings on the back railing. There'd been a positive shift in my relationship with Mum and with Chloe when they'd carved them before my wedding, but it was incredible how much my relationship with both of them had moved on since then. So many times, I'd been tempted to walk away and say 'no more' but I'd hung in there, convinced they could overcome the challenges making them lash out, and they both had. Now I reaped the rewards.

'The fragrance stays in the hand that gives the rose,' I said, looking over to the meadow.

I turned at the sound of footsteps and smiled at Josh holding Thomas.

'We were missing you, but we can leave you to your chat with Thomas senior if you'd like.'

I shook my head, smiling. 'No, it's good that you're here. I was just thinking about how good things are with Mum and Chloe, how Gramps's phrase about the rose was so right, and how that phrase came from Gwendoline.'

Josh passed our son to me and I kissed his soft head as I gazed out over the meadow once more.

'I love it here so much,' I said. 'It truly is a magical place.'

Josh slipped his arm round my waist. 'I agree. Anything can happen. And it has!'

Hedgehog Hollow was the place where we'd found love, welcomed new arrivals, discovered family secrets, held our wedding, chased our dreams – and Thomas Mickleby's – of having a family and brought home our Christmas miracle. And none of it would have happened without Thomas, Gwendoline and Terry.

'Do you think you will tell their story?' Josh asked.

'Terry clearly wanted me too and, after everything he's done for us, how could I deny him that? But for now, I want to relax and celebrate everything we've achieved so far.'

Josh stroked Thomas's head and tenderly kissed me.

'Ready to go back to the party?' he asked.

'Ready.'

As we set off down the steps, I took one more glance back at the meadow and, for the briefest moment, I'm sure I saw the three of them standing there, Gwendoline between Thomas and Terry, their arms round each other.

I blew them a kiss and pressed my hand against my heart, forever grateful to those three wonderful people for the love, friendships and animals they'd brought into my life. I *would* write their story. One day.

ACKNOWLEDGMENTS

Oh, my goodness, I can't believe I've just written the fourth book in the Hedgehog Hollow series! What started out as an exercise on my Master's in Creative Writing to put a character in an uncomfortable setting – a woman being bridesmaid for her cousin's wedding when she was secretly in love with the groom – has certainly taken on a life of its own! I hope you've enjoyed reading it as much as I've enjoyed writing it.

This is a fictional series, but I undertake a considerable amount of research to ensure I accurately capture the plight of hedgehogs and the many dangers they face. I love that, in a work of fiction, it's possible to learn so much too. Thank you to everyone who has taken hedgehogs to their heart and who has been inspired to help in whatever way they can.

In *A Wedding at Hedgehog Hollow*, the community rally around Samantha when the Grimes family do their worst again. As an author, I'm part of two invaluable communities: a community of writers who are exceptionally supportive and a community of readers whose enthusiasm for a particular book and/or author can make such an incredible difference. For the latter, particular thanks to the members of Facebook groups Redland's Readers, The Friendly Book Community, and Heidi Swain and Friends, for the book love and recommendations.

We ran another 'name the hedgehog' competition for this book and our randomly selected winner was Mrs Pricklypants, courtesy of

Rachael MacKay. Congratulations Rachael! Absolutely loving that name.

The hedgehogs look forward to welcoming you back for book five and, if you've not taken a trip to Whitsborough Bay yet, they'd encourage you to do that. Who doesn't like to be beside the seaside?

Big hugs

Jessica xx

ABOUT THE AUTHOR

Jessica Redland writes uplifting stories of love, friendship, family and community set in Yorkshire where she lives. Her Whitsborough Bay books transport readers to the stunning North Yorkshire Coast and her Hedgehog Hollow series takes them into beautiful countryside of the Yorkshire Wolds.

Sign up to Jessica Redland's mailing list for news, competitions and updates on future books.

Follow Jessica on social media:

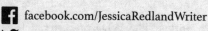

facebook.com/JessicaRedlandWriter

twitter.com/JessicaRedland

instagram.com/JessicaRedlandWriter

bookbub.com/authors/jessica-redland

ALSO BY JESSICA REDLAND

New Arrivals at Hedgehog Hollow

Family Secrets at Hedgehog Hollow

A Wedding at Hedgehog Hollow

Chasing Dreams at Hedgehog Hollow

Christmas Miracles at Hedgehog Hollow

The Escape to the Lakes Series

The Start of Something Wonderful

Boldwood

Boldwood Books is an award-winning
fiction publishing company seeking
out the best stories from
around the world.

Find out more at
www.boldwoodbooks.com

Join our reader community
for brilliant books,
competitions and offers!

Follow us
#BoldBookClub